WE ARE ALL
GOOD PEOPLE
HERE

Also by Susan Rebecca White

A Place at the Table
A Soft Place to Land
Bound South

WE ARE ALL GOOD PEOPLE HERE

SUSAN REBECCA WHITE

ATRIA BOOKS

New York   London   Toronto   Sydney   New Delhi

ATRIA
BOOKS

An Imprint of Simon & Schuster, Inc.
1230 Avenue of the Americas
New York, NY 10020

First Atria Books hardcover edition August 2019

ATRIA BOOKS and colophon are registered trademarks of Simon & Schuster, Inc.

For information about special discounts for bulk purchases, please contact
Simon & Schuster Special Sales at 1-866-506-1949 or business@simonandschuster.com.

The Simon & Schuster Speakers Bureau can bring authors to your live event. For more
information or to book an event, contact the Simon & Schuster Speakers Bureau at
1-866-248-3049 or visit our website at www.simonspeakers.com.

Manufactured in the United States of America

1   3   5   7   9   10   8   6   4   2

Library of Congress Cataloging-in-Publication Data

Names: White, Susan Rebecca, author.
Title: We are all good people here / Susan Rebecca White.
Description: New York : Atria Books, 2019. |
Identifiers: LCCN 2018043103 (print) | LCCN 2018046884 (ebook) |
ISBN 9781451608953 (eBook) | ISBN 9781451608915 (hardcover) |
ISBN 9781451608922 (paperback)
Classification: LCC PS3623.H57896 (ebook) | LCC PS3623.H57896 W42 2019
(print) | DDC 813/.6—dc23
LC record available at https://lccn.loc.gov/2018043103

ISBN 978-1-4516-0891-5
ISBN 978-1-4516-0895-3 (ebook)

To Sam

We can never be gods, after all—but we can become something less than human with frightening ease.
—N. K. Jemisin

Part One

Belmont Girls

Chapter I

BELMONT

Roanoke, Virginia, 1962

Daniella's father steered the Dodge Pioneer up the serpentine drive of Belmont College, home to more than five hundred girls renowned for their Beauty and Brains, or at least that was what the boosterish tour guide who had shown Daniella around the previous spring had claimed. Just as the main quad came into view—a pleasing vista of faded brick buildings with white columns, the Blue Ridge Mountains serving as backdrop—they passed a gang of cheering students holding signs painted with the school colors of green and white: "We Love Our New Girls!" and "Honk If You're a Monty!" and "Welcome to Heaven!"

Daniella's father beeped his horn at the cheering girls, causing them to yell all the louder.

"How fun!" remarked Daniella's mother, a woman who should have graduated from a school like this but had dropped out of Sweet Briar (only an hour's drive away) after her second year, when she became pregnant with Daniella's older brother, Benjamin, by the visiting history professor, the handsome, young, and Jewish Dr. Gold. The Golds parked in the visitors' lot and, passing other pretty, fresh-faced girls carrying suitcases and pillows—many of whom were followed by their fathers, lugging trunks—they made their way to Monty House, the redbrick Colonial that was to be Daniella's new home. There was a portico out front and a large Palladian window above the open front door. Waiting just inside was a stout woman who wore her silver hair in a bun at the nape of her neck. She introduced herself as Mrs. Shuler, Monty House's dorm mother.

A faded Oriental rug, so thin in spots it was almost translucent, partially covered the dark wood floor of the entryway. Against the wall ticked a grandfather clock, and beside it hung an oil portrait of Georgina March, whose father founded the college. The whole place smelled of oranges, as if someone had polished all of the wooden surfaces with citrus oil. Mrs. Shuler noted that supper would be served at 6:00 p.m. in the dining hall and told Daniella that her room was on the second floor, the fourth on the right past the front staircase. Daniella's roommate had already arrived. All Daniella knew about her was that her name was Evelyn Elliot Whalen, she went by "Eve," and she was from Atlanta. Moments later, when Daniella walked through the open door of her new room, she was practically tackled by Eve, who flew through the air to envelop her in a hug. She smelled of roses—Joy perfume Daniella would soon learn and which she, too, would start wearing.

"You are Daniella, right?" Eve asked, no longer embracing her, but with both hands resting lightly on Daniella's forearms, which were tan from tennis.

"Indeed, I am," said Daniella, trying to sound breezy but feeling a little overwhelmed.

"Oh, I'm so excited to meet you! I don't mean to be such a spaz, but I've been looking forward to this moment all summer! I *thought* I was going to room with Tate Pennington, but then she ended up going to Agnes Scott at the last minute to be near her boyfriend at Tech. And I was secretly so excited because that meant I would get to meet a whole new person!"

Daniella's mother smiled brightly at her daughter.

"Well," said Daniella. "I hope I don't disappoint."

Eve waved away that bit of blasphemy as if clearing the room of an unpleasant odor. She was taller than Daniella, at least five foot eight, and while she was far from overweight, her hips were curvy and her body was, if not large, *present*. She was not a girl who would ever fade into the background. She wore a kelly-green sleeveless shirtdress and a pair of Keds printed with watermelon halves. Her shoulder-length blond hair was teased and curled, so that it formed a bump on top, secured with a barrette, and flipped under at the ends. Daniella teased her brown hair, too, only first she straightened it using the comb attachment that fit on the end of the hose of her hair dryer. Left to its own devices it frizzed.

Eve had already set up her bed with a white eyelet spread and pink-and-green decorative pillows. On the far wall of the room, sitting on an antique coffee table, was a silver tea set on a silver tray. Eve noticed Daniella looking at it. "Grandmommy gave it to me. I guess there's a tradition of girls hosting tea for each other?"

Eve conveyed this information with enough of a raised brow to let Daniella know that she recognized it was all a little silly. Daniella's father stood off to the side, his lips pressed together in amusement. But Daniella's mother was clearly delighted.

"Is that Strasbourg?" she asked.

"Yes, ma'am," said Eve.

"Daniella! Strasbourg is the pattern Mother Scott left you! Can you believe it? You two are a match made in heaven."

"Oh, we're going to have a ball!" gushed Eve.

After hugging her parents good-bye and watching them drive away, Daniella returned to Monty House to settle in. Eve was just finishing unpacking her trunk full of beautiful clothes. Daniella admired Eve's Burberry trench coat (the same one Audrey Hepburn made famous in *Breakfast at Tiffany's*) and the rainbow of cashmere twin sets Eve hung in her closet, along with a little fox fur stole Eve's grandmother had given her to wear to formals on chilly evenings. Daniella had her own collection of cashmere twin sets, but she owned three, not ten, and it had never even occurred to her that someone might bring a fur to college.

That night after their dinner plates were cleared and scoops of vanilla ice cream were served, Daniella and Eve lingered in the dining hall talking, long after the other girls had left. At one point Eve walked to the kitchen where the cafeteria ladies were cleaning up, taking her and Daniella's empty bowls of ice cream with her. Daniella assumed she was bussing their table, but instead Eve returned carrying a half-pint carton of milk, a can of Hershey's syrup, and one of their old bowls, which now contained a heaping second serving of ice cream. Eve then proceeded to make a milk shake for the two of them, dumping ice cream, milk, and chocolate syrup into a water glass, then swirling the concoction furiously with a spoon. After she drained her half of the shake, Eve patted her own stomach, saying that she'd better watch out or she would turn into a fat pig.

"Don't say that about yourself," scolded Daniella. "You're beautiful." Eve looked at her, surprised.

"Aw," she said, and looped her arm over Daniella's shoulder, giving her a little sideways hug.

Later, after hanging the framed Audubon prints of hummingbirds that Eve had brought and organizing their desks, the two girls stayed up till 3:00 a.m. talking, long after their other hall mates, who had joined them for a spell, had wandered back to their rooms. As the night progressed, Daniella surprised herself by telling Eve the awful secret that she hadn't shared with anyone: that she was almost certain her father was carrying on an affair with Dr. Spool, the new lady professor in the history department at George Mason, where her father taught. That past spring Daniella had surprised him by showing up at his office one afternoon after tennis practice. She had wanted to talk to him honestly, and without her mother around to interject, about whether she should go to Barnard or Belmont the following year. His door was closed, but the department secretary had assured her that he was in, so she knocked until he answered. When he finally opened the door, Dr. Spool had hurried out of his office, her blouse haphazardly tucked into her pencil skirt, her cheeks flushed.

Eve shared a shocking revelation of her own: Her mother's best friend—Eve's "Aunt Pooh"—had died in a plane crash that summer, a chartered plane filled with Atlantans returning from a European art tour. Upon take-off in Paris, the plane had caught fire.

Eve blinked and her eyes pooled with tears. "You cannot imagine. So many of my parents' friends died. It was just—it was biblical. Like a flood swept over Buckhead, wiping away so many good people."

They continued to share the details of their private lives, Daniella telling Eve of the chronic nightmare she had been plagued with ever since she was nine years old, when Julius and Ethel Rosenberg were sent to the electric chair for being communist spies, the Rosenberg children losing both of their parents in the course of a single day. In her nightmare it was her own parents who were dragged away by the police, all the while Daniella screaming that they were innocent, that she needed them, she needed her mom and her dad. "My father is Jewish," Daniella explained. "And while I was raised Unitarian, the fact that the Rosenbergs were Jews haunted me, as if *that* were the real reason they were killed."

When the subject turned to sex (both girls confirmed they were virgins), Daniella confessed that over the summer her high school boyfriend had unhooked her bra and cupped her breasts in his hands. Eve said that one summer when she was twelve she hid in her brother Charlie's closet and watched him change into his swim trunks so that she could see what a penis looked like. He was sixteen, and she was fairly certain he knew that she was in there, watching, though neither of them ever said anything to the other about it.

Both girls had older brothers, but neither was particularly close to her sibling. Eve reflected on how differently she and her brother were raised, that when Charlie got in serious trouble her father would hit him with a belt, but that he never hit her. She said she always felt guilty when Charlie was punished, but she noticed, too, that as they grew older her father listened to Charlie more and more, treating him like a man, whereas she felt she would always be cast as the family's "baby," adored but never particularly respected.

Daniella said that she didn't know if her father really respected her mother, that when he spoke about politics or other matters of importance at the dinner table it was her and her brother he addressed, and not his wife, even though she had, in fact, been a stalwart volunteer for JFK's presidential campaign. But it seemed as if Daniella's father just couldn't stop seeing his wife as the pretty college girl he had once seduced.

"At least your dad talks to you," said Eve. "My dad would never even consider that I might have an opinion about that stuff." She raised her legs and crossed them beneath her, intending to sit Indian-style on her bed, but just as she did she passed gas, loudly. Daniella wasn't sure what to do—it had been drilled into her to ignore such things—but Eve started laughing so hard she snorted. And so Daniella started laughing, too, and then Eve passed gas again and it made Daniella laugh even harder, and Eve pointed out that when Daniella laughed her nostrils vibrated.

In the basement of each residence house lived a maid. The maids were there to straighten the common areas, to assist with afternoon tea, to clean the girls' bedrooms, to do their laundry, even to do their ironing. A sophomore informed them, "If you need a dress or a blouse pressed, just leave it hanging on your door and it will be returned the next morning, wrinkle-free, presto change-o!"

Miss Eugenia lived in the basement of Monty House. She was an older woman, though Daniella could not say how old. Like all of the maids at Belmont, she wore a knee-length black uniform with a white apron tied around her waist, thick white hose covering her brown legs. Any time Eve saw Miss Eugenia she would grin and say, "Hey!" as if she were encountering a favorite cousin at a family reunion. Miss Eugenia always smiled politely and answered with a formal greeting, and she always called Eve ma'am. Eve told Daniella that she couldn't see a maid without thinking of Ada, who had practically raised her back in Atlanta, spending five days a week at the Whalen house, letting Eve watch soap operas with her while she ironed the family's clothes, fixing chicken and dumplings for dinner—Eve and Charlie's favorite—on nights when their parents were out.

Eve and Daniella started bringing cookies down to the basement any time Eve's mother sent some of Ada's from home, in an attempt to "Only Connect," the E. M. Forster edict that the dreamy youth group leader from Daniella's church back home had adopted as his motto, and that Eve had latched on to as well under Daniella's influence. In early October, Eve's father sent a half bushel of Winesap apples from Ellijay, Georgia, where he had spent the week hunting. The apples were a perfect balance of sweet and tart, and so fresh the juice ran down their chins whenever they took a bite. Eve put most of the apples out in the common room for the other girls to enjoy, but she and Daniella decided to bring half a dozen down to Miss Eugenia.

It was midafternoon, the calmest stretch of the day. They found Miss Eugenia sitting in her lounge chair watching *Central Hospital* on the little black-and-white television that she kept on her dresser. "My baby," she called it. Though her door was open, Eve knocked anyway.

Eugenia jumped and quickly stood. "Lord, I'm sorry," she said. "Did I not hear the bell? What you girls need?"

Every room at Monty House had an interior doorbell. If a girl needed something she just pressed the doorbell and Miss Eugenia would arrive.

"Not a thing, Miss Eugenia," said Eve. "We just wanted to bring you some apples."

"No, thank you, honey," said Eugenia, sitting back down and returning her attention to the TV screen.

"But they're so good! My daddy sent them fresh from Ellijay."

"I ain't got nothing but fake teeth in here," said Eugenia, tapping at her top tooth. "Cain't bite an apple."

"Oh, I'm so sorry," said Daniella.

"Wait, is that Dr. Lance Patterson?" asked Eve, pointing to the handsome man on the TV screen.

"It sure is, honey, and he supposed to be dead."

"I know!" said Eve, making her way into the room and sitting down on the end of the narrow bed. "I watched all last summer."

"Well, what happened is his cousin buried him alive in that cave, but what his cousin didn't know was there was an old hobo already living in there, and that hobo fixed it up so they could get water from a little drip that came in through the rock, and he had all kinds of canned goods for them to eat. Dr. Patterson lived in that cave for six months, honey, six months! Till one day there was an avalanche and he just tumbled right out."

"Oh my Lord," said Eve, covering her mouth with her hand, the opal and diamond ring her mother had given her in honor of her sixteenth birthday twinkling in the television's soft glow.

After that, Eve would go to Miss Eugenia's room to watch *Central Hospital* any afternoon she wasn't in class. Miss Eugenia didn't exactly invite her, but she didn't seem to mind the company, either, even offering Eve some of her Kraft caramels, which she sucked on like hard candies since she wasn't supposed to chew them with her false teeth. Sometimes Daniella would go down, too, to try to talk with Miss Eugenia during the commercials. Daniella wanted to know where she was from, and did she have a husband, and did the two of them have children, and how much did she get paid for cleaning up after the Belmont girls?

Miss Eugenia spoke easily about her four children and three grand-children, all of whom lived nearby in Roanoke, except for her oldest grandson, who had enrolled in the Army, but she would never give Daniella a straight answer about her salary. "I get by," she would say.

Later Eve told Daniella it was bad manners to pry, to which Daniella responded that southern manners helped keep segregation in place. "My dad says it's all part of an elaborate code to keep the racial lines firmly drawn."

"That's not true," said Eve. "Manners are about making other people feel at ease."

"Yeah, I'm sure Miss Eugenia feels really *at ease* with what she gets paid," Daniella retorted. But then she wanted to take back her words, because Eve looked as if she might start to cry.

"Lord, I miss Ada," Eve said the first week after Thanksgiving break. She told Daniella that besides a brief stay at her family's farm in South Georgia, where she caught up with her brother and her cousins and even went hunting with the men, she had spent most of her time in Atlanta following Ada around like a dog, just going from room to room with her, getting in the way. She even offered to help clean, but Ada told her to quit being foolish.

"You've influenced me, you know," Eve said. "I asked Ada how much she gets paid."

"What did she say?" asked Daniella.

"That it was none of my business."

"You could ask your dad."

"I did. He said she probably doesn't get paid enough, but that Mother can't pay her more because then the other maids would start demanding more from their employers and Mother would be in trouble with all of her friends. So they try to make up for it in other ways. Like Daddy puts money in a savings account for her, and Mother often gives her old clothes that are still in really good condition, stuff she would normally take to the Nearly New."

"Kind masters," said Daniella.

Eve frowned. "They *are* kind. Don't be mean."

"Sorry," Daniella said, feeling a little stung. They always talked honestly about their families, about what they did and did not like about them. Eve had never accused her of being mean before.

"Ada tickled my arm just like she used to when I was little. It was heaven. Did you ever play that game? Where you close your eyes and the person runs her finger up your arm and you're supposed to say when she hits the vein at the crook?"

Daniella shook her head no.

"Lord, what did you Unitarians do at spend-the-nights?" said Eve. "Here, sit down. Let me show you."

Daniella sat on her bed and Eve sat beside her. "Now close your eyes," said Eve. Daniella obeyed, and Eve ran her fingers up the underside of Daniella's forearm, starting at her wrist and working her way toward the elbow. "Tell me when I get there," Eve said. Daniella felt a light, tickling sensation in the middle of her arm and told Eve to stop. She looked down and was surprised to see that Eve's fingers were a good two inches below where she thought they would be.

"You moved them!" said Daniella.

"I didn't. It's some weird nerve-ending thing. If you practice, you'll get better. Ada let me practice again and again, and it felt so good. And then she scratched my head like she used to do when I was a little girl. I asked her if she wanted me to rub her feet and she said I was too old to be doing that, that it wouldn't be right."

Eve looked so sad after talking about Ada that Daniella suggested she write her a letter to let her know how much Ada meant to her. Eve pulled out her box of monogrammed Crane stationery and threw herself into the task, while Daniella went down the hall to see if there was a game of bridge in session. She had never really played before coming to Belmont, but it turned out she was a natural.

When Daniella returned to their room, she could tell from Eve's wet lashes and ruddy cheeks that she had been crying.

"What's wrong?" Daniella asked, sitting on the edge of the bed beside her friend. Eve reached for a tissue and blew her nose, then told Daniella, in a shaking voice, that she realized she *still* didn't have Ada's address. She had meant to ask Ada for it in Atlanta but had forgotten. So she decided to address the letter to Ada in care of her mother. She started addressing the letter: "Miss Ada . . . ," and then she realized she couldn't remember Ada's last name. She knew she had learned it before, but she could not think of what it was. And suddenly the lopsidedness of it all struck her in a way that it never had before.

"She used to rub my tummy while I sat on the toilet and cried, because I was constipated, and I don't even know her last name."

After that, Eve joined Daniella in her efforts to try to find out more about the lives of the Belmont maids. How many worked at the school? Did they all know one another? How many hours a week did they work? Were they given lunch breaks? What happened if someone got sick? What happened if someone got pregnant? What happened if someone needed to take time off to care for a sick family member—would her job be waiting for her when she returned?

They tried to talk with the maids who worked in the other dorms, but Eugenia was the only one who told them anything at all, and that was only during *Central Hospital*'s commercial breaks. Eve had asked Eugenia if she would show them pictures of her family. The only pictures hanging on the wall of Miss Eugenia's room were of Jesus, Dr. Martin Luther King, and the president. Miss Eugenia opened the top drawer of her dresser and brought out a portrait taken at her church. There stood a younger Miss Eugenia in a large hat, flanked by her three daughters, all with somber faces. Below the women was an older man, presumably Miss Eugenia's husband, who was in a wheelchair. Daniella knew Miss Eugenia had a son, but he was not in the picture.

"What happened?" asked Eve, pointing to the wheelchair. Miss Eugenia explained that Franklin had been shot in a hunting accident years ago. The wound had gotten infected, and he ended up having to have his leg amputated, just a week shy of his twenty-third birthday. "He got a wood leg, but he says it's real uncomfortable, so mostly he sticks with the chair."

"Has he had trouble finding work because of his leg?" asked Daniella.

"He tried to go back to work at the factory, but he couldn't 'cause of the stairs. He had a little shoeshine business downtown, but then that diner came in—Lester's—and they run him off, even though he had paid good money to rent that corner. He thought about finding somewhere else to set up his polish, but his arthritis started acting up real bad. So we both real grateful I got this job, honey; we surely are."

"But when do you see him?" asked Eve.

"Every Sunday. And my daughter Gwinn, she look after him during the week."

"But couldn't you go home each night and come back every morning?" asked Eve. "That way you'd get to see him more."

"What if one of y'all got sick in the middle of the night?"

"We would go to the infirmary," said Eve.

"What if one of y'all rips a hem just before one of your formals over at Hampden-Sydney?"

"We'd go to the dance with a ripped hem," said Eve. "Big deal."

"All I know is my job is to take care of you-all, and that means round-the-clock."

The show had come back on, so Eugenia quit talking. By this point Daniella had become interested in the story, too, in what Dr. Lance Patterson was going to do to extract revenge on the cousin who tried to bury him alive. She noticed that Eve wasn't really paying attention.

• • •

At dinner Eve brought up the plight of the maids with some of the other girls from Monty House, as it was a Thursday, when everyone was required to sit at a table with their dorm mates. The Monty House girls made up four tables in total, but Mrs. Shuler sat at Eve and Daniella's, leading the girls in grace before the casual meal of chicken salad, fruit cocktail, corn muffins, and chocolate chip cookies.

"Seriously, y'all. If we banded together and said that we don't need them to stay overnight, they might be able to go home and see their families," said Eve. She was animated as she spoke, wearing her dad's old plaid flannel shirt—which she rarely took off—with a blue-and-white-striped skirt zipped over her jeans to comply with the school's dress code for dinner.

"I agree," said Daniella. She was buttering a corn muffin, served savory, not sweet like her mother made at home. When Daniella first commented on the lack of sugar in the Belmont corn muffins, Eve told her that no self-respecting southerner would eat a corn muffin that was sweet. For a moment Daniella had felt wounded, the seed of insecurity her mother had planted long ago sprouting. (Countless times during her life her mother had said some version of, "I worry that it will always be a struggle for you to feel as if you belong, because you are half-Jewish.") But then she looked at Eve and realized she was being affectionate and laughed, allowing herself to be delighted once again by her friend.

"But Eve," said Lane Carmichael, "what if I'm getting ready for a formal and the zipper on my dress breaks? If the maids have all gone home, who's going to fix it?"

"Yes, and I love how Miss Eugenia puts out milk and graham crackers before we go to bed," said Eleanor Morgan, who had removed every piece of celery from her scoop of chicken salad.

"You can't pour yourself a glass of milk and get some graham crackers out of the box?" asked Eve.

Eleanor rolled her eyes. She was a prim girl, someone who always sat ramrod straight. "I simply don't think it's wise to do anything controversial before rush."

"Are you serious?" said Eve. "First of all, rush isn't until next semester, so who cares, and second, I would think the best of Belmont would want to do all they can to help the women who help us so much."

Daniella knew that when Eve said "the best of Belmont" she was alluding to Fleur, the local sorority that Eve's mother and grandmother had been members of during their Belmont days.

"It's December, Eve. Next semester is just around the corner," said Eleanor. "And we're not all double legacies. Some of us can't afford to be as blithe as you."

"What does that have to do with trying to be decent and kind to Miss Eugenia?" implored Eve.

"Girls," said Mrs. Shuler. "Let's move on."

Eve stopped talking, but Daniella knew that she wasn't going to move on, indignation burning her cheeks.

After dinner Daniella asked Eve if she wanted to go to the library with her to study, but Eve demurred, saying she had things to do in their room. When Daniella returned a few hours later, her face flushed from the brisk mountain air, Eve held up a piece of her heavy stationery, upon which she had written a letter to Dr. Dupree, the headmaster of Belmont. Eve read the letter to Daniella. In it she stated that the policy of twenty-four-hour maid service was outdated and unnecessary and that the maids themselves had to find people to take care of their own families in their absence. Mrs. Eugenia Williams, for example, had a crippled husband who was left home alone while she served 10:00 p.m. snacks of milk and graham crackers to the girls of Monty House. Eve suggested an alternative, that the maids work from 8:00 a.m. to 4:00 p.m. and then anyone who wanted to earn overtime could stay for an evening shift.

When Eve finished reading, she looked at Daniella expectantly. Daniella didn't say anything.

"What?"

"It's great, Eve. It really is. I'm just not sure if you should send it."

"Why on earth not? You just said it was great."

"Well, if you do send it, don't use Eugenia's name. Or check with her first—make sure she's okay with it."

"I'm a concerned student! I have every right to send it! And none of those other girls give a damn. That idiot Eleanor Morgan just wants to make sure someone is there to pour her milk and serve her graham crackers and probably burp her before she goes to bed at night. We need to be the voice for Eugenia and all the other cleaning ladies. Aren't you the one always telling me, 'Do not be too timid and squeamish about your actions'?"

Thanks to the Unitarian Church, Daniella had memorized lines and lines of Emerson, which Eve was now parroting back to her.

"I just think you need to make sure your ducks are all in a row before you start shooting."

"'You cannot do a kindness too soon, for you never know how soon it will be too late.'"

Emerson again. Eve was a quick study.

Eve posted her letter in the campus mail the following day. For the next week, if Daniella checked their mailbox before her, Eve would race in from class and go through the letters on her desk, looking for one on Belmont stationery. "Nothing?" she'd ask, and Daniella would say, "Nothing."

"Well, damn."

Eve was still going down to Miss Eugenia's room to watch *Central Hospital* most afternoons, but Daniella spent every afternoon in the library, writing papers and studying for exams. Eve told Daniella that she hadn't mentioned the letter to Miss Eugenia, saying she didn't want to disappoint her if nothing came of it, which she was beginning to think would be the case.

On the Thursday before Christmas break, Daniella, who had taken her last exam the day before, turned in her final paper of the semester. Her parents weren't picking her up until Saturday, so she had a day and a half to play. The sky was blue and the December air was crisp but not too cold—the perfect weather for a hike along Lazy Creek, which ran through the campus and then continued to wind all the way to the base of Mount Illahee.

Daniella's appreciation for the surroundings of Belmont had deepened. She loved the crisscrossing of bare tree limbs, the mountains that held the college within their embrace, the stillness of a winter day. Earlier that week, Eve's mother had sent peanut butter fudge—made by Ada—and Daniella imagined munching on a piece of it as she and Eve hiked, following the circuitous path of the half-frozen creek.

She just hoped Eve was done with her papers and exams as well. She couldn't quite remember her friend's schedule but was pretty sure she would be finished by Thursday, too. Daniella went back to their room, but Eve wasn't there. Glancing at her watch, she realized it was *Central Hospital* hour. She headed down the basement stairs, hurrying as she got near the bottom, because she could hear keening, like a cat in heat.

It was Eve, slumped on the floor, clutching her knees to her chest, her hair in her face, crying and hiccupping, her back against the wall. A cold certainty settled over Daniella as she walked toward her friend. She knew that Miss Eugenia was not in her room; she knew that Miss Eugenia would no longer be returning to Belmont. When she peeked inside, she saw that the bed had been stripped and Miss Eugenia's pictures had been removed: the one of Jesus with a halo, the one of Dr. Martin Luther King, the one of President Kennedy. There was no TV set on the dresser, no chipped cup on the bedside table, no worn slippers peeking out from underneath the bed. There was no sign of Miss Eugenia at all.

Daniella walked toward Eve and slid her spine down the wall so she could sit beside her. "What happened?"

"I got here right as she was finishing packing. She barely looked at me,

Daniella. Said she'd been fired for being an 'agitator.' Said she was given the afternoon to get her stuff and find a ride home."

"Oh, Eve."

Eve, her cheeks stained with tears, her breath hot and foul, looked at Daniella. "I did this. I made this happen. It's my fault."

Daniella kneaded Eve's shoulders, which were bunched, tense. She imagined absorbing some of Eve's pain into her own hands. "It's not your fault," she said. "I promise. This is all much bigger than you are. This stuff has been happening for a very long time. Just ask my father, the historian."

"Well, I never knew about it," said Eve, and in that moment she sounded like a haughty child.

Daniella tried not to think of Miss Eugenia carrying an old suitcase down the basement hall, on her way to the parking lot to wait for one of her daughters to come pick her up, to drive her toward a bleaker, starker future. For a moment, Daniella felt a cold, calm anger toward Eve, her silly friend who was so naïve she thought she could splash and kick her way into an ocean of oppression and instantly change the tide. But then she looked at Eve, saw her weeping, saw that she was deep in grief. Daniella, so full of instant indignation, deflated. She understood that she was as responsible as Eve. Before the two girls met, Eve was blissful in her ignorance. And Miss Eugenia had a job.

Chapter 2

FLEUR

Roanoke, Virginia, 1963

While Belmont did not have national sororities, there were three local ones on campus: Fleur, Pansy, and Carnation (Phi Lambda, Pi Alpha, and Chi Alpha, though nobody called them by their Greek letters). Eve's mother had been a Fleur during her two years at Belmont, and her maternal grandmother had been the chapter president when she was an undergraduate, so naturally Eve was expected to "pledge the bouquet." In truth it seemed that every girl going through rush hoped for a bid from Fleur, though the more prudent ones claimed they just wanted to "find the right sorority home for me."

For decades, rush had occurred during the very first week of the fall semester. A few years back, the school had decided to delay it until two weeks after Christmas break to let the new girls settle into college life a bit before they were subjected to the frantic four days of selection and rejection. But as soon as everyone returned to campus from the holiday, rush began in earnest.

The night before the first round of parties, Mrs. Shuler gathered her freshmen in the parlor for hot chocolate and vanilla wafers. Everyone was abuzz with nervous energy, for Monty House, the oldest dorm on campus and filled with the daughters of Belmont alums, was known as the "Greek house"; while only about half of the girls at Belmont ended up joining a sorority, nearly every girl who lived in Monty House did. Eve and Daniella had already spent the afternoon speculating about who might end up where, Eve insisting that Eleanor Morgan would pledge Pansy, which was known to be prissy. Mrs. Shuler, wearing a tweed dress with her hair pulled back in its trademark bun, stood by the baby grand piano and called the girls to attention.

"I know you all have a lot to do before tomorrow," she began. "So I will keep this brief. Sororities can be an enriching part of college life, but I want you to remember that, above all, you belong to Belmont. Do not let your sorority affiliation replace your dedication to your academics or your loyalty to school. And tomorrow, as you go to your first round of parties, just be yourself. Act natural. Remember that the girls inside the sorority houses are just as nervous as you are, for they, too, are being evaluated by you. My hope is that every one of you will find the perfect sisterhood, regardless of reputation, and that not *too* many tears are shed in the process."

She lifted her hot cocoa mug in the air and said, "Cheers."

Eve turned to give Daniella an exaggerated look of horror. "Gee, now I'm not nervous at all!" she joked.

Mrs. Shuler had been a Carnation when she was at Belmont, and the rumor was that she had never quite recovered from being cut from both Pansy and Fleur. That was why she was constantly reminding the girls that they belonged to "Belmont first." Her antipathy toward the more popular sororities seemed to be confirmed when she pulled Daniella aside as she was filing out of the parlor and urged her to "think about Carnation."

Daniella, who might not have even gone through rush had she not landed in Monty House with Eve, *was* thinking about Carnation. She was thinking that she did not want to join it. She wanted to be in Fleur with Eve, though she had no family connections, was not southern, and had not attended an elite prep school like Eve had. She didn't even realize she was supposed to have letters of recommendation until it was too late to try to secure them. Eve had them, of course, but she claimed they didn't matter.

"I only have them because Grandmommy insisted," she said. "But you don't need them. Midge Miller was in Charlie's class at Coventry and she was a Belmont Fleur. She told me that with local sororities, recommendations really don't matter. What they look at are your grades and your extracurriculars."

When it came to that, Daniella was on more sure footing, something Eve reminded her of any time she expressed doubt that she was "Fleur material."

"Are you kidding me?" Eve said. "You're so precious, you've got a four-point-oh, you're on the tennis team, and you're my roommate!"

"Just being associated with you is powerful enough to get me in?" joked Daniella, though really, she was hoping Eve was right.

"I don't mean that, of course. I just mean that given my family's history, it's pretty likely I'll get a bid, and everyone knows you're my best friend, so of course we'll be seen as a matched set."

"Like salt and pepper shakers," joked Daniella.

"*Sterling* salt and pepper shakers, dahling," joked Eve. "Only the best."

Each day of rush, the girls would gather first in the Blue Room, a formal parlor in the Admissions Building, which was rumored to have a bullet hole in the wall marking the long-ago suicide of a Belmont girl that was now covered up by a portrait of Dr. William March, the college's founder. The Blue Room was where the Rush Counselors would hand the girls their daily envelopes. On the very first day the envelopes simply contained a list showing the order in which the potential pledges (referred to by the sorority members as "pee-pees") were to visit the houses, since every pee-pee visited every house during the first round. After that, cuts were made, the very most after that first round as a way to encourage those girls who weren't really "sorority material" to drop out of rush altogether before becoming too invested.

The parties were orchestrated as precisely as a military campaign: the first an afternoon tea, the second skits, and the third Song Night, the only party held after dinner, when everyone wore a formal dress and the sorority members courted the pee-pees with candlelight, dessert, and songs of sisterhood. After Song Night concluded, the pee-pees, still in formal dress, would gather once again in the Blue Room to list the sororities in order of their first and second choice. The Rush Counselors urged the girls not to worry: As long as they were invited back to at least one of the three houses for Song Night, they *would* get a bid. That was a rule of the college. Indeed, many girls *only* got asked back to one house on the final night—usually Carnation—and so they had to decide right then and there if they wanted to join that house or if they wanted to drop out of rush altogether.

Very, very rarely, a girl wouldn't be asked back to any house for Song Night at all. It was rumored that that was why the young woman had killed herself so long ago in the Blue Room: She had received an empty envelope after the second round. But the Rush Counselors assured the girls that such an outcome was extremely unlikely; everyone just needed to trust the system and not think about which sorority was "popular," but rather which was a good fit. Everyone cries at least once during rush, they said, but ultimately, the system works.

Daniella and Eve chose each other's outfits for the first party, the afternoon tea, both wearing knee-length skirts embellished with one crinoline apiece, and a cashmere twin sweater set, Daniella's baby blue, Eve's pink. Eve, who as a double legacy could afford to be a little cavalier, wore a pair of saddle oxfords, while Daniella wore flats. They set their hair in rollers the night before, which meant Eve's flat hair curled up at the ends while Daniella's waves were tamed straight.

There was a nervous sense of anticipation as the girls gathered in the Blue Room to learn the order in which they would visit the houses. Eve and Daniella were scheduled to visit each house at different times, which was probably good, because Eve would likely try to crack Daniella up while she was making small talk with a sorority member. The three houses sat next to each other, up a little hill behind the library. They were all brick, all Colonial in style, and for rush the exterior of each was decorated with an archway of balloons and a big welcoming banner. Fleur's archway was made of light pink and white balloons, the Fleur colors, and its banner featured a painted straw basket filled with flowers in an array of pinks, reds, and whites, each petal created by a scrunched-up piece of colored tissue paper held in place with glue.

The interior of the Fleur house was a study in good taste, all Oriental rugs and fine antique furniture gleaming with polish—the entirety of Belmont was redolent of citrus polish—save for the very modern Eames chair in the living room. Most of the girls in Fleur came from money, and nearly every member was some sort of campus leader: the student body president, the head of the Junior Achievement Society, Miss Illahee, which was Belmont's version of a beauty queen, although she couldn't only be beautiful but also had to have breeding and brains. Daniella was greeted by an attractive brunette named Lauren, who, after learning that Daniella had grown up in D.C., asked if she had ever met JFK. Daniella was pretty sure they weren't supposed to talk politics, but who didn't love the young, handsome president? And so she told Lauren about how her mother had poured herself into volunteering for the Kennedy campaign and how he had once stopped by the campaign office and shaken her hand. Lauren gave out a little yelp and said that her mother had volunteered for Kennedy, too, but golly, had never gotten to meet him!

Daniella's conversations at Pansy and Carnation were dull in comparison. She told the girls that she lived in Monty House, that her dad was a professor, that yes, the weather was gorgeous, and that she most certainly was looking forward to Illahee Day, that much-anticipated but unknown day in spring when all of the girls would be surprised by a bugle call in the morning, announcing that classes were canceled so everyone could go and climb Mount Illahee.

At Carnation, Rachel Tennenbaum asked if she had attended any services in Roanoke. Daniella said that she didn't realize there was a Unitarian church in town, and Rachel had answered that she meant the Reform synagogue.

The girls were encouraged to dress informally for the next round of parties—Daniella and Eve were both invited back to all three houses—so they each wore capri pants paired with a popover top, Eve's pastel plaid and Daniella's turquoise blue. Lauren, the girl Daniella had chatted with about Kennedy at the Fleur tea, played Dorothy in the sorority's *Wizard of Oz* sketch. "There's no place like Fleur; there's no place like Fleur!" she chanted, while clicking the heels of her ruby slippers. Later she winked at Daniella from across the room while Daniella spoke with a perfectly nice if slightly ditzy girl named Bev, who had been two grades above Eve at their private school in Atlanta and had an obvious crush on Eve's older brother, Charlie. "He's just so all-American!" Bev gushed.

After skit day the girls who had been invited back to all three houses had to eliminate one of them to get the choice down to two for Song Night. Eve and Daniella both dropped Carnation, keeping Pansy and Fleur, but agreeing that Fleur was the only one worth joining.

When they returned to Monty House, Eve stopped at the shared phone in the hallway in order to call her grandmother in Atlanta, who had insisted that she check in with her after each rush event. A few minutes later Eve returned to their room, flopped down on her bed, and sighed. "Grandmommy pretends to want to hear all of the 'fun' details about the parties, but she's really just making sure I pledge Fleur. It's like she thinks I'm going to pledge Pansy to rebel or something."

"*Would* you pledge Pansy? If you didn't get a bid from Fleur?" asked Daniella.

"I guess, but I don't think that's going to be an issue."

"Not for you, obviously, but I could get cut."

"You keep saying that, but you're going to be fine, really. I mean, look at you—you're so pretty and wonderful. You're a shoo-in."

The next morning Daniella was awoken by a noise, but she was in such a deep slumber that it took her a moment to realize the noise she was hearing was someone knocking on the dorm room door. Eve remained asleep. Daniella opened the door in her nightgown, trying to be as quiet as possible so as not to disturb Eve. There stood an ashen Mrs. Shuler beside Daniella's Rush Counselor, Peggy.

Peggy looked as if she were attending a funeral. Daniella felt as if her knees might buckle.

They had been told that if anything "unfortunate" occurred during rush, your counselor would come to you, so you wouldn't have to show up in the Blue Room with all of the other girls only to leave in humiliation when you were handed an empty envelope. And here was Peggy. Surely she had not come to see Eve.

"Would you come talk with me downstairs, please?" asked Peggy.

"Let me get a robe," said Daniella, her voice sounding far away even to herself.

She went to her closet and grabbed the pink fuzzy robe her mother had given to her as a going-away present before she left for Belmont. She knotted it tightly around her waist and followed Peggy and Mrs. Shuler down the stairs and into the little den off the parlor where Daniella sometimes studied. The den had wood-paneled walls and elk horns mounted over the fireplace.

Peggy sat beside Daniella on the couch. "I'm sorry to have to tell you this," she said. "But you have been released from Pansy and Fleur."

Even though Daniella knew Peggy's arrival could only mean news of this sort, her words didn't make any sense. Released from both? But Lauren had winked at her during the *Wizard of Oz* skit!

"I'm so sorry, Daniella; I really am. Sometimes there are quirks that just don't make any sense."

"Oh my God," said Daniella, flush with humiliation. Neither house had asked her back for Song Night. Neither house wanted her. Should she have jettisoned Pansy and kept Carnation instead, since Carnation was known to be the least choosy? But she hadn't made a connection with anyone there, had found the girls awkward and difficult to talk to. And Lauren from Fleur had winked at her. Wasn't that a sort of promise? Did that not count for anything?

"I was blackballed?" she asked.

"I really don't know what happened. It's just an unfortunate, awful thing. But think about this—you have the tennis team, which will be starting up soon, and there are plenty of other organizations you may join—the literary society, the drama club, the Illahee Climbers. There are *so* many ways, with or without a Greek affiliation, to be a well-rounded Monty."

Mrs. Shuler, who had remained quiet up until that point, finally spoke. "Daniella, dear, when I was a student at the Madeira School I was taught a very wise mantra: 'Function in chaos, finish in style.' It is your choice to function during this chaotic moment, and I imagine that if you do, you will most certainly finish in style."

Daniella didn't know what to say. Everyone in Monty House would know she had not been asked back to Song Night. And surely everyone on campus would soon know, too. Yes, there were plenty of Belmont girls who didn't go through rush, for either financial or personal reasons, but it was different to have tried to join and been blackballed. Daniella couldn't exactly claim indifference the way those other girls could. Would anyone believe her if she said she had dropped out of rush to focus more on her studies? No. It was a small campus and the girls at Fleur and Pansy knew what happened. Should she transfer dorms, maybe to Hanker House, which was known to be a little bohemian and contained the fewest members of the Greek system? Should she transfer colleges altogether? Would Eve still want to be friends with her, Eve who would surely receive a bid to Fleur and leave Daniella behind, their friendship only a brief distraction before she met her real sisters?

"So I just don't show up in the Blue Room today?"

"That's right," said Peggy. "Don't come to the Blue Room. Do something nice for yourself instead. Take a long, hot shower; get yourself an ice cream."

"Because that will make things all better," Daniella said, unable to stop herself.

"I think you will find that sarcasm will not help your situation," said Mrs. Shuler, to which Daniella wanted to scream, *I'm functioning, you bitch! I'm functioning in chaos.*

"Okay, thanks. Thanks for telling me," Daniella mumbled, and she rose from the couch and walked in a haze of tears back to her room, where she found Eve still asleep, her long blond hair fanning out around her head on the pillow. Sitting on the edge of her friend's bed, she shook her shoulder.

"What is it?" Eve asked, her voice kind and concerned even in her half-awake state.

"I have to tell you something. Something bad."

With a snap Eve was sitting up in her bed, alert. "What? What happened?"

"I'm not going to be a Fleur. I'm not going to be in any sorority." As soon as she spoke the words aloud she started to cry, staccato little sobs that sounded like hiccups.

"What are you talking about?"

"Peggy came to tell me this morning. I'm not invited back to Song Night. No one wants me."

"But it doesn't make any sense. You're perfect for Fleur. You *are* a Fleur!"

"It's because my father is Jewish," said Daniella, and as soon as the words left her mouth she realized they were true. That was why Mrs. Shuler told her to "think about Carnation." That was why Rachel Tennenbaum was asking her about Reform services in Roanoke. Everyone at Belmont thought of her as Jewish whether she called herself Unitarian or not, and Carnation was clearly the only sorority that accepted Jews.

"That's absurd," said Eve.

"Why then?"

"I don't know. It doesn't make any sense. I know a couple of the older girls in Fleur from Coventry. Maybe I could ask one of them what happened."

"You know you're not allowed to make contact with anyone in the houses until after bids are given. Besides, you don't need to ask. I know. It's so clear to me now."

"I refuse to believe that's the reason. It's just too ludicrous for words. I mean, isn't the whole motto of Fleur that it takes every type of flower to make a beautiful bouquet?"

"Yeah, a Methodist flower, and a Presbyterian flower, and an Episcopal flower . . ."

"I mean, maybe some girl in Fleur had it in for you, was jealous or something, and insisted they cut you, but that doesn't really make any sense. I mean, if that were the case, why not drop you after the first round? And it's not like you're going out with anyone's ex-boyfriend or anything."

"It happened with *both* sororities, Eve."

"Wait! I just thought of something. How many letters of recommendation did you have?"

"I didn't have any, remember? They're local sororities; you told me they weren't necessary."

"That's got to be it! I must have been wrong. I mean, I had three letters for each one! And I don't even want to be in Carnation or Pansy. But my grandmother insisted on it, so maybe recs were more important than I realized. It must have been a stupid technicality. We just need to get you some recs, and then you can go through rush again next year. Or maybe even get a snap bid before then."

"I really don't think it was a matter of recs," said Daniella, even though a small, dumb part of herself was hoping that Eve was right, that there was some mundane reason why she had been cut; some small mistake that, once rectified, could reopen the door to Eve's world.

Eve went to Song Night without Daniella and, of course, was offered a bid to Fleur the next day. That night a woven basket was placed in front of their door, filled with twenty-four intricately constructed paper flowers, each one personalized with the name of a girl in the Fleur pledge class. Up and down the hall, girls had their own straw baskets of flowers—or paper cutouts of pansies or carnations—decorating their doorways, all but Natalie, the only girl in Monty House who had not gone through rush at all. Chapter meetings were every Monday and so it would just be Natalie and Daniella left in the dorm while everyone else toddled off to their sorority.

Eve told Daniella that as soon as she got to know a few more of the older girls, she was going to find out what had happened, find out what Daniella needed to do to get in. Daniella appreciated Eve's loyalty, but she also knew that her friend might let things slip as the semester rolled on. Eve had sisters now, a whole pledge class to befriend; what did she care about a girl who was cut before Song Night?

But true to her word, if Eve was eating lunch with a group from Fleur or walking through campus with one of them, she would always wave Daniella over, throw an arm around her, introduce her all around. The older members of Fleur were nice to Daniella, though it was awkward talking to them knowing that they knew she had been cut—that they had cut her. Worse was running into Lauren, the JFK fan who had winked at her while performing her skit. Whenever Daniella would pass her on campus, Daniella would look away, as if she didn't see her, but one day she happened to be walking alone to the library when Lauren sidled up next to her, matching her stride.

"Look, can we talk?" Lauren asked.

"Sure," said Daniella, but she kept walking at the same pace, worried that if she were to stop and turn to face Lauren she would burst into tears.

Lauren reached over and put her hand on Daniella's arm. "Can you just stop for a minute? Sit down?"

There was a bench nearby. Lauren dusted off the seat before they sat.

"I'm so sorry about what happened. I'm not supposed to say anything, but I need you to know that we wanted you. We all wanted you. It's just, there's this group of alums that kind of controls things, and they said 'no.' They said we could only have twenty-four pledges tops, that if we had more than that the sorority would lose some of its exclusivity, and that everyone we offered a bid to . . . everyone had to have letters of recommendation. And you didn't. We tried to argue with them, but they were resolute. I'm so sorry."

Had Eve been right? Had she been rejected simply over a technicality? Why, then, had Mrs. Shuler encouraged her to "think about Carnation"? She hadn't had recommendation letters for Carnation, either. But maybe that was what made Carnation different from the other two; maybe its requirements were less stringent.

"The school should have told us," Daniella said. "They should have let us know so that everyone had a fair chance."

Lauren looked pained. "It wasn't fair at all," she said. "And again, I'm just so sorry."

And then she got up quickly and hurried off, and the next time Daniella saw her, Lauren gave only the most cursory of smiles.

Eve, of course, was elated to hear about Daniella's conversation with Lauren, though Daniella made her swear not to tell anyone else about it. "I told you!" she said, and then her eyes lit up even more. "Daniella! This means all we need to do is get my mother to write you a Fleur rec and the next time they give out snap bids you can get one. Did I tell you that's how Aunt Pooh got in? She had mono during rush, but later that year Fleur just offered her a bid after someone dropped out."

Daniella still felt uneasy. If what Eve was saying was true, then why did Lauren seem so pained during their conversation? If Fleur wanted her and she just needed to have a letter of recommendation to get a bid, then why didn't Lauren tell her that, tell her the exact steps she needed to take?

There was one member of Eve's pledge class whom Daniella really liked, a girl named Katharine Ridley from Alabama who lived just down the hall from them in Monty House. Katharine—Kitty—was goofy like Eve and always seemed glad to see Daniella. As the semester continued, the three of them grew close, and eventually Daniella allowed Eve to tell Kitty about the conversation she had had with Lauren about the alumnae group and recommendations. After that, any time it was just the three of them, Eve and Kitty would openly discuss how to get Daniella a bid sooner rather than later.

"I think they offer snap bids after Easter break," said Kitty, "because that's just after midterm grades come out and some girls are forced to drop because they're failing. That's probably our best option."

"And I asked Mother to write Daniella a letter of recommendation," said Eve. "So we've got that taken care of."

"Y'all, I don't even know if I want to join anymore. Seriously, it would feel really queer after they rejected me."

"Oh, please," said Eve, waving away Daniella's words, as she always did when Daniella mentioned her doubts about trying to join Fleur. "Lauren said they all wanted you. It was just a stupid technicality."

"Here's the thing," said Eve to Kitty. "If they know they are going to lose girls after Easter, why not go ahead and fill up? Why not just offer Daniella a snap bid as soon as they receive the letter from Mother?"

"Let's ask Mandy about it," said Kitty. "Maybe she knows." Mandy was their pledge trainer. Like Eve, she was from Atlanta, although she had gone to the Lovett School and not Coventry.

That night after chapter meeting, Eve returned to their dorm room in a foul mood. She wouldn't tell Daniella what was going on, only said she was sick of all the bitches at Belmont, then stormed off to the phone down the hall to make a call. From inside their room Daniella could hear Eve yelling. Eventually Mrs. Shuler came up and gave Eve a demerit, told her she must calm down or she was going to hang up on whomever Eve was speaking with. Eve returned to their room flushed and steely eyed.

"Well, that's done."

"What's done?" asked Daniella, looking up from her book.

Eve flopped down on Daniella's bed, as Daniella's was made and Eve's was not. "I approached Mandy tonight. I asked her point-blank if you could get a snap bid after your letter of recommendation arrives, and she pulled me aside and told me that she was going to tell me something completely confidential that I couldn't share with anyone. And then she told me that, just like Lauren said, the girls in Fleur totally loved you and wanted you as a member, but that they weren't allowed to offer you a bid because you're Jewish. Apparently there's a local alumnae association that is really adamant about allowing only Christian girls in the sorority, and they sent some representative over before Song Night to vet Fleur's choice of girls. And I can only presume that's what happened with Pansy, too. God, I'm just so sick I can hardly stand it."

Daniella felt an odd combination of both embarrassment and validation. She *had* been right. It *was* because she was Jewish. They didn't want her because she was Jewish.

"Did you tell them I'm Unitarian?"

This was something of a joke, but Eve did not laugh.

"I called Grandmother to tell her I'm dropping out."

"What? You can't do that!"

"That's what Grandmommy said. She told me I was making a 'grave mistake' that I would regret for the rest of my life. She told me not to expect her to pay my tuition if I drop."

"Then you have to stay in."

"No, I don't. My parents will pay it if she doesn't. She's just a mean old bitch; she really is."

Daniella looked at Eve, whose face was locked in defiance. "Don't drop out for me, okay? It really doesn't matter all that much. All it means is I don't go to chapter meetings and I don't have to pay dues."

"It means so much more than that and you know it," said Eve.

Clearly it did, because the next evening Eve's grandmother showed up, having been driven to Roanoke from Atlanta in her pale blue Lincoln Town Car. Daniella happened to be returning to Monty House from tennis practice when "Grandmommy" arrived. She watched as the colored driver parked on the gravel in front of the house. He got out of the car and walked around to open the rear door of the sedan, holding out his gloved hand to help his tiny passenger emerge from the back seat. Though Daniella had never met her, she knew immediately who it was. Grandmommy wore the Fleur colors, a bright pink jacket over a light pink dress, her elfin feet strapped into pale pink heels, her Fleur pin secured close to her heart. Around her neck were three thick strands of pearls, and in each ear a pearl so fat it must have popped open the oyster it grew in.

Daniella ran up the front steps to find Eve and warn her, but Eve was not in their room. Surely she was with Kitty down the hall, but Daniella hesitated to go look for her, indulging for a moment in the fanciful thinking that if she did not help it along, perhaps this ensuing drama would not unfold. It was all so humiliating, to be the source of so much trouble.

A few moments later there was a knock on her dorm room door, but when Daniella opened it she was faced with Mrs. Shuler, not Eve's grandmother.

"Is Eve here, dear?" Mrs. Shuler asked.

"Try Kitty's room," said Daniella.

Mrs. Shuler turned with a sigh and headed toward Kitty's room, knocking on the door, then speaking quietly with whomever answered. And then Eve shot into the room, as if launched by a slingshot.

"Oh my Lord, oh my Lord, oh my Lord. Grandmommy is here, as in right now, and my hair is a mess and I haven't taken a shower in three days!"

Eve was wearing dungarees and one of her dad's old shirts, her greasy hair pulled back into a low ponytail. She looked pretty, but not at all like a debutante.

"How can she be mad you're not ready for her? She didn't tell you she was coming."

"'A lady is always dressed for visitors,'" said Eve. "One of Grandmommy's rules." As she spoke she was tearing off the flannel shirt and putting on first her soft pink cashmere shell and then the matching cardigan. She slid off the dungarees and slid on an A-line skirt, then shoved her feet into a pair of kitten heels that happened to be resting beneath her dresser.

"There's nothing I can do about the hair, but how does the rest of me look?"

"Good. You should put on a little lipstick, though."

"Right." Eve ran a tube of pink lipstick across her lips, rubbed them together, then headed out the door. "I would invite you to come with me, but I promise, it's not going to be pleasant."

Daniella did not know what to do with herself while she waited for Eve to talk with her grandmother. She felt antsy sitting in the room, but she felt embarrassed venturing outside of it. The school was so small, surely news had gotten around that Eve was dropping out of Fleur because of her and that Eve's grandmother had come all the way up from Atlanta to talk her out of it.

She was causing so much trouble. She was keeping Eve from the institution that nearly all of the women in her family belonged to. An institution she might have belonged to as well, if only she could have better hidden her Jewishness. *Oh God.* What was she even thinking—that she would change her last name? Use her mother's maiden name instead? Wear a cross around her neck? No. She would *not* be ashamed of who she was. She would *not* be ashamed of her father—she loved her father; he was the smartest person she knew, and he made her feel smart, too.

She wondered again if perhaps she should transfer to a different college. She had been accepted at Barnard, but her mother had worried about her living in New York City and Belmont had such a good tennis team and such a lovely campus—and was closer to home. But maybe a place like Barnard was a better fit. There would certainly be more Jewish girls there. She wondered if she would need to apply again or if the fact that she had been admitted once would be enough. She supposed she could have her father telephone the admissions office or perhaps ask a dean at Belmont about doing so. She would miss Eve, miss her terribly, but they were from different worlds, and she didn't want to continue causing Eve angst.

By the time Eve returned to the dorm room, Daniella had pretty much decided she was leaving Belmont. Eve's eyes were red from crying, but she was smiling. "Would you come downstairs and talk to Grandmommy? She wants to meet you."

Why hadn't it occurred to Daniella that Eve's grandmother might want to meet her? She was still in her tennis clothes, still sweaty from practice, her hair pulled back in a ponytail. *Oh well.* She smeared on the same lipstick Eve had used, shrugging at her reflection.

She and Eve walked down the curved front staircase to the parlor, where Grandmommy waited, perched atop an antique armchair. Miss Louise, who had replaced Miss Eugenia, was pouring the old woman a cup of tea from the silver service that belonged to the house, bequeathed by a childless alum who had no one to pass her treasures on to. Every surface of every piece of the silver was imprinted with flowers. During their first days at Belmont Eve had identified the pattern for her—Repousse by Kirk. "Repousse is one you either love or you hate," Eve had declared. Daniella loved it.

"Cream or sugar, ma'am?" asked Miss Louise.

Grandmother waved away the offer, imperious as a tiny queen. "Neither. Eve, would your friend like a cup of tea?"

"No, thanks," said Daniella, but she was so nervous her words were barely audible.

"Speak up, dear," said the woman.

"No, thank you," said Daniella. She had no idea if she was supposed to sit or wait until she was instructed to do so. Suddenly, her rebellious side took over and she thought, *Oh, to hell with it,* and just plopped down on the sofa across from the old lady. Eve sat down beside her, so close their thighs nearly touched.

"It's nice to meet you, Mrs. Elliot," she said. "Eve speaks so highly of you."

"I hear you are from Washington, D.C.?"

"Georgetown, actually."

"Georgetown has some lovely old homes."

"It does," said Daniella. She wanted to tell her that she grew up in one of them, but she held back. She did not want to pander.

"And my granddaughter tells me you were raised Unitarian?"

"Guilty as charged," said Daniella. "Weaned on Emerson."

"Well, that's just fine. A little unorthodox, but fine. And why did you decide to come to Belmont from all of the way up in D.C.?"

Daniella resisted the urge to remind Mrs. Elliot that Georgetown was closer to Roanoke than Atlanta was. She knew Mrs. Elliot was not talking about geographic distance, but rather culture. "I love tennis, and I was offered a spot on the team. And my mother attended Sweet Briar, so it seemed nice to have a similar experience to hers."

"Sweet Briar is a fine institution. And tennis is a wonderful game! I always told my children that as long as they learned to play tennis and golf they would do well in the world."

"Well," said Daniella, "I'm one for two."

The old woman smiled and looked at Daniella directly for the first time. Perhaps she was being paranoid, but it seemed to Daniella that Eve's grandmother lingered for an extra second on her nose, weighing it, determining just how "ethnic" it was.

"You seem like a perfectly lovely girl. I understand now why my granddaughter is so fond of you. And you aren't flashy at all. There's really no need for the alumnae group to be concerned. I'm going to talk to them and things should open up for you at Fleur, all right, dear?"

It was as if one half of Daniella split from the other, because there was a part of her, sitting in the formal parlor of Monty House, that felt such pride at having passed muster with Eve's grandmother, as if being deemed not too Jewish were a great accomplishment. And then there was another part of her that wished she knew Hebrew—or, better yet, Yiddish—so she could curse the old lady in the language of her ancestors. "Not too flashy." What the hell did that mean?

But it was Eve who spoke, her voice quiet at first, contemplative, as if she were formulating her thoughts while she said them aloud. "Grandmommy, did you know beforehand that the Fleur alumnae would insist on Daniella being blackballed?"

"Why, I didn't give it any thought," said Grandmommy, but the expression on her face was furtive.

"But you knew that Daniella and I were going through rush together, and you knew that her father was Jewish and her mother was Methodist and she was raised Unitarian. I told you all about it over Christmas dinner, and you told me about the Jewish doctor you once met on a cruise ship to England. You said, 'Some of them are perfectly fine people.'"

"Clearly they are," said Grandmommy, smiling affectionately at Daniella, as if the two of them were old friends.

"You knew. You *knew* she would be rejected. And I bet Mother never wrote her a letter of recommendation, did she?"

"Well, now we are seeing to it that she is accepted."

"Oh, it all just makes me want to scream!" Eve cried, the force of her convictions propelling her right out of her chair, so that she was standing, flush with indignation. "You know what? Daniella can join Fleur if she likes, but I don't want to have anything to do with it."

Eve's grandmother jerked her neck up sharply in order to glare at Eve. "Don't be such a child," she said.

"Don't be such a bitch," Eve responded.

Daniella was sure the old lady would heave herself out of her chair, march over to her impertinent granddaughter, and slap her. Or at least beat her fists against her shoulders, as Eve was a head taller than she was. But instead her eyes pooled with tears and her lips started trembling. And then tears were running down her face, and she was shaking her head and saying, "Well, I never. I never."

Eve remained standing. "Oh, Grandmommy," she said, her voice not at all sorry, only exasperated.

A feral look crossed over Mrs. Elliot's face as she turned her gaze upward to address her granddaughter, index finger wagging. "I nearly died when I gave birth to your mother. Do you hear me? I lost so much blood I nearly died. But it was worth it because she was my own, my flesh and blood, my child, and she went on to have children of her own. And you—you nearly killed her when you came out, but it was worth it, too, because you were flesh from her flesh, blood from blood. And how do you repay us? By turning your back on your family, by turning your back on all we hold dear."

"I didn't ask to be born into this family," said Eve, and she walked out of the room, leaving Daniella alone with Grandmommy, who sat very straight in her chair, lips trembling as she dabbed at her eyes with a white handkerchief she had pulled from her pocketbook, its sides embellished with antique lace.

Chapter 3

TRANSFER

Atlanta, 1963

"That girl has too much influence on you," said her mother as she and Eve sat on the back porch overlooking the rear of the Whalen estate, which they referred to as "The Compound." The manicured yard complete with cutting garden and greenhouse eventually gave way to woods that led to a rippling creek. It was the second week of April and nearly everything was in bloom, including the creamy white flowers on the dogwood trees, Eve's favorite. Beyond the woods were the stables and the tennis courts, out of view from where Eve and her mother sat. And beyond that was Grandmommy's "cottage," which wasn't a cottage at all, but rather an old barn converted at great cost (though no Whalen would ever be so gauche as to speak of money) into a window-filled, high-ceilinged home that included two bedrooms, a full bath with a claw-foot tub, and a small kitchen so that Grandmommy could heat up food prepared by Ada on evenings when she did not want to join the rest of the family in the main house for supper. So far she had stayed away during Eve's trip home for Easter break.

"Mommy, she's my best friend. She's like Aunt Pooh was to you."

"More like Aunt Jew," muttered her mother, but she said it softly enough that Eve wasn't sure she heard the words right, and so she ignored them, because she was doing everything in her power to persuade her parents—her mother, really—that she should switch schools for her sophomore year, transfer to Barnard with Daniella. She had history on her side, to an extent: The women in Eve's family typically didn't attend Belmont all four years. They went to Belmont, joined Fleur, and then transferred after two years to the University of Georgia, where they would pledge a national sorority, though none so beloved as the bouquet.

"If you don't let me transfer, I might be too upset to go to any deb parties this summer," Eve threatened.

"Don't you dare even suggest such a thing," warned her mother.

"I'm serious, Mommy. If you make me go back to Belmont without Daniella, I'll probably be so melancholy I'll have to miss a bunch of the parties."

"I presume you're arguing that the converse is true, that if Daddy and I were to allow you to transfer to that school up north you would fulfill your duty as a member of the Atlanta Debutante Club, acting with honor, grace, and good cheer?"

"I would," Eve said, and recognizing that a deal was being ironed out, she arranged her face so that it projected earnest conviction.

"Daddy and I will discuss it," her mother said, before adding her final condition. "But before we do I want you to apologize to Grandmommy for your appalling behavior toward her when she came to see you in Roanoke."

The following morning, Good Friday, Eve was greeted in the kitchen by her mother, holding a wicker basket filled with warm blueberry muffins, wrapped in a blue-and-white-checked napkin.

"Run these to Mother while they are still warm," instructed Mrs. Whalen.

"Can't I have a cup of coffee first?" asked Eve.

Ada, who was rinsing off dishes in the sink, dried her hands with a towel, preparing to fix Eve a cup.

"There's coffee at The Cottage," Eve's mother said.

The Cottage was covered in weathered gray shingles, the door painted robin's-egg blue. The Town Car was parked in the driveway, and not in the garage, which meant she must have an appointment that day, perhaps at the beauty parlor to get her hair fixed for Easter, or maybe someone was hosting Bridge Club. As Eve walked by the Lincoln she saw Willie sitting inside, wearing his tweed driver's cap. He tipped his hat and smiled when she waved.

Eve knocked on the front door, but no one came to greet her. She leaned back on her heels, waiting her grandmother out. She was certain Grandmommy had watched her approach from the living room, as she had seen the curtain jerk. *Oh, well. Let her play her games.* Eve knocked once more, and after a few more moments Grandmommy answered, wearing a navy-blue dress printed with pink flowers and sturdy blue heels, pearls around her neck and in each earlobe.

Grandmommy did not acknowledge Eve exactly, just stood erect in the doorframe, blinking, as if Eve were delivering a parcel and Grandmommy was simply waiting for her to hand it over.

"I'm sorry I was so rude when you came to Belmont. I was feeling protective of Daniella, but I know that's no excuse."

Grandmommy's facial expression did not change. She stood, impassive, for what seemed like a very long time before allowing Eve the slightest smile.

"Well," she said. "I appreciate how fond you are of your friend, but you shouldn't have disrespected your grandmother."

"No, ma'am, I shouldn't have." Eve affected a look of contrition and then held up the wicker basket filled with blueberry muffins. "Muffin?"

Grandmommy glanced at the slender gold watch around her wrist. "I suppose there's time for one before my appointment," she said. "Though really I shouldn't. I'm trying to reduce."

"Why?" asked Eve, walking into the house even though she hadn't yet been invited inside. "Who cares?"

"I shouldn't care about my appearance simply because I'm of a certain age?" Grandmommy asked, but Eve could hear bemusement behind the admonition.

"I don't mean *that* of course," said Eve. "I mean you're already tiny as a bird. You should enjoy yourself. Have a muffin. Have a muffin with butter!"

"Oh, all right, you naughty thing," said Grandmommy. The truth was, prior to Eve dropping out of Fleur she and her grandmother had always gotten along well, had been close. Indeed, Eve was named after her—Evelyn Elliot.

They sat at the little bridge table in the living room, eating their muffins on Grandmommy's casual china, spreading their butter with a sterling Strasbourg knife, the same pattern as the tea set that Grandmommy had given her to take to Belmont, an item she most certainly would not be displaying at Barnard, though she wouldn't be sharing that with her grandmother.

"You're still a Fleur, by the way," said Grandmommy, giving Eve a conspiratorial little grin.

"No, I'm not," Eve said. "I officially dropped out. Signed the papers and everything in front of Fleur's president, Bunny."

"Bunny Malone never filed your resignation," Grandmommy said.

"What?"

"Dear, if Bunny was instructed to tear up your resignation papers, you had better believe she did. Regardless of whether or not you choose to associate with Fleur while you're at Belmont, *officially* you are still a member in good standing. I know that doesn't mean much to you right now, but one day you will be happy to have the sisterhood in your corner. If nothing else, you might have a daughter who wants to join."

"Oh, for goodness' sakes, Grandmommy, you are incorrigible."

"Friendships come and go, my dear, but Fleur is forever."

That summer Eve returned to Atlanta to make her debut. All debs were required to volunteer a certain number of hours a week, which Eve did at Piedmont Hospital, donning a pink-and-white "candy striper" pinafore and checking in on patients to see if they needed water or perhaps wanted to play a hand of cards. She was so friendly and engaging that some of the patients began asking for her by name. Sometimes she would catch a ride to the hospital with her father, whose obstetrics practice was in the adjacent medical building. Other times she would drive her brother Charlie's MG convertible, as Charlie was in Europe that summer, touring the sites before he began law school at Emory in the fall. She spent the rest of her time swimming at the Driving Club. After completing her laps she would bob by the side of the pool, holding on to the edge with one hand, sunglasses on over her bathing cap, studying the Negro employees. They were all so deferential, all "Yes, ma'am" and "Yes, sir," as if there was nothing they would rather do than swap out fresh towels for used ones and bring glasses of iced tea to white people. Surely they were burning up in their starched uniforms, despite the explanation her father once gave when, as a girl, she commented from the back of his Coupe de Ville about how hot the maids must be walking to the bus station in the summer sun. "Colored people don't get as hot because they are originally from Africa," her father had explained. "They are biologically engineered to be comfortable in the heat."

Back then she had believed everything he said. Now she was uncertain of almost all he had taught her. Surely the uniformed workers at the Driving Club resented the white ladies prancing around in their daring two-pieces, diving in the water whenever they needed to cool off.

Did they resent her? Did they hate her?

She tried to shake away those worries. Daniella had, as gently as possible, cautioned her that racial inequality wasn't an easy thing to put right. That had been the problem with the letter she had sent to Headmaster Dupree about Miss Eugenia. She could see that now. Sure, her moral indignation was justified, but it cost Miss Eugenia her job. Fresh shame washed over her every time she pictured the look of despair on Miss Eugenia's face as she carried her well-worn suitcase out of her emptied room. She thought she would never get over the shame. But Daniella had reminded her that the issue of racism was much bigger than Eve and her guilt. The issue was that they lived in a country where Negroes were treated as second-class citizens. Bringing about equality was what mattered, not Eve's sad feelings about the situation.

Still, she couldn't help but wonder if Ada had ever actually loved her.

Over the course of the summer Eve tried to be as accommodating as possible of her parents and grandmother, for fear that her mother might change her mind at the last minute and refuse to let Eve board the plane that would take her to Manhattan. And when Daniella called long-distance, in tears, to tell her that she wasn't going to be able to come down to Atlanta to attend Eve's deb party, the low-country BBQ that Eve's parents were hosting along with the parents of five of her girlfriends from Coventry, Eve was quietly relieved, knowing she could fake it better without her enlightened friend around. Daniella was a senior counselor at the summer camp she had attended in the Berkshires ever since she was twelve, and Eve's party coincided with their all-important Peace Olympics. Daniella swore she would come another weekend, and she did, but it was an uneventful one with no deb events scheduled, and so the two friends spent most of their time driving Charlie's convertible to The Varsity for onion rings, which Daniella proclaimed the best she had ever had.

Eve did as she had promised: fulfilled her duty as a member of the Atlanta Debutante Club, acting with honor, grace, and good cheer. And honestly, some of the parties were really fun, including her own, at which the guests ate pulled pork doused in vinegar sauce, along with boiled shrimp, corn, potatoes, and sausage, before dancing to Carolina beach music. And she had to admit the dresses her mother bought for her were beautiful. Still, her thoughts lay mostly with what was ahead—college in New York City. She hadn't even seen Barnard in person, but she'd memorized every detail of the photos in the brochure that the college sent. And of course she adored New York from what she had seen of it on-screen, especially in *Breakfast at Tiffany's* and *BUtterfield 8*. Since Daniella had almost gone to Barnard instead of Belmont in the first place, she was able to tell Eve all about it. Those final few weeks of their freshman year, their acceptances to Barnard pinned to the corkboard in their room (the corkboard Eve had once imagined showcasing all of their pictures and paraphernalia from Fleur), she basked in the tutorials Daniella offered about the world they would soon be entering.

"Barnard's campus is attractive, stately," Daniella lectured as they walked the short distance from Monty House to the dining hall, the setting sun ablaze with pink and orange. "Not nearly so gorgeous as this, but having New York City at our fingertips will make up for it!"

Daniella also told Eve that there would be a lot of Jewish girls at Barnard, her words sounding almost like a warning.

"Good," Eve had shot back. "My best friend's Jewish."

"I'm beginning to think that's the thing you like most about me," Daniella said, linking an arm through Eve's as they strolled through the bucolic campus they would soon leave behind.

It wasn't so much Jewish girls that Eve noticed when she arrived at Barnard as northern girls, northern girls who operated from a different code of conduct than she had been taught. That first month of school she was always getting her feelings hurt, which was funny considering that the summer before she had felt as if she were constantly bruising the feelings of her fellow debutantes. Try as she had—and she had been truly trying, since her future at Barnard depended on it—she had never displayed the proper level of enthusiasm over a girl's gown, or the darling little favors passed out at this party or that, or the particular shade of coral nail polish that would match both the lipstick and the skirt. But in New York things were reversed, and she was forever feeling like a rube. Like the time she casually mentioned that in high school she had been a fan of Pat Boone, and suddenly everyone in the common room where they were gathered was groaning in disgust, with Abby, who wore her dark hair long and straight and was somehow on the Pill even though she was not engaged, proclaiming, "I would honestly rather die than listen to that shit."

But Abby, who was biting and sarcastic and always seemed ready to insult Eve, wasn't really representative of Barnard girls. Abby was actively mean while the others were just . . . brash. Bold. Opinionated. Utterly confident in their opinions about *everything*, from the type of sandwich to order at Chock full o' Nuts (the nutty sandwich, of course), to the *utter* brilliance of *Marjorie Morningstar*, to whether or not Thich Quang Duc's self-immolation in Vietnam was admirable or simply insane (the girls were split on that one). Eve admired their bedrock confidence, but she didn't know how to make inroads with them, these girls who had already gone through freshman year together. She had Daniella, thank God, but Daniella had started dating a handsome sophomore from Columbia, Pete Strum, who was forever whisking her away from Barnard altogether, taking her down to the Village for romantic dinners at some little Italian hole-in-the-wall they called "our place."

Things got better when she took the job at the Hungarian Pastry Shop on Amsterdam Avenue, not because she needed the money—her father sent her a generous allowance—but because she needed something to claim as her own. The Hungarian Pastry Shop was catty-corner from the Cathedral Church of St. John the Divine, which Eve loved for its sheer size and majesty. Some of her co-workers were actually from Europe, if not Hungary.

Ozge from Istanbul taught Eve to boil her coffee with cardamom before pouring it into a tiny teacup, a single sugar cube placed at the bottom. Chloe from Paris got her hooked on Gauloises. Eve had smoked occasionally at Belmont, at parties and such, but at Barnard she smoked all of the time. It seemed everyone in New York did. The Hungarian Pastry Shop would fill with smoke as students from Barnard, Columbia, Teachers College, and Union Theological Seminary wrote papers or polemics or poems or put their heads together to talk heatedly about whatever news, often of racial oppression in the South, caught their attention.

One night around dusk when she was on a smoke break outside, a rugged, handsome man, not much taller than she, stopped and asked if she had a light. She handed him a box of matches from the front pocket of her skirt. She had swiped the matchbox from Daniella, who had brought it home from "her" Italian place downtown, Mother Bertolotti's.

The man managed to light the match on his first try, something she could never do, especially with that particular box, as the strip was too slick. He exhaled a series of smoke rings before motioning across the street to the cathedral, asking, "Don't you think they ought to do something useful with that place?" He had the faintest trace of a southern accent. He sounded like her uncle who lived in Charlottesville.

"Excuse me?" she said.

"Someone ought to knock it down and turn it into a park, or affordable housing, or a community center—something that actually serves the people of Harlem."

"St. John the Divine?"

"Yep."

"Knock it down? Are you crazy?" she asked, thinking he must be joking, but what a queer thing to joke about. "The whole place is a work of art. And it's a *church*. I'm not sure what's more useful than that."

"Yeah, it's awfully useful to sit around eating wafers and lighting incense. Think about it: The church is responsible for either instigating or overlooking pretty much every evil perpetuated. You know the German Lu-theran Church was in lockstep with the Nazis."

"Not Bonhoeffer's church," said Eve, pleased with her knowledge of the German pastor and dissident who was eventually arrested for trying to assassinate Hitler. A professor from Union had given a talk on Bonhoeffer that she and Daniella had attended.

"Sure, but Bonhoeffer was executed by the state. So basically, what he shows is that the church can either be complicit and go along with the bas-tards in charge, or it can martyr itself and its followers. How about saying, 'Screw you!' to Big Brother and also having a little fun?"

"I'm not following," Eve said. "How does saying, 'Screw you!' to Big Brother help with affordable housing?"

"Not just pretty but smart," he said.

He was not dressed like a Virginian, or, at least, any Virginian she knew. He was dressed like a beatnik, wearing a black turtleneck over jeans, his dark curls long enough so that he could push them behind his ears.

Her co-worker Donovan, who wore funny-looking leather sandals over black socks, stuck his head out of the shop's door: "Break time's over, Eve."

Eve took one last drag of her cigarette before crushing it beneath her foot.

"Eve, huh?" said the man.

"Yep."

"I'm Warren."

"Hi, Warren."

"So if I come inside and order a hot cocoa from you, will you give me extra marshmallows on top?"

"We don't sell hot cocoa. Maybe try Schrafft's."

Schrafft's was a lunch place that catered to ladies who took off their white gloves before nibbling at chicken salad followed by butterscotch sun-daes. He acknowledged her insult with a smile, showing off the straightest teeth she had ever seen.

"You like to ball?"

"Come again?" asked Eve, thinking he was referring to a new cocktail or perhaps had somehow intuited that she was a debutante and was teasing her about the parties.

"Well, yeah, with me you probably would."

Eve looked at him blankly.

"Ball, screw, get laid, you know?"

"You better be glad I don't call the police," she said, and turned to march inside with all of the self-righteousness the moment called for.

"Just messing with you, kid!" he called after her. In that moment he sounded like her brother, Charlie.

Later, after her shift ended, she sat side by side with Daniella on her twin bed in their dorm room and told her about her exchange with Warren.

"I've seen him!" Daniella exclaimed. "He's a junior at Columbia. Short, kind of muscular, really good-looking?"

"Disconcertingly so," said Eve, going on to describe his sleepy brown eyes, his white teeth, his dark curls worn a little too long to be respectable.

"Yep. That's Warren St. Clair. From some old Richmond family, I've heard. Supposedly he was a protégé of C. Wright Mills. I think he rode motorcycles with him. He's really brilliant but pretty wild. When you sleep with him it's called getting 'St. Claired.'"

"I'm not going to sleep with him!"

"I don't mean you, goose; I mean girls in general. He has a reputation. Abby told me all about him. She met him at some CORE thing."

"What's CORE?" asked Eve, thinking that surely Abby had been St. Claired.

"Committee of Racial Equity? Or maybe Congress of Racial Equality?"

"Daniella! Why aren't we in that?"

"Don't you think we should get a little settled before we jump into anything, learn the lay of the land?"

"But that's just it!" cried Eve. "That's the problem. We get too settled, and then we stop seeing how unfair everything is. Did I tell you that I found out about Medgar Evers's death through Ada? I walked into the kitchen one morning last June and I could tell she had been crying. I kept asking her what was wrong, and she finally showed me the headline of the colored newspaper she takes, along with a picture of Evers's wife and three children. And then my parents came down for breakfast and all they could talk about—well, all my mom could talk about—was how tacky the decorations had been at Mary Louise Bennet's party the night before. The whole thing just made me sick."

"We can find out when the next CORE meeting is," said Daniella.

"Let's."

But life got in the way. There were papers to write and film screenings to attend (after Godard's *Breathless* was shown on campus Daniella had to talk Eve out of chopping off her hair à la Jean Seberg). And then Eve had to fly home for the Halloween Ball, of all things, where she was officially presented as a member of the 1963 Atlanta Debutante Club. All the while Pete, who was now very much Daniella's boyfriend, tried to caution the girls against joining CORE, which he considered radical.

"A lot of its members are admitted communists," he told the two of them over beers at the West End.

"So what?" Daniella challenged.

"Ask the Rosenbergs how well the Communist Party worked out for them," Pete retorted.

Daniella's face turned red. Without a word she stood up and walked out of the bar.

"You're a real jerk," said Eve as she gathered her pocketbook to go after her friend. "You know she has nightmares about the Rosenbergs."

"Damn. I know. I *am* a jerk, Eve. Stay here. I'll go get her."

He was out the door before she could protest. Suddenly she was alone at the table, a nearly full pitcher of beer her only company. It seemed that lately Eve was always alone, that Daniella was always running off with Pete. It made no sense to Eve that Daniella was dating him. Well, actually it did. He was attractive—tall and lean with reddish-brown hair and horn-rimmed glasses that he was perennially pushing back on his nose. He had elegant hands and long fingers, the sort that might effortlessly play scales up and down the piano. He was always polite, always deferential, and he looked at Daniella as if she had hung the moon. Yet the two of them were so different. In addition to being a WASP from Connecticut (a term Eve had learned from Daniella), he was a member of the Columbia Young Republicans, though he always stressed that he was a moderate and did not approve of that "nut" from Arizona, Barry Goldwater. Still! He wasn't planning to vote for Kennedy the following year when Kennedy would be up for reelection. He thought that Kennedy was all style and no substance.

That Daniella was dating him, was in love with him, felt like a betrayal. Hadn't Eve left behind the WASPy world of Fleur and Belmont in order to join Daniella at Barnard? And then what did Daniella do as soon as they arrived in New York? Link arms with a man who would have fit in just fine at Hampden-Sydney, back in Virginia.

She craned her neck toward the door, hoping to see Daniella and Pete returning. Instead, she locked eyes with Warren St. Clair, who had just walked in. He wore a leather jacket over a black T-shirt, jeans, and work boots. She thought of Pete Strum's pressed button-downs and smiled, giving Warren a half wave. Just then a girl Eve had seen around campus but did not know by name ran up to him and they embraced. Eve watched as Warren patted her rear. She imagined what his hand might feel like on her own bottom.

He extricated himself from the girl and walked toward Eve, squeezing into the booth beside her even though the opposite bench was empty.

"Drinking alone, eh?" he said.

"Pretty much," she said. "My friend has abandoned me for a Young Republican."

"Well, fuck 'em and the polo ponies they rode off on."

She knew, even as she laughed, that she was betraying Daniella, but here she was in New York, away from all that was familiar, and Daniella, who was supposed to be her anchor, kept floating away.

Eve and Warren had emptied the pitcher of beer by the time Daniella and Pete returned, arms around each other, happy once more.

"It's the Young Republican!" heralded Warren as the couple sat down across from them.

Daniella shot Eve a look of incredulity.

"I was just telling my friend Warren here about Pete's campus involvement," she said.

"Heck, I'm not ashamed!" said Pete, meeting Warren's disdainful gaze. "Anything you want to know, just ask. It's a good group of fellows."

"What's your take on the Negro situation?" asked Warren.

"Jim Crow is a damned shame, of course, but these things take time. You can't just put a gun to someone's head and say, 'Integrate!'"

"Seems to me that's exactly what it's going to take," said Warren.

A week later, Eve was headed to her last shift at the Hungarian Pastry Shop before the Thanksgiving break, which she would be starting early, having booked a ticket to fly home the following day, a Saturday, skipping her Monday and Tuesday classes. Her mother had insisted, even though Eve argued against going home for Thanksgiving at all, considering that she had just been to Atlanta for the Halloween Ball and she would be returning so soon for Christmas. But then her mother started talking about how Barnard was just too far away and that maybe she would be better off finishing her degree at the University of Georgia, and Eve had quickly acquiesced.

She had made it nearly all the way to work when an odd feeling came over her, a sort of internal catch-up of what was going on all around. She looked up from the sidewalk—she had been brooding about her upcoming trip—and noticed that everyone walking by appeared stunned, was crying, or both.

"Excuse me, do you know what's going on?" she asked a colored woman walking down the sidewalk in the opposite direction.

"Someone shot President Kennedy," she said, her voice clipped, northern.

When Eve arrived at work, all of the other employees were huddled around the portable television that someone had brought up from the back office. She watched as Walter Cronkite gave an unconfirmed report that the president had died and then a few minutes later confirmed it. Cronkite's words did not make sense. She could feel a sob in her chest, which she pushed down, not wanting to break down, not here. Instead, she washed the dirty coffee cups in the little sink behind the counter while silent tears ran down her face. President Kennedy was so young, so dashing and hopeful. He had little children, little children who no longer had a daddy.

When she finished the dishes, she turned and walked out of the café without saying good-bye to anyone, without punching out. She didn't care if she was fired. She walked back to her dorm as fast as she could. She needed to see Daniella.

She found her friend in the common room, crying with everyone else, even Abby, who usually made a point of being tough, stoic. Eve walked straight to Daniella, who was sitting on a couch, and collapsed beside her, resting all of her weight against her friend's side. She thought of how Daniella's mother loved Kennedy so much that she had spent all of her spare time volunteering for his presidential campaign and so Daniella had spent her weekends volunteering as well. She thought, too, of how Pete had not been a particular fan of Kennedy's, had thought his containment strategy for communism weak, had thought he had more charisma than actual substance. She wondered how much comfort Pete would be able to offer Daniella.

As these thoughts went through her head, Abby went to her room and placed *The Freewheelin' Bob Dylan* on the record player, setting the needle to "Blowin' in the Wind" and turning up the volume as loud as possible. Eve loved the song, but at that moment it annoyed her, as if Abby thought they were in a movie, as if they needed a soundtrack for their grief. Eve didn't want to hear anything intended to capture the moment. Instead, she felt a strong urge to go to church, to be among incense and ritual, to pray for the president's widow and two young children. She held Daniella's hand in her own and asked if it would bother her to go to St. John the Divine.

"Why would that bother me?" Daniella asked.

"Well, it's a church," said Eve. "A Christian church."

"God is God," Daniella said, sounding annoyed. In a kinder voice she added, "You keep forgetting about us Unitarians. We don't deny anyone their divinity—even Jesus."

This was one of many not-too-funny Unitarian jokes that Daniella had told before, including one about burning a question mark on somebody's front lawn, though Eve could never remember exactly who was burning the question mark, the Unitarian or the vigilante. In any event, she half-smiled at Daniella's remark, and then the two of them went to their shared room, Daniella to change out of her tennis clothes and Eve to blow her nose and run a brush through her hair. They left Brooks Hall and made their way to the eerily empty street, walking down Broadway to 112th, which took them to the enormous stone cathedral.

As they approached the entrance, Eve spotted Warren, wearing the same black turtleneck he had worn when she first met him at the Hungarian Pastry Shop. He was sitting on the cathedral's front steps, smoking a cigarette. Eve had an urge to make contact, but not knowing what to say, she only nodded in his direction. He nodded in return, offered a weary smile.

She and Daniella walked through the massive front doors, large enough for an elephant to pass through. Eve heard organ music. They joined the other souls in mourning, some sitting, some kneeling in prayer, everyone dwarfed by the magnitude of the place. Eve dipped her hands in the font of holy water, flicking the water on her skin, thinking it might somehow protect her. They chose seats about halfway down the aisle. Eve bowed her head. Daniella grabbed her hand and held on tight as if they were walking in a fast current and might otherwise lose each other.

Chapter 4

CORE

New York City, 1964

On their way out the door after the meeting, Eve grabbed two application forms from the woman who had come from the national office to tell them about the Mississippi Summer Project. She and Daniella could look over the application at the West End, where they were meeting Pete for beers, Pete who would inevitably bring along a fraternity brother of his in yet another attempt to set Eve up, no matter how many times Eve told both him and Daniella that she was not interested in dating a Sigma Chi. Before exiting the building the girls buttoned up their coats and wrapped their scarves tightly around their necks; still, their exposed cheeks turned red from the cold March air as they walked at a fast clip toward the West End.

Warren had also been at the CORE meeting, positioned on the other side of the room, and though seeing him made Eve's stomach flip, she had only slightly lifted her hand to give a half wave. He had his arm slung around Abby's shoulder. Never mind. There were more important things at stake, like the action CORE was planning for that summer, sending hundreds of college students to Mississippi to join the Student Nonviolent Coordinating

Committee (SNCC) field officers already stationed there. Once in Mississippi, they would canvass the state, urging Negro residents to register to vote.

"Of course, the Mississippi registrars will refuse to process their forms," the woman from the national office had explained. "But if enough people are denied, we'll have a federal court case on our hands."

They arrived at the bar before Pete, so they grabbed a booth and ordered beers. Even though she had been to the West End a dozen times before, Eve was suddenly cognizant of how far she had come from her upbringing: Not only was she hanging out at a bar, but she was also—at least at that very moment—unaccompanied by a man. And once the waitress brought the Blatz she ordered, Eve would crack it open and drink it straight from the can.

Daniella did not seem as convinced as Eve that going to Mississippi was a good idea. She hadn't said no but had not expressed any enthusiasm when Eve tried to impress upon her the importance of their going.

"Do you not want to do it?" Eve finally asked, halfway through her beer. She had shed her coat, revealing a black cashmere turtleneck that she wore over a heavy tweed skirt.

"It's not that," said Daniella, who drank her beer from a glass. "I just think we need to seriously consider how dangerous it's going to be."

"We should only take actions that are safe?" asked Eve.

"Of course not. I'm just saying that we should really think it through. I hate to bring it up, but we don't want to rush into things like we did with Miss Eugenia."

It was kind of her to say "we" when really it had been Eve who had rushed into things.

"This isn't the same as interfering on behalf of Miss Eugenia," Eve argued. "This isn't just me with some half-baked plan. CORE has been around for twenty years. They're smart, they're organized, and they know what they're doing."

WE ARE ALL GOOD PEOPLE HERE 61

"We also need to think about whether or not *we* could handle it, not to mention our parents, who would surely be worried sick all summer."

"That's a gas. As if Patty and Lem would let me go."

"You would go without their knowing?"

"I can always find a reason for being in Mississippi. There was a girl in Fleur from Greenwood. I could tell them I'm staying with her, doing the deb circuit or something."

"Are you talking about Caroline Foster?"

"Yeah."

"Do you remember the first time it snowed at Belmont and she came out of the dorm in a full-length mink coat and mink hat?"

"Caro was *very* concerned about the cold," said Eve.

"I *think* I want to do it," said Daniella slowly. "I just have to sit with it. Make sure it's something I'm actually capable of."

"I don't think we know what we're capable of until we try," said Eve.

"That's probably right," conceded Daniella, and then her attention shifted from Eve because Pete had entered the bar and was rushing toward them, apologizing for running late, eager as always to kiss his girl. Behind him trailed a tall man wearing a varsity jacket—Eve's consolation prize. The boys sat, introductions were made (Pete's friend was named Tad), and more beer was ordered. Eve's mind wandered as Pete and Tad discussed *Dr. Strangelove*. She was thinking of what she would say in her CORE application, how she would write of what happened to Miss Eugenia.

She would tell of how Miss Eugenia's firing haunted her, how she would lie in bed at night worrying about how she and her crippled husband were supporting themselves now that she had lost her job. She would write of how she would do anything to take back having sent that letter, to have been more strategic, smarter, wiser. She was wiser now. She wanted to make up for what she had done. Perhaps by going to Mississippi she could help mend the tear. Perhaps going to Mississippi would render her a little less complicit.

Chapter 5

LETTERS HOME

Leflore County, Mississippi, 1964

June 14, 1964

Dear Eve,

Just a quick note to say I arrived in Ohio for the volunteer training. Western College's campus is beautiful and things feel very peaceful here—a sharp contrast to what will greet us in Mississippi, I'm sure.

Are you feeling better about things? I wish you were with me. Whoever made the decision not to accept your application was an absolute idiot. I think of your wonderful heart, and how fully you would have given it to this mission.

Please forgive me for going on. My conscience told me I had to. I miss you already.

Love,
Daniella

July 2, 1964

Dear Daddy,

I am sending this directly to your office because I worry it might be too much for Mother to bear. I will send a lighter note to the two of you at home. Of course if you feel obliged to share this with her, I understand. I'm sure both you and Mother were thrilled that President Johnson signed the Civil Rights Act today. I was happy, too, of course. I just wish I had more confidence that it would make a difference to the people down here.

As our bus crossed over the state line, we were greeted by a billboard that read: "Welcome to Mississippi, The Magnolia State." Beneath the sign were two Highway Patrol cars that pulled out and followed us for the rest of the trip. I should not be telling you this, I suppose, because I know that like Mother, like all of us, you are worried sick about those who have gone missing: Michael Schwerner, Andy Goodman, and James Chaney.

The levity I felt at the beginning of the summer, when I first pulled into Western College, is long gone. It began to erode the very moment I checked in, when I realized how frosty relations were between the white volunteers and the Negro field officers from SNCC. Tensions escalated the evening Bob Moses, the brilliant man behind this whole thing, played a movie produced by CBS Reports about the disenfranchisement of Negroes in Mississippi. There was a clip showing this absurd-looking Mississippi bureaucrat, with a potbelly so large it looked like he might topple over from the weight of it. He's a county registrar in Mississippi and therefore uses his power to systematically deny Negroes their constitutional right to vote. He's a man who surely uses the word "nigger" freely, spits tobacco on the floor, and calls any effort to bring the vote to Negro people a "communist plot." He looked like such a cartoon version of a dumb, racist villain that all of us white college students just started laughing. Six SNCC officers stormed out of the room.

Afterward everyone stayed and talked. It was very heated. Someone from SNCC said, "You people are going to get us killed!" and then another said, "You white folks don't understand; you are going to have to live like black people when you're down there. You don't get to make up the rules. You don't get to decide what's what. The danger is very, very real." We ended up staying in that auditorium for over two hours talking. I think it helped to open things up between us, to release some of the tension.

And then Michael, Andy, and James went on down to Mississippi early, to investigate a church bombing that occurred in Meridian. A call came to Michael's wife, Rita, who was still at Western, saying that no one had heard from any of them. Honestly, we all expect the worst. Still, most of us boarded the bus that would take us to Mississippi anyway.

We are deliberately scattered throughout the state, living in the homes of different families (all Negro, of course). Bob Moses said we needed to "melt away" into the Negro community, that they would house and harbor us.

My hosts for now are the Lewises. They have taken me in at great personal risk. All of us volunteers are achingly aware that while we will leave at the end of the summer, the Negroes welcoming us into their homes will remain, and surely face retribution. Do you know that two years ago the state shut down the commodities program—which gives surplus food to poor colored families—as retaliation for a group of eighteen Negro Mississippians trying to register to vote?

The Lewises' house is comprised of only two rooms. The boys sleep on the floor so that I can have the mattress they usually share, which is thin, lumpy, and narrow. Mr. Lewis (James) farms on rented land, and Mrs. Lewis (Hattie) cleans house for a white woman in town. And by "cleans house" I mean she does everything from scrubbing the toilets, to cooking the food, to caring for her "Boss Lady's" three young children, sometimes staying overnight in the maid's room when her employers drive over to Doe's (a steakhouse in Greenville) and don't get back until late, or decide to go all the way to New Orleans for a night on the town. Of course, they don't tell Hattie when they decide to do this; she just knows that if they're not home by eleven or so she is expected to spend the night and fix them elixirs in the morning to help with their hangovers.

If Hattie's employers discover that she is hosting me, there might well be hell to pay. Same with the white man who is renting James his farmland. Ironically, the

Lewises are probably best protected by the bigotry of their bosses. They don't like to visit what they call "N-town." (Although of course they don't use an abbreviation.)

The Lewises have two boys, James Jr. ("Jimmy") and Jonah. They are eight and six, respectively. Jimmy is a card, whereas Jonah is serious and eager to learn. That said, Jimmy is quite brilliant. I taught him a few knock-knock jokes and now he tells them all the time, making up his own punch lines. Here's one he made up the other day after we finished eating:

"Knock-knock."

"Who's there?"

"Overall."

"Overall who?"

"Overall that was a fine supper!"

The other day I recited as much as I could remember from The Cat in the Hat to James and Jonah, and they loved the whimsy of it. They had never heard of Dr. Seuss. There are no libraries for colored people down here, and the textbooks the state provides are secondhand copies of fourth-rate textbooks. One of the other volunteers, Ellen, got her hands on a history book used in the colored school, and it was appalling. It was filled with quotes about how plantation slaves were looked after kindly, with all needs provided. How, content with their lot, they would sing happy songs as they worked the fields.

Before I came to Mississippi, I would have laughed at such an absurd claim, same as I laughed at that absurd county registrar. But none of it is funny anymore, not when you start to love the very real people who are so brutally oppressed by such ludicrous ignorance. (Though it's not just ignorance, is it? It's deeply entrenched evil, camouflaged by some sentimental fantasy of moonlight and magnolias.)

Bob Moses amazes me. After all he has endured, after all he has seen as a black man trying to register voters in Mississippi, he still has it in him to say, "White Mississippians are more oppressed, in their ability to speak, than Negroes." For instance, one white couple who has lived here forever invited one of the white organizers over for coffee, just to ease tension. Now they are facing bomb threats, and someone killed their dog. I heard they are planning on moving out of state.

I should add that the field secretaries from SNCC are doing all they can to protect us. We are warned never to walk alone. We are reminded to remain focused on the task, not to shoot our mouths off at some racist provocateur. I am definitely learning self-control. It reminds me of the lessons taught during that unit on Buddhism they did at the UU church during my senior year of high school. I wish I could go back and take that class again! At the time it didn't seem to apply to my life. Detachment from outcome? Humility? Those were lessons my seventeen-year-old self could not really comprehend. But wow, do I need them now.

Do you think you might have Mother send my copy of The Cat in the Hat, as well as any other childhood books that might be lying around? I'd love to offer James and Jonah a little "library." Ferdinand would be a great choice. I'm so grateful I thought to bring Annie Allen by Gwendolyn Brooks with me. When I shared it with Hattie, she was just stunned. "Someone published a book of poems by a colored woman?" she asked. "Not only that," I said. "But it won the Pulitzer, one of the most prestigious prizes in literature."

What is stunning to me is the fact that after all the Lewises have been denied, after all the humiliations they have endured (Mr. Lewis bows and tips his hat to every white man who crosses his path, not out of deference but self-preservation), their souls are very much intact. They humble me. And I'm thankful to you, Daddy, for supporting my doing this. Not all of the volunteers here have parents as supportive as you and Mother.

Your loving daughter,
Daniella

July 22, 1964

Dear Eve,

You would love Jimmy and Jonah Lewis, the two little boys I'm staying with—along with their parents, Hattie and James. They live in Leflore County, just outside Greenwood, where Caro Foster at Belmont was from, though granted, her Mississippi is not the same one the Lewises live in—or rather it is, just the flip side of the coin.

My mom sent a care package for the boys containing *The Cat in the Hat, Green Eggs and Ham, Make Way for Ducklings,* and *The Snowy Day. The Snowy Day* was an inspired choice, as the little boy in it, Peter, is colored. You would not believe how delighted Jimmy and Jonah were by that! They loved the Dr. Seuss books, too, especially *Green Eggs and Ham,* which they thought the height of comedy.

Well, cut to about a week later when Lew Feinstein stopped by the house to pick me up for canvassing. Lew is from Brooklyn and, as you can probably tell by his surname, is an actual true Jew, whereas I am just sort of a half-ass one (as Lew likes to joke). Lew grew up in a very religious family, and while he himself doesn't keep kosher, his parents do, and he still doesn't eat pork of any kind. I'm sure you can imagine how difficult that is down here, where nearly every cooked vegetable is seasoned with a piece of fatback. Indeed, surely Lew has eaten pork in Mississippi——he just doesn't know it.

So Lew was at the house and we were about to leave for the day to go canvassing. Hattie had packed us some sandwiches. (I pay her $5 a week for room and board.) Well, what do you know, the sandwiches were filled with deviled ham. We wouldn't have even known what was in them except that Hattie was so excited that she announced it. Ham is a big deal down here, even from a can. Lew gets this funny look on his face, but he obviously doesn't want to say anything. But Hattie notices and sort of forces it out of him, and he ends up telling her that he doesn't eat ham because he's Jewish. Jimmy, who is eight, has just been sort of hanging around the whole time watching all of us "grown folk" talk. He asks, all incredulous, "You don't eat ham?" And Lew says, "I don't." Jimmy asks, "You do not like ham?" and Lew says, "I do not," mimicking the sort of strange way Jimmy put it. And then Jimmy says, "Would you eat it on a boat? Would you eat it with a goat?" And suddenly I catch on. He's doing a riff on Dr. Seuss!

What a smart, smart child he is. Hattie ended up sending Lew off with a tomato sandwich, and the two little boys got to split the deviled ham.

I miss you, dear Eve. I wish you would write and tell me everything that is happening in your life. Every day I hope to receive a letter from you saying that all is okay between us. This summer is already heartbreaking enough. Please don't let it divide us.

Love,
D

August 1, 1964

Pete,

I told myself I was not going to write you, but I can't get your words about the southern Negro out of my mind, especially in light of what happened to me recently. You told me "those primitive and uneducated people" were not yet ready for the vote. That the situation in Mississippi was all very "sad," but granting a "virtual child" voting rights would only result in poor governance and state-sponsored "giveaways." Do you realize that was the night I decided to end our relationship? The moment you said those words my feelings for you just clicked off. Even though I had been so in love, even though a part of me still longs for what we once had.

Let me tell you about primitive Mississippians. Let me tell you about the white people who gathered around the courthouse on the day that I, along with a group of volunteers, accompanied a group of elderly Negroes to register to vote in Leflore County. Let me tell you about being spit on and called a "commie nigger lover," and how the registrar pulled me aside and asked me to tell him about "how big a nigger penis is" because he knew "sexual relations" were going on between "you white college gals and them niggers you live with." He then walked over to our group of elderly Negroes, pulled out his pistol, and asked, "Alrighty, which one of you wants to register first?"

Or let me tell you about what happened to me a week ago. Lew (my field partner) and I were canvassing, and he stayed behind at the home we had just visited to see if he could help this little boy put back together an old rocking horse that had broken. I went on to the next house (a shack, really), which wasn't too far down the road. It was stupid of me to be out walking alone, and something the SNCC officers have repeatedly warned us against, but I just wanted to get on with the canvassing. I am absolutely possessed with a sense of urgency when I'm doing it, like if I can just knock on enough doors I can make a difference. (Though the sad truth is very few of the people we talk to will attempt to register, even with our urging. The risk of doing so is just too great.) So I was walking down this dusty road by myself when I hear a motor behind me. I turn around and see that it's a brown pickup truck with a Confederate flag plate on the front bumper. The truck passes me at a crawl before stopping just ahead of where I am. There are four white men in the truck, two in the cab, two in the bed, all young—in their late teens or early twenties. One of them isn't wearing a shirt, just a pair of cutoff jeans. I keep my head down and keep walking, but the one without a shirt jumps out of the cab. He's lean, with tan skin, and he's got snuff stuffed into his lower lip. He walks right up to me and gets so close I can see the sheen of sweat on his skin. I want to step back, but I'm afraid if I do so he'll attack. He is clearly dangerous. He smells musky, and he's almost twitching with energy.

"Ain't this our lucky day," he says, with a look that is both a sneer and a grin. "We've killed plenty of niggers before, but we ain't never killed a nigger-loving white lady."

He pulls a pistol from the back pocket of his shorts. He puts the pistol to my head. I can feel it there, cold and heavy. And I think, "Oh my God, this is it." And in that moment I have the oddest reaction: I hope that my parents won't be too devastated by my death, and I recognize that the world will keep spinning after I'm gone. And I am also exquisitely aware that I would choose to go to Mississippi again if I could do it all over. That my life will hinge on this summer, whether I live past it or not.

He looks me in the eye and he pulls the trigger. And the trigger goes click. "Well, damn," he says. "I meant to load my nigger-lover bullets, but I guess I forgot." I am wearing a sleeveless top, and he puts his hands on my shoulders, as if he's going to *shove me, then taps my bare skin with his fingers, turns around, and jumps back into the truck as they drive off.*

A few nights later I went to a mass meeting led by Fannie Lou Hamer, a sharecropper severely beaten and then kicked off her land for trying to register to vote in 1962. She now works as a field secretary for SNCC. She is Mississippi through and through, with a deep, powerful voice that makes you sit up and listen whenever she talks. She said, "I've been tired a long time in Mississippi, but just because I am tired don't mean it's time to quit. Now is the time to keep fighting. Now is the time to shine the light of truth on what we've suffered down here, on what we've endured." And then she starts singing, her voice expanding with every verse: "This little light of mine, I'm gonna let it shine." Soon everyone has linked arms and is singing along with her, except I can't sing, because the words catch in my throat when I try, so I cry instead, just weep, as the voices of everyone else in that room wash over me.

What I'm trying to say, Pete, is that you have it backwards when it comes to who is primitive in this equation. You really, really do.

D

August 4, 1964

Eve,

I got your letter. I know that you gave up Fleur for me, and Belmont, too, to an extent, and that was huge. But Eve, I didn't ask you to drop out of either. I never made that demand of you. You chose to do so. And I think that after a little time has passed you will see that it wasn't fair of you to demand that I stay home from Mississippi simply because you weren't going. The state of Mississippi, the state of civil rights in America, it's so much bigger than our friendship. We have to de-personalize. We have to recognize that this isn't about a club I got into and you didn't. Otherwise our activism is just child's play.

I'm sorry. I'm frustrated. Tensions down here are high, and sometimes it feels hard to breathe. I'm sure you've been following the news, and so you know that today they found the bodies of James Chaney, Andrew Goodman, and Michael Schwerner.

D

August 5, 1964

Dear Mother and Daddy,

I am sure you heard that the bodies of Michael, Andy, and James were found. Andy's and Michael's bodies will be flown to New York. James will be buried here. The national media is hounding Rita Schwerner. They want to make the story about this poor little white woman who lost her husband. But she won't let them. She keeps reminding them that had it only been James—a Negro—who died, the media wouldn't be paying attention at all. She refuses to sink into her own grief. She will not lift her eyes from the goal of this project—to bring the vote to Missis-sippians, so that the systematic brutality enacted by white supremacy can be driven out. Perhaps she thinks that if voting rights are guaranteed, her husband's death will not have been in vain.

I used to believe we could beat this awful system. I am not so certain anymore.

Here's something I've been thinking about regarding white Mississippians: Yes, some of them are simply trying to survive; they know that if they were to speak out against Jim Crow, they would be terrorized by their own community. But for many, I think that their hatred stems from the fact that they understand, at least on a subconscious level, the degree of cruelty they have inflicted on the Negro for hundreds of years. They feel that if they were to lose their power, to give the Negro the vote, the liberated Negroes would oppress them in the same way.

There is no way the Lewises or the Hamers or Bob Moses or Julian Bond or any of the other Negroes I have met down here would ever inflict such suffering on another sentient being. But the problem is, white supremacy doesn't understand empathy or love. It only understands power and dominance.

I am not sure I understand much about love these days, either, but I have come to understand something about forging on. We are holding our state convention in Jackson tomorrow. We are going to elect a slate of delegates to attend the Democratic National Convention in Atlantic City. Our hope is to unseat the official delegates sent by Mississippi, as we believe they are an illegitimate body, considering that half of the population was barred from voting.

You would have thought that finding the bodies of those three men would have demoralized us, but I think everyone knew, deep down, that Michael, Andy, and James were dead. Now we have proof. And now we are more determined than ever.

Your loving daughter,
Daniella

August 7, 1964

Pete,

You don't need to come down here. You don't need to rescue me. There are only two weeks left anyway, and besides, you aren't part of the program. This isn't just a "free-for-all" that any well-intentioned person can join. Remember, Eve applied and wasn't accepted.

The letter you sent was lovely, and yes, I accept your apology. You are right— you didn't understand. Thank you for recognizing that. It means more than you know.

Don't come to Mississippi, but if you want, you could come to the Democratic National Convention in Atlantic City. I'll be going up there along with our elected delegates for the Mississippi Freedom Democratic Party. The idea is that we can unseat the delegates that Mississippi is sending. It's a long shot, but I am hopeful it *might work. Our legal argument for seating our delegates is sound: Over half of the population of Mississippi was denied the right to vote, so how can the all-white delegates Mississippi is sending be legitimate in any way?*

You could join me there. I have no idea if there will be any hotel rooms available, but surely you could figure something out. I don't really know where to tell you to meet me, but I think if you just look out, you'll see us. The delegates from the MFDP are mostly Negro, and mostly sharecroppers, maids, hairdressers, etc. We will not look like your "typical" group of politicos, thank God.

You flatter me in your letter, Pete, but you have to understand: I walk away from Mississippi at the end of the summer, but the Lewises and every other Negro family that hosted us do not. They are the heroes. And besides, I think that if you had been raised by my father, and if you had seen firsthand what happened to Miss Eugenia when Eve (stupidly, naïvely) tried to advocate for her, you might have come down here, too.

Perhaps I will see you in Atlantic City? I hope so.

D

September 3, 1964

Dear Eve,

I've called your house several times, but your mom always says that you are "unavailable," either out with friends, or back-to-school shopping, or napping. I know she is just making an excuse because you don't want to talk. Oh, but Eve, we have to move past all of this! I have so much to tell you, so much to discuss. And I want to hear about you—are you still seeing Warren? Last spring you were talking about volunteering with the Columbia Citizenship Council and tutoring children in Harlem. Are you still planning to? I hope so. God knows Harlem is suffering. Is Warren still a member of that Columbia group speaking out against our involvement in Vietnam—what is it called, ICV? I think I would like to go to one of their meetings this year, at least find out more about their position. Maybe we can go together.

Oh, Eve. I feel bereft without you in my life, and I'm so sad we aren't going to be rooming together this year, though of course it's nice we each got singles. I admit I let my feelings grow hard toward you earlier this summer when you were still mad at me for going to Mississippi without you, but now I just miss you. I want my friend back.

I miss our long talks. Here is what I would say if I were sitting next to you on one of our beds, smoking cigarettes and hearing the sounds of Dylan coming out of Abby's room for the ten thousandth time: Negroes are the only ones who really understand race in America. They are the only ones who go through every day of their lives in colored skin, skin they cannot peel off just to have a temporary respite from the abuse it brings. They are the ones who can teach us about oppression in America, because they live on the receiving end of it. And they are the ones who can teach us about resistance, about standing up for human rights.

Those of us with white skin can empathize, can stand in solidarity, but we can always trick ourselves into thinking things aren't so bad. We are allowed to make up stories about "the race situation" because we don't have to bear the burden of it on our own bodies.

Here is something else I would like to talk to you about: I am not sure we made any real change this summer. Positive change, that is. Three of us died. Countless were beaten. (Lew got the back of his skull split open with a railroad spike—he had to have twenty-two stitches.) I was threatened with a gun, pointed at my head. An unloaded gun, it turned out, but I didn't know that during the endless seconds it was held against my temple. The families we stayed with will surely face retribution from their white employers, their white landlords, the white law enforcement, now that most of us are gone and the national media has turned its attention to other matters. And we did not, after all, unseat the Democratic delegates sent from Mississippi. I'm assuming you followed all of that on the news? What a joke. The DNC offered us two seats—two seats out of seventy. We turned them down. Took the "moral victory." Is there any such thing?

Did you watch Fannie Lou Hamer testify in front of the select committee when we were vying for the seats? She was so powerful that LBJ called an emergency press conference during her talk so that the cameras would move off her and onto him. And then do you know what that jackass did? He announced that it was the nine-month anniversary of Kennedy's death. That was his big press conference. By the time they turned the cameras back to the select committee hearings, Fannie Lou had finished speaking. But it didn't matter. Stations replayed her testimony again and again. (Please tell me you saw it!) There she was, with a voice that did not waver, speaking of how she was brutally beaten by the police after she tried to register to vote in 1962. "How many beatings will I have to take?" she asked those well-heeled committee members. Lew, who stayed in Mississippi during the convention, said that the Negroes watching Miss Hamer testify could not believe that one of them, a poor farmer, a colored woman, was speaking on national television about their lives, was captivating the nation with the truth.

Throughout the convention she kept saying, "When you tell the truth, you've got nothing to hide."

Well, she was right. We had nothing to hide. But that didn't stop the Democratic Party from shutting us down. Even though our supporters lined the boardwalk in front of the convention center with poster boards reading: "One Man / One Vote" and "I Support the MFDP."

Oh, Eve. My heart is so heavy. What a wasted opportunity. If they had seated us, if they had refused to seat the "Dixiecrats" from Mississippi, not a one of whom represented their state's Negro citizens, God, it would have changed things. Just thinking about the loss makes me cry.

My father told me not to despair. My father reminded me that because of our actions, the nation had to turn its eyes to Mississippi. The nation had to tune its ears to Fannie Lou Hamer. My father says that change will come, eventually, as a result of all of this. I would say that I "pray" that he is right, but Unitarians aren't that big on straight-up praying, you know—we'd rather attend a seminar discussion on the psychological benefits of prayer! (You didn't think I'd get through this letter without at least one Unitarian joke, did you?)

Something else happened in Atlantic City. A minor event compared to the delegate fiasco, but an important one all the same—important to me at least. Pete showed up. Pete showed up with a sign of support, a placard that read: "I Support the MFDP." He stood on the boardwalk for hours with that sign before I ever saw him. And here's something I didn't tell you—I had broken up with Pete at the beginning of the summer. I'm sure you remember how unsupportive he was of us—of me—going to Mississippi. He felt I was putting my life and the lives of the Negroes in Mississippi in danger. He said why not work on "fixing" Harlem first. He said something about uneducated colored people not being "ready" for the vote. I know. It was awful. I broke things off with him after he said that. But then we ended up exchanging letters over the ten weeks I was down there, and I guess the stories I shared shifted something in him, allowed something—empathy, I suppose—to blossom. And there he was, standing in solidarity in Atlantic City. Can you imagine what his mother, Stockton, president of the West Hartford DAR, would say?

Pete asked me to marry him. Our engagement is assuredly not the most important event of the summer, and yet, I am happy. Thrilled in fact. We will not get married until after I graduate from school, so it's a long way off. And the wedding will be small, unless Pete's mom manages to talk me into something bigger. But I'm happy, Eve. Grateful for the life Pete and I will build.

Do you think you might be my maid of honor?

I miss you,
Daniella

Chapter 6

CALLED HOME

New York City, 1968

Eve would not be a "Good German." She would not get lost in a fog of rationalizations. She would not, when the Vietnam War finally came to an end, clear the condensation from her glasses and cry, "I never knew; I never knew the terrible things we were doing!" as the "Good Germans" had once done. She knew. She knew what American soldiers were doing to villagers in Vietnam, knew what they were doing to children in those villages. Children. She knew that napalm burned between 1,500 and 2,200 degrees Fahrenheit and if you tried to wipe it off it only spread, until eventually flesh melted from the bone.

Children suffered this death, delivered by bombs dropped from the sky by her country. Her country.

Warren had a book of photographs, purchased in Paris, showing scenes from everyday life in Vietnam after the French had finally retreated and before the Americans arrived. She could not stop studying its pages. She was especially drawn to a picture of two dozen children or so, bunched shoulder to shoulder in disorderly rows, widemouthed and laughing, two of them mid-clap, captured in the middle of delight, their bare feet on the dirt, or perhaps it was sand. What were they laughing at? What was bringing them such delight? Anything and everything. Children were delighted so easily—this she knew from her own teaching.

Only a few years after that photo was taken, the Americans would arrive. She thought of the boy in the photo who was clowning around with his hands on top of his head, reminding her of Malcolm, her own class clown. She imagined a boy like him walking down a dirt road, taking lunch to his father. She imagined a noise coming from above, the child looking up to the sky. Spotting it. Spotting the plane overhead. She imagined him watching as bombs tumbled out from its insides. How graceful the bombs might look, falling. How elegant. And then the fire, gasoline mixed with a rubber perfected in the labs of Dow Chemical, creating a viscous, burning gel that stuck to the flesh.

Her parents were shocked—shocked!—by those who lit *themselves* on fire in protest, burning themselves to death, first Thich Quang Duc in Vietnam, protesting the treatment of Buddhists under the South Vietnamese government, but soon followed by American martyrs, so overcome with the evil America was perpetuating—in their names—that they made the ultimate sacrifice, their flaming bodies demanding that we pay attention to what was happening, pay attention *now*.

She remembered talking to her mother soon after the suicide of Norman Morrison, a thirty-two-year-old Quaker who, in 1965, set himself on fire just outside Robert McNamara's office at the Pentagon, his baby daughter covered in kerosene before he handed her to a bystander.

"What a sick, sick man," her mother had said. "To kill himself in front of his baby. And he had two other young children at home, and a wife! Imagine a father doing that to his family."

"What a sick, sick nation we live in," Eve had answered. "To bomb innocent Vietnamese villagers in the name of freedom. Imagine doing that to an autonomous country halfway around the world."

"You do not understand the very real threat of communism," her mother had rebuked. At the time, Eve had just rolled her eyes, but were they to have the same conversation today (they wouldn't—Mrs. Whalen flat-out refused to engage in political discussions with Eve), she would tell her mom that she now considered herself a communist. She no longer simply wanted the United States to withdraw from Vietnam. She wanted the National Liberation Front to win. She wanted colonized people all over the world to break free, to smash imperialism, to be autonomous, to live as they so desired.

She did not start from this place. She had once been a liberal, like Daniella and Pete, who had once been a Young Republican. Daniella and Pete had marched down Fifth Avenue two years ago along with tens of thousands of others, demanding that the United States withdraw from Vietnam. She had not marched in their group but had seen them among the other Barnard and Columbia students. The banner they held read: "Unitarian Universalists for Peace."

Eve was with people from the Independent Council on Vietnam—ICV—Warren, Abby, David, Mark. They carried signs, too. Warren's read: "Not with My Life You Don't." Hers, cut into the shape of a stop sign, simply read: "Stop War." Abby, ever the provocateur, carried a poster board that read: "Girls Say Yes to Guys Who Say No." But the most compelling sign she saw was held by a black man in a group of black marchers: "The Vietcong Never Called Me a Nigger."

There were so many people at the march—young, old, black, white, college kids, working class—she honestly believed that LBJ would listen. (How could he not hear their chants? "Hey! Hey! LBJ! How many kids did you kill today?") Back then she believed that the United States was a good nation that had made a bad decision in entering the Vietnam conflict but that, when faced with the will and the conscience of its people, would reverse its course, correct itself, take a dose of painful medicine and recognize how brutal it had become. Warren had laughed at her naïveté. The

United States had always been a brutal country, he said, beginning with the genocide of the American Indians. And then the country itself—the actual White House, for fuck's sake—was built by enslaved humans, kidnapped from their home country and brought here in chains, kept in submission by the lash and the noose.

Back in the spring of Eve's sophomore year, Warren had convinced her to tutor kids in Harlem through a program called the Citizenship Council. "Don't be such a child," he had said when she sniffed that she didn't know if they would want her. After all, CORE had just rejected her application to go to Mississippi for the summer. But Warren was right (Warren was always right), and so she had signed up. Shortly after she joined, one of the Council leaders, David Gilbert, told her the story of how he had come to see the link between the shameful treatment of blacks in America and villagers in Vietnam. David had arrived at his tutee's apartment in Harlem upset because he had just read a newspaper account of a massive bombing in Vietnam. He said to the child's mother, "Our government is bombing people on the other side of the globe for no good reason."

"Bombing people for no good reason, huh?" the mother had said. "Must be colored people who live there."

Many of the members of ICV were Jewish. Abby's father had immigrated to America in his teens, but many of his relatives, including his brother, stayed in Poland. They all died in the concentration camps during the Holocaust. "We didn't know!" the "Good Germans" had cried when they were forced to tour Buchenwald shortly after the Allies declared victory. The "Good Germans" walked past piles of emaciated corpses, shielding their eyes, ducking their heads. Eve had seen the pictures. She had imagined her own mother taking such a tour, claiming ignorance as she held a hand-kerchief over her nose.

She would not be a "Good German." She would not, as Pete and Daniella had chosen to do, slide into cozy domesticity, hide out in the universities, get a mortgage, buy a car. Pete and Daniella were married now, both enrolled in graduate school at Emory, Pete studying history, Daniella studying law. She and Warren had gone to dinner with them a couple of months ago, when they were up north visiting Pete's parents in Connecticut. It had been the first time Eve had seen Daniella since the spring of 1966, when they had graduated from Barnard. Three days after graduation, Daniella married Pete. Eve refused to attend the wedding, even though Daniella had asked her to be her maid of honor.

For their reunion dinner, Daniella had suggested they meet at some Chinese place in Harlem, and Eve and Warren had agreed since it was near their apartment. But the place was an embarrassment—an Americanized version of "the Orient" where the host wore a red silk dress and the piped-in music was of the Frank Sinatra variety. They didn't even offer chopsticks; Warren had to ask for them. "Bet they don't have a copy of Mao's Little Red Book, either," Warren had whispered to Eve, making her laugh.

Daniella was wearing the big diamond ring Pete had given her for their engagement, an heirloom piece crafted in 1912 that had belonged to Pete's grandmother. Eve once cared about such things. Her own mother had a similarly impressive ring, though it was made in the late 1930s, an era not known for its opulence. But the diamond was of a respectable size. As a girl Eve had dreamed of the day she would get engaged, a handsome man offering her a ring with a big rock sparkling from its center (the diamond needed to be more than a carat, but not much larger or it would run the risk of being gauche). But now it struck her as immoral to wear something of so much value when there were so many impoverished people in the world. She suggested Daniella give the ring to the Panthers.

"I hardly think they would want it," Daniella had said, eating her lo mein with a fork. "Aren't they all about autonomy and self-determination?"

"They are, sure," Warren said. "But they'd deign to hawk it for cash."

He wore his own ring, given to him by a North Vietnamese commander

he met while on a secret trip to Cuba. It was made with the metal of a
downed American fighter jet.

During dinner Daniella told Eve that their old friend Kitty Ridley had
moved to Atlanta but that she was now Kitty Steed, having married her
English professor during her junior year at Belmont.

"I take it she dropped out?" asked Eve.

"No, she graduated. She said she just didn't take any classes from her
husband once they were married. He's teaching at Emory now. They actually
seem really happy."

"I wonder which young student he'll fuck next," Eve mused.

Daniella raised a brow but didn't say anything. "Oh, and I keep meaning to tell you, I ran into Charlie in Virginia Highlands, at Moe's and Joe's,
which is kind of a hangout for Emory law students. I met his fiancé, Fig."
Daniella gave Eve an amused look.

"God. Their wedding is next weekend."

"You going?" asked Daniella, her voice suddenly tight.

She shook her head. Daniella sighed, seemingly relieved. Jesus, Daniella
was *still* upset that Eve hadn't attended her wedding. Wasn't Daniella the one
who used to tell her to de-personalize, that the movement was bigger than
any individual drama?

"She told me it was *quite* a feat to find a lipstick that matched the color
of the bridesmaids' dresses."

Eve couldn't help but laugh. Of course Charlie would choose to marry
a girl who went by "Fig," a girl who was concerned about her bridesmaids'
lipstick matching their dresses. She probably had her silver pattern picked
out for her the day she was born. Granted, so had Eve, not that she would
ever use it. Indeed, she had sold the silver tea set that Grandmommy had
given her, had sold it and given the money to Warren to help finance his
Cuba trip.

Just as Daniella had done, Fig had asked Eve to be the maid of honor in her wedding, the invitation issued through Eve's mother during one of their increasingly tense phone calls.

"That's ridiculous," Eve responded. "I haven't even met her."

"Of course you have," said Eve's mother. "We invite her family to our Christmas party every year. And she was a cheerleader at Lovett, just two grades above you. You would have seen her at the Coventry-Lovett game."

"She must not have made much of an impression, because I don't remember her."

"Do you realize what a terrible snob you've become, darling?"

"I learned it from the best, Mommy," said Eve, her throat tightening the way it always did when she argued with her mother. "In any event, tell Fig I'm not going to be able to make it to the wedding. There's too much shit going on up here."

Eve's mother immediately hung up the phone. Any time profanity slipped through Eve's lips, her mother hung up on her, as if bad language simply burned her delicate ears.

"It's *almost* comical how outraged your mother becomes over the stupidest things," Warren told Eve when she relayed their conversation.

He was right. Both of her parents were outraged by the wrong things. They were outraged the previous Christmas when the Driving Club put up a red tree ("So tacky," her mother had moaned), but they certainly weren't outraged over Vietnam. Her father had been a medic during the Second World War, and he saw the current conflict as a continuation of the United States' benevolent presence on the world stage. Besides, his son was not at risk of being sent over there. Charlie had graduated from Emory Law School in 1966, just as he turned twenty-six, placing him outside of any danger of being drafted. Eve had a cousin who was in the National Guard, but so far he had only been sent as far as Houston. She knew of a few boys from Coventry who had enlisted, one in the National Guard and two in the Air Force. She didn't know anyone who was a ground soldier.

That is, except for Ada's only son, Albert. He had been drafted in 1966. And unlike Charlie, Pete, and Warren with their student draft deferrals in hand (Warren was getting a master's in sociology at the New School), Albert had no choice but to serve or face a long jail sentence.

"Can't you get him into the National Guard?" Eve had pleaded with her father on the phone after he casually mentioned that Albert's draft number had come up.

"The wait list for the Guard is miles long."

"Don't you know someone on the draft board?" she had asked.

"Sweetheart, our country is at war. Albert is of age. It is his duty and responsibility to serve. And you know about the G.I. Bill, don't you? When Albert comes home he will be able to enroll in college, paid for by his service."

"*If* he comes home," Eve had said.

He did not. Ada didn't even have the comfort of having his body to bury. Small in stature and quick-footed, Albert had been a "tunnel rat." A booby trap went off while he was underground, so that he literally walked into his grave.

Her mother would sometimes mail newspaper clippings, most of them announcing that some person Eve had known a million years ago had gotten married. So Eve was not surprised to receive Charlie and Fig's wedding announcement, which had run in the *Atlanta Journal.* The picture of Fig and her ten bridesmaids was in black and white, so Eve was unable to tell if her new sister-in-law had pulled off a successful lipstick match. When she showed the picture to Warren, he commented on how many people could be fed with the money spent on that one lavish reception.

"It's not like your family is a bunch of pious monks," Eve said, feeling defensive despite herself.

"Of course they aren't. Shit, my dad will be the first with his back against the wall when the revolution comes," said Warren. "But until then, I'm happy he sent me this."

He showed her the check for a thousand dollars, ostensibly as an early Christmas present, though really, his father sent checks every few months. Eve's did, too.

Eve hated that they needed money from their parents. It wasn't as if they were lazy. It wasn't as if they were "flower children," dropping out of society and living off the land. They wanted to change society. They wanted to dig out the rot. Their latest project was the founding of a community school in the basement of a Friends meeting house in the Bronx. Called The Children's Place, it welcomed four- to ten-year-olds. It offered open admission, so that anyone who wanted to enroll could. There were no set classes, but Eve was there to offer instruction in literature and writing if the children so desired, and Jane, a math major from Barnard, was there for numbers and equations, while Warren offered assistance with social studies and history. The kids determined what they did each day, and if what they wanted was to read the funny pages, fine. They'd read the funny pages. Eventually, some of them would get bored and ask one of the adults to teach them something. More and more frequently the children asked her to help them make "story books." She would ask them questions about their lives and write down whatever they told her. Then she would give them the pages so they could illustrate them as she hovered nearby, in case they needed reminding of what was written on each page. Later she would read their stories aloud during circle time. Three of her kids who hadn't known their letters when they first enrolled at The Children's Place could now read.

One early December afternoon Eve arrived home from teaching exhausted. The kids had decided to have a naked day, which was always tedious because it meant sorting all of the clothes they tossed on the floor and making certain they didn't run outside to dance in the snow. For starters, she didn't want them to catch a cold, but also, she had to be careful not to do anything that would attract the attention of the authorities, who might come barging into the school demanding licenses and other bureaucratic bullshit. Walking into the apartment she shared with Warren and a rotating parade of others, she went to the kitchen sink, overflowing with dirty dishes, and got herself a glass of water. Then she went to the living room, pushed the sleeping bag off the sofa (some guy who'd gone AWOL from basic training was staying with them for a few days), and pulled her stash out from the rosewood box that sat on the coffee table. Last year she had bare-knuckled her way through quitting tobacco, but pot was a different story. With great care, she rolled herself a well-deserved joint. Just as she was bringing a match to its tip, the phone rang. She ignored it, lit the joint, and inhaled. The phone rang five times, stopped, and then a minute later started up again. She sighed, answered.

It was her mother. "Eve, I have some bad news. Mother has died," she said. "A sudden heart attack. She was absolutely fine yesterday and now—gone."

"Oh no," said Eve. "I'm so sorry." How could Grandmommy no longer be alive? It seemed impossible that such a formidable person could have succumbed to something so ordinary as death.

"How soon can you get home?"

"Oh, Mommy, I don't think I'm going to be able to make it. I've got a class of twenty kids that need me up here. But I'll be with you in spirit, I promise."

"God dammit, Eve, if you don't come to this funeral I will see to it that your father never sends you another check again. I swear I will."

She had never heard her mother curse. She brought the joint to her mouth, thinking. The last thing she wanted was to return to Atlanta, even to bury Grandmommy. It was just too hard, too disorienting. It was like being the guest of some hausfrau during World War II, being fed schnitzel while you knew that, a few miles away, innocents were being gassed. But without her parents' money she could not do her work at the school. She could not do her work to end imperialism. As embarrassing as it was to rely on their largesse, in an exploitive, capitalist system what other option did she have?

"Warren's coming with me," she said. "We'll need two tickets from JFK. Nonstop."

They had gotten high just before boarding their flight. As their plane started its final descent into Atlanta, they raced up and down the aisles grabbing drinks off people's trays, like crazed stewardesses. Indeed, passengers must have mistaken them for overly zealous employees of the airline, for no one said a word to them about their crazy-motherfucker actions, even though their actions were intentional, political: White Bread America went along with all sorts of atrocities, from Jim Crow in the South to the war in East Asia. Acting like crazy motherfuckers was a form of resistance.

They walked off the plane, attracting only a few glances. Eve's father was waiting for them at the gate. It had been a long time since Eve had seen him. He looked older, heavier, the bags under his eyes prominent.

"What happened to your hair?" he asked as he took her duffel bag from her.

She had cut it short, as short as Jean Seberg in *Breathless*, only she was not trying to be chic but rather utilitarian.

"It's easier," she said. "No fuss, no muss. Saves on shampoo, too. This is Warren."

This was her father's first time to meet—not her boyfriend exactly; they weren't exclusive—her lover. She wondered how Warren would appear to her if she were meeting him for the first time. Her father probably assumed he was a hippie, but he resembled a hippie only in that his hair was a little long. Otherwise he looked like a manual laborer in his uniform of jeans, work boots, and flannel shirt, a small SDS button pinned to it.

Warren held out his hand. "Nice to meet you, sir," he said.

"The pleasure is mine," said Eve's father, shaking Warren's hand heartily. Eve gave Warren a hard stare. *Sir?*

Once at the car, Eve insisted that Warren take the front seat while she rode in the back. It would be easier to avoid being questioned by her father that way, should he want to hit her with some version of "What exactly are you doing with your life?" Of course, he might interrogate Warren, but she doubted he would. Her father was known as a "consummate gentleman." In his study was a framed quote by Theodore Roosevelt: "Courtesy is as much the mark of a gentleman as courage." They zipped up I-75, the interstate so empty it almost seemed as if they were driving through a ghost town. As they drove, her father told them there would be a viewing that night at Patterson Funeral Home and then the service itself would be at All Saints' the following afternoon at 1:00 p.m.

"Your mother asked that I suggest you shave your legs," said Eve's father. "But I believe I'll leave that between you and your God."

"My god doesn't give a shit about hairy legs," she said.

"Hmm," murmured her father. "Well, I guess that settles that."

How could it feel both so good and so awful to be back home? Her mother had freaked out about her hair, of course, actually shrieking when she first saw it. But she pulled herself together pretty quickly, probably helped by the fact that Warren was, inexplicably, acting like an Upstanding Young Man. In addition to calling her father "sir," he referred to her mother as "ma'am" and even pulled the chair out for her when they sat down at the kitchen table for a very early supper of hamburger soup and biscuits. (Was Warren just fucking with them? Was he hoping to get something out of her dad, money maybe?)

Casual though the meal was, her mother still put out silver flatware, not her ornate pattern, but the Fairfax, whose simple design paired well with the simple food. The weight of the sterling soup spoon felt good in her hand. She hated that it felt good in her hand. She hated that earlier, after unpacking, she had stood underneath the showerhead in her childhood bathroom for thirty min-utes, just luxuriating in the hot water. At their New York walk-up they never got hot water for more than five minutes, and never with so much pressure.

Her mother had hung a robe for her on a hook on the bathroom door, and she had set out lotions and cotton balls and nail scissors, along with a new razor blade and shaving cream. She was anything but subtle. God forbid Eve embarrass her mother with unshaved legs at Grandmommy's funeral. God forbid her mother give serious thought to anything other than how things appeared.

They gathered in the vestibule before heading for the viewing. Eve did not know Warren owned one, but there he was in dark suit and even a tie. When she asked about it, he told her it was left over from his boarding school days. Fig and Charlie, the very newly minted Mr. and Mrs. Charlie Whalen, ar-rived at the house, even though their Garden Hills starter home was closer to Patterson's than The Compound.

"Sister!" Fig said the moment she saw Eve, arms outstretched to em-brace her. Fig wore a little black-and-white tweed suit. Her hairstyle was not dissimilar to how Eve used to wear hers, back in the days when she had added height with a teasing comb and lots of hairspray and then curled the ends so they flipped out. Now she didn't even have enough hair to fit around the rod of a curling iron. Eve wore a black turtleneck and a long black skirt, her feet tucked into a pair of clogs, an old pea coat, bought cheap from the army surplus store, draped over her arm—the same coat she had worn to countless demonstrations against the war.

"Hi, Fig," she said, hoping her sister-in-law's embrace wouldn't last too long.

"Oh, it's so good to see you!" exclaimed Fig. "And I love your darling haircut. It looks like Mia Farrow's in *Rosemary's Baby*. Did you see that movie? I had nightmares for weeks!"

"Nothing that happened in that movie is worse than what's going on right now in Vietnam," said Eve.

Fig stared at her for a moment. Then she blinked, linked her arm through Eve's, and whispered, "You might just be right."

At the viewing Eve spent a long time looking at Grandmommy's waxy face, her rouge applied in two round circles on her cheeks. She had always been so careful to look put together, elegant. Eve felt a shiver and put on her coat, grateful that she had thought to bring it with her.

Grandmommy was being buried in a pleated pink silk dress, with a small cream-colored Bible—just the New Testament—in her manicured hands and her Fleur pin attached to the dress slightly above her bosom, close to her heart. Eve wondered if Grandmommy's belief system would soon be buried, too, if the old world had to die before a new one could burst forth into being. She thought of how her grandmother used to invite her over to her "cottage" for tea parties when she was a little girl, how she would serve Earl Grey from a sterling pot, and then dilute the black tea with lots of milk and sugar for Eve. She would serve petits fours from Henri's bakery, too. Eve used to love those cakes. She remembered how her grandmother would sometimes even have an extra cake for Eve's cherished doll, Annabelle, and how she and her grandmother would secretly nibble at it and then praise Annabelle for eating her confection all up. She felt tears well in her eyes. She couldn't believe her grandmother was no longer on this earth.

And yet it was time for the old woman to go! It was time for the world she lived in, the things she believed in, to be rendered to dust.

Wiping away her tears, Eve left the coffin to look for Warren. He was standing with Charlie. She wondered what in the name of God they might be talking about. The war, probably, as Warren didn't speak of much else. Her brother was almost a head taller, but he looked gangly and almost goofy next to Warren with his simmering intensity. She walked over to them. They were discussing Hank Aaron and the Braves. Eve could care less about sports. She found herself tuning out until she realized Charlie was talking to her.

"Sorry?"

"Fig and I saw your old friend from college a few months ago. We ran into her at Moe's and Joe's. Dani something?"

"Daniella. She mentioned running into y'all when I saw her in New York. She's in her third year at Emory Law, you know."

Even though Charlie had been the one to pull Eve into the conversation, he looked past her while she spoke, scanning the crowd, a habit that had always driven her crazy.

"Help me out with something," said Charlie, making brief eye contact with her before continuing to scan for people more important to talk to. "Why, exactly, is she in law school?"

"Um, so she can be a lawyer?"

"Sure, but how is that going to work? I mean, I suppose she could be an associate at a firm for a few years, but what happens when she wants to start having babies?"

"Are you kidding? Mom could have had a full-time job for all the time she spent with us when we were little. Daniella will just hire someone like Ada to take care of her kids—if she has them at all."

"I just don't see it," said Charlie, looking at Warren, as if he might offer confirmation. "I don't see how a woman could put in the hours needed to be a really successful lawyer."

"I told you, she'd hire someone like Ada."

"Ada might have helped out when we were little, but when we were sick, Mom was there."

She thought of the chicken and rice soup her mother made every time either she or Charlie had a bad cold.

"Chuck's got a point," said Warren. "I mean, isn't becoming a mother sort of the pinnacle of a woman's life? Is Daniella really going to skip out on that? Isn't her Young Republican husband going to want a brood of rug rats all his own?"

Warren still referred to Pete as "the Young Republican" even though it had been years since Pete claimed loyalty to the GOP.

"All I'm saying," Charlie lectured, "is that I think it's dangerous when we get away from our innate roles. Daniella's bright, no doubt, but she essentially stole a spot in her class that should have gone to a man who will one day need to provide for his family."

"You're a chauvinist pig," said Eve. She pointed at Warren. "You, too."

"I would be willing to bet one hundred dollars that she quits five years into whatever job she gets in order to start pushing out babies," said Charlie.

Warren laughed.

"Hilarious," muttered Eve, and she walked away from both of them, toward the other side of the crowded room. Several people cast sideways glances at her as she made her way through. These were people she once knew, but she had no intention of talking to any of them. What would she say? "Hi, Mrs. Calhoun! I find your entire way of life offensive!"

She imagined that most people in this room felt the same as Charlie did about women pursuing serious careers, not to mention nearly every man in Daniella's law class. *God, poor Daniella.* For a moment she ached for her old friend, who must be under such scrutiny so much of the time. But then she reconsidered. The truth was Daniella probably deserved whatever shit she got. Not because she was "stealing" a spot in her law school class, as Charlie claimed, but because she was of the erroneous belief that she could change the system from within. When it came to the system, the only thing you could "change from within" was yourself. Entering the system would change *you.* You would acclimate to its norms.

• • •

She saw Fig standing by herself near the guest book, smiling bravely but looking uncomfortable. It was hard to believe Fig was only twenty-six. She looked like a matron. It was her tight hairdo, her fussy little suit.

"Do you need a drink as much as I do?" asked Eve as she sidled up next to her.

"Lord, yes!" said Fig. She glanced at Eve, smiling, but then her expression shifted into something different—confusion and surprise.

"What?" asked Eve. But before Fig could answer, Eve's mother was storming toward her, her cheeks flushed, her eyes hard.

"I cannot believe you."

"What?" Eve had no idea what was going on, this sudden onslaught of fury.

Her mother took her pointer finger, the nail painted bright red, and jabbed it into the lapel of Eve's pea coat. "This," she said. "You found this an appropriate accessory to wear to Mother's funeral?"

Eve looked down and saw the button she had pinned to the coat, which said in small print: "Fellatio is fun. Cunnilingus is cool." Someone had given her the button months ago; she had gotten so used to it being on her lapel that she had forgotten about it.

"I didn't even realize I was wearing it. It was just left on from a long time ago. Don't worry, Mother. I bet no one here even knows what those words mean."

"I know what they mean! Your father knows what they mean! And I promise you everyone else in this room knows exactly what those words mean. They mean: *I don't give a damn about my grandmother.* They mean: *I don't give a damn about my family.* You just despise us, don't you, Eve? There is no conclusion other than that. You despise your own family. You want to humiliate us at every turn. Well, congratulations. A-plus!"

"Mommy, I didn't mean to wear it. I promise. I'm sorry. I'll take it off. I'll throw it away."

"Don't bother. And you and Warren don't bother coming back to the house. It was a mistake to ask you to come home."

"Mommy—"

Her mother turned and walked away. Eve looked at Fig, whose face was frozen in shock. But then Fig turned to her, put her hand on Eve's forearm.

"She's lashing out because she's grieving," she said. "Why don't you come and stay with Charlie and me for the night? The guest bed is all made, and then tomorrow after the service maybe you can go back to your mom's house and clear things up."

She had to admit that Charlie and Fig's house was adorable, a white cottage with window boxes filled with boxwoods and paperwhites on the first floor and dormer windows popping out of the roof on the second. It reminded her of the house the Anderson family lived in on the TV show *Father Knows Best*. She wondered when Fig would have a baby, make Charlie a father.

They went inside and Fig led her and Warren to the guest room upstairs, hesitating for just a moment before saying, "There's a pullout bed in the living room if y'all would rather not share?"

"Fig, we've been sharing a bed for years now," said Eve, and her mind flashed to that first night with Warren, the night she discovered that Daniella planned to go to Mississippi without her. She had gone alone to the West End, where she had hoped to find Warren, where she had lingered at the bar until he showed up. And he did, as if she had conjured him. She thought of how bold she had been, approaching him as soon as he walked in the door, how she had looked him straight in the eye and told him she wanted to go home with him, and how, soon after, they were naked together in his bed. He had plunged right into her, and she had felt a tearing pain. And the pain, somehow, felt good, as if she were ripping herself away from some former self, some naïve, girlish self who believed in loyalty above all.

Fig continued to fuss over things, pulling an extra blanket from a shelf in the closet and putting it at the foot of the bed, checking the medicine cabinet to make sure it contained extra toothbrushes and toothpaste.

Because all of their clothes were at Eve's parents' house, Fig dug up some comfy things for them to change into—a pair of sweatpants from Fig's PE days at college, along with an old Agnes Scott T-shirt. She gave Warren a pair of Charlie's sweats and one of his old Phi Delt sweatshirts.

"Look at us," said Eve, twirling in front of Warren. "It's like we're in disguise."

They went into the living room where a Christmas tree stood on display, bejeweled with colored lights. It was a Fraser fir, the same kind Eve's mother always insisted on, though the elder Mrs. Whalen was of the firm opinion that the tree should not be put up until Christmas Eve. Charlie, his tie removed but dress clothes still on, had lit a fire and was now pouring drinks, Scotch on the rocks for all. Her brother handed her one, and Eve made her way to the sectional sofa, where she sat down with a sigh.

"How about some music?" she asked Charlie.

"What do you want to hear?"

"Do you have any Dylan? Maybe *Blonde on Blonde?*"

"I've got *Dylan's Greatest Hits.*"

Of course, Charlie had his Greatest Hits. God, he was so derivative. But never mind. When he put the album on, the opening song was the same as the opener on *Blonde on Blonde*, "Rainy Day Women #12 & 35."

"Well, they'll stone you when you're trying to be so good. . . ."

Ain't that the truth, Eve thought, remembering her mother jabbing her finger into her chest, infuriated over a tiny button that Eve hadn't even realized she was wearing, a button that encouraged people to have fun with their bodies.

Warren sat next to her. She was annoyed at him for siding with Charlie at the viewing, but it was still nice to feel his leg against hers. "Do you have a joint?" she asked.

He pulled one from behind his ear, like a magician with a trick hat.

"Where's Fig?" asked Warren.

"She'll be here in a minute," Charlie said. "She's just putting together something for us to eat." He settled into the armchair across from them, legs spread wide, drink balanced on his thigh. He looked extremely comfortable inside his own house. He looked like the king of the castle.

"Do you have a light?" asked Eve.

"Sure," he said, putting his drink down on the floor and walking to the stone fireplace. He pulled a glass ashtray and a Zippo from the mantel, where several silver-framed photographs were on display, including his and Fig's engagement portrait.

"You don't mind, do you?" she asked, waving the joint in his direction.

"What is that, marijuana?" asked Charlie.

"Yes, Charlie. It is a marijuana cigarette, and after you smoke it you are going to become both a communist and a practitioner of free love."

"When did you become such a smartass, Sis?" Charlie asked.

She lit the joint, inhaled. She held the smoke in her lungs for a moment, then pushed it out.

She passed the joint to Warren, who took a hit before reaching across the room to give it to Charlie.

"I can't," said Charlie, waving away the offer. "I might run for office one day."

"He's adorable, isn't he?" Eve asked Warren.

Fig, who had changed into black capri pants and a thin gray sweater, walked into the room and set a tray down on the coffee table. On it was a bowl full of saltines next to a white dip with little green flecks in it, along with serving knives and paper napkins.

"Cream cheese and olive," said Fig. "It's yummy."

Eve dipped a knife into the cream cheese mixture and spread it onto a saltine. It *was* yummy, creamy and smooth with little salty nuggets of olive mixed in.

"Do you want a hit?" Warren asked Fig.

Fig glanced at Charlie.

"You have to ask his permission?" Eve asked.

"No, I just, I wanted to see if Charlie was doing it or not."

"I'm not, but you go ahead if you want to, sweetheart."

Fig sat on the sofa next to Eve. Warren handed Fig the joint, reaching over Eve to do so.

"You just put it to your mouth like a cigarette, but hold the smoke in your lungs before exhaling," said Eve.

Fig took a hit, coughed, and blew the smoke out. "Wow," she said. "Now I've smoked marijuana."

Warren smiled, amused. He grabbed a saltine and dragged it through the cream cheese and olive.

Fig passed the joint back to Eve, who took a hit and passed it on to Warren.

"This is perfect stoner food," said Warren.

"Thanks," said Fig, who had turned to sit sideways on the sofa so that she could face Warren and Eve, her knees pulled into her chest like a young girl. "So what's it like to live in New York? I've only visited once, when I was twelve. We saw the Rockettes and went ice-skating at Rockefeller Center. We had a ball."

"We pretty much avoid the tourist stuff," said Eve. "We're mostly just teaching at the school and organizing against the war in Vietnam."

"What does 'organizing' entail?" asked Charlie.

"We help out guys who have been drafted and can't, in good conscience, serve. And also guys who are in the Army and want to leave."

Charlie shook his head, though he didn't say anything.

"Let me guess," said Eve. "You disapprove."

"It just seems like you're doing the enemy's job so well that we should fight you instead of the Vietcong," Charlie said.

"Depends on who you think the enemy is," said Eve.

Charlie left to go to bed shortly afterward. Eve couldn't tell if he was upset by their conversation or just genuinely tired, but in any event it was just she, Fig, and Warren left in the living room, passing the joint around, Fig getting more proficient at smoking each time it circled back to her.

At some point Fig took her hair down from its tight little updo and restyled it into a simple ponytail. She was very pretty. Mrs. Whalen had told Eve, with no small amount of pride, that Fig had been on the Homecoming Court when she was a senior at Lovett.

"I admire y'all so much," Fig proclaimed. "You're really doing something with your lives. You're taking a stand. And you're living in New York! It must be so thrilling to live there, even if you don't . . . you know . . . tour the sites."

"I'm sure Charlie could practice law in Manhattan," suggested Eve.

"He doesn't want to leave Atlanta. He says the social 'infrastructure' here is too compelling, that between y'all's family history and the Driving Club directory, he's just one drink away from everyone who matters."

"That sounds *exactly* like something my brother would say," said Eve, standing so that she could retrieve more saltines from the kitchen.

"Fuck Charlie," said Warren, turning toward Fig so that he was looking directly at her. "What do *you* want?"

Fig held his gaze for a moment before answering. "Adventure," she said.

Fig continued staring at Warren, her lips parted slightly. Warren reached over and put his hand on her leg.

"Excitement," added Fig, twisting a piece of hair that had escaped from her ponytail. "Something different."

And then Warren moved toward Fig, leaning in so close that his lips were grazing hers. Eve watched from where she stood halfway between the couch and the doorway, frozen, as Warren rested his hand lightly on Fig's cheek, a move Eve remembered from when they first kissed, a move that was so small, so incidental, and yet felt so proprietary. And now Warren was kissing Fig, while motioning for Eve to come back to the couch to join them. For a moment Eve felt herself pulled toward Warren's desire.

But then she glanced at the fireplace and caught sight of their engagement portrait on the mantel, its silver frame gleaming. The two of them looked so happy, sitting side by side on a bench by the Duck Pond, near where they now lived. Soon their wedding photos would also be on display, but those probably hadn't even come back from the photographer yet.

Ah, fuck the system, right? Break every taboo. But she couldn't. She couldn't do what Warren wanted. She couldn't act like a crazy motherfucker when it came to her brother's wife, even if her brother's wife was a willing participant.

"I'm exhausted," she told them. "I'm going to bed."

Fig looked up at her, her eyes searching and uncertain. "I guess we should all call it a night?" she asked, hesitant.

"You two can do whatever you want," Eve answered.

Eve walked away, heading for the stairs that would lead to the guest bedroom that Fig had meticulously prepared for them. She turned around once at the doorframe, watched Warren's hands on Fig's waist, his fingers encircling her.

Chapter 7

SMASH SESSION

Atlanta, 1970

Eve sat on the back steps of the house, opening the latest letter she had received from her father, her father who didn't even know she had moved back home and was living not ten miles from him. As always, her father had used his Crane stationery, and had addressed the letter to her old apartment in New York, the Morningside Heights walk-up where she and Warren and an assortment of others had lived, off and on, since college. Though Eve was no longer living there, members of the collective still used the New York apartment. Any mail from her family was immediately forwarded because it often contained money.

The house they were renting in Atlanta was a baby-shit-yellow brick ranch on Euclid Avenue, sandwiched between two crumbling Victorians. Long ago this downtown neighborhood was fashionable, but its status had tanked with the rise of the automobile and suburbia, and now, more than half a century later, the grand old Victorians were abandoned or turned into boardinghouses.

Eve pulled the ivory-colored card from the envelope and opened it, hoping a bill might fall out. Nothing. She ran her fingers over the front of the card, engraved with her father's initials, *LRW*, standing for "Lemuel Richard Whalen," her father's middle name the same as the pig president's. Her father was one of the pigs, yes, but Eve still believed he was better than Nixon. This belief of hers, that there were different levels of culpability, got her into trouble during Smash sessions, the point of which was to smash any remaining bourgeois notions and attitudes the members were holding on to. Smash the past in order to build the future. Smash the past in order to resist imperialist control. Smash the past in order to destroy the idea that because the members of their collective were white and almost all of them were from wealthy families, they could return to the straight life whenever they wanted simply by washing their faces and tucking in their shirts.

Well, fuck that. A true revolutionary could never go back. The Panthers couldn't go back. Fred Hampton sure as shit couldn't go back. Nat Turner couldn't go back, but neither could John Brown, because though he was white, he had been irreversibly committed. He had been willing to die for the cause. The members of Smash believed it was better to die in honor than to live as their parents did, anesthetized by liquor and Valium, getting and spending, the sweat and blood of colored people past and present allowing them the luxury to believe that they *deserved* their good fortune, that they had somehow earned it by virtue and hard work, when really they "earned" it through exploitation.

Eve knew that she had not been born innocent. But she was committed to change. She was so committed that when Smash decided it needed a cell in the South, to fight racist America at ground zero, she volunteered to go. She thought of herself as a double agent, once intimate with the enemy. How strange to be back in Atlanta, chosen as their base city because it had a sizable enough counterculture that they wouldn't stand out. They would be mistaken for hippies, though they were nothing like hippies. "Peace is for pussies," Abby liked to say.

Eve hated leaving her job at The Children's Place. She had loved working with young children, loved their curiosity and exuberance. She had become known as the Reading Lady, because nearly every child she encountered learned how to read. It was really just a matter of paying attention: paying attention to what kind of stories they liked, to whether or not they mixed up their letters, to whether or not they might need glasses to help them see. She studied their sweet faces, noticed the varying colors of their skin tones, tried to notice everything. It was their faces she saw when she thought of the children in Vietnam burned by napalm or shot dead by U.S. soldiers. (That photo from the massacre at My Lai, the mother holding her toddler, both about to be killed. It was too much. It was unbearable.) Black or Vietnamese, it made no difference to the men in charge of her country. Both were expendable.

In Atlanta they were learning judo, karate, how to load a gun quickly, how to aim, how to shoot. "*Piece Now*, motherfuckers." That's what Warren always said, Warren who had brought her into Students for a Democratic Society, before he became disillusioned and left, giving the splintering factions the middle finger on his way out the door. Especially Jeff Jones and Bernardine Dohrn, with whom he had some sort of falling-out, probably over sex, but maybe it was just over power. Who knew? Some from SDS had morphed into the Weathermen. Just a few months earlier three of them—Diana, Terry, and Ted—had blown themselves up while building a bomb they intended to detonate elsewhere. The rest disappeared deep underground, not a trace left behind.

Eve had known all three who had died. Not well, but well enough to cry when she heard the news.

Warren kept a stolen box of dynamite in the rusty storage shed behind their rental house, along with some copies of *Popular Mechanics* and *Science of Revolutionary Warfare*. He said it was time the American people got a taste of their own medicine in retaliation for what they were allowing to happen, daily, in Vietnam. "We have to blow things up to start all over," Warren said. "But we have to know what the fuck we're doing."

• • •

She read her father's letter quickly, made a sound of disgust, and put it back inside its envelope, which she folded in half and slipped into her back pocket. Scanning the yard, she spotted the skinny orange cat that sometimes came around, a cat who was seemingly afraid of no one or thing, despite the fact that he weighed all of ten pounds. Once Eve spied him having sex. It happened so fast that she wasn't sure what she'd seen before he sprinted away from the other cat. The Smash Collective believed that's how humans should fuck, too. Monogamy was just a way to keep the imperialist system going. To have a girlfriend or a boyfriend is to set yourself up. Eve remembered Warren explaining this to Daniella and Pete at that shitty Chinese restaurant in Morningside Heights Daniella had insisted on going to.

"Say the pigs held Daniella hostage," Warren had said. "You're going to do whatever they want to release her, right? But if you were to say to them, 'Hey, man, I have no girlfriend, I have smashed monogamy; I will not let her fate tie me to your imperialist, bullshit system.' They wouldn't be able to use you, see?"

Daniella had remained quiet, but Eve knew what she was thinking: that Warren was a blowhard and a jerk. Daniella had said as much the first time Eve admitted she had slept with Warren, that she had lost her virginity to him.

"Oh, sweetie, not him!" Daniella had cried, and Eve had hated her for her casual judgment.

Once Eve and Daniella had been as intimate as lovers, just without the sex. For a time Eve took a certain pride in how close they were, how it was Eve and not Pete whom Daniella clung to after they learned of JFK's death, how it was Eve who had finally dragged Daniella to a CORE meeting, even though Pete warned them not to get wrapped up in that "communist organization."

Then betrayal. First Daniella went to Mississippi without her—when it was Eve who told *her* about the Mississippi Summer Project in the first place, when it was Eve who insisted they both apply! And then Daniella agreed to marry Pete, who as far as Eve was concerned represented everything Daniella had taught her to mistrust in the first place.

For most of Eve's family, Atlanta was a small, interconnected world centered on four locations: Piedmont Hospital, where Dr. Whalen delivered the babies of their friends and social equals; the Driving Club, where a million years ago Eve grudgingly made her debut; All Saints' Episcopal Church, where once a week the Whalens swallowed their wine and wafer; and, most important, The Compound on Northside Drive that covered twelve acres of Buckhead real estate and nearly stretched to Chastain Memorial Park. During Eve's childhood the extended family would gather at The Compound each week for Sunday supper. Eve's mother never did much in the way of cooking, but she served Ada's dishes with pride, especially her fried chicken, which Ada soaked for a day in buttermilk before frying in hot grease.

Eve missed Ada's fried chicken, not that she would ever admit to it, she who lived primarily on rice, beans, and oatmeal. She missed Ada, too, and on occasion even thought about trying to visit her but didn't think she could trust Ada to keep secret her whereabouts. Besides, Eve wasn't sure where she lived. Ada used to have a house in Peoplestown, which was only a few miles from where Eve was staying now. When Eve was growing up, Ada would sometimes bring tomatoes from her garden, fix Eve and Charlie BLTs or tomato sandwiches for lunch. But Eve had read in *The Great Speckled Bird* that much of Peoplestown had been torn down to make way for the downtown connector, where Interstates 75 and 85 merged. She imagined Ada's house had probably been demolished.

Eve thought of how she ached for Ada during her first year at Belmont, the first time she had ever really been separated from her. She had been so glad to see her when she returned to Atlanta that summer, feigning the part of enthusiastic debutante in order to fulfill her half of the bargain she had struck with her mother, her mother who had immediately whisked her away to J. P. Allen to purchase a closetful of dresses and outfits for a summer of parties, including a long white dress that would have suited a bride. Indeed, the long white dress had cost as much as a bridal gown. When she and her mother had returned from buying it she had confided to Ada that she thought it was obscene to spend so much money on clothes. Ada had given her an inscrutable look that made her feel as if she had done something wrong, though at the time she couldn't quite figure out what it was.

Once Eve had dreamed of being a bride, of having her wedding portrait displayed in a sterling-silver frame on top of the Steinway. When she later confessed this to Warren, he told her that she was barking up the wrong tree if she thought someday they'd get married. She'd laughed it off, asked if he really thought she wanted to join such a sexist institution. Hell no. She was just trying to show him how far she had come.

Even though they were *not* a couple, were *not* tied to each other in any formal way—as mandated by Smash—she loved Warren, loved his fiery intensity. Warren said that the two of them really shouldn't be in the Atlanta collective together, that they should have split up. They proved their loyalty to the cause by sleeping with everyone, sometimes switching partners, sometimes in a group, a collection of bodies being entered and explored by different hands, mouths, cocks. Sometimes Warren left for weeks at a time, to a collective in Detroit, she thought, though she did not know for sure. All Smash information was on a need-to-know basis.

The orange cat had made his way stealthily toward her and was now butting his head against her hand. She stroked the underside of his neck, and he began to purr. Eve had always loved cats. On her seventh birthday she had been given a gray-and-white kitty she named Ivan. From the time she returned home from the Coventry School to the time her mother or Ada tucked her into her canopied bed at night, Ivan stayed near. When she took a bath Ivan perched on the side of the tub, watching the water shift with her movements. Once Ivan jumped in the water, then somehow managed to leap out, a furious bullet of wet fur. After that he was more careful, but he still waited for her on the edge of the tub while she bathed. When she got out he would lick the water off her feet.

The cat was purring loudly now, rhythmically. As she stroked his fur she noticed that it wasn't solid orange, but tabby stripes of different shades of red.

"Who's a pretty boy?" she asked as she rubbed the cat's back with more force. Hair fell off him while she stroked. She had half a mind to go inside and get a brush, but then she remembered that she didn't own one. Nobody in the house did.

She heard a noise behind her and, turning, saw that Mack was awake. Abby and Jane must have still been sleeping off last night. Warren was at *The Great Speckled Bird* dropping off a Smash Manifesto he hoped they would run. Mack sat beside her on the back steps and began rolling a cigarette on the leg of his work pants. Soon he would turn them into cutoffs in deference to the impending Atlanta summer, but it was only May and the heat was not yet oppressive.

Usually the collective smoked weed—the herb of the proletariat—but Mack loved tobacco, couldn't seem to give it up no matter what kind of abuse he endured from the rest of them. Tobacco was a dirty product sponsored by the state to opiate those who labored, to give them a little pleasure during the workday so they would not revolt against the capitalist system, and the members of Smash berated Mack for his cigarette addiction the same way Abby berated Eve for her "rich girl" trip. Little rich girl who brought a sterling silver tea set with her to Belmont College. God, why had she shared that detail with Abby her first year at Barnard?

Mack struck a match against the sole of his work boot. He lit the cigarette, took a deep inhale, then exhaled in the direction of the cat.

"Bring you anything?"

Eve shook her head.

The week before, the cat had brought her a large, dead gray rat, dangling limp from his mouth. Eve had wanted to scream but had forced herself not to, knowing that such a reaction would smack of bourgeois squeamishness, and besides, the cat was only trying to bring her a gift.

The cat carefully made his way over to Mack, bumping his head against Mack's hand, making Mack rub him whether he wanted to or not.

"You better be glad we don't eat you, man," Mack said to the animal.

"Gross," said Eve, and immediately regretted expressing disgust. Warren always said that the wrong things disgusted Americans. Americans were disgusted by a little mold on a piece of white bread, but not by the mutilation of the flesh of Vietnamese children.

"I'm sure the Vietcong have eaten their fair share of kitty," Mack said. "Protein's protein."

That night they sat on the floor of the living room in the ranch house, eating brown rice and black beans off dirty plates with chopsticks. Warren vented about the pussies at *The Great Speckled Bird* who had declined to run his incendiary manifesto that claimed revolution was not going to come without blood in the streets. "Alternative paper, my ass," fumed Warren. "Those motherfuckers are all talk, talk, talk. Then they pussy out whenever anyone calls for direct action."

"Ah, the mighty lion roars," said Abby. Abby's favorite charge to levy against Warren was that he, too, was all talk and no action. Sometimes during Smash sessions she would refer to him as the Cowardly Lion from *The Wizard of Oz*.

"Yeah, and we're getting sick of your chauvinist trip, man," said Jane. "*The Great Speckled Bird* isn't made up of pussies. It's made up of pigs. White, male pigs."

"Yeah, pussy power, motherfucker," said Abby. She had deep red marks up and down her arms and presumably on other parts of her body as well.

Mack had matching ones. The two of them had been pairing up a lot lately, and everyone in the collective knew that Abby liked to scratch. Jane and Abby stood, unbuttoned their pants, and slid them off their hips. Neither wore underwear. "Who wants some pussy with their dinner?" asked Abby.

"Right on," said Mack. He walked on his knees over to Abby, buried his face in her crotch, and then roared as if having swallowed some powerful elixir. Without thinking, Eve shook her head. Abby could always be counted on to take things a step further and Mack could always be counted on to follow. During their last confrontation with the police, Abby had bitten an officer in the arm when he tried to arrest her. In shock he had released his grip, and she had gotten away, joking later that the pigs might make a plaster mold out of the bite marks, to identify her by her teeth.

"What about you, Eve? No pussy power?" asked Abby.

"I'm down with it," she said.

"Then show us," said Abby.

"Yeah, show us your pussy! Show us your pussy!" Jane chanted.

Eve stood, unbuttoned her pants, and pulled them down along with her underwear, revealing a triangle of pale, blond pubic hair.

"Look at that bourgeois muff," said Abby. "I bet you're proud of how blond you are. I bet you're proud that your blood is Aryan and 'pure.'"

"We need to get a big, black stallion to come fuck Eve," said Warren. "Then she might get off her elitist trip."

Eve pulled her pants back up. "Fuck you," she said to him. "I'd love to fuck a big, black stallion. He'd sure as shit be better than any of you motherfuckers."

Warren laughed and Eve drew an inward sigh of relief. She'd gotten him off her back. During Smash sessions Warren was harder on her than he was on anyone else, enumerating the ways in which she still held herself above the group, still saw herself as special, wasn't yet committed, wasn't yet ready to die for the cause.

"I'm still hungry," said Jane, picking up a leftover grain of rice with her finger.

"Of course you are, you fat bitch," said Abby. Though Jane was now as sinewy as the rest of them, she had been chubby in college and Abby never let her forget it.

"Fuck you," said Jane. "I want noodles. Wet, slippery noodles."

"How 'bout some Vietcong cat?" asked Abby.

"How we gonna get that?" Mack asked. It sounded to Eve as if he were saying a line from a play he was performing.

"Maybe there's one in the kitchen," said Abby. "Just waiting to become cat suey."

"Cat suey!" cried Jane.

"C'mon!" yelled Abby, standing and racing toward the swinging door that divided the living room from the kitchen. Everyone stood and followed. Eve followed, too, though she was the last to enter the kitchen with its filthy black-and-white-checkered floor. Lying motionless on the wooden table where Warren often wrote his manifestos was the little orange tabby, his head twisted halfway around, making her think, for a moment, of the Cheshire Cat in *Alice in Wonderland*.

"Mack said Eve was growing attached," said Abby. "So. Time to smash the cat."

The scratches on their arms—they were from the cat, fighting for his life. Eve felt tears push against her eyes.

"That is some *heavy* shit," said Warren.

Eve looked at him, desperately, pleadingly, as if he could somehow stop this, rewind to an earlier time, resurrect the cat. He held her eyes, and in that moment she thought he might save her.

"Dig it! White Bread Americans lavish their pets with food and treats and treat black and brown people like shit. Well, fuck that! And fuck any taboo that keeps us from revolution."

Abby turned toward Eve, as serious as a drill sergeant. "You need to skin the cat."

Eve's stomach flipped and she put her hand instinctively against her abdomen. "I don't know how," she said, but of course that was a lie. She had told them the story of skinning a rabbit after one of her father's hunts, during a Thanksgiving spent at their family farm in South Georgia. Her father had shown her how to do it.

Abby walked to the sink and dug a knife out of it, rinsing it off under hot water, then wiping it against the leg of her pants. Handing it to Eve, she said, "First cut is the hardest."

The cat no longer looked like the animal she had stroked earlier that day. There was the broken neck, of course, but also, he looked so diminished, shrunken in his skin. Eve didn't know how to cut him without holding him, and she did not want to touch him. She looked at Warren. His eyes bore into her, encouraging her to do it, to recognize that disgust is something a true revolutionary has to push beyond. Recognize that protein is protein, that cat is no different from rabbit or chicken. Recognize that if she could do this act, she'd be able to do anything, fight back when being arrested, put Warren's dynamite to good use, be the front line in the war against the system, no longer allowing the black and brown people of the world to take all of the blows.

Eve walked to the edge of the table, standing above the cat with knife in hand. She was afraid he would be stiff when she touched him, but his body was looser than she had feared. Rigor mortis must not have fully set in. She set the knife down and repositioned him so that he was splayed on his belly, limbs sticking out on all four sides. She thought of her father instructing her on skinning the rabbit, guiding her: "Pinch the fur on its back and make a small cut," he had said. She felt bile rising in her throat as she pinched the cat, gathering enough loose skin so that she could pierce it without danger of cutting into the flesh. She made a slit with the knife, big enough to work her fingers into. Even if she vomited she would not stop. She took a deep breath and hooked her fingers under the skin. Once she did this, the worst was over. As long as she skinned him, someone else could deal with the head, the feet, the guts. With two sets of fingers under the skin, she pulled one toward the rear and the other toward the head. At first nothing happened, but then she heard a tearing noise as the skin began to come off the body in two pieces.

"Ho, Ho, Ho Chi Minh! Ho, Ho, Ho Chi Minh!" cried the others, and suddenly Eve felt powerful. She kept pulling, kept tearing. She remembered her father showing her how to work the legs out and then tug hard to tear off the hide, though the fur would remain around the little foot. It disgusted her, yes, but disgust was a privilege, a lie of the bourgeoisie. Protein was protein. This was the most real thing she had ever done in her life, and doing this meant that she could do anything.

The members of the collective cheered and whooped and hollered as she kept going. Abby suggested they eat the cat raw, but Eve, still working, said no, once she finished skinning the animal, she would let Abby gut it, and then they could make a feast of it, braise it with potatoes and onions and eat the stew the following night for dinner. For once Eve had the upper hand, and Abby had to go along. When she finally finished, she placed the dirty knife beside the skinned animal, and the group roared their approval.

She was feeling good, if a little weak. She stumbled backwards and rested her body weight against the counter by the sink. She slid her hand into the back pocket of her jeans, feeling the folded card from her father. She remembered its first line and how reading it that afternoon had only confirmed how little her family understood her, how little they understood the import of the mission she was on.

"Eve," the letter had begun. "We are beginning to think we have lost you for good."

Chapter 8

V.C.

Atlanta, 1972

Usually Warren was in decent spirits when he ventured to Manuel's Tavern, ready to laugh at the dumb-ass liberals and bait Oscar about Vietnam. But not tonight. A few hours earlier, Eve had laid some heavy shit on him, not to mention the shit that had gone down last week. God, he had acted like an idiot—so impulsive, so undisciplined, everything he warned the other Smashers not to be, not that Smash really existed anymore, his comrades having mostly scattered, the majority going underground, while a few pussies turned themselves in, hoping to reintegrate with "society."

It wasn't exactly as if they had been living aboveground for the last four years. Ever since the Democratic Convention in '68 there had been outstanding warrants for their arrests, making it necessary to lie low and use aliases when filling out forms and such. (His favorite alias was Fred, as in Frederick Douglass, whereas Eve often went by Harriet, for Harriet Tubman.) But he had viewed this as an inconvenience, not a catastrophe. After all, the warrants were for relatively minor things: disturbing the peace, resisting arrest, failing to show up for a court date. Until now he had always been smarter about his more committed actions.

He had gone to Detroit last minute to help out the Army of Brothers, a black nationalist group known for its militancy. The Brothers had been planning a direct action for months when their driver—a white guy—had bailed. They needed someone to drive the getaway car, and the driver had to be white because white guys didn't arouse the suspicion of the police the way black guys did. And so they contacted Warren.

After he had successfully made the transfer, he was taken back to the safe house where he had left his truck. He stayed there for a few hours, smoking a little weed with two of the Brothers, an honor that, as a white man, he did not take lightly. It was a little after midnight when he started the long drive back to Atlanta; he popped some bennies to keep from falling asleep at the wheel. He spent the drive thinking about what he and Eve might do next now that Smash was breaking up, now that Eve was souring on the movement, was beginning to grumble that at twenty-eight she should not still be living in such squalor, was beginning to question whether or not any of their actions had done any good. She had gotten it into her head that they should either commit to one grand gesture that "really counted" or walk away. Hell, he could get on board with stepping away from things for a while. Things *had* started to feel stale, redundant, even boring. Which, if he was honest with himself, was probably why he was volunteering to do things like drive a getaway van for an armed robbery.

Maybe it really was time to take a break. Throw away the paper, move to the country, eat a lot of peaches—just like the John Prine song. Hell, they could leave the goddamn country if Eve wanted. They could move to Algiers, get brown as berries under the Mediterranean sun.

What he wasn't willing to do was turn himself in, act contrite, maybe serve a little time, and then sign up for the great American sleepwalk. Eve didn't want that, either; he knew it.

•   •   •

He was a little south of Lexington when he realized his gas tank was almost empty. He spotted a single self-service pump attached to a small restaurant. He couldn't make out the name of the place because the rising sun was in his eyes. He filled his tank and then stepped inside to pay. *Jesus.* The place was a goddamn tribute to the Confederacy. A Rebel flag flew from the corner behind the cash register. A sheath of uncut Confederate dollars was hung on the wall, framed behind Plexiglas. A portrait of Robert E. Lee was displayed above one of the two booths. A bumper sticker on the cash register read: "If I'd known it would be like this I would have picked my own damn cotton."

He should have just turned around and walked out. But he had already filled his tank, and he didn't want a cop chasing after him for nine dollars' worth of gas. There was no one at the register, but when he walked over to the food counter he saw a heavyset white man kneeling to stock the refrigerator near the grill.

"Help ya?" the man asked, standing. He grabbed a laminated menu from the counter and handed it to Warren.

"This your place?" Warren asked.

"That it is," the guy said. "Best dang burger in Kentucky."

"I don't eat meat," Warren said, which was only half-true—he ate anything when necessary—but he wanted to fuck with the guy.

"Guess this ain't your place then, is it?"

"Guess not. I got $8.67 worth of gas."

"Alrighty." The man walked slowly to the register, rang in the amount, took Warren's ten-dollar bill, and handed Warren the change. Only then did he give Warren an obvious once-over, his eyes lingering on his long wavy hair, which he had pulled into a low ponytail.

"You ain't from round here, is you?"

"Nope."

"Why don't you get on then," the guy said. "Before someone shows up and asks why I'm doing business with a commie fag."

"Right on one count," said Warren.

The two men stared at each other across the register, as if they were in a Western and were about to draw their guns. Indeed, Warren had a gun on him, a handy little Smith & Wesson 9mm, tucked into his waistband. He was willing to bet Big Boy was armed, too. Armed to the teeth, most likely. Neither said a word, the only sound the radio, which sat behind the cash register and was playing gospel music—and not black gospel, either, but that insipid, warbling, white shit his grandmother used to listen to on Saturday nights. Both men remained quiet while the gospel quartet sang, "I'm learning to lean, learning to lean on Jesus," and then without even thinking about it, Warren whipped out his pistol and held it to Big Boy's head, told him to put his hands on the counter and not move an inch.

The man's hands were surprisingly small, his fingers plump as little Vienna sausages. Warren noticed he wore a gold wedding band. "I want you to open your register and give me what's in there," said Warren. "And if you pull any shit I swear to God I will blow your fucking head off."

The man had just started moving his hand toward the register when Warren struck him with the butt of his gun. It landed with a dull thud against the side of his head. The man slumped over on top of the register. *Oh fuck.* Warren hadn't meant to do that, but when he saw the man move his hand, it had occurred to him that maybe he was reaching for his gun, or tear gas, or, hell, some kind of panic button that alerted the redneck posse.

Warren was contemplating trying to get into the register himself when he was interrupted by a high, sweet voice: "Hey, Dad, I got the—"

He turned around and saw a young boy, seven or eight years old, standing in the doorframe of the kitchen holding a carton of hamburger buns, eyes wide, mouth shaped into the proverbial O of shock.

Fuck. There was a fucking witness. A kid. A fucking kid. Warren saw Big Boy's chest rise and fall. He was still breathing. He would be okay. He turned to the kid, pointed the gun at him, and told him to get down on the floor and close his eyes.

"Start counting," Warren said. "Count slow. And you better count to five hundred before you get up or I'll come back and blow your old man's brains out."

And then he ran to the truck, started it up. On instinct he headed back toward Lexington—the opposite direction of where he needed to go. Once he had driven a few miles north he pulled off the highway onto a deserted road, changed the license plate (he kept spares under the seat), changed his shirt, then hit the road again. Just outside Lexington, he pulled into a big truck stop with a convenience store and private showers. Why the fuck didn't he stop there for gas in the first place? He bought shaving cream and a razor, along with a pair of scissors. In the shower he shaved off his beard and chopped his hair so close to his scalp that you could barely tell he had curls. He toweled off, and then wrapped the shorn locks in a bunch of toilet paper before stuffing them into a trash receptacle. After asking around for the nearest Greyhound station, he managed to hitch a ride there with a guy in a rig heading for California later that afternoon. He abandoned the truck in the parking lot of the truck stop, a bummer, but there were always casualties in war.

It was dawn when the Greyhound finally pulled into the downtown Atlanta station. He had hitched his way back to the house on Linwood Avenue, shorn as a plebe. When Eve woke up he told her he'd been threatened at gunpoint when he stopped for gas in Kentucky and had fought back and as a result he had to change his look and ditch the truck. Warren thought she might be excited by the danger of it all, but Eve was less sympathetic than he would have liked. Her lack of sympathy only heightened his anxiety about the whole thing, and for the next few days he kept expecting to hear the police knocking at his door, child witness in tow, still holding that carton of hamburger buns.

He kept trying to make plans with Eve about how they were going to slip off the grid for good. They needed to work on securing airtight IDs. They needed to secure money, of course, and they needed to figure out where to live. Warren thought somewhere in Mendocino County might work, away from the more obvious hot spots of Berkeley and San Francisco. He had stayed in the town of Mendocino one summer; often the fog was so thick it obscured everything in its view, making it the perfect place for a fugitive.

Whenever he introduced the subject of Plan D—Plan Disappear—the name they had coined years ago, knowing that eventually that time might come, Eve was dodgy. That night she had dropped her bombshell. She was pregnant.

They were sitting on the back steps of the house they were renting, off Ponce de Leon, where they had moved just a few months ago after returning to Atlanta, just the two of them this time. Warren was smoking a joint, but Eve had waved it away. They watched as skinny old J.T., who rented the efficiency unit in the basement, made his way out his door wearing jeans and a Hampton Grease Band T-shirt. J.T. worked the graveyard shift at the Mead distribution center and therefore never complained about noise—usually loud music but sometimes the occasional fight—coming from their place in the middle of the night.

J.T. looked ill, his shoulders hunched as he hacked into his fist.

"Are you okay?" asked Eve. If they were still eating meat she would probably offer to fix him chicken noodle soup.

"Got me this cough that won't go away," said J.T. "But it ain't nothin' a drink won't fix." He flashed a crooked smile at Eve before heading down Linwood. When he hit Ponce he turned, and was soon out of sight.

"So whose is it?" Warren asked.

"Yours, you ass. You and J.T. are the only people I ever see."

"Oh, is the deb too proper to fuck poor white trash?"

She stared at him for so long he started to feel uncomfortable. "You're a fucking elitist," she said, but it was more like she was saying it to herself. "After all this, you're still a fucking elitist."

"Oh, did I offend you? Is a lady never supposed to mention that there's a class system in America?"

"I want to keep it," Eve said, steely.

"You know that's impossible," said Warren. "So just get that thought out of your head."

"I want to keep this baby and I want us to do whatever we need to do to give it a normal life."

"Babe, you opted out of a normal life a long time ago."

"You act like we're these mighty revolutionaries, but all we do is play games. We've done nothing to put a stick in the wheel of the war machine. You realize that, don't you? Sure, we'll have group sex and lug around a box of dynamite from hovel to hovel, but none of it matters. We never actually do anything—we haven't done anything that matters since The Children's Place."

Warren opened his mouth to object, but Eve, who was on a roll, wouldn't let him talk. "Acting like 'crazy motherfuckers' doesn't count. It didn't stop My Lai. It didn't stop Fred Hampton from being murdered in his bed. It didn't stop Nixon from invading Cambodia. It didn't even stop Calley from having his sentence reduced and being allowed to serve it from his fucking apartment at Fort Benning instead of Leavenworth where he belongs!"

She was back to Calley again. She was obsessed with Lieutenant Calley. Even though Eve knew that the slaughter he led of more than five hundred villagers in My Lai was just one of many war crimes committed by American troops in Vietnam, she was fixated on it. Probably because she had memorized the pictures printed by *Life* magazine in 1969, showing toddlers clinging to their mothers before they were shot, showing the corpses of villagers, from infant to elderly, piled in a ditch, showing the roar of fire as every home and hut was burned to the ground. A few weeks ago, he had idly joked that the two of them should bomb Calley's apartment at Fort Benning, and Eve had jumped all over the idea, had said that making Calley pay would actually amount to something, would actually make a difference. To which Warren had replied that she was a fucking idiot if she thought they could bomb an Army base, a *Fort*, for fuck's sake, and get away with it.

Warren reached over and put his hand on top of Eve's. They had spent so many years claiming they weren't a couple, and now it was just the two of them, the two of them in it together, the two of them against the world.

"Think about it, babe," he said gently. "No one would have even paid attention to My Lai if it weren't for us. Do you think a mainstream rag like *Life* magazine would have printed those photos if we hadn't been resisting the war for so many years? Fuck, no. We were the vanguard. We forced the mainstream, kicking and screaming, to see the truth."

"So our whole point was to help other Americans become outraged, too? Terrific. I'm so glad I gave up my life for that."

He stared at her. Did she really think that was all Smash added up to?

"They didn't even press charges against Jane when she turned herself in. She just paid a fine for failure to show up in court and was free to go."

"Jesus, Eve! You shouldn't be in contact with her. You need to be careful about who you communicate with."

Eve startled them both by opening her mouth and screaming as loud as she could, screaming for so long that surely her throat hurt afterward. And then she was crying, crying and hiccupping. But still she spoke, her words interrupted every few seconds by little gasps for air. "God, I am so tired of all of this, Warren. I am just . . . so tired . . . of all the bullshit. I don't even care if I have to go to jail. I just cannot . . . I will not . . . continue living this way with a baby. You can disappear into some stolen identity if you want, but if all we are going to do is to keep dicking around, I'm done."

Did Eve not realize that he, Abby, and Jane were behind five—five!— bombings that took place around Atlanta in 1970? They had become so proficient at building explosives that *none* of their actions resulted in casualties, *including* the bombing of the lobby of the Georgia State Capitol that had shut down the place for two weeks for repairs. (Jane, whose mathematical brain made her a bomb-building wizard, had convinced him and Abby that symbolic bombings were just as effective as ones that might rack up collateral damage.) Did Eve really consider such forceful protests *dicking around*? As a matter of self-protection, none of them had shared any details of their direct actions with the rest of the group, going so far as to rent a motel room, away from their Euclid Avenue headquarters, every time they built a bomb—but wasn't it obvious that they were the merry pranksters behind such glorious displays of chaos? And hadn't they all celebrated the news of the Capitol bombing with stolen steaks, Champagne, and an orgy?

And what of the funding for the Army of Brothers? Wasn't funneling more than $5,000 into their coffers doing something? The omitted details of the gas station debacle in Lexington would upset her, of course, but she sure as shit couldn't write them off as toothless. He considered, for a moment, telling her everything but deemed it too great a risk. Eve seemed ready to bolt. He would not give her information she might use as a bargaining chip were she to surrender to the police.

Instead, Warren held the joint to his lips, took a hit. "You're done?"

"I am done."

"Welp," said Warren. "It's been nice knowing ya."

Of course, it hadn't ended that easily. Eve had started sobbing, had begged him again to surface with her and help her raise the baby. "The cops don't have anything on us, just little stuff, and I seriously doubt they'll press any charges," she pleaded. "And we'll figure out a way to keep fighting, just aboveground."

He held her for as long as seemed necessary and then told her that he needed to get out of the house for a bit and think things over. She had nodded, agreed that it was a good idea for him to clear his head, said she might drive over to Jane's and see if she might crash with her. "Clear my head, too, you know?" He didn't try to talk her out of it, even though he knew it was stupid to show up at a former comrade's house. What if the house was being watched? Unlikely, but still.

· · ·

Warren hadn't been at Manuel's long when Oscar lurched in, dragging his sack of resentments along with him. Oscar was almost always at the bar, though occasionally he got so drunk and belligerent that he was kicked out for the night. Why Manuel Maloof didn't ban Oscar for good was a mystery, but he supposed the old lefty had a soft spot for losers. Oscar had served two tours in Vietnam and had clearly left most of his brain behind in the jungles of Southeast Asia. Or maybe he had always been an idiot. When he wasn't bitching about his rotten family in Cleveland who wouldn't even give a guy a bed to sleep in, he was bragging about how many "gooks" he had killed.

"You sure picked a funny bar to come to," Warren would say.

Oscar would answer, "Beer's beer, man."

Warren didn't like the crowd at Manuel's any more than Oscar did, though for different reasons. Manuel's was the watering hole for Atlanta's Democratic establishment. Jimmy Carter had announced his decision to run for governor at Manuel's, and pretty much every local Democratic politician met there to drink and bitch. Warren considered them all chickenshits, with their tepid ideas about reform and their squeamishness around revolution. The piggy businessmen at the Driving Club—where Eve's dad belonged—probably had more balls than these losers, but beer's beer, man, and Manuel's was a short walk from their house. Better yet, since Eve wouldn't go inside the place if you put a gun to her head (she said her father knew too many of Carter's people and she would be recognized), it served as a retreat when they weren't getting along. Plus, he enjoyed baiting Oscar.

Normally Oscar sat at the corner barstool, but it was taken, so Warren waved him over to sit by him.

"I don't sit next to hippies unless they buy," whined Oscar, and Warren resisted the urge to tell him that he wasn't a hippie, was nothing like a hippie. Instead, he motioned the bartender over and ordered two whiskies.

"Look who's buying you a drink, Oscar," said Warren. "It sure as shit ain't Uncle Sam."

The whiskies were placed in front of them. "To the flag," Oscar toasted, and Warren clicked glasses with him, all the while picturing the Vietcong flag in his head.

"So how's ol' Uncle Sam treating you, Oscar?" Warren asked. "You glad you risked your life for him? You glad you gave all you got, including your goddamn teeth?"

Oscar wore a set of VA-provided dentures, though Warren was never clear on whether he lost his teeth during combat or if they had just rotted over the years from neglect. Some nights, when Oscar was in a more contemplative mood, he would pull his dentures out and rest them on a napkin on the bar, his jaw strangely slack while he stared off into the distance.

"Fuck you, man," Oscar answered. "We would have won already if it weren't for you fucking traitors with your nigger marches."

"Is that right, Oscar, is that right?" Warren cooed, though really, he wanted to punch the guy in the mouth. "I served, too, you know. Yep. Dedicated my life to the cause I believe in." He held up his dog tags that had *Minh, Ho Chi* engraved on each side, twirled them in front of Oscar's nose.

Oscar never seemed to remember having seen them before. He squinted at the letters until he could make them out and then slurred, "You goddamn commie!"

"You're goddamn right!" Warren answered.

This was their standard banter. In fact, Warren was pretty sure they had exchanged the exact same lines the last time they saw each other. But tonight Oscar was pissing him off more than he was amusing him, or maybe he was just pissed off to begin with.

Nigger marches, for fuck's sake.

He had always known Oscar to be a reactionary blowhard, sure, but he tried to think of Oscar as a victim of the system, a poor kid from the Midwest who didn't know any better than to show up at the induction center when his draft number came up.

But re-upping for a second tour threw a wrench in that theory, didn't it?

"So how come you went on two tours, man? They hold a gun to your head?"

Oscar slurped his whisky. "Nah, man. I liked it. Liked how nuts it was. Shit, it would be out-of-your-skull boring for days on end, and then, suddenly, without even realizing it, you were in the middle of combat and there was shit flying all around you and you were shooting as fast as you could, and then you looked up and you'd killed more gooks than you could count and you were still alive, man. You were still alive."

The seed of an idea took root in Warren's brain.

"You see any action like what happened in My Lai?"

"Shit, man. I would have done the same damn thing if I'd been there. I *did* do the same damn thing, all over that country. I mowed the Vietcong *down*."

"How'd you know they were VC?" Warren asked. He already knew how Oscar would answer, but he wanted to hear him say it.

"How did I know? Because they had slant eyes. Because they all had fucking slant eyes."

"You're a real class act, you know that, Oscar?"

"Go on and judge, you pussy. You think you could tell the difference between a peasant and a VC? The peasants *were* the VC. Shit, they'd offer you a light in the morning and set a booby trap to blow you up at night. Lieutenant Calley is a goddamn hero. The fact that he's sitting behind bars right now is the real crime."

Warren didn't bother to correct Oscar, to tell him that Calley wasn't behind bars, was under house arrest in the comfort of his own apartment, in this very state. Instead, Warren got quiet. Quiet and calm. He thought of what Eve once told him when they were frying rice in a skillet full of hot oil. "Be careful when the oil gets still," she had said. "When it's still, it's dangerous."

He was becoming very, very still as he mapped out his plan. Most likely Eve would not be at home when he returned from the bar. Most likely she would be spending the night at Jane's, sipping a cup of herbal tea and plotting her retreat.

But Warren was still on the front lines. He was in the middle of a battle. A stealth battle, but a battle nonetheless. It was almost funny. Here sat Oscar in some comfortable bar in Atlanta, Georgia, and he didn't even realize a VC was sitting right beside him, inviting him back to his place, telling him he had a six-pack there, a six-pack and a joint, just ready to be lit.

Chapter 9

GHOSTS

Atlanta, 1972

That afternoon, Norah Pringle, a junior from White Oak, a new progressive high school in Druid Hills, had come to Daniella's office at Henritz & Powers to interview her. On the phone Norah had said that she wanted to talk to Daniella about being a "barrier-breaking female attorney in the Deep South." Daniella corrected her, saying that Atlanta was not the Deep South, it was the New South, and if Norah didn't know the difference between those two concepts, then White Oak was not doing its job when it came to teaching social studies. Daniella forced a laugh after that, hoping to soften her words. She knew that among the secretaries at the firm she had a reputation for being a bitch, a fact she hated but did not know how to avoid, not if she wanted to have any authority at all.

Daniella had greeted the girl in the lobby and introduced her to Miss Betty, who was in her sixties and had run the front desk since she was widowed after the Second World War. Miss Betty was professional as always, despite Norah's outrageous outfit—bell bottoms pressed so tight against her pelvis they revealed the dip of her vaginal lips, and a Rolling

Stones T-shirt with its arms cut off, the better to show off her armpit hair. As Daniella raced the young woman to her office, trying to avoid any of her colleagues (in particular Bob Powers, known as a stickler for office decorum), she tried to suspend her judgment of the girl. After all, it had only been two years since she was dismissed by the judge her first day in court for wearing a pantsuit instead of a skirt.

Still, Daniella couldn't help but find the girl irritating. It didn't help that Norah's first observation, upon seeing Daniella's office, was to remark that it wasn't a corner one. Or that she dropped into the chair across from Daniella's desk and kicked her feet up over its side, as if she were in the high school smoking lounge, ready to shoot the shit. Or her compulsion to yell "sexist pig!" at every anecdote Daniella shared about being the first female attorney at the firm—how clients were always assuming she was the secretary, how clients would go behind her back and ask to be switched to a male attorney after meeting with her.

Daniella didn't want to come across as a scold, but she did try to impress upon the girl that shouting "sexist pig!" at stories of discrimination wasn't really going to change anything. Instead, Daniella explained, you had to work for change at both the institutional and the individual level. For Daniella this meant pushing for Georgia—and every state—to ratify the ERA and continuing to be superlative at her job, so good that Henritz & Powers would suffer were she driven out, so good that some of the clients who had initially asked for a man to work on their case ended up requesting Daniella specifically.

"Yeah, but aren't you just falling into the trap of tokenism?" the girl asked. "Like, if you're five times better than anyone else at the firm, sure, maybe they'll let you stay, but will that really change anything about the system, about how women are treated in general? And you won't ever make partner, will you?"

"It matters to have a woman in the room who isn't just taking notes or bringing coffee," Daniella said. "As for making partner, I don't think that's an impossibility."

Daniella was not bullshitting; she believed every word she said. Change would not happen without women who held power in the workforce. She knew this. Yet the girl's words still bothered her, hours after the interview concluded. *Was* she simply a token? *Did* her presence at Henritz & Powers matter? Daniella had decided to go to law school because of her time in Mississippi, realizing that the only way to change the system was to change the laws. Then the sweet old judge she had clerked for during her first year out of Emory Law had suggested she apply for the position at Henritz & Powers, assuring her that ultimately she would make real and lasting change by being the first female associate they ever hired. And of course the money was good, which mattered, since Pete was still in grad school. But other than a pro-bono case now and then, most of Daniella's work consisted of writing contracts for big companies when they decided either to merge or to dissolve.

Pete had managed to hold on to his ideals more solidly than she had her own. The dissertation he was writing helped tear a hole in the myth of Reconstruction after the Civil War: That it had been a terrible time of scalawags and carpetbaggers come to take advantage of the broken South, using the newly freed Negroes as pawns who didn't know any better than to be used. Instead, Pete was documenting what a time of great hope and democracy it was for those formerly enslaved, until the compromised election of 1876, when the white southern Democrats agreed that Rutherford B. Hayes could take the presidency if federal troops left the South. After the federal troops retreated, God help the black people left behind as white terror began once again, a terror that continued through that summer she had spent in Mississippi, nearly ninety years later.

The research and analysis Pete was undertaking was both necessary and important, and it demanded nearly all of his attention and time. All spring he had spent his nights working late at Emory's Woodruff Library. In the earliest days of their marriage, she would bring him cookies from Rhodes Bakery when he stayed late working, and he would do the same for her during exams, though he usually brought her a burger and fries from George's, which they would eat on the steps of the law library, enjoying the night air, the brief break. But now when Pete worked late, she tended to stay at the office and work late, too. She liked the quiet, when no one else was around except for the night janitor, emptying trash cans.

It wasn't until she had put away her brief and was walking through the underground lot to her car that she realized why the young girl from White Oak had left her feeling so agitated: She reminded Daniella of Eve. Physically, the girl was Eve's opposite: dark haired, wiry, sharp featured. But her arrogance, her perpetual sense of outrage, the way she just threw herself into a chair without asking if it was okay for her to sit there, she was Eve all over again.

Daniella started up her green Volvo 142, a gift from Pete, with help from his parents, when she graduated from law school and was inducted into the Order of the Coif. The last time she had seen Eve was several years ago in New York, when she and Pete met Eve and Warren for Chinese food. Eve spent the entire night either complaining that the restaurant wasn't authentic enough or nodding along with whatever nonsense Warren spouted, even fawning idiotically over the ring he wore, which he claimed was made from the metal of an American fighter jet, shot down by the North Vietnamese. Later that night, in their small hotel room at 96th and Lexington, Pete had told her that he almost walked out of the restaurant when Warren started boasting of his ring, staying only because he knew how important Eve's friendship had once been to Daniella.

Back then Eve was teaching at a newly formed "free" school in the Bronx, and Daniella could tell just from listening to Eve talk about her students that she was an excellent teacher, observant, empathic, and effective. But she was pretty sure Eve was no longer teaching. She had heard from a mutual college friend that Eve was now completely entrenched in some militant faction of the antiwar movement, the Weathermen, or something like them. Pete called such groups "Hoover's Favorite Radicals," as he believed that their ilk did more damage to liberal causes than J. Edgar Hoover could ever possibly do himself.

When Daniella graduated from law school, she somehow convinced herself that since her own life was progressing, Eve's must be, too, and so she had phoned Eve's childhood home in Atlanta, looking up the number in the white pages. Eve's mother had answered, and while she exclaimed in all of the right places when Daniella reintroduced herself and informed Mrs. Whalen of her new last name, Daniella detected emptiness behind the manners. When she finally asked about Eve, Mrs. Whalen's response was cold: "We have not heard from her in a year."

Daniella was driving down Peachtree now, past the Fox Theatre and the Georgian Terrace. Normally she would cut over on Tenth to make her way to Morningside, but instead she continued north on Peachtree, thinking she might drop by Oxford Books, which had recently opened in Buckhead. She was not ready to go home to an empty house. Better to find a new novel to read and maybe have a coffee at the bookstore's café, The Cup and Chaucer, which reminded her a little of the Hungarian Pastry Shop in New York, where Eve once worked.

Oh, Eve. Why was she preoccupied with thoughts of her old friend, and why did it still hurt to think of her? Perhaps because she had yet to find anyone to fill her place. As the only female attorney at her firm, she had to be careful in her dealings with her male colleagues, lest one of them think she was interested. And she couldn't really befriend the secretaries, even though her formality with them had earned her a bad reputation. Her old friend Kitty was in Atlanta but was now the mother of four children, ages one, three, four, and five. While Daniella and Pete enjoyed the occasional supper at Kitty and Jim's house, it was a noisy place where adult conversation was impossible, with one child after another constantly interrupting. For her part, Kitty seemed happy as a clam, the central figure in all of those young people's lives, living in her picturesque two-story house on a quiet street near Emory, where the window boxes were filled with seasonally appropriate flowers and tricycles and bicycles littered the driveway.

She certainly understood Kitty's draw toward hearth and home. Didn't she spend what little free time she had decorating their Morningside Tudor-style cottage that she and Pete had bought for a song? (Twenty-six thousand dollars, to be exact, the entire sum given to them by Pete's parents.) She and Pete had gone to Danish Modern on Piedmont and purchased a teak sideboard and dining room table, along with eight Eames dining room chairs. In the living room was the old upholstered recliner from Pete's childhood home and a Pfister modular sofa Daniella had paid too much for, but she didn't care because she adored it, loved its clean lines and handsome leather.

Their light brown ceramic dishes came from Heath, purchased direct from the factory in Sausalito during their honeymoon in the Bay Area. In Sausalito, they also bought a copper sculpture that hung on their kitchen wall—three figures standing by a bus bench, holding umbrellas.

Pete did most of the cooking during the week, that or they would go to George's for a burger. But on Saturday nights she liked to embark on culinary projects, making something complicated from Julia Child's *Mastering the Art of French Cooking* or Claudia Roden's *A Book of Middle Eastern Food*. Too often it was just Pete and her eating their boeuf bourguignon or lamb tagine. Pete had good friends from the history department, and she liked them fine, but they all had wives with babies, with whom she felt obligated to chat about vegetable purees and Montessori preschools, all the while girding herself for that awkward moment in the conversation when one of the women would ask Daniella when she and Pete were going to have kids. It wasn't that she didn't want to become a mother; indeed, she very much wanted to meet the child she and Pete would make. But she could not fathom how she could have a child and stay at the firm. She was already working impossible hours, and if she had any hope of making partner she needed to keep it up. And even though she was ambivalent about the very nature of the work she was doing, the idea of being kicked off the partner track because of biology filled her with rage, a rage so intense she tried to avoid feeling it at all. Better to leave the wives in the kitchen and go join the men, as they tackled the weighty subjects of the day—Nixon, Kissinger, the upcoming retrial of Daniel Ellsberg—not to mention the respective subjects of their dissertations.

Of course, most gatherings usually ended with everyone sitting around the living room smoking a joint, but that presented its own set of problems. The last time they had entertained three couples at their house, Bernie Fisher, outrageously stoned, had suggested they do a "partner swap" for kicks. If Pete hadn't been so stoned himself he would have been aghast. Instead, he just leaned back against the couch and laughed, while shaking his head "no." Absolutely not.

She pulled into the Peachtree Battle Shopping Center parking lot, hoping the lights of the bookstore were still on. She did not want to go home alone to an empty house. She did not want to simply do her nighttime rituals, get into bed, and then wake up in the morning to face the same routine all over again. She wasn't unhappy, exactly, but she wasn't exactly happy, either. Was adult life supposed to be happy? Mostly she was just uncertain how she had gotten where she was, the sole female attorney in a prestigious Atlanta firm, married to a rising academic star to whom Emory would surely offer a tenured professorship. Was this success? Surely this was success. Did loneliness always accompany success? Probably.

Oxford Books was a respite. And the store was still open, thank God, open until 10:00 p.m. according to the sign on the door. She took in the wood chip smell of all of those new books. She stood still for a moment before detouring from her usual destination—Fiction and Literature. Instead, she found the Poetry section. Still on a nostalgia trip, she wanted to thumb through Gwendolyn Brooks's *Annie Allen*. She had left her copy in Mississippi with Hattie Lewis. She wondered how Hattie and James were doing. They had kept up with each other through letters for a few months after Daniella returned to Barnard, but after a while their correspondence petered out.

She picked up a collection by Denise Levertov titled *Relearning the Alphabet*. Norah from White Oak had mentioned it that day, had said the poems were "far out." She was flipping through the pages when she noticed, out of the corner of her eye, a thin woman with short dark hair, the color so monotone it appeared to be dyed. She, too, was holding a book of poems, *The First Cities*, by Audre Lorde. Daniella kept looking. That nose, those long fingers. The woman looked like Eve. But it couldn't be Eve—not in Atlanta, not in Buckhead.

"Eve?" she asked. She could not help herself.

The woman looked up from her book of poems and locked eyes with her. My God, those were Eve's eyes, brown-green with a sunflower in the center. The corners of her mouth turned up slightly.

"Is it really you?" Daniella felt the push of tears and she wondered, for a moment, if she was hallucinating.

"What are you doing here?" Eve asked Daniella, as if she were the one out of place.

"I live here. In Atlanta. I'm an attorney with Henritz & Powers. My God, Eve, it is you! I can't believe it!"

The woman blinked, and the spell was broken. "I don't know what you're talking about," the woman said, slipping the Audre Lorde book back onto the shelf and then hurrying toward the door. Daniella, the Levertov poems still in hand, ran after her but was stopped by a clerk at checkout.

"You can't take merchandise outside before purchase!" called the clerk, who wore a McGovern button on her vest, the wings of a peace dove spread above the letters. Pete had a matching sticker on the bumper of his car.

"Sorry," said Daniella, tossing the book onto the nearest shelf. She ran out onto the sidewalk by the parking lot, looking in every direction, but Eve was gone, as if absorbed by the dark night sky.

Chapter 10

RETAINER

Atlanta, 1972

Daniella awoke with the disorienting sense that *something* of import had occurred last night, but she couldn't recollect what. It was like the mornings after a fight with Pete—their fights were rare but fraught—when she woke up knowing something was off but not being able to remember exactly what until a few seconds later. (These days when she and Pete fought it was usually over whether or not to have a baby.) And now came clarity about the night before: For the first time in four years, she had seen Eve. Probably. Maybe.

She glanced at the clock on her bedside table. 7:25 a.m. In five minutes, her alarm would sound. She turned it off and rose from bed, taking care to be quiet so as not to wake Pete, who was asleep, curled up on his side, his reddish-brown hair just beginning to show flecks of gray near the temples. He was only twenty-nine, but the men in his family went gray early. Their cat, Argus, who was especially beloved by Pete, was waiting on the other side of their closed bedroom door, mewing for his daily dish of wet food. Argus kneaded their heads at night, keeping them awake, and so finally Pete had agreed to shut him out of the room when they went to bed, though he hated doing so and would often remind Daniella not to slip on Argus's tears when she opened the door in the morning.

Belting her robe around her waist, she walked into the kitchen to feed Argus and start a pot of coffee. Pete ordered Kona beans from some roaster in New York, which was a ridiculous expense but something she agreed to because the smooth, chocolaty coffee really did taste better than the stuff you could get at the A&P. Once the coffee was brewing she opened the front door to get the paper. They took the *Atlanta Constitution*, which had a more liberal editorial page than the *Atlanta Journal* and was delivered first thing in the morning, whereas the *Journal* didn't come until the afternoon. Pete thought they should subscribe to both for "balance," but Daniella held firm in her refusal, saying two papers was a waste.

She pulled the paper out of the newspaper holder to the side of the mailbox and waved hello to Fran across the street, who was also in robe and slippers and also fetching the paper. A Quaker, Fran had recently left her husband, announcing that, after twenty years of marriage, she had finally reached the conclusion that "Norman is a real asshole."

Who wasn't leaving their spouse? On their short street alone four couples had split up. Four! Recently she had gotten together with some of the girls—women—who had lived in Monty House during her one year at Belmont: Lane, Eleanor, Kitty, and a woman named Beatrice whom she had never really known. Out of their group of five, three were going through a divorce—only she and Kitty had no plans to end their marriages! She had even heard that Eve's brother, Charlie, and his wife had divorced. Apparently she had moved to San Francisco and gotten involved with est.

What would it be like to divorce Pete? What would it be like to lose a leg?

Back in the kitchen she poured herself a cup of coffee and then a bowl of cereal. Pete had cornflakes with milk every morning, often with a banana sliced on top. She had adopted a similar ritual, only she preferred raisin bran. Standing at the counter to eat, she unrolled the newspaper.

Above the fold was a photo of a burning house. The headline read: "Explosion and Fire in Poncey-Highland; Man's Body Found; Police Suspect Bomb; Possible Link to Antiwar Radicals."

Her mind immediately went to Eve. She had seen Eve, long-lost Eve, radical Eve, the night before. And this morning there was news of a bombing that had killed someone. Her heart was in her throat as she skimmed the article, alert for pertinent details. The explosion appeared to have been caused by a homemade bomb, the damage most severe on the main level of the house. In the burned-out basement of the building, the intact remains of a man believed to be John Travis ("J.T.") Higgins were found. Mr. Higgins, a longtime employee of Mead Paper Company, rented the basement efficiency. Mr. Higgins's supervisor confirmed that, while he typically worked nights, he had called in sick that evening, saying he had been to Grady Hospital, where he was diagnosed with pneumonia. The owner of the home, Patrick Daly, who lived in Decatur, described J.T. as "a real good guy, salt of the earth." He said J.T. had been renting from him for years now, whereas "those two hippies, a fellow and a girl," had only lived in the upstairs unit for three months. He had been there a few weeks ago, trying to fix a leak that was causing damage to J.T.'s ceiling. No one was home, but you don't mess with water, so he had entered without their permission, noticing with disgust the posters he saw hanging on the walls: All leftist propaganda, including one showing a revolver with "Piece Now" printed below it. He thought of evicting them right then and there but knew he probably didn't have the grounds. Plus, they had paid several months' rent up front.

Daniella, who had been standing at the counter, felt her knees nearly buckle. She needed to sit. She made her way unsteadily to the breakfast table, sinking into one of the kitchen chairs. *Breathe*, she told herself. *Breathe*.

The "girl" described by the landlord must have been Eve. Otherwise, it was too much of a coincidence that Daniella had seen her last night. So the "fellow" was surely Warren. For, as much as Warren and Eve liked to deny that they were a couple, they had been inextricably linked since Eve and Daniella's last year of college. And "Piece Now" sounded exactly like him.

Did Warren and Eve build the bomb together? Did it accidentally detonate, killing them both? The article said that the police suspected they would find more casualties. My God, was Eve dead?

Or maybe Eve had already built the bomb by the time Daniella saw her at Oxford Books. When did she see her? Eight p.m.? Eight thirty? Neighbors reported first hearing the explosion around 10:40 p.m. Perhaps Eve and Warren built the bomb, but then Eve made herself scarce, leaving Warren in charge of planting it—driving it over to, say, the Boeing Headquarters, because surely he hadn't intended to blow up his own place. Maybe Eve helped build the bomb, then headed off to Buckhead, a place so close to her estranged home that no one would think to look for her there, the prodigal daughter lurking around the periphery of all that was once familiar.

In that case, Eve might still be alive. But she would also be a murderer.

Pete walked into the kitchen wearing his blue-and-white-striped pajama bottoms but no pajama top, revealing the scantest sprinkling of reddish chest hairs. He headed toward the coffeemaker but then stopped, studying Daniella, who was still hunched over the kitchen table, now rubbing her temples with her fingers.

"You okay?" he asked.

Daniella held the paper out for him to take. "I'm almost positive I saw Eve last night at Oxford Books."

She watched as Pete scanned the article. "Shit," he said after a few moments.

"I know. It had to be Eve, right? It had to be Eve and that idiot Warren."

"Are the investigators absolutely certain it was a bomb? And not a gas leak?"

"I don't think the paper would have led with the word 'bomb' if they weren't pretty damn sure it was one."

"God." Pete furiously scratched his head, tousling his already unkempt hair, messy from sleep. He walked to the coffeemaker and poured himself a cup, then came and sat at the table with Daniella. "Eve frustrated me, endlessly, but I can't see her building a bomb."

"I can," said Daniella, in a small, pained voice. "She could become so overtaken with indignation and outrage. I can see her justifying it somehow."

"I don't think we know enough yet to draw any conclusions."

"I know. Should we drive over there? Linwood Avenue is, what, two miles away? Maybe we could talk to a cop, figure something out."

"I imagine the street is completely blocked off and completely secured."

"I keep trying to think of someone we know at the paper, someone who might know more details."

"I could drive downtown and see if the street edition has more information. It's got a later print time."

"Yes! That's brilliant. Please do."

"I can check the West Coast sports scores while I'm at it," Pete joked.

Daniella gave him a half smile. "Hurry back."

While Pete was on his mission, Daniella had another cup of coffee, got dressed, and then phoned the answering service at work, leaving a message for her secretary that she would be coming in late. She hung up quickly, not wanting to tie up the phone for any longer than necessary, just in case Eve might be trying to call. Of course, that was probably wishful thinking, as it seemed a distinct possibility that Eve had died in the explosion, that her remains simply hadn't been found or identified by the time the newspaper story went to print. And even if she was alive, would she really contact Daniella? Other than the night before—assuming the woman she saw at Oxford Books really was Eve—they hadn't talked in more than four years.

Daniella had just started pacing the living room when Pete returned with the street edition of the paper. "They found out more," he said grimly. She grabbed it out of his hand and sat on the sofa to read, Pete sitting beside her.

Soon Argus was on his lap, purring loudly. The paper did, indeed, have additional news. It now seemed very likely that the bombing was tied to some radical faction of the antiwar movement. A pair of dog tags and more human remains had been found among the rubble. They read: *Minh, Ho Chi*, the name of the now-deceased president of North Vietnam. An unidentified investigator speculated that the bomb was probably intended to go off elsewhere, its detonation an accident, an eerie parallel to the 1970 11th Street townhouse bombing in New York that had killed three members of the Weathermen, two of whom were engaged in the act of building the bomb when it exploded.

Ho Chi Minh dog tags. Jesus. Warren had Ho Chi Minh dog tags. He had shown them to her during that awful dinner in New York years ago; he had twirled them in front of her as if to elicit shock. She hadn't given him the satisfaction. She had simply murmured, "Hmmm," and turned to Pete to ask him to pass the soy sauce.

Was Warren dead, his body ripped to pieces and mixed among the rubble?

There had been so many bombings over the last few years—including several in Atlanta in 1970, the most significant an explosion at the State Capitol that shut down the place for weeks. It seemed there were reports of bombings all of the time. But with a few infamous exceptions, they were mostly symbolic, causing property damage, not death. Last night's bombing had killed a man living in the basement. And it had presumably killed Warren, too. And maybe Eve. *Oh God, please don't let it have killed Eve.*

Did Warren (and Eve?) know that J.T. worked nights and that was why he (they?) detonated the bomb at that time? But surely, as the paper had speculated, the intention hadn't been to blow up the house where they lived. Surely the bomb was intended to blow up something else.

She turned to Pete. "Do you think I should call the police and let them know I might have seen Eve last night?"

"Hmm. Since you can't be sure it was her, I don't think you're under any legal obligation to report it."

"I don't necessarily mean a legal obligation, but a moral one."

Just then the phone in the kitchen rang. Daniella jumped, causing Argus to leap from Pete's lap and run away. She rushed to answer it, hoping against all odds that it would somehow be Eve on the line. But no, it was just Sandy, her secretary.

"I'm sorry to bother you at home," she said. "But a Mrs. Katharine Monty phoned. She said her case was urgent and you would know what it was about."

But she didn't know what it was about, didn't know a Katharine Monty. Daniella was a corporate lawyer. Her clients were all men. Was there a chance that Katharine Monty was actually Eve, posing as their old friend Kitty, her last name a reference to their dorm at Belmont? If so, Eve was still alive!

After ending the call, she quickly dialed the number Sandy had given her. After ten long rings, someone picked up.

"Monty residence. May I ask who is calling, please?" It was Eve's voice, repeating the exact refrain she used to use when answering the shared phone in the hallway at Monty House.

"This is Daniella Strum. I'm trying to reach Katharine Monty."

"Daniella! It's me. Kitty. Listen, I can't talk now, but is there any chance we could meet for coffee?"

It was most definitely not Kitty.

"Are you okay?" whispered Daniella, as if her sotto voce might throw off anyone who might be tapping the call.

"How about the Majestic?" answered Eve.

The Majestic was a diner on Ponce that stayed open twenty-four hours a day and smelled always of bacon.

"Meet in an hour?" asked Daniella.

"Okay."

She hung up. *My God.* She was going to meet Eve. Eve who might be involved in the explosion that killed J. T. Higgins and surely killed Warren St. Clair.

She wondered if she was obligated to call the police, but she wanted to speak to Eve first, learn everything she could about what had happened. If she were Eve's lawyer she would have attorney-client privilege. She would offer to be her lawyer. Her phone rang again. It was her secretary.

"Your client Mrs. Monty phoned again."

"Yes?"

"She said to cancel your prior plans, that she'll meet you at your usual place instead."

"Did she give any other specifics?"

"She said you would know where that was."

"Okay, thanks," said Daniella, and then thinking she should somehow explain things, she added, "She's a little eccentric, but she's loaded, so she's a good client to have."

She walked back to the living room, where Pete was still sitting on the sofa, studying the newspaper photo of the destroyed house as if it might tell him something if he just looked close enough. "Where is my usual place to meet Eve?" she asked.

His eyes widened. "She's alive?"

"Yes. She called, gave an alias."

"Thank God."

Daniella felt that she might start crying, and so she made a joke instead. "Perhaps I should first try the Driving Club?"

"Didn't you once tell me she took you to The Varsity a lot when you visited her in Atlanta?"

"That's it! I mean, I can't ever remember calling it 'our place,' but I did insist she take me there a bunch of times, and it's so busy and crowded it's easy to blend into the crowd."

She went to her room, applied a light dusting of powder to her face and a little lipstick. She then went to Pete's home office, where she kept a filing cabinet of her own. From the cabinet she pulled out a client agreement form.

• • •

It was only 10:45 a.m., but the lines at The Varsity were already long. Perhaps there was a convention in town. Back when Daniella visited Atlanta during the summer before they transferred to Barnard, she had made Eve take her to The Varsity three times in as many days and one more time on the way to the airport. But now that she lived within a couple of miles of it she never went. Same with the Krispy Kreme on Ponce, where the clerk plucked hot doughnuts off the conveyer belt just as soon as they rolled under a cascade of glaze. Maybe Krispy Kreme was where Eve wanted them to meet. Was *that* their "usual place"?

She would stay until eleven, and if Eve didn't show up she would head over to Krispy Kreme. She kept her eyes trained on the door, looking for the woman she had seen the night before. She had already scanned the lines that had formed at the counters. But maybe Eve was already seated in one of The Varsity's many dining rooms. And then she saw her walk through the door, her short hair covered by a floppy straw hat decorated with a yellow ribbon, as if she were playing at being the belle she once had been. She wore a loose dress in a floral pattern with a Peter Pan collar. She looked as if she were going to a Junior League meeting.

Daniella did not wave her over but walked up beside her instead. "Excuse me," she said.

"Daniella!" said Eve, as if she were surprised to see her. "It's Kitty! Kitty Monty. What a wonderful surprise!"

Eve held open her arms and Daniella stepped into them, holding on tight. Through the fabric of Eve's tent dress, Daniella felt the small, hard bulge of her friend's abdomen—a sign of malnutrition?—made more noticeable because the rest of her body was so skeletal.

"Will you join me for lunch?" asked Daniella, playing along as best she could.

"You know, I'm kind of craving something else," said Eve. "Do you think we could go to the Waffle House? The one in Avondale?"

"Seriously?"

"It's a good idea to zig and zag," said Eve quietly. "Why don't you get in line and order something to go, then meet me there in thirty minutes."

"Okay. Sure." She stepped in line behind a black family, the two children wearing sweatshirts advertising Atlanta. She imagined they were out-of-town tourists, visiting all of the sites. Out of the corner of her eye she saw Eve exit through a different door than the one through which she had entered, as if she were an old hand at subterfuge.

Eve was already in a booth sipping a Coke when Daniella arrived at the Waffle House in Avondale half an hour later. Daniella sat across from her. The place was nearly empty.

"God, I haven't had one of these in years," Eve said, sipping her soda through a straw.

"Too decadent for the comrades?"

Eve gave a weak smile. "Pretty much."

"Look, before we start, I think I should offer to represent you as my client. That way whatever we discuss is protected by attorney-client privilege."

"Do you need money for our attorney-client privilege to go into effect?"

"Do you have money for a retainer?"

"I've got about three hundred dollars on me."

"Okay, we'll set the retainer at one hundred dollars, you can sign this form, and we should be good."

As Daniella was getting the form out of her briefcase, Eve looked at her shyly. "Wow. You're, like, the real thing."

"That's what happens when you go to law school," Daniella answered. "So I'm presuming you know about the explosion that took place last night on Linwood Avenue?"

Eve's eyes filled with tears. "Warren and I had a fight last night, a big one, and I slept over at a friend's. When I tried to return to the house this morning, around eight thirty, the street was shut down. There were fire trucks and police cars all over and someone said a bomb had gone off."

"So, what did you do? Ask around? Find a newspaper?"

Eve shook her head. "I guess I should have, but I didn't. I just—I was in shock. I mean, Warren must have been behind it, and if he was there when it went off . . ."

Eve looked at Daniella plaintively and said in a choking voice, "Don't tell me yet. I don't want to know just yet."

"Okay. We can take it slow. Let you digest things bit by bit. You say you went by the house around eight thirty this morning. But I didn't get your call until around nine forty-five. What were you doing between the time you went by the house and when you called me?"

"I was at a church. Hiding out. I hadn't stepped foot in a church in I don't know how many years, but I went up to Druid Hills Presbyterian, just a couple of blocks from where we lived. The sanctuary door was unlocked. I couldn't believe it. I went in and sat at a pew and thought of the words to every hymn I could remember. Somehow doing that made it so that I could breathe. I sat there for a long time, letting the hymn verses run through my head, and then clear as day I heard this voice say, 'Call Daniella.' And so I left the sanctuary and found a pay phone. I looked up your firm in the white pages. Kept calling until someone finally answered."

If Eve was telling the truth, then that meant she didn't know anything about J.T. "Do you know a man named J. T. Higgins?" asked Daniella.

"Yeah, he lived in the basement of our house. Not *our* house really, we just rented it." She caught her breath, raised a hand to her mouth in surprise. "Oh God. . . ."

"His body was found among the rubble."

"That can't be! It has to be a mistake! He worked the graveyard shift. Always."

"He called in to work sick. He had pneumonia."

"Oh my God. I saw him. I saw him yesterday and he looked terrible."

Daniella motioned to Eve to keep her voice down.

"I asked him if he was okay. Oh my God, poor J.T."

"They think there was probably another person killed in the explosion. They found a pair of dog tags engraved with the name of Ho Chi Minh."

"Warren," Eve confirmed. "I knew it."

"I'm sorry," said Daniella, watching as tears ran down Eve's face, as she wrapped her arms around herself, as she opened and closed her mouth, like a fish pulled from water.

Neither spoke for a few minutes, as Eve wept and Daniella watched, periodically handing her napkins from the dispenser on the table so she could blow her nose, wipe her face. When she finally seemed to be under control, Daniella asked her to describe, in detail, her whereabouts from the night before. She was not at all convinced that Eve was telling her the whole truth.

"I was with Warren, at the Linwood house. And then sometime around seven, I drove to the bookstore, where I saw you. Afterward I went to my friend Jane's—she lives near Piedmont Park. Jane used to be in Smash, but she dropped out a little over a year ago, turned herself in and everything. I went to her house because I wanted to leave Smash, too. I wanted to know how she did it."

"What exactly *is* Smash?" asked Daniella.

Eve sighed. "It's a collective—a tribe. We thought—oh God, Daniella, it sounds so dumb saying it out loud. We thought we could bring down the United States government by bringing the war home, by being the vanguard who would force people to pay attention to the atrocities being committed in our name in Vietnam. We thought we would start the revolution and then working-class and black kids would join with us. . . ."

She paused, rubbed her temples with her fingers, looked pleadingly at Daniella. "I promise, at one point it all made sense. Everything was just going to hell in this country and we thought the revolution was at hand. I don't even know who was in Smash other than a handful of guys who circled in and out of our apartment in New York, plus Warren, Abby, me,

Jane, and a guy named Mack. Like I said, Jane surfaced. Mack took off for Canada, I think, and Abby went underground. For all I know, that was the entirety of the collective, though Warren always said there were Smash tribes in every city."

Just then the waitress arrived at the table, dressed in uniform, holding a pen and an ordering pad. "Welcome to Waffle House," she said. If she noticed that Eve had been weeping, she gave no indication of it. "What can I get you?"

Daniella hadn't even looked at the menu. She scanned it briefly while Eve ordered hash browns.

"Covered and smothered?" asked the waitress.

"Just plain," said Eve.

"Grilled cheese and a Coke," said Daniella, adding, "Thank you."

After the waitress walked away Daniella leaned forward in her seat. "Look, I'm going to ask you some tough questions, and I need you to be completely transparent with me so we can figure out the best plan for going forward."

Eve nodded, lip trembling.

"Did you or any other members of your collective plant bombs other than the one that presumably went off last night at the Linwood Avenue house?"

Eve shook her head. "Not that I know of. Warren did keep dynamite, and a book on building bombs, but the book was more a historical artifact than anything, written about seventy years ago. Warren really loved the old-school anarchists, J. H. Most and Emma Goldman and such, and that book was his homage to them. I do remember Jane and him poring over *Popular Mechanics* magazines, back when we were all living together in a house in Little Five Points. That was around the time of the Weathermen townhouse explosion; I think they were just trying to figure out what might have gone wrong with their bomb. And I remember Warren and Abby once getting into a discussion about how you could use a drugstore alarm clock with the minute hand removed to set off a blasting cap. But that was all I ever heard or witnessed—just talk. I never saw Warren, or anyone else for that matter, making a bomb or in possession of one."

"Eve, from what you're describing it sounds like he most *definitely* knew how to build a bomb. Come on. Be honest with me. Be honest with yourself. You said the two of you had a fight before you went to the bookstore. Are you absolutely sure it wasn't over the bomb he was planning to detonate?"

Eve shook her head. "I promise, the only thing Warren was planning was to go underground. We were already pretty much off the grid, but he wanted to truly disappear, like with a new birth certificate and everything."

"So what was your fight about?"

"I told him I was done with Smash. I told him I wanted to turn myself in, that I wasn't going to have a baby and be looking over my shoulder all the time, afraid of being exposed."

Oh. She was pregnant. Of course. *That* was the protrusion Daniella had felt when they had hugged.

"How far along?" asked Daniella.

"My period's been irregular for a while now, so I don't know for sure, but I think about two months?"

"How did Warren react to the news of your pregnancy?"

More tears fell from Eve's eyes. "He wanted me to have an abortion. We know a guy."

"Are you considering it?"

"I have no business having a baby. I know that. But I can't have an abortion. I just can't. Everything has been dead in me for so long, and now there's this life taking root. I'm not going to kill it. I'm not going to be responsible for killing one more thing."

Jesus, who else had Eve killed? Daniella must have shown her alarm, because Eve grabbed her arm. "I don't mean literally. I mean, killed one more part of myself."

"Look, you really can tell me anything," said Daniella, steadying herself.

"I'm acting as your attorney. And with all of the switchbacks about where we were meeting today, it's pretty obvious you think you're being followed."

"The brown shoes are everywhere," said Eve. "The good thing is they're so fucking obvious they're pretty easy to spot."

"What are brown shoes?"

"*The* brown shoes. You know: Hoover's guys, the Feds."

Jesus. Was she wanted on federal charges?

"Tell me what you could be arrested for," said Daniella. "Tell me what they've got on you, so we can figure out how to go forward."

"I just want to go home," said Eve, burying her head in her hands. "I'm just so tired and I want to go home."

"Look, if the FBI were to walk in right now and recognize you, would they arrest you for the murders of J. T. Higgins and Warren St. Clair, or would they charge you with, say, evading arrest during a protest?"

"Daniella, I swear, I didn't know anything about the bomb that went off last night. I knew that Warren had a supply of dynamite, and I knew that he liked to talk of just 'blowing up the whole system,' but I thought he was all talk. I really did. A month or so ago he even talked about driving down to Fort Benning, figuring out where Lieutenant Calley lived, and blowing the place up. But he had no plan. He just liked to talk a big game."

"Wait. He talked about bombing Fort Benning? Eve, you have to tell me these things! That could have been where he planned to detonate the bomb last night, and he accidentally set it off before he left the house."

"I'm telling you, he was all talk."

Their waitress returned carrying a grilled cheese and soda for Daniella and hash browns for Eve.

As soon as she was out of earshot, Daniella said, through clenched teeth, "Warren clearly *wasn't* all talk, and the dynamite clearly *wasn't* just some prop, because at some point he must have used it to build a bomb— the bomb that went off in the Linwood house, killing not only him but J. T. Higgins. That was action, Eve. That was murderous action."

"I never thought he would go through with anything. I really didn't. He was . . . I don't know, kind of a pussy when it came to actual violence. The rest of the group gave him shit for that all the time. Abby used to call him the Cowardly Lion."

"So maybe he was building the bomb to prove that he wasn't all talk."

"But there was no one left for him to prove himself to! I'm telling you, everyone had bolted. It was just the two of us. And I just keep thinking about how upset he was with me for choosing the baby over him, for leaving him, just like everyone else had. Maybe he just, I don't know, felt so alone that he built the bomb with the intention of killing himself, not knowing poor J.T. was at home. . . ."

She paused for a moment, tears spilling down her cheeks. "I'll never see him again."

Daniella grabbed both of Eve's hands in her own. "I know this is really hard," she said. "And I wish we had more time for you to take all of this in. But I need to ask you something: Would you be willing to share everything you know about Warren with the authorities, including that he talked about bombing Fort Benning?"

"I don't know. It feels like I'm throwing Warren under the bus."

"Honey, Warren is dead. He's already under the bus. There's nothing you can do to hurt him."

"But is it wise to mention the Calley threat? Wouldn't *I* be in more trouble if I told them I knew about his plans, even if I didn't think he would go through with them? Like you said, Warren's no longer here . . . so why reveal anything I don't have to?"

"Because they need to understand why he was building the bomb in the first place," said Daniella. "Because they probably need to put some extra security on Calley, just in case Warren was working with someone else we don't know about."

Daniella paused for a moment, hesitating, but then pushed through her apprehension. "Also, I'm wondering if it's possible that the reason you

decided to leave Smash was because Warren's talk was turning from theatri-
cal to deadly."

The two women stared at each other for a long, intimate moment.

"Yes," said Eve, nodding along. "I knew it was time to get out when
Warren started talking about bombing Calley. I just needed to figure out
how to do it. I was scared to tell him I was leaving, so I needed to find a
smart way to extricate myself."

Oh God, what had she just done? Was it moral to plant a rationaliza-
tion in a client's head? Was it legal? Daniella took another bite of her sandwich, tasted the molten goo of the American cheese, the crisp of the fried
bread. She washed it down with a sip of Coke as she watched Eve pick at
her hash browns like a small child faced with soggy broccoli.

Dammit. She was a lawyer; Eve was her client, and she was going to represent her to the best of her ability.

"Here's what I think our plan should be: I'm going to contact Bob
Powers, one of the partners at my firm, who can help with the details of
your surrender. He's old-school, he's well connected, and he knows proto-
col. He'll be a good person to have in your corner, and I have a hunch he'll
be interested in your case."

"Why?"

"Just a feeling. I've heard him lament that chivalry is dead, that sort of
thing. I think he'll feel chivalrous helping you. After we contact Bob, we're
going to contact the police, assuming Bob agrees that's the best way to
proceed. We'll tell them that you are going to turn yourself in for any outstanding warrants. More important, you are going to tell them that you are
willing to share any and all information that you have about Smash, including, of course, that it was you and Warren St. Clair living in the house on
Linwood Avenue and that you knew he kept dynamite but did not believe
he was building a bomb, until he 'joked' of trying to kill Calley at Fort Benning, at which point you still didn't know if he was serious or not. But you
decided it was time to surface, turn yourself in to the authorities. Hopefully

your friend Jane will be willing to confirm that you spoke with her about turning yourself in *before* the bomb exploded."

"I don't know how I'm going to make it through this," said Eve. "I'm just so tired. I just want to sleep."

"You're going to pretend your life is a movie," coached Daniella, "and take it scene by scene. Our meeting right now is one scene. The next will be consulting with Bob Powers. Then the next scene will be dealing with all legal matters. I'll be with you the whole way. All you have to do is show up. Just show up, and life will push you forward."

Chapter 11

LIFEBOAT

Atlanta, 1972

It had been seven years since Robert Benno Powers—Bob—made partner at Henritz & Powers at the age of thirty-four. No doubt the fact that his late father had been one of the firm's founding partners helped when Bob finished law school and applied for the position of associate, but making partner was certainly not a fait accompli. He had been expected to work diligently and without complaint, which turned out to be a very good thing, as legal work and playing squash were the only two things he could manage with any competency during the immediate years following Marian's death.

In 1958, the summer after Bob received his law degree, also from Emory, more than four hundred guests packed the pews of St. Philip's for his and Marian's wedding, which was followed by a blowout reception at the Driving Club. Four years later, Marian had died in the plane crash at Orly Airport in Paris. She was one of 103 members of the Atlanta Arts Association on that plane, all of whom were taking part in a month-long European art tour.

Though Bob could not take a month off work to accompany her, he had encouraged her to go. His work was so all-consuming that he couldn't even take a week off to join her at the tail end. But just because he had a demanding job didn't mean she should deny herself the experience of a lifetime, especially since they wanted to start a family soon. Why not take a grand tour before motherhood, enjoy one last fling before full adulthood kicked in? Besides, her best friend, Betty Miller, was going, and the two of them could keep each other company. As for Bob, he would miss Marian, of course, but he wouldn't have time to feel lonely, as he was helping with a major bank merger and was going to be working around the clock.

Well, and then there was Stella, with her bright red lipstick and curly yellow hair. She had a little girl's voice and a high-pitched laugh, which Bob knew would irritate him if he ever spent any real time with her, her flighty demeanor so different from Marian's soothing, steady countenance. Their entanglement was insignificant, beneath him—still, he had let himself stray. He figured that he and Stella could enjoy just a few more encounters and then he would end things before Marian returned, would end things for good and settle fully into his adult life. Three weeks into the trip, Marian telephoned from Paris. He was surprised she would make such an expensive call, but he understood once she shared the news that they were going to have a baby. "I suspected before I left," she said. "But now I know for sure."

He did not ask how she knew. Men did not ask such questions of their wives. Instead, he asked if she was well enough to finish the trip, if she would like to fly home early. She had laughed off his concern, told him she felt perfectly fine, was experiencing only mild nausea, usually in the middle of the afternoon, which she found she could fend off if she drank a little soda. Bob hung up the phone feeling that the pieces of his life were locking into place. He and Marian had recently purchased a two-thousand-square-foot bungalow in Ansley Park, just two blocks from the imposing brick fortress in which he had been raised and where his mother still lived. It was in this pleasing craftsman-style bungalow where they would raise their first child, with more surely to follow.

He had met Stella a few months before Marian's trip to Europe, at the bakery counter at Rich's Magnolia Room. He had stopped by on his way home from work to pick up the coconut cake he had ordered for Marian's birthday. They were having his mother and her parents over to supper to celebrate—Maggie was fixing Marian's favorite, beef tenderloin—and they would drink Champagne with the cake because Marian had spent a semester in Paris her junior year at Emory and henceforth adored all things French.

Bob had no intention of flirting with the pretty clerk who rang up his order. But she was just so bright and cheerful, a confection as pretty as the cake inside the box she was handing to him. He asked if she had baked it herself. She laughed and batted her eyes. And so it began. Just before Marian was to return from Europe, he brought Stella a parting gift, a Whitman's Sampler and a hundred-dollar bill. When she realized he was breaking things off, she chased him out of her apartment, pelting chocolates at him as he scrambled to exit. Later that night, the whole thing struck him as so comical that he wished he could share the story with his wife. Marian was such a practical girl that he could almost imagine her understanding what had happened, shaking her head at his naughtiness, forgiving him by bedtime.

She was to return on a Sunday, the day after he ended things with Stella. It was not until weeks later that the remains of her body were flown home for her closed-casket funeral.

Of course, Bob blamed himself for his wife's death. If he hadn't started things with Stella, he surely would not have encouraged Marian to go away for a month on her own. If he hadn't started things with Stella, he might have concluded that he *could* take the time away from work, at least for that final week of the tour. If that were the case, he would have died along with her, holding her hand as the flames consumed the plane. The three of them would have died together, though no one but he and Marian would have known of the child growing inside her. But surely she had told Betty Miller, whose hand she had probably held at the end instead of his.

Some evenings, after a second glass of Scotch, he sat alone in his leather chair in the living room and wondered if it were possible that he had made it all up—the wedding, the pregnancy, the fact of Marian herself.

When his mother died a few years later, he sold the bungalow and moved into her stately home, designed by renowned architect Neel Reid, in the Georgian Italianate style. It was comforting to return to the house he grew up in, the much-loved only child of a nervous mother and a courtly father. As the 1960s dragged on, his once-lovely neighborhood deteriorated. Some of the beautiful old Ansley Park homes were divided up and rented out as boardinghouses, while Piedmont Park became overrun with hippies and bikers. As a child he had played in Piedmont Park, had spent many weekends on its golf course with his father. Now he avoided the place, saw it only from the vantage point of the Driving Club, which overlooked the public park.

He supposed that if he dwelled on his life for too long he would come to the conclusion that he was lonely. But he had been raised not to dwell. He had been raised to get on with things, to make his bed in the morning, to finish everything on his plate without complaint or excessive praise, to say "yes, ma'am" and "no, sir."

Bob would work late on Friday nights, have a Scotch at the club, have another drink at home while reading—he preferred dense histories, particularly if they were about Churchill. On Saturday mornings he played squash, and then he typically spent his afternoons doing personal bookkeeping: going through bills, balancing his checkbook, studying his investments. Sometimes he would meet his old fraternity brother Fox McGee for a burger and beer at George's or a seafood supper at Bill McKinnon's place.

Often he just stayed home and read. Sunday mornings he went to services at St. Philip's. Maggie would be back on Mondays and she would grocery shop for him and make sure he had something to eat each night.

Years passed. Life went on. His personal life was predictable, contained. Gone were the flirtations that he used to engage in, his monasticism atonement for past sin. World events did not cause much of a disruption for him, though he was disheartened by the assassinations of the Kennedy brothers, one at the beginning of the sixties, one at the end, and irritated by those fools protesting the Vietnam War. It wasn't that he had a strong opinion about the war; it was more that he felt that if the commander in chief thought the United States should be over there, then we damn well should be. When he saw protesters on the nightly news he just shook his head. Children. They seemed like children. As if you could change the human condition by offering a flower to a soldier. As if war were something new.

He liked his work. He liked drawing up airtight contracts. He liked building model airplanes and working on crossword puzzles. He liked the lady lawyer they hired in 1970, though the only reason they hired her was because nervous old Samuel Sneed thought they needed to get in front of any risk of a discrimination suit. Still, he recognized that she was diligent and smart, if a bit formal.

So it had surprised him when one day, rather out of nowhere, she had asked if she could speak with him alone. She had never initiated contact, and he wondered if she was going to tell him that she was pregnant, something the managing partners all assumed would eventually happen and would signal her imminent departure. (He had come to accept that a smart young woman such as Daniella Strum might want a career right out of law school; he could not accept a mother choosing to spend her days in an office with men instead of at home with her child.)

But Daniella wasn't meeting with him to tell of a pregnancy. Instead, she wanted to tell him about a new client of hers, Eve Whalen, who had somehow gotten herself brainwashed by one of the more radical antiwar groups and now had rightfully come to her senses and wanted to return home. Daniella explained that she had met with Eve that morning and that Eve was now waiting at Daniella's house while she sought his counsel. She knew this was all terribly last minute, but was there any chance he could meet with Eve at her home in Morningside, now?

He didn't have much scheduled for the afternoon, save for a deposition, and he could get an associate to handle that. He asked Daniella for her address and told her to give him an hour while he tied up loose ends at the office.

He was happy to help. He knew her parents, for goodness' sake, had gone to their annual Christmas party for years now, could even remember a party some time ago when Eve was home from college and making her debut. She had been a very pretty girl. He remembered that.

The interior décor of Daniella's house was rather *ethnic*, what with the African masks hanging in the living room and the abundance of textiles that seemed to be from the Far East, but Bob admired the craftsmanship of the house itself—a well-maintained mock Tudor cottage with half-timbering, an arched front doorway, and casement windows with diamond panes.

Eve was already seated in the living room, wearing a faded Barnard T-shirt and a pair of jeans, her legs tucked beneath her, her dark hair cut short. She looked up and smiled at him, and suddenly he felt so dizzy that he almost had to catch himself on the doorframe.

She looked like Marian, dark-haired Marian, still in her twenties, still beautiful, still very much alive.

If Daniella had noticed how startled Bob was, she didn't let on. "Eve, this is Bob Powers, one of the managing partners at the firm."

Eve locked eyes with him. "Thank you for coming, Mr. Powers. I think you know my parents?"

"Call me Bob, please. And yes, your parents are wonderful people."

She was not Marian. Of course she was not Marian. But she looked so much like Marian that he was having trouble keeping his thoughts organized. Had her hair always been so dark? He had a memory of her as a blonde. Perhaps she had dyed it. She was, after all, a fugitive.

"I've got coffee," said Daniella, heading toward the kitchen.

Eve didn't say anything, just remained looking at him, tentative, like a shy kitten.

"Coffee?" he asked her.

"I wonder if she has any tea," she said in a soft voice.

"I'll check," he said, and walked to the kitchen where Daniella was arranging grapes, cubes of cheddar cheese, and Triscuits on a platter.

"Perhaps tea would be more calming?" he suggested.

"I've only got herbal. Sleepytime or Red Zinger."

"A cup of coffee for me and an herbal tea for Eve, whichever one you think is best. This house is an architectural gem, Daniella, beautifully restored."

"That's all Pete's doing, my husband. Normally he'd be here for you to compliment him—he doesn't teach on Fridays, and he usually works at home. But he decided to go into the office today, just to assure he doesn't overhear anything that's confidential."

"Prudent," Bob said.

They sat in the living room and nibbled on grapes and cheese, sipping their coffee and tea. Eve didn't say much, but Daniella shared her game plan with Bob, and he agreed that the best course of action was for Eve to turn herself in for any outstanding warrants and to offer any information she had on Warren and Smash, including his talk of bombing Calley's apartment, the talk that had triggered her to make plans for her own surrender, aware that Warren really had gone off the deep end. After being questioned by the police, she would, they hoped, be released to the custody of her parents, whom they planned to call later that day.

Throughout their discussion, Daniella kept pushing Eve to tell her more details about her time with the Smash Collective, as if she was certain there was something Eve was not admitting, as if she could trip the poor girl up by asking the same questions again and again. It was good legal strategy, frankly, and it was probably good practice for when Eve would surely be interrogated by the authorities. Still, Bob hated for Daniella to make Eve so uncomfortable.

Eve told them that she had moved to Atlanta from Manhattan a few years ago, living in a dilapidated ranch on Euclid Avenue, near Little Five Points. But in 1971 she had returned to New York, back to the apartment in Morningside Heights where members of Smash often crashed. There she had lived with Warren and Abby for more than a year, taking temporary jobs to earn money while plotting a revolution that she was now certain would never come. "I don't even think I want it to come," she added.

Good girl, Bob thought.

"But why did you return?" demanded Daniella, still playing the devil's advocate. "Why were you in Atlanta on the night that Warren, the man you have been involved with for nearly a decade, blew himself up in the house the two of you were renting?"

Bob worried that Daniella was coming on too strong.

Eve looked down at the Oriental rug that covered the floor of Daniella's living room. "Smash was ending. It was obvious we didn't know what we were doing anymore, if we ever did. But Warren couldn't let it go. A few months ago he asked me to move back to Atlanta with him. He had this theory that the revolution was going to start in the South. I agreed to come because . . . because my world had gotten really small and Warren was pretty much the only person remaining in it. But a part of me was also thinking that maybe if I got to Atlanta I could reconnect with my parents. I could reconnect with everyone important—with you."

She looked straight at Daniella when she said this, and the two women held each other's gaze for a long moment.

"But once I got here," Eve finally continued, "I didn't know how to do that. What was I supposed to do, just ring the doorbell after how many years? Just say, 'Mom, Dad, here I am! Your prodigal daughter returned at last!'"

"Well, yes," said Bob. "Your parents would delight in your return. You allude to the prodigal son jokingly, but they would have reacted exactly as the father did in the parable. They would have thrown open their arms and called for a celebration. They would have been so grateful their daughter had come home to them."

She looked at him with tears in her eyes.

"You told me that just a few weeks ago Warren talked of bombing Fort Benning in order to kill Lieutenant Calley. Are you sure you two didn't come to Atlanta for the express purpose of doing just that?" interrogated Daniella.

"The Calley talk was new. And it terrified me. When he started talking about that—that's when I decided to leave."

"You had no idea he was planning on setting off a bomb on the very night you wandered around Buckhead, on the very night I saw you at Oxford Books, during which time Warren was presumably at the house the two of you shared, counting out sticks of dynamite?"

"Daniella, please," Bob interjected. "I understand that you're trying to prep her for questioning, but how many times does she have to tell you she had no knowledge of Warren being in possession of a bomb? Mercy. Eve is our client, not a hostile witness. We're all good people here, all trying to muddle through this the best we can. You don't have to keep badgering the poor girl."

Just as Bob predicted, Eve's parents rushed to Daniella's house as soon as she phoned to tell them that she was in Atlanta. After a teary reunion, Eve followed them back to The Compound in her little American Motors

Gremlin, her only remaining belonging, as everything else she owned had burned in the fire. The following day, Bob drove Daniella to the Whalens', where they would pick up Eve and accompany her to the police station so that she could turn herself in. Both Mr. Whalen and Bob had spoken privately with the police chief and were assured that Eve's surrender would be kept under wraps, that no reporters would be on hand to scream questions and snap pictures.

The Whalens' home wasn't visible from the street, but after driving through a veritable forest they arrived at the stone house on the hill, which looked smaller than it actually was, probably because it was surrounded by so much undeveloped land.

"I've always thought this was one of the best pieces of property in Buckhead," said Bob.

They parked in the front drive. Bob started to walk to the door, but Daniella stopped him. "Let's go around back. I still remember Patricia Whalen telling me years ago that the front door is just for 'party guests and solicitors.'"

They walked around back to the kitchen door. Bob knocked on one of its glass panes. Through the glass he could see Eve sitting at the kitchen table, sipping a cup of coffee with her parents. She raised her hand at the sound of his knock as her mother rushed to the door.

"Bob Powers!" she cried, her eyes springing with tears as she grabbed both of his hands. "Words cannot express my gratitude. Thank you for bringing us back our daughter!"

Patricia Whalen wore a navy St. John knit suit. Her hairstyle looked the same as always, a sort of short, fluffy helmet around her head, locked into place with Aqua Net, the smell of which made Bob think of his mother.

Dr. Whalen had stood when Bob and Daniella entered and was still standing now, wearing a blue blazer with gold buttons over khaki pants.

"Bob!" he called. "So good of you to come. And Daniella, too. Can Ada get either of you a cup of coffee?"

Dr. Whalen motioned to a small, trim Negro woman standing by the counter. She had perfect posture and wore a pale blue maid's uniform with a white apron, very proper, though her hair was worn in a short Afro, a becoming style for her angular features, but which Bob found vaguely unsettling.

"No, thanks," said Daniella. "It's good to see you again, Miss Ada."

"It's good to see you," she answered. "Thank you for bringing our baby back."

"Coffee, Bob?" Dr. Whalen asked again.

"I'm good, thank you."

Bob watched Daniella walk to the kitchen table where Eve was sitting. "How are you feeling?" she asked.

"Nervous. Terribly nervous."

Eve looked beautiful in a pale pink baby-doll dress, her short hair fluffed and shellacked into a style not dissimilar from her mother's. The dress was youthful looking, a smart choice, Bob thought, before he realized that it was probably not a choice exactly, but an item of clothing that happened to be left over from her college days.

"Baby," said Dr. Whalen, striding to the table where he stood behind Eve, placing his hands protectively on her shoulders. "Nothing bad is going to happen to my little girl. Believe me when I say that I know everyone worth knowing in this town: judges, lawyers, everyone. Now that you've come home, we can protect you. Now that you've come back home, everything is going to be okay."

Chapter 12

MRS. POWERS

Atlanta, 1972

Eve and Bob married within six weeks of their first meeting. In the wedding photo, taken in Judge Chambliss's chambers at the downtown courthouse, it was impossible to tell that Eve was pregnant under the silk Missoni caftan she wore, pale blue and decorated with pink and orange birds, the sleeves fringed.

"I won't wear white," she had told Bob. "I just can't."

Bob understood the shame she felt and did not argue. He hoped that as the years passed Eve would be able to forgive herself for embracing such unsavory people and positions during her youth, that she might come to understand that her sweetness and innocence had been used against her, that she had been taken advantage of.

The fact that she had gotten pregnant a little before the wedding was not a cause for great concern. Indeed, Bob's new mother-in-law, upon learning that she was soon to have a grandchild, had said with a wink, "The first baby doesn't always take nine months." If Patricia Whalen had really thought about it, she surely would have determined that Eve must have been pregnant *before* she met Bob. But Patricia clearly did not want to think about it. Daniella knew, of course, but everyone else assumed the baby was simply the product of a very whirlwind romance. As Eve's pregnancy progressed, even Bob began to feel as if the baby really was his, if not biologically then spiritually.

Eve had told him she was pregnant during their first dinner together, the day after she had turned herself in and was informed that all outstanding charges would be dropped and no new ones pressed, as long as she was willing to share any and all information she had on any member of Smash, living or deceased. And as long as she was willing to testify for the state should a fugitive member be caught and brought to trial.

Bob had taken her to Jim White's Half Shell at Peachtree Battle Shopping Center, where she had ordered the flounder and he the stone crabs. She had turned down the glass of wine from the bottle he had ordered, a Chablis recommended by Jim White himself. It was then that she told him that she was expecting and that the child was Warren's, Warren who had blown himself to pieces only a few days previous. She told him that Warren had wanted her to get rid of it—that he knew someone who could perform the abortion, but that she just couldn't destroy the life growing inside her.

"Of course you can't," he said, resting his hand on top of hers.

She smiled.

"You know," he said, and then he paused, his confession poised on the tip of his tongue. Was he really going to share his most shameful secret with this woman he barely knew? But he felt he *did* know her. He felt, in fact, that he had been waiting for her ever since he lost Marian. "None of us are perfect. That's the human condition. I was not faithful to Marian. I was unfaithful even while she was in Europe, on the tour that ended in her death. I've always felt that if I had been a better husband, maybe, maybe she wouldn't have signed up for such a long trip abroad, and then she wouldn't have been on that flight, and her life wouldn't have ended so tragically, so early."

"My mother's best friend died at Orly, too," said Eve. "My aunt Pooh."

They were holding hands now, holding hands and looking into each other's eyes.

"You know what, Bob? It was a fucking fantastic adventure they were on. *Fucking* fantastic. Marian would have seized the opportunity to take an art tour of Europe regardless of whether or not you were a perfect husband. Don't you think?"

He was grateful for her reassurance and the fact that she did not judge him for his past sins. Still, he cringed at her crass language. But how could she help it? She was still shedding the trappings of the seedy underworld she had been pulled down into, all the while offering him absolution.

"Eve," he said gently. "You don't have to use their vulgarity anymore. You don't have to pretend to be some Marxist lunatic in order to survive. You're out. The nightmare is over."

She looked momentarily confused. He imagined how hard it must be for her to trust that the underworld wasn't going to suck her back in.

"Thank you," she finally said, letting out a long sigh. "Thank you for that. Thank you for not just seeing me as who I was—when I was with them. God. I wish Mother and Daddy could see me through your eyes."

Here was a girl as beautiful as Marian had been, a girl who, like him, knew what it meant to experience exile, to suffer.

"When I see you, dear Eve, I don't picture what you might have once done wrong; I see a woman taking great risks to save herself. And her child," he continued, smiling.

She started crying, dabbing at her eyes with her white napkin, gazing at him with a look of pure gratitude through her tears.

"Don't think of this baby as his," he said suddenly. "He gave up paternity the moment he suggested you terminate. This is *your* baby, growing in *you*."

And when he proposed just a few weeks after that first dinner, he asked if he might claim the baby as his, as theirs.

On their wedding night, after they consummated their marriage, he told her, "You are now flesh of my flesh, Mrs. Evelyn Whalen Powers, till death do us part." How could that *not* include the child that was growing within her? Later even the baby would cooperate, maintaining the illusion of Bob's paternity by arriving three weeks later than expected.

After a grueling labor that left Eve so depleted of blood she had to have a transfusion, baby Anna was delivered at Piedmont Hospital on December 1, 1972. Nine pounds and two ounces of perfect pink flesh, she had heart-shaped lips and cornflower-blue eyes. Her full name was Joannah Ella Powers, Joannah after Bob's mother and Ella in honor of Daniella. Anna was an easy baby who slept through the night after two months. Eve claimed she was most content when placed on a blanket in the backyard, observing the goings-on around the huge white oak tree that offered so much shade. Birds flitted on, off, and around the branches, all while baby Anna watched. "Our little birder," Eve said. Bob thought that Eve should have help, and Eve finally agreed when her parents suggested that Ada switch with Maggie, so that Ada, who had practically raised Eve, could help raise Anna.

"We have to pay Ada a true living wage," Eve had insisted, and Bob smiled indulgently and agreed to pay her sixteen dollars a day, nearly a 100 percent raise.

Ada worked for the Powerses five days a week, from nine to five. During the hours that the baby slept, she cleaned and prepped food for the family's supper. Bob encouraged Eve to use her free time to join a tennis team or perhaps the Junior League. Eve balked. "Babe," she said. "I'm really not Junior League material. They're not exactly looking for someone who once had an outstanding warrant for her arrest."

Bob assured her that if she wanted to join the Junior League, she most certainly could (his own mother had once been the president of the Atlanta chapter). But if she felt it wasn't a good fit, that was fine; she would soon enough find a group she felt comfortable joining. And indeed, shortly after that conversation, she deepened her involvement at St. Luke's Episcopal, the downtown church she insisted they transfer their membership to, saying All Saints' was her parents', St. Philip's was his and Marian's, and St. Luke's could be their own.

A member at St. Luke's had recently started a soup kitchen in the church basement. Eve would go there to serve the homeless two mornings a week, a form of penance, it seemed to Bob. She spent a lot of time painting, too, setting up an easel in the upstairs sun porch of their Ansley Park home, just off their bedroom. She painted portraits mostly, picture after picture of baby Anna, as well as portraits of the homeless men she fed at St. Luke's. For Eve's birthday, Bob signed her up for painting classes at Callanwolde Fine Arts Center, located in the old Candler house where his parents had once attended parties when it was a private residence.

Every month or so Eve got together with Daniella, either the two ladies on their own or joined by Bob and Pete. When it was the four of them they would go to the Colonnade (Bob and Pete both loved their chicken livers) or to Nino's, but when Eve and Daniella were on their own they liked to go to Gene & Gabe's, a flamboyant place where the atmosphere was a little swishy for Bob's taste.

Three months after Eve delivered Anna, she came home from dinner with Daniella, thrilled to inform Bob that Daniella was expecting.

"How wonderful that you girls will be able to share the experience of motherhood," Bob said. "Though I suppose this means we'll soon be looking for a new associate."

"Daniella says she'll go back to work as soon as she can," said Eve. "I was surprised, too. But here's a thought we had at dinner: What if, once Daniella goes back, she drops the baby off with us during the day? We'll have to ask Ada, of course, but I'm sure she won't mind. Daniella says she'll pay her extra, and Anna's going to need a playmate soon enough. It's perfect, really. Daniella's baby will only be a little younger than Anna is."

"Fine by me," said Bob. "Let's just hope Daniella has a girl, so there won't be a little football player running circles around our daughter."

"Oh, Bob," said Eve, her eyes shining with happiness as she put her arms around him. "I feel like my life is finally coming together."

Part Two

Their Daughters

Chapter 13

ASTRAL PROJECTION

Atlanta, 1983

I don't remember Mom talking so much about money when Dad was alive. But I was only six when he died, so maybe she did and I was just too young to notice. After Dad's accident, she started talking about money all of the time. I remember her bringing it up as soon as we returned home from Mimi and Papa's house, where we had gone for two weeks after the funeral so that Mom could let her own mother take care of us.

"You and I are a team, Sarah," she said, placing a bowl of Campbell's Chunky beef soup in front of me for dinner. "And as a team we're going to need to tighten our belts."

"What do you mean?" I asked, digging around with my spoon for a carrot.

"Just that we are going to have to keep on a tight budget and not buy anything unless we really need it. And we probably won't be going on any more fancy vacations. And I'll hold off on buying that Mercedes convertible."

Mom was joking about vacations and the Mercedes, trying to make me smile. She always said people who drove luxury cars were silly—even though her best friend, my aunt Eve, drove a Mercedes. And we never went on fancy trips, just to Georgetown to visit Papa and Mimi and up to Connecticut to visit Grammy Strum. Well, and we always went to the beach for a week each summer, but it was Daddy who loved the ocean—much more so than Mom ever did—so I figured we probably wouldn't be going to Florida anymore. Turned out I was right about that.

Soon after Mom's talk about tightening our belts, she installed a mini fridge and a hot plate in the guest room, which was in the basement, and started renting it out as a studio apartment. It had its own bathroom and its own entrance, so we didn't really notice our tenant, a shy graduate student in the English department at Emory. Mom also stopped getting her hair colored. She still looked pretty, but she looked a lot older now that her dark hair was streaked with so much gray, especially when she stood beside Aunt Eve, whose hair was always bright blond.

Mom and Eve are like that—opposites. Like, they each say no to opposite sorts of things. Mom says no to private school, cable television, Jordache jeans, Laura Ashley bedspreads, anything that she thinks "costs too much money," which is pretty much everything.

Aunt Eve rarely says no when it comes to buying little things for Anna and me, unless she decides something is "age inappropriate." On Wednesday afternoons, which she keeps open so she can spend special time with us, she usually takes us shopping—sometimes to Lenox Square Mall, sometimes to Peachtree Battle Shopping Center. Usually when we go to Lenox, we just browse at Rich's and Davison's, get ice cream at Häagen-Dazs, and play with the puppies at the pet store. But the last time we were there, Aunt Eve bought Anna the coolest jacket. She said it was an early birthday gift, though Anna's birthday was months away. The jacket was made of pale pink satin with a life-size Jordache horse head embroidered on the back. I really wanted the matching one in lavender, though I acted like I didn't care that much about it, because I could tell Aunt Eve felt guilty about buying something so nice for Anna in front of me.

She probably *would* have bought me the lavender one, but she knew Mom would have thrown a fit.

On the days when we go to Peachtree Battle Shopping Center, we'll hit Baskin-Robbins first (Aunt Eve says the three of us are "a bunch of ice-cream addicts"), then spend the rest of the afternoon at Oxford Books. While Aunt Eve knows not to buy me clothes, she buys Anna and me as many books as we want. If we want to buy four or five apiece, Aunt Eve won't even blink. She'll just say something about how wonderful it is that we are both such "avid readers." That is, unless we try to get her to buy us a Lois Duncan thriller, which she swears will put "sinister ideas" into our heads and give us nightmares. I've already read three Lois Duncan books, and while they creeped me out, they didn't give me nightmares or anything. Still, Aunt Eve refused to purchase *Stranger with My Face*, even though I promised her that Mom wouldn't mind.

The next weekend Mom took me to the public library so I could check out a copy. In that way, Aunt Eve is the one always saying no while Mom says yes. Like, Anna can't walk *anywhere* by herself even though she's almost eleven and Aunt Eve refused to let her go see *Poltergeist*, even though Mom took me to see it.

Last night, after I was supposed to be asleep, I finished *Stranger with My Face*. It's about a girl, Laurie, who was adopted when she was little. She lives in this seaside village where everyone knows everyone. One night her boyfriend thinks he sees her out on the beach with another guy. But Laurie was home sick. It turns out that Laurie has a twin sister, Lia, who she was separated from when they were just babies. And Lia knows how to astral project, which is when you sort of will your soul out of your body, so that your soul is free to travel anywhere. When Laurie's boyfriend thought he saw her on the beach with another guy, it was Lia he was seeing.

Well, it turns out that Lia is evil. She killed her foster sister and is now in a mental institution. But Laurie doesn't know this. Not yet. All she knows is that Lia is teaching her how to astral project. It takes a long time for Laurie to learn, but finally she does. And then when Laurie's soul is outside of her body, astral projecting, Lia's soul jumps into it and takes over. Luckily, her little sister recognizes how different "Laurie" is acting and together with Laurie's boyfriend, Jeff, they figure out how to drive Lia out with the Navajo charm Laurie was given earlier in the book.

Aunt Eve was right; the book *did* scare me. So much so that after I finished I crept into Mom's bed and slept curled up next to her. But it also made my brain spin with ideas. I wasn't thinking about Laurie and Lia's story so much as I was thinking about astral projection and how I might learn to do it. If I could figure it out, I could go anywhere and my mom wouldn't even know. I would just do my projecting at night while she slept.

The thing is, I don't really want to visit my grandparents or go to California or anything like that. I want to project myself to the place where the souls of dead people go. I'm not talking about heaven. I'm not even sure heaven exists. But I have this idea that Dad's soul is sort of hanging around *this* world, hoping to catch glimpses of Mom and me. Maybe I could find him—just to say I love him. Just to say how sorry I was that I acted like such a brat the last time I saw him.

I was mad because he was going to this stupid book reading instead of going with Mom and me to see *Bon Voyage, Charlie Brown* like we'd planned. The chair of the history department at Emory was the one giving the reading. Dad explained that he had forgotten about the event when we made plans to go see the movie, and he was really sorry for the mistake, but he was up for full professor that year and he needed to do everything he could to get on the chair's good side. He asked me to please understand. He asked me to please give him a hug good-bye. I wouldn't.

"Love you, Sarah!" he called as he left the house. "Poop the door!"

That was an old joke from when I was really little and thought that saying "poop" was funny whether or not the sentence made any sense. But I didn't even smile or look up. I just kept my eyes on the floor. And then on his way to the reading, someone ran the light at Piedmont and Monroe and hit his car. We hadn't even left for the movie when we got the call. Mom and I rushed to Crawford Long, where they had taken Dad. He was in the intensive-care unit. They finally let Mom in, but I wasn't allowed. Something about kids and germs. Mom gave me money to get a Sprite out of the machine while she was gone. Later, after the doctor came to tell us he had died, Mom still didn't want me to see him. She said his body was just too broken. She said it wasn't really him lying there, anyway. That it was just his shell.

"Then where's Daddy?" I asked. "If that's not him?"

"I don't really know," she said. Then she added, "Wherever God is."

It was the middle of the night when we got back to our house. Aunt Eve was waiting for us. Mom had called her from the pay phone at the hospital. Even though it was really late, Aunt Eve had fixed us pimento cheese sandwiches. I didn't think I was hungry, but I ended up eating two.

The funeral was held at St. Luke's because Aunt Eve was a member there and could arrange everything easily, and though Mom sometimes went to services at UUCA—the Unitarian church in Atlanta—she had never actually joined. Mom told Eve that she didn't really care where the service was held as long as whoever presided over it didn't try to convert new members during the homily by telling everyone to accept Jesus or else. "You know it's not that kind of a church," Aunt Eve had said.

The priest told stories about Dad, gathered from his colleagues at Emory, from Aunt Eve and Uncle Bob, from Grammy Strum, who stayed at Eve's house while she was in town for the funeral because Mimi and Papa and Mom's brother, my uncle Benjamin, who we almost never saw (he married a Japanese woman and lived in Kyoto), were all staying with us. And of course he told stories he learned from Mom. One of my favorites was about their first date.

They were both in college in New York. Mom was all dressed up in a silk blouse and a skirt with a crinoline underneath, and Dad had on a skinny tie. They were walking down Broadway, on their way to the subway station, when they heard mewing from behind some garbage cans. When they looked, they found a tiny orange-and-white kitty, defenseless and alone. They had dinner reservations in the Village, but of course they couldn't leave the pitiful thing behind, so they got an empty cardboard box from a nearby liquor store and took the kitten back to Dad's dorm, where Mom wasn't allowed to go into his room with him because she was a girl. Dad ended up getting a friend to watch the kitty while they went to dinner, but not before Mom was kept waiting in the lobby for over twenty minutes. Still, Mom said his tender heart made her fall in love with him that very night.

I slept over at Anna's house a lot the year Dad died. One time when I was there and couldn't sleep, I got out of bed and started walking around. It was really late, past midnight, and the house had a quiet, hushed feel to it. I wandered downstairs and found Aunt Eve sitting on the sofa in the den, just staring off into space, a drink in her hand. She looked very far away, but then her eyes focused on me and she was back.

"Sweetie, are you okay?" she asked. And for some reason I told her all about how bratty I had been the last time I saw my dad.

"Oh, bless your sweet heart," she said. And then she told me about how, during her wild, hippie days, she almost never came to Atlanta to visit and never saw her grandmother, who she was named after and who lived in a "darling" cottage on her parents' property. And then one day her grandmother suddenly died, and it was too late. She had no choice whether or not to see her again.

"The death of someone you love is so, so painful. And what you're going through is so real," she told me. "But I promise, your father knows you love him and he knows what a good girl you are. Your daddy is looking down at you from heaven, and he is so proud of what he sees."

"Do you really believe in heaven?" I asked.

"I really do, sweetheart, and I believe your father is there."

I started crying, so relieved by Aunt Eve's words. Whenever I asked Mom about heaven, all she could say was, "I don't know, honey. I just don't know."

Anna's neighborhood, Ansley Park, is really near ours, but it's even nicer, with really big houses. I think Anna's is the prettiest of all—it looks like something out of one of those *Masterpiece* programs Mom watches on PBS, tall and grand with huge front windows and columns. Mom says it's "Georgian," but Uncle Bob says that's not quite accurate; it's a "Georgian Italianate Revival." In private, Mom says Bob is full of himself. When she's feeling really mean she calls Aunt Eve a "limousine liberal," but Eve doesn't actually have a limousine or anything.

Mom and Aunt Eve have known each other forever, and Anna and I are always asking them to tell us stories about their college days. Our favorite is the one where Mom wasn't let into any of the good sororities at Belmont because she's half-Jewish and how Aunt Eve dropped out of the very best one, Fleur, to show how wrong it was that they wouldn't let Mom in. The girls in Fleur were supposed to be her "chosen sisters," but Mom was her "*real* chosen sister." The next year the two of them transferred to Barnard, where Mom met my dad at Columbia.

Mom says that she and Eve drifted apart after she met Dad. She says she was so head-over-heels in love with him that she let a lot of things drop from her life, and she knows she hurt Eve's feelings when she did. And then she was in law school, which she said kept her just as busy as falling in love with Dad had. Plus, Mom said that Aunt Eve was really wild for a couple of years, a "free spirit," which is hard to imagine. She's always so polished and put together. Eve says back then there wasn't a protest march she didn't join and that she "grew unaccustomed to regular bathing." Eve always shakes her head when talking about her hippie days, as if she can't believe she was ever like that, either.

• • •

Miss Ada has taken care of Anna and me since we were babies. She took care of Aunt Eve starting from when she was a baby, too. Aunt Eve says Ada is family, which I'm sure makes Miss Ada feel good, because Miss Ada lost her only son, Albert, in the Vietnam War. I once tried to interview her about him as part of my fourth-grade Forgotten American Notables Project. But Miss Ada said I was poking at a past that she didn't like to talk about.

What Miss Ada *does* like to talk about are vegetables and how I should eat more of them. There is nothing she loves more than a vegetable! She says she practically has a whole garden growing in pots on the fire escape outside her apartment. She's even in the "Green Thumb Club" at her church. Last summer she tricked me into eating a tomato. I told her I didn't like them, that they were slimy and gross. She claimed that I hadn't ever had a real one because all I had eaten were ones from the grocery store. She said a real tomato is sweet and tastes like stored-up sunshine. She said she'd share one of her homegrown tomatoes with me if I promised I'd actually try it and not just "turn your head after giving it a sniff."

This all happened while Anna was away at summer camp in North Carolina. Anna wanted me to go with her, but Mom said that, while she had certainly loved summer camp as a girl, Anna's was too expensive for our budget and too WASPy for her taste and that if I wanted to go to "socialist summer camp up north" one day when I was older she'd think about it. Then she made me promise not to tell either Anna or Aunt Eve that she had said that.

Ada held the tomato in her hand, her fingers thin and delicate, and had me smell it. I said it smelled like dirt, and she smiled, saying yes, it did, that it smelled like rich, beautiful soil.

"Course this is from a pot," she said. "I used to have a proper garden, back when I had my house on Ormond. But a pot will do. Long as you've got enough sun and a place to mound some dirt, you can grow a tomato."

Mom had told me all about Ada's old house. It was downtown, in a neighborhood called Peoplestown, which always made me think of my Little People figurines. Mom said the Georgia Department of Transportation knocked down most of the houses on Ada's street. Then they just built the interstate right on top of where Miss Ada used to live. Mom said that never would have happened if the people in Peoplestown didn't happen to be mostly black and poor.

Miss Ada took two slices of Pepperidge Farm white bread, spread each one with Hellman's, and placed a thick slab of tomato on one of them, seasoning it with salt and pepper before putting the other slice of bread on top. I was hooked the moment my teeth sank into the fluffy bread and bit into the firm, juicy tomato that Ada had somehow convinced me tasted like the sun itself.

Mom is not nearly as good a cook as either Miss Ada or Aunt Eve. Actually, she can make a few things that are really delicious—like her brownies, which are the same ones Katharine Hepburn used to make (Mom clipped the recipe out of a magazine)—but she doesn't usually have the time. She says she's more a "microwaver than a cook." But tonight she fixed meatballs, which she served with Prego spaghetti sauce and noodles and that yummy garlic bread that you buy pre-made at the grocery store and just heat in the oven. Mom said there was something important that she needed to talk to me about. I thought she might say that she had decided I could apply to Coventry, the private school where Anna goes. I've been wanting to go there ever since Anna got to take creative writing for a whole semester (for an hour every day!) and got to write about anything she wanted as long as she used lots of action verbs and description.

Instead, Mom told me that she's thinking about quitting her job at Henritz & Powers, where she's worked since before I was born and where Anna's dad is a partner.

"You're not going to be a lawyer anymore?" I asked.

"Of course I am, sweetie. I just want to work with different people."

"Will you make more money?"

Even though Mom said that she earned a decent salary, she was always worried about money.

She took a long sip of her wine. "Probably not. I've applied for a position at the Southern Center for Human Rights, where I'll be helping defend indigent men on death row. If I'm offered the job and I take it, it will mean a pay cut. But the work I will be doing will be really important."

"What's 'indigent'?"

"It means really poor. I'll be helping defend men who didn't get a fair trial in the first place, often because they were too poor to hire a decent lawyer."

"And if you win, will the men pay you?"

Mom laughed. "God, no. These men have nothing. The Southern Center for Human Rights will pay me a salary. Not a great one, but enough to get by."

"Are you at least going to be working less?" I could hear my voice getting louder. Mom used to say that was a sure warning sign that I was headed for a tantrum. But I hadn't had a tantrum for years, not since I was little.

Mom took another big sip of wine. From the expression on her face I already knew the answer.

"So you're quitting your job and going to work for really poor people who can't pay you. And you're going to be working *more*?"

"I know, honey. It will be a sacrifice for both of us. But if there's one thing your father's death taught me, it's that our time on this earth is short, and the only thing that really matters is that we make our lives count while we're here. Even though the work will be hard, I'll be happy doing it. It will really fulfill me."

"But why can't *I* fulfill you?" I asked. "Why isn't it fulfilling enough to be my *mother*? Why do you care more about men in prison than you do about me?"

I was too upset to stay at the table. I ran out of the kitchen and to my room, where I slammed the door and lay on my bed, trying to remember how to breathe.

Mom didn't come after me. I knew she wouldn't. She said that she learned a long time ago that when I was "all worked up" I needed some

"Sarah time" to get myself back together. She was right. I couldn't stand it if people tried to talk to me—or, worse, touch me—when I was upset. I just needed to lie on the bed and count my inhales and my exhales like Mom taught me to do: in for four, and out for four; in for four, and out for four.

Why would Mom give up a good job when she was already so worried about money as it was? Why would she want to take a job that would make her have to think about the death penalty all the time? A couple of times a year she went with a group from the Unitarian church to the prison in Georgia where they execute people. They would go on the nights when there was an execution, and they would hold candles and pray until it was over. She would always come back from those trips so sad. She said she would be happy in her new job, but how could that be? She was going to be sad all of the time, just like she was during that first year after Dad died.

Why couldn't Mom just be happy being a mom, like Aunt Eve was? Mom had told me that back during the Vietnam War, Aunt Eve went to protests, just like Mom and Dad did. But now her number one job was being Anna's mother. Now she was always thinking about Anna, was always so concerned with how she was doing. Like how she immediately hired a tutor when Anna made a B-minus on her math test. And she still sits down with Anna every night after dinner, just to see if she has any questions about her homework. And every year she plans Anna's birthday party for months and the parties are always perfect. I still remember the party Anna had when we were in second grade, a "doll party" based on our very favorite book at the time, *The Best-Loved Doll.* We each brought our favorite doll, and there was a miniature cupcake for each of them and a big-sized cupcake for each of us. There were even miniature teacups and party hats. And at the end, Aunt Eve gave us all paper dolls she had made that looked like us. Mine looked so much like me that Mom put it in a frame.

I wished we could switch moms—just for a little while, like in the movie *Freaky Friday.* If I had Aunt Eve for a mother and Anna had Mom, it would be so great! Anna could walk anywhere she wanted; she could read every single Lois Duncan book; she could go see *Poltergeist* and whatever other scary movie she might want to watch. I wouldn't care about stupid movies or not being able to watch something on TV; I would just soak up all of Aunt Eve's attention. I would appreciate every surprise gift, every tennis lesson, every vacation to Sea Island or retreat to North Carolina for summer camp, where I would live in a cabin in the woods with seven other girls and learn which tribe I had been assigned to for Color Wars.

All of a sudden and without even planning it, I was willing my soul out of my body, willing my soul to travel to Aunt Eve's house in Ansley Park, thinking, somehow, that maybe Anna and I wouldn't have to trade places. Maybe I could just share Anna's body with her. Anna was always so generous; maybe she would let my soul just sort of slide in next to hers. I wouldn't stay for long, just for a little while. I was picturing Anna's room, picturing her high-framed bed, the bumper stickers she had pinned to the corkboard on her door, including the one Uncle Bob bought for her that she thought was so funny but that never made sense to me that said: "Don't steal. The government hates competition."

My body began to shake, starting with my toes and working up through my legs. And then everything locked up. I could not move a single muscle even though I was straining with all of my might to do so.

I was paralyzed.

I don't know how long I was frozen, but with a jerk I could suddenly move again, and I sat up fast but then had to lean back against the headboard because I felt dizzy. I was having trouble breathing. I couldn't seem to get enough air in my lungs. I started crying, which only made it harder to breathe, but still I cried louder and louder, my sobs becoming more and more choked.

And then Mom was beside me on the bed, letting my body slump against hers, holding me in her arms. "Breathe, baby, breathe," she said, repeating those words until I once again could.

Chapter 14

CREDIT

Atlanta, 1983

For years, Daniella believed that if she gave everything she had to the firm, made herself absolutely essential, she would one day be made a partner at Henritz & Powers. It wasn't so much the financial gain she craved—though the security would have been nice—but the recognition of her effort and skill. But no matter how hard she worked, no such payoff came, only empty platitudes and last year's request from Bob to bring her "wonderful brownies" to the firm Christmas party, which was catered, making the request even more infuriating. So she plotted her escape and applied for the salaried position at the Southern Center for Human Rights.

She was stunned by how upset Sarah was when she learned that the new job at the SCHR would pay less than Daniella's current position. It would be a significant pay cut, yes, but it wasn't as if her new position was going to put them in the poorhouse. It wasn't as if she and Sarah were at risk of going hungry. She owned the Morningside house outright, and the rental income she received for the basement studio helped offset the property taxes. And Sarah was at a good public school where she was in the Gifted and Talented program, excelling in her classes, and where she was certainly learning more about the diverse makeup of the city than Anna was at the posh, protected Coventry School.

Was it normal for a ten-year-old to be so focused on money? Perhaps it had been a mistake for Sarah to have spent so much of her childhood with Eve, Eve who seemed to feel that any outing with the girls that did not result in the purchase of a "little happy" wasn't worth making. Had the exposure to so much wealth and excess taught her daughter the wrong values?

She thought of what Pete would say. She talked to him sometimes—to his spirit, his memory. She talked to him most often in her bed late at night when her mind raced with worries. Surely he would tell her that Sarah was not inherently selfish, that her hysterical response to the news that Daniella would be making less money was completely normal, a *big reaction to a big change*. He would remind her that for Sarah, who had lost her father so unexpectedly, change was inherently scary. *She's a good kid*, he would tell her. *You're doing a good job.*

Pete had always possessed more faith in their parenting skills than she had. Of course, it had been easier for him to assume they were doing a good job; he wasn't breaking any rules when he became a father. It was absolutely expected that he would enjoy both fatherhood and a career that gave him some vestige of authority in the world. But the same assumptions did not apply to Daniella. For her, the choice not to quit when she had Sarah, or at least cut back on her hours, was unorthodox at best. So from the moment she returned to work full-time, when Sarah was three months old, she was going off script, at least for a woman from her upper-middle-class background. Working-class women, of course, always went back to work.

Daniella felt certain she was a good lawyer, but she was not always so certain that she was a good mother. The self-doubt could be intense. At her worst moments she accused herself of pawning Sarah off, letting a black woman do the thankless task of childcare while letting a rich white woman spoil her.

Well, there was some truth to that.

Funny that she hadn't even considered taking Sarah to a therapist until more than three years after Pete's death, when Sarah had what Daniella assumed could only be a panic attack upon hearing that Daniella planned to change jobs. She supposed that in those first few years of widowhood she was too lost in her own grief to think about finding professional help for Sarah. And honestly, until lately Sarah had seemed okay. She brought up her father easily and often, and she loved to look through old photo albums, studying the pictures of him, particularly Pete and Daniella's wedding album, when the two of them were so very young. Weren't such reactions normal and appropriate—even healthy?

Daniella had consulted the guidance counselor at Sarah's school for the name of a good child psychologist. She was told that Dr. Ruth Stein was the best. Dr. Stein (who had told Daniella during their first phone consultation to "call me Ruth") was an attractive woman in her late forties or early fifties with shiny, dark chin-length hair. Daniella only met her briefly before Sarah's first session, when Ruth appeared in the waiting room outside her office to shake Daniella's hand and usher Sarah in. Sarah spoke with Ruth alone during her first three visits and didn't offer much to Daniella about the sessions other than to say that she liked going to them. (After that first appointment, Eve volunteered to drive Sarah to see Ruth.) But for the fourth visit, Daniella was asked to join. She took the afternoon off work to do so.

Upon entering the office, Daniella immediately noticed a large bowl of Hershey's Kisses on the coffee table near Sarah, along with several clear glass bottles placed throughout the room, each filled with the balled-up aluminum foil wrappers. She observed that her daughter already had two balled-up candy wrappers on her lap.

Once Daniella settled herself on the couch beside her daughter and reached for her own Hershey's Kiss, Ruth cut to the chase. "Sarah has a lot of anxiety around scarcity. She is afraid that the things she loves will be taken away."

"Is that right, sweetheart?" Daniella asked. Sarah nodded, her eyes on Ruth and not Daniella.

If she had been alone with Ruth, Daniella would have asked exactly how it was that she was supposed to deal with Sarah's worry that the things she loved would be taken away. Something Sarah desperately loved—or rather, a person Sarah desperately loved—*had* been taken away.

But Daniella was pretty sure she was not supposed to point that out.

"I think Sarah needs some reassurance that her life will not be upset by you switching jobs," Ruth continued.

All three were quiet for a moment, and then with a start Daniella realized that both Sarah and Ruth were waiting for her to say something.

"Honey," she said, turning to look straight at Sarah. "Assuming I take the position, which I believe I will, the basic facts of your life will not change. You will still be my beloved daughter. You will still be a fifth grader at Morningside Elementary. You will still go to Aunt Eve's house after school. Ada will still try to get you to eat more vegetables. We will still watch *Family Ties* every Thursday night. And I will still love you more than anything else in the world."

Sarah turned and made eye contact with her, smiling shyly. Daniella allowed herself the private acknowledgment that, in that moment at least, she had said the right thing.

They went on to discuss more ideas for how Daniella could make the transition easier for Sarah. They agreed that she wouldn't talk about her cases at home (they were too scary and sad) and that as long as Sarah was in bed by 9:30 p.m. Daniella would save any work she needed to do at night until after Sarah was asleep. That way the early evenings could be theirs. And twice a month she and Sarah would have a Saturday-night date, doing something fun, just the two of them.

The weekend after that session, Daniella and Sarah were all set for their first date. *The Sound of Music* was airing on television, starting at 9:00 p.m., and they planned to watch it while eating Domino's pizza followed by popcorn and M&M's. But first Daniella needed a shower, having played tennis that afternoon at Piedmont Park with her old friend from Belmont, Kitty.

Daniella took a leisurely shower, toweled off, and then sat on her bed with a towel on her head, rubbing Jergen's lotion into her legs and listening to H. Johnson's *Jazz Classics* on the radio. She liked the music, but it was Johnson's commentary that she loved, that and his mellifluous voice, which always left her craving a cigarette. She kept a pack of Virginia Slims in the drawer of her bedside table for when the urge really hit. Just as she was reaching for the drawer handle, Sarah burst into her room. Her daughter knew that she smoked occasionally, but she highly disapproved. Daniella was glad she hadn't yet retrieved the package.

"Aunt Eve is here," Sarah said. "And she seems upset."

"She's here right now?"

Sarah nodded. "She says she needs to talk."

That was odd. Eve and Bob had a standing date at the Coach and Six on Saturday nights, where they were always seated at the same table and began their evening with a cocktail.

"Tell her I'm getting dressed, but I'll be out as soon as I can."

Sarah glared at her with locked jaw.

Daniella glanced at her watch, which she had put on the bedside table before showering. She put it back on her wrist. It was only 8:15.

"Sweetheart, I promise I will kick Eve out at nine if I have to. I'm not forgetting about our date."

"Okay. I'll order the pizza. Can we get a large?"

Daniella walked into the kitchen having hastily dressed in sweatpants and a T-shirt. She had taken a minute to blow-dry her hair so that it wasn't dripping wet, but the ends still dampened the shoulders of her shirt. Eve, her eyes puffy, was already sitting at the table, having helped herself to a Tab from the fridge. Or maybe Sarah had gotten it for her, Sarah who was sitting at the dining room table in the adjacent room, pretending to read one of her Sweet Valley High books.

"Sarah, honey!" called Daniella. "Why don't you go to my room and watch TV while Eve and I talk."

"Pizza's on the way" Sarah said, her voice tight. "And the movie starts at nine."

"I wouldn't miss it for the world, sweetie. Just give us a few minutes."

Sarah walked to the refrigerator and grabbed a Coke, then took the bag of Fig Newtons from the pantry. Daniella didn't bother reminding her that they were soon going to eat, her silence a peace offering for letting Eve barge in on their special night.

As soon as she was certain her daughter was gone, she asked Eve what was wrong.

"It's Ada," Eve said.

"Oh God, has something happened?"

"No, nothing like that. She's found a house she wants to buy, in Kirkwood, near a new MARTA station."

"That sounds promising. God, her commute time would be so much shorter if she could take the train to Ansley Park."

"I know. Believe me, I know. The problem is, she can't afford to buy the house outright, so she needs a loan."

"I imagine it will be difficult for her to secure a loan on a housekeeper's salary."

"She's actually found a place that will give it to her, some little credit union in Little Five Points."

"I know that place! Very community oriented. I think the Mennonites helped get it started. Or maybe it was the Quakers. Anyway, how wonderful that they're willing to make the loan!"

"The problem is they won't give Ada the loan outright. She has to have a co-signer, even though she actually has a bit of money saved for the down payment, and from what I can tell she could actually make the mortgage payments based on her salary. We pay her a lot more than the going rate, you know."

"Couldn't you or Bob co-sign the loan? Surely it's not much of a risk if Ada earns enough money to make the payments."

"That's the problem. Bob won't do it. He just refuses, and nothing I say can convince him otherwise. Ada gave him the address of the house and he went and looked at it with Buddy, our handyman. He said that even without going inside he and Buddy saw lots of things wrong with it, including the fact that the brick piers it's built on seem to be crumbling and it needs a new roof. He says that Ada would be getting in over her head, that the house needs way too much work for a single woman working as a domestic to keep up with. He even suggested that Ada could live in our garage apartment if she needs a better space that's closer to work."

"Where the girls have a playroom?"

"Yes, but we would fix it up."

"I take it Ada wasn't interested," Daniella said, pressing her lips together to avoid saying anything about Bob that she might later regret.

"No, she wasn't."

"How heartbreaking for Ada."

Eve, who was starting to cry, dug around in her purse for a Kleenex, which she used to blot her eyes. "I've never heard her so excited in my life as when she was telling me about this house. It's owned by a woman who goes to her church and is also on the Motherboard, which I think is some sort of a leadership position. She's moving in with her daughter and son-in-law, and would love a fellow church member to buy the home from her, so she's offering Ada a good price. Ada even said there's a sunny spot for a garden in the back, and you know how gifted Ada is at growing things. Oh, Daniella. This is the first time she's ever directly asked me for anything. But Bob just refuses. A flat-out 'no.' And the terrible thing is, his reasons for saying no make sense. It *would* be awful for Ada to get in over her head. Bob says he's only looking out for her, but I don't know. I just don't know."

Daniella looked at Eve, who had torn the Kleenex she was holding into tiny little strips. Her hair was pulled back into a ponytail, so different from the more formal style she normally wore, and she wasn't wearing any makeup. She looked younger than usual. She looked more like the college girl Daniella once knew.

"What's the sale price?"

"Nineteen thousand dollars."

"Old homes almost always have a ton of stuff wrong with them. My God, this place was a mess when Pete and I first bought it, but we just chipped away at the problems bit by bit. Don't you think Ada could do that?"

"It's a moot point. Bob won't sign."

"But surely you have nineteen thousand dollars of your own. Why not give Ada the money she needs to purchase the house outright?"

"She would still have to pay for taxes and upkeep."

"But she has to pay rent now. There's not going to be a scenario where she doesn't have to pay anything. And this way she'd own something, which I would think Bob would approve of. Isn't he always going on about the importance of ownership and private property?"

This was as close as Daniella would come to criticizing Bob in front of Eve.

"I don't have a job. I don't just have nineteen thousand dollars to give. I don't have unfettered access to money like you do."

"I'd hardly qualify what I earn as 'unfettered access to money.'"

"Of course not. All I mean is that I don't have my own money. Bob writes me a check every month for our household expenses. It's a generous check for sure, but it hasn't left me with an extra nineteen thousand dollars lying around. And the money I've received from my parents is tied up in investments that Bob handles."

"What about co-signing the loan and just not telling Bob?"

"Why would the credit union offer me a loan? I have no income. And even if they did allow me to co-sign, I couldn't do that. It's just—it's not how my relationship with Bob works. He would be so upset to know I went behind his back about something so significant. I mean, I know plenty of women hide things when it comes to their husbands and money—Mother certainly did—but this is a different situation than, say, buying an expensive dress and tearing up the receipt."

"What if you don't lie to him but just . . . stand up to him? Say, 'Hey, Bob, listen up! Either we are going to give Ada the money to buy the house outright or you are going to co-sign the loan with her.'"

During the ensuing silence, Daniella thought she heard a noise from the other side of the kitchen door, a sort of popping sound. She wondered if Sarah was positioned there, eating her Fig Newtons and listening in. She wondered what Sarah would think of all this.

When Eve finally spoke, her voice was steadier than before, more forceful. "I'm sorry, Daniella, I really am, but I'm not going to choose to do something that would sabotage the peace that Bob and I have found with each other. What kind of thanks would that be after all he's done? My God. I was drowning and he saved me. I'm not going to turn around and throw sand in his eye. But listen . . . if you think it's a good idea for Ada to purchase the house . . . maybe you could co-sign the loan?"

"God, I wish I could afford to," said Daniella.

"Bob said last year was a great one for both you and the firm."

Oh, fuck you, Bob, Daniella thought. She wanted to tell Eve that she was leaving her job for a position that paid significantly less in order to use her law degree to help people, rather than continue using it to help corporate executives find "creative solutions" to ease their tax burden. But if she told Eve all that, Eve would surely tell Bob, and that was *not* how she wanted to handle her resignation.

Besides, she didn't have to justify her financial situation to Eve. Eve might claim that all of her money was tied up in investments, but the point was, she had money to tie up. She had so much money that Bob could probably retire and they would still be able to live as lavishly as they did now. Whereas Daniella was the sole provider for Sarah.

And Eve, who had literally never held a job outside of pouring coffee and teaching in some half-baked, unaccredited "free" school, wanted *her* to co-sign a loan with Ada when she and Bob probably spent nineteen thousand dollars on vacations alone last year.

Daniella voiced none of this, saying instead that as the sole provider for Sarah, she didn't feel comfortable taking on a house loan with Ada.

"I am so sorry," she said. "I feel terrible."

The two women looked at each other for a moment. It occurred to Daniella that they each wanted reassurance from the other. And then the doorbell rang and Sarah, who surely had been eavesdropping from the other side of the door, burst in, demanding money to pay for the pizza. Eve gathered her purse and stood, announcing that she would "skedaddle" so the two of them could enjoy their evening together. Daniella was glad to see her go.

Chapter 15

CHANGE COURSE

Atlanta, 1983

I was at the dining room table finishing up my homework when I heard the back doorbell ring. Aunt Eve was putting away clean dishes in the kitchen, so I knew she would answer it.

After a moment I heard Aunt Eve exclaim, "What a surprise to see you in the middle of the day!"

And then I heard Mom's voice, saying that she had taken the day off.

I stood and went to the kitchen, which smelled of rosemary and browning butter from the turkey breast Miss Ada had put in the oven for dinner.

"Hi, sweetheart," Mom said when she saw me. I smiled at her.

"Can you stay for a few minutes?" Aunt Eve asked. "Have a glass of wine? I've got lemonade for the girls."

"Have you finished your homework?" she asked me.

"Most of it," I answered.

"Hmm," she said. "We should probably get home so you can get everything finished before dinner."

"Mom, I go to public school, remember? All I have to do is finish filling out this stupid worksheet and then I'm done."

Anna had tons of homework every night from Coventry and was practically two grades ahead of me in every subject. It drove Mom crazy when I pointed out how much harder Anna's school was, because she knew I was a "natural learner" (as my report cards often stated) and would love to go to a place that was really, really challenging. But any time I mentioned the possibility of applying to Coventry, Mom went off on a lecture about how there was a "hidden curriculum" at private school that she didn't want me exposed to, which meant she thought they taught you how to be a snob. Except Anna wasn't a snob. Anna was sweet and fun, and if you asked her for something she would just give it to you. Once, a couple of years ago, I asked her for the Pink & Pretty Barbie she had just gotten for her birthday, and she just handed it over. Except Mom made me give it back.

"A glass of wine would be lovely. I actually have some news to share. Good news, I think."

"Well, let's make it Champagne then! Sarah, go get Anna. I'll open a bottle of sparkling Martinelli's for the two of you."

"I don't think that's necessary—"

"I love Martinelli's! I'll go get Anna!"

I ran up the back staircase and raced into Anna's room, with its four-poster bed, pink-and-white floral Laura Ashley bedspread, and pink princess phone, which I was so, so jealous of. "Our moms want to make a toast!" I shouted. "They've got Martinelli's!"

Anna was sitting on her bed, where she always did her homework, working on a set of response poems to the novel *Bridge to Terabithia*, which she warned me not to read because the girl in it dies and she thought it would make me too sad about my dad. Anna was really good at writing poetry and had even won a contest at school for a poem she wrote about whales.

"Oh, good!" she said.

We raced downstairs just in time to hear the pop of a Champagne cork and then Aunt Eve laughing. "Why can I not do this without spilling it all over myself?"

"Because you're a spaz?" joked my mom.

Aunt Eve looked up from the foaming Champagne bottle as we walked into the room. "Anna, honey, would you get me a dish towel?"

Anna walked to the cabinet where they kept the towels and fetched one for her mom, who dabbed at the Champagne bottle with it. She had already put out four flutes. She filled two of them with Champagne and the other two with Martinelli's, which she also opened with a pop.

"So what are we toasting?" Aunt Eve asked once we were all standing by the kitchen table holding our glasses. Just then Miss Ada walked into the kitchen.

"Ada! Will you join us?" asked Aunt Eve. "I know you're not a drinker, but we've got delicious sparkling apple juice!"

"I'm just here to check on the turkey, ma'am."

Miss Ada didn't look at Eve when she answered, just headed straight toward the oven, where she punched a button on the panel to turn on the oven light, opened the door, peeked inside, then shut the door again, heading back out of the room carrying herself elegantly as always. If she was aware that Aunt Eve looked crushed, she sure didn't show it.

Aunt Eve bit her lip.

"Well," said Mom, after Miss Ada was gone. "Here goes. I quit my job. As of the first of the new year, I will no longer be working for Henritz & Powers."

"Daniella, that's wonderful!" cried Aunt Eve. "I'm sure Bob is heartbroken that you're leaving, but this is a good, good thing! You've been so overworked and now you'll actually have time to relax a little!"

We all clinked glasses and took a sip.

"Honestly, my new job is going to keep me just as busy," said Mom.

Aunt Eve looked startled. "New job? You've already got a new job? I thought you might take a little time off."

"If only my bills would take a little time off," Mom said.

"Of course, I'm sorry! I didn't mean to be insensitive."

"It's fine," said Mom. "And actually, I'm taking a pay cut so it's almost as if I'm taking time off—ha, ha, ha. I'm going to be working for the Southern Center for Human Rights. I'll be defending indigent men on death row."

"Well. I suppose that's admirable."

Mom took a seat at the kitchen table. "You 'suppose'"?

Eve walked to the pantry, where she retrieved a tin of cheese straws, which she opened and placed on the kitchen table before sitting down next to Mom. "You don't get sent to death row for nothing, after all. It's usually for a pretty grisly crime. My goodness, Daniella, what if they asked you to defend someone like Wayne Williams, someone who . . ."

Aunt Eve glanced nervously at Anna and me. ". . . hurt all those children."

Just hearing Wayne Williams's name spoken aloud made my throat tighten, made me feel like I couldn't breathe, like I was about to have a panic attack. There had been so many young black boys killed in the city over the last few years. Many of them had been strangled to death. They had finally caught Wayne Williams for the murders and sent him to jail for life. Still, it was really scary, even if I didn't live in the same area where all of the murders were happening, even if it wasn't white girls like me who were being killed.

"For starters, Williams wasn't given the death penalty, but a life sentence. So that's kind of a moot point. Also, he wasn't actually charged with murdering a child, but rather two adult men—the other murders were just sort of pinned on him so the city could close the case. The point is whether or not a defendant gets the death penalty is almost always based on race and income level. And you know that the state can use the death penalty to intimidate people they view as a threat. Think about Angela Davis back in the day."

"I'm just thinking about those poor children," said Aunt Eve. "I'm just thinking about justice for their families."

"I agree! And I'd say their families *haven't* really received proper justice, because while I think it's likely Wayne Williams is guilty of the murders he was convicted of, it's highly unlikely he was *the* child murderer. But that's just one highly sensationalized, highly publicized case. A lot of the men I'll be defending are completely anonymous and unknown by the public, and some of them are guilty of nothing more than being black and poor. Seriously, Eve, it's appalling. Besides, no matter how heinous the crime, the death penalty is barbaric. It just makes no sense for the state to say that murder is illegal, except when they are the ones doing it."

"But what if it's a deterrent?"

"Research shows it's not."

"I guess all I'm saying is that I feel a lot more sorry for the victims of crime than I do for the people committing them."

"Jesus, Eve, have you become a Republican, too?"

Mom had told me that Uncle Bob had officially declared himself a Republican back when Ronald Reagan was running against Carter, but Eve and my mom had remained committed Democrats.

"I admit, I had serious concerns about Reagan when he first took office, but don't you think he's done a good job? Don't you think he's given the American people a much-needed sense of optimism? Honestly, Daniella, just put aside your prejudices long enough to really listen to him. That's what I did, and I have to say, he makes me feel really hopeful about the state of things."

"Really? You've fallen for his imperialist nostalgia shtick?"

"I haven't fallen for anything. I just appreciate that he's returned our country to the moral standards we once had."

"Are you fucking kidding me?" asked my mom, and Anna and I both looked at each other with wide eyes. Mom sometimes cussed, but never in front of Anna. She and I both knew that Uncle Bob and Aunt Eve were really careful about what sort of language Anna was exposed to.

"Daniella! Please. Little girls! Big ears!"

Aunt Eve probably didn't even think Anna knew the word "damn."

"Eve, do you remember what you were doing, oh, a little over eleven years ago?"

"Of course I do. That's my whole point. Because here's the truth, Daniella: I *never* would have become that way if I hadn't gotten brainwashed by Warren and the whole counterculture movement. I regret it. I really do."

"The cause was good; you just went off the deep end. But that doesn't negate the injustice of Jim Crow or the fact that our country had no business being in Vietnam. You just got wrapped up with the wrong people."

"The whole movement was the wrong people! And we weren't just protesting our involvement in Vietnam—we wanted the Vietcong to win. We acted like they were these scrappy, virtuous heroes. But they were brutal, monstrous! My manicurist, Linh, was telling me all about how the North Vietnamese imprisoned her father after the war for having had ties with the South. They starved the man! They beat him. They kept him in solitary confinement for years. Years! They were breathtakingly cruel, and we adored them."

"Eve, sweet friend, the majority of us protesting the war didn't adore the North Vietnamese," said my mom. "We just wanted the U.S. out. We didn't want any more of our American soldiers to die for what was a civil war in a country that had *nothing* to do with us."

"You say that now."

"I am absolutely certain I would have said that then. I *did* say that then. You just weren't listening."

Eve and my mom glared at each other.

"Who's Warren?" Anna asked, and I watched as Aunt Eve's expression shifted from mad to worried.

"Just an old beau of your mom's," Mom answered quickly. "Your pretty mother always had boys chasing after her. It was hard to keep up with them."

Chapter 16

BLAST FROM THE PAST

Atlanta, 1984

Driving home after completing her errands, Eve felt enchanted with the world. It was April, and everything was in bloom. The crocuses had been the first to push through the dirt, popping up among the beds in front of their house. Whenever Bob spotted one he would say, "There's a crocus amoke us." Nonsense, but it made her smile.

Today the whole world made Eve smile. Ansley Park was beautiful in every season, but spring was its glory: the flowers on the dogwood trees unfurling, the bright pink azaleas ablaze in nearly every yard. She loved how close Ansley Park was to the actual city—she could practically touch the Atlanta skyline from her bedroom window—and how convenient it was to everything: walking distance to the Driving Club and just a short drive to St. Luke's and Ansley Mall. Easter would be here on Sunday, and she had a woven straw basket all ready to fill for Anna, though of course Anna, at age eleven, no longer believed in the Easter Bunny. Who cared? Her daughter still believed in Cadbury Creme Eggs and jelly beans.

Once upon a time she had turned up her nose at "the straight life."

But now she felt so grateful for it: the order, the rhythm, the pride of being a responsible adult. She liked that her life with Bob gave her structure, boundaries, two straight lanes to drive within. She liked that the gutters were cleaned the moment they became full, the grass mowed whenever it grew a half inch too tall, the furnace filters replaced on schedule. She liked, indulgent though it was, that she had a standing appointment with Jeffrey every six weeks for a haircut and highlights, and another standing appointment with Linh for manicures and pedicures. Bob admired pretty feet and hands, so why not oblige?

Of course, she recognized how privileged her life was. She knew most people did not get to live like this. In response, she and Bob contributed generously to a multitude of charities, from CARE USA, which was close to her heart, to the American Cancer Society, which was close to Bob's. (His mother had died from ovarian cancer.) They gave to a number of other non-profits as well, including St. Jude, Big Brothers Big Sisters, and the YMCA of Metro Atlanta. And of course they made and fulfilled their hefty annual pledge both to St. Luke's and to the Coventry School. She volunteered as much as she could at Coventry, as well. Any time moms were asked to help set up for an event or help spruce up the playground or serve on a planning committee for some auction or another, Eve signed up. She loved stitching herself into the fabric of her daughter's life in that way. She intuited that she should seize this time, her daughter's childhood, as the years would quickly pass. Indeed, Anna was starting to grow breast buds.

Eve wished she had had more than one child. Two would be nice; three would be ideal. Three kids made a real family, a brood. But like her mother and her grandmother before her, she had not had an easy time giving birth. When Anna was eventually pulled out with forceps, she was perfect, save for her temporarily misshapen head. But Eve had lost so much blood that she required a transfusion. And despite the fact that the doctor had performed an episiotomy to try to minimize tearing, she had torn so badly that she ended up with fourth-degree lacerations. It was a painful recovery. But by

the time Anna was eighteen months old, the memory of the pain had re-
ceded and Eve was ready to try for a second. It took nearly a year and a half
of trying before she was finally rewarded with the call from her doctor's
office confirming she was pregnant. She was thrilled, but the pregnancy
turned out to be ectopic, and she had to have emergency surgery, which
resulted in the removal of one of her fallopian tubes. Afterward, she was
urged by her doctor not to get pregnant again. Bob agreed. "Sweetheart," he
had said, "another child is not worth your life."

She wondered, after her fallopian tube was removed, if God was pun-
ishing her for past sins. Or maybe she had simply messed up her body with
too many drugs, which was a sort of indirect punishment, inflicted by her
former, careless self. Or maybe the women in her family simply did not
birth children easily. She and Bob considered adopting a second child, but
Bob was wary. "You never really know what gene pool you might be tapping
into," he had said.

She did not remind him that he had chosen to tap into a dubious gene
pool when he assumed paternity of her daughter, who at the time was only
the size of a grape in her uterus. Bob knew, of course, that Warren was
Anna's biological father, but everyone else—save for Daniella—believed
that she and Bob had gotten pregnant during their whirlwind courtship,
Anna included. Anna had been upset enough earlier that year when she and
Sarah did the math and realized that unless Anna was born *really* premature,
she had been conceived *before* her parents were actually married. Eve had
spent a long time assuring her daughter that, while after the wedding was
of course best, it really was okay if a baby got a little head start during the
engagement.

There was absolutely no reason for Anna to know the sordid details of
her conception. Warren was dead, obliterated, and Bob loved her as much as
any father could possibly love a child, especially when Anna did something
particularly delightful: brought home straight As once again, or won the
poetry contest held by the elementary school at Coventry, or just looked

pretty and innocent dressed for church on Sunday, wearing a Laura Ashley floral dress with a square neckline.

Despite the disappointment of only having one child, life was good. So good, in fact, that it sometimes stopped her breath. She was so grateful to have this second chance. She was amazed that not only did she survive the madness of her years with Warren, but that she had somehow been allowed to reenter society, to become a central figure in the Atlanta world she had once so arrogantly disparaged.

She turned into the driveway of their house, which had once been Bob's house and before that his parents'. She loved that it was stately, that it was architecturally significant, but she had insisted on softening its facade with thoughtful landscaping. Her landscape designer, who had legally changed her name to Honey Butterfly—also the name of her company—made certain there was something in bloom every season but winter, and even then she greened up the windows on the front of the house with boxwood wreaths.

Eve parked at the foot of the driveway to retrieve the mail, then drove up the gentle hill where a riot of tulips—reds, yellows, purples—bloomed in intentionally haphazard arrangements in the front yard. Pulling the Mercedes wagon into the two-car garage behind the house, she contemplated its second-floor space, which Bob referred to as a "bonus room" and which, for the past several years, the girls had used as a playroom. Soon she would convert it into a guest suite, as the girls didn't really play anymore, now preferring to talk on the phone with their friends, paint their nails, and read endlessly.

Letting herself in through the back door, she found Anna and Sarah at the table drinking Sprites (Anna was allowed two a week) and eating toasted bagels topped with cream cheese and pineapple chunks.

"Hey, sweet girls!" she called, dumping the mail on the counter and walking over to give them each a kiss. She loved her daughter most of all, of course, but she loved Sarah, too, loved her the way she might love a particularly close niece. (She had no nieces and nephews. After Fig left Charlie, he had devolved into a perennial bachelor, dating increasingly younger women as the years went by.)

"Where's Miss Ada?" Eve asked, hearing the pitch of her voice go up when she said Ada's name. Things had not been the same ever since she and Bob had told Ada they couldn't help her get a loan for a house. The warmth that Eve had always felt radiating from Ada had simply been turned off, which honestly seemed a little unfair given that Eve paid Ada significantly more than any of her friends paid their maids. Did that not count for anything?

"Upstairs, I think," answered Anna, glancing up from the book of Mad Libs she and Sarah were filling out.

"Okay, now I need a noun," Anna said.

"'Fart,'" said Sarah. "As in 'a fart,' not 'to fart.'"

Anna looked at her friend with delight but swatted her on the arm. "That's rude, crude, and socially unacceptable!" she proclaimed, a phrase she had picked up from her teacher, Mrs. McDonald.

"The whole point of the game is to be rude, crude, and socially unacceptable!" cried Sarah. "Right, Aunt Eve?"

"Perhaps you could land on 'rude' without crossing all the way over to 'crude,'" Eve bargained.

"Okay, fine. A burp," conceded Sarah, and then burped loudly to make sure everyone got the point.

"You two," said Eve, laughing along with them as she pulled a Tab from the refrigerator and gathered up her mail, including the new *Southern Living*, to take with her to the sunroom. The bills she left for Bob.

She sat in her armchair in the sunroom (there were two matching armchairs, upholstered in Pierre Deux's Fontenay Linen, one strictly hers and the other strictly Bob's) and flipped through her magazine while sipping her diet soda. There was a recipe for an Italian cream cake with cream cheese frosting that looked divine—maybe she would fix it for Easter dinner, along with a spiral-sliced ham, macaroni and cheese for the girls, slow-cooked green beans for Bob, and a big, fresh salad with avocados and mandarin oranges for her and Daniella. Eve always invited Daniella and Sarah to Easter dinner. She considered asking Bob to bring along one of the single men from his golf group—several were recently divorced—in an attempt to set Daniella up, but she knew that was a fool's errand. Bob's golf friends were his age or older, and Daniella often made disparaging comments about men who dated younger women, either forgetting about the fact that Bob was twelve years her senior or not forgetting about it at all. (Would she rather Eve have raised Anna as a single mother and not provided her with a loving, stable, two-parent family?)

Of course, the real deal breaker for Daniella, when it came to any of Bob's golf friends, would be their politics. Eve had plenty of friends who still considered themselves Democrats even though their husbands had started voting Republican, but Daniella was such a purist, there was no way she could live with such a compromise. A month ago the *New York Times* had run an article about the white southern migration from the Democrat to the Republican Party, as a surge of former Democrats had cast their ballots for Reagan in 1980 and continued to offer the president their full-throated support. Bob, who was the newly elected national committeeman of the Republican Party of Georgia, was prominently featured in the piece. His great-grandfather had been a Democratic senator from Georgia, and Bob had voted Democrat in every election until 1972, at which point he wrote in "Mickey Mouse" instead of either Nixon or McGovern. He had voted for fellow Georgian Jimmy Carter in 1976, of course, but in 1980 he had finally said to hell with it and switched parties, casting his vote for "someone who was actually proud of our country." It was a trend piece, not a deep investigation, but it was of added interest that she, Bob's wife, had been active in the antiwar movement during the 1960s and had voted for Carter in 1980 but was planning to support Reagan in his upcoming bid for reelection.

Eve was uncomfortable with the article, wary of it shining a light on what she had come to think of as her "lost years." But Bob was thrilled with how the piece turned out, saying that the brief mention of Eve's ideological turnaround only drove home the point that Reagan was a "big tent" leader. The evening after the *Times* piece ran, Eve had attended a gathering of Atlanta-area Fleur alums (it turned out Grandmommy had been wise to stop the mailing of her official resignation), and she was practically greeted with a standing ovation.

"And your family looks so darling in the photo!" exclaimed Ginny Simmons, whose son, George, was a grade above Anna at Coventry.

Daniella's reaction had not been to applaud. She had telephoned Eve that same night, after Eve returned from the alumnae event, and when Eve answered, the first words out of Daniella's mouth were, "Please tell me this is some sort of elaborate prank you're playing on me."

"People change, Daniella," Eve had said. "You have to allow for people to change."

"'*I was once something of a radical, but now I realize the system works*'!" said Daniella, parroting Eve's quote in the *Times* back to her.

"I stand by my words," said Eve. "The system has flaws, of course, but it *does* work. It's a work in progress."

"Would Ada agree that the system works after the state tore down her house, after her son was sent to die in an unjust war?"

"Well, that's exactly it, isn't it?" replied Eve. "Ada is actually a perfect example of government overreach. You let the government have too much power and look at what it does to its citizens."

"The fact that Ada has been screwed by our country has much more to do with black people not being guaranteed their constitutional rights than with government overreach."

"Plenty of white boys died in Vietnam," retorted Eve.

"So what are you getting at here? What exactly is your point? Are you saying the answer is to rely solely on the kindness of individual citizens to help each other out? That sure worked well during Jim Crow. That sure stopped a lot of lynchings! And gee, come to think of it, that sure worked well for Ada when she asked you to co-sign for her loan!"

Eve hung up the phone. She just hung up on Daniella.

They didn't speak to each other for a week, other than a cursory "hello" if Eve happened to be home when Daniella came to fetch Sarah after work. But then one evening, Daniella arrived with a vase of daisies for Eve. "I'm so sorry," she said. "I can be such a judgmental bitch."

"Don't use that word," said Eve, though she was really just parroting Daniella, who years ago had promised never again to call a woman by the slur a man might use while beating or raping her.

"I'm sorry I was so judgmental," said Daniella. "You have every right to vote however you want."

Eve had hugged her friend tight, so grateful that only a week had gone by with the two of them on the outs. She found it was easy to forgive Daniella for her biting accusations. Her words had hurt, but not nearly as much as it would hurt to become estranged again, as they had been for so long during Eve's lost years. Besides, Daniella hadn't co-signed the loan with Ada, either. It helped to remember that.

She put down the *Southern Living* and turned to the other mail, tearing open the large envelope from Camp Manataka, where Anna would be going for a full month this summer instead of two weeks, as she had the previous summer. Inside were registration forms. She would fill them out when she had Anna's immunization records and such in front of her. Lord, she would miss her daughter while she was off in the mountains of North Carolina. But Sarah would still spend weekdays at her house. Perhaps she would see if Sarah might like to take tennis lessons while Anna was away. She could sign her up for them at the Driving Club and either Sarah and Ada could walk there or Eve could drop Sarah off.

Eve wished that Daniella would take more of an interest in Sarah's extracurriculars. Daniella was a good mother, yes, loving and honest and (Lord knows) open with her daughter, but Eve didn't think she did enough special things for her. It was almost as if Sarah were a physical manifestation of Daniella's political views. Take Sarah's clothing: Daniella dressed her mostly in consignment-store finds, though surely she could have occasionally afforded to buy her something new from the mall. Granted, Daniella purchased a lot of Sarah's clothes from Sweet Repeats, which was upscale and stocked really cute stuff. Still, a brand-new dress, purchased just for your daughter, was a special way to let her know she was loved.

Far worse was Daniella's stubborn insistence that her daughter attend public school, even though Sarah was so very bright and would surely thrive at an academically challenging school like Coventry. Gracious, the child had taught herself to read at age four! And there was the science kit she requested for her eighth birthday, which included a real embalmed frog and tools for dissecting it. Sarah had spent countless hours occupied with the contents of that kit, even after Anna had lost interest and wandered away.

Surely if Daniella wanted to send Sarah to private school, either her parents or Pete's mother would pay for it. But Daniella was stubborn. Daniella was a purist, with her heartbreaking job, her small house that she made even smaller by renting out the basement, her refusal to cover up the gray that had now pretty much taken over her once-brown hair. It was easy to feel like a sellout around Daniella. It was easy to feel inadequate when your best friend was on a mission to be like Jesus. Not that Daniella would ever do something so pedestrian as to join a mainline church. (*But she didn't co-sign the loan*, Eve reminded herself. *She didn't co-sign the loan.*)

Enough about her old friend. Eve had her own life to attend to, her own family to manage. She opened the last piece of mail addressed to her, a letter with her name typed on the front and no return address. Most likely it was a solicitation, another nonprofit asking for money. She unfolded the letter and began to read:

Dear Eve,

Or should I say DeeDee, Mary Jane, or Harriet? Might one of your former aliases help you remember who you once were? I certainly received an eye-opening update on who you have become. A whole article in the New York Times, featuring none other than our little Evelyn Whalen from Atlanta, Georgia. Your mother must have been so proud! Three cheers for you!

Tell me, baby, is Robert Powers, committeeman of the Georgia Republican Party, aware that his little debutante-in-training has a living father who might not be so fucking keen on a B-movie actor occupying the White House? And you! Voicing your support for that moron! For fuck's sake, Eve, do you not remember what your beloved Ronnie said back when he was governor of California, when asked how he would respond to riots in Berkeley in 1969?: "If it takes a bloodbath, let's get it over with, no more appeasement."

And people called us radical—Jesus H. Christ!

I'm not saying I don't understand your decision to swim in the mainstream. Shit, we all do what we need to do to survive. (And yes, obviously, I survived, and at a huge cost.) But to become a mouthpiece for the Republican Party of the South? Are you fucking kidding me? Have you ever heard of the term 'the Southern Strategy,' first employed by your good pal Richard Nixon? To refresh your memory, here it is: Get white southerners to migrate to the Republican Party by quietly affirming their racist beliefs.

You have certainly fallen right into their trap, baby. I mean, goddamn.

Okay, fine. Whatever politics you choose to support in 1984 are really none of my goddamn business; I know that, I really do. Whatever gets you through the night and all that. But Anna is my business. She is my daughter, whether Robert Powers, GOP spokesman-at-large, admits it or not.

Even though the family picture in the paper is small, I can see you in Anna. And I can see me, too. Am I right that she has my eyes? Do something for me, Eve. Do me this one favor if you do nothing else. Send me a photograph of her. A school picture, a vacation shot, whatever. Just let me see my daughter without Bob Powers's arm around her.

You were right to have kept her. I will give you that. And while I'm sure Bob Powers makes a fine provider, don't you think she needs to know who her real father is? I'm assuming she has no idea. I'm assuming Daddy Powers passes himself off as her progenitor, or perhaps she thinks her father is dead and that Daddy Powers adopted her.

I'm not saying you need to tell her who I am. At least not now. I'm just saying I would like for the two of us to exchange letters. You could say I was an uncle, or a second cousin. I could send a present and you could insist that she write a thank-you note. (I know you, baby. I know the world you returned to! I know you would insist on the thank-you note!) And I could write her back and we could begin a simple correspondence. Nothing scary. Just a way for a man about to turn forty to make some contact with his own flesh and blood.

You can send the picture to P.O. Box 3455 / 195 41st
Street / Oakland, CA / 94611

Think about it, Eve. It would certainly be easier
than me coming to Atlanta.

Eve's hands were shaking as she let the letter fall to her lap. Warren St.
Clair was *alive*? No. He couldn't be. He absolutely could not be. He was in
the house on Linwood Avenue when the bomb went off. He had to have
been. They had found his Ho Chi Minh dog tags among the rubble. How
could anyone walk away from that? Panic blossomed like a spiky flower in
her chest and she thought of the bottle of Valium she had in her medicine
cabinet upstairs. Instead, she walked on shaky legs to the liquor cabinet, a
heavy piece of furniture on the opposite side of the sun porch stocked with
crystal stemware and drinkware and all manners of alcohol. A drink. She
would have a drink. A drink would help.

Chapter 17

PHOTOGRAPH, MEMORIES

Atlanta, 1984

That night she lay beside a sleeping Bob, her mind racing despite the fact that she had taken a Valium. She had hidden Warren's letter in the antique stationery box that she kept in her study. That was where she kept the one photo of Warren that she still had, the one object from that time that had not been destroyed by the bomb that ripped through the Linwood house. She had taken the photo with her to Jane's house that last night she saw Warren, the night she had told him she would not get an abortion. They were breaking up, yes, but she had no reason to think she would never see him again. Yet somehow she must have known.

After placing Warren's letter underneath the felt lining of the stationery box, she had taken out the photo and studied it. It had been a long time since she had looked. The girl in the picture (could that militant creature really be her?) wore her hair so short she looked as if she were a cancer patient, and her thinness added to that impression. She was not smiling in the photo, though Warren was, an arrogant smirk that suggested he alone had all of the answers. She held the photo up closer, studying his features. Anna *did* have his eyes—not in color, but in shape. How had she not noticed that her daughter had Warren's eyes? She had not wanted to notice, of course. She had not wanted to think of Warren ever again, and yet a memory surfaced so quickly she could not push it back down in time. It was after everyone else had abandoned Smash and just she and Warren remained. They were moving from New York down to Atlanta, traveling in Warren's old pickup. Eve hated driving with Warren because he wouldn't talk to her. (Whereas other times, especially when they were around other people, he often wouldn't shut up.) But during road trips he would either space out, presumably lost in his own thoughts, or become completely absorbed in whatever music was blasting from the radio. If she tried to start a conversation he would wave away the attempt, adding, "I don't like to talk while I'm driving."

She always felt so alone during their drives, so erased. She thought that perhaps Warren might make an effort to talk if she brought up how much his silences bothered her *before* they started their trip. So the night before they left New York, she told him how she felt and asked if he would please, please engage with her during the drive. He had thought for a minute and then said, "Give me a blow job and I will."

And she had. My God, she had.

She couldn't look at his photo anymore, and so she dropped it back in the box, along with the letter she had just received from him—if it was actually Warren who had written it. She had spent the rest of the night trying to distract herself from thinking about him, from thinking about his body on top of hers. His pushy, hairy body.

She had kept busy filling out Anna's camp forms, then organized her study, then cleaned out the refrigerator. But now here she was in bed, unable to escape her thoughts. Warren St. Clair was supposed to be dead.

There was absolutely no way for him to walk away after the bomb exploded. Unless he wasn't there when it exploded. Unless he had put his dog tags around someone else's neck. *Lord.* But who would do that, who would agree to act as Warren's body double?

Maybe it wasn't Warren writing her. Maybe Warren *was* dead and it was someone else, someone who knew her history, posing as Warren. Maybe Abby. But why would Abby stir the pot? Abby had already brilliantly reinvented herself, having resurfaced a year after Eve. Just as Eve had, Abby turned herself in to the authorities, and though it was believed that she had participated in several "symbolic" bombings during her time underground, bombings that only damaged property, not people, most of the charges were dropped. She ended up serving just nine months in a federal penitentiary in Connecticut for the few minor offenses the FBI was able to charge her with (the FBI had broken so many laws in pursuing radicals that very little of their evidence was admissible in court). Upon release, she went to law school. Now she was a professor of constitutional law at UC Hastings.

Abby would not risk her prestigious new life to send Eve a forged letter. Why would anyone but Warren send it? But how could Warren still be alive? Even if he had somehow managed to fake his own death, how could he have survived underground for so long? Well, he was a St. Clair, and his father did send him money during his Smash days. So maybe his father was continuing to support him now.

She felt the first stab of a blinding headache. Stress-related migraines, her doctor had said during her last checkup, adding that she should try to take it easy and writing her a prescription for a higher dose of Valium. How was she going to tell Bob about the letter? She had to, didn't she? She had to let Bob know that Warren was alive. But if Bob knew, wouldn't he, as a lawyer, be mandated to alert the authorities? Weren't there strict guidelines around such things? Or maybe he could keep quiet because of spousal privilege. She could ask Daniella for clarification on the law. But Daniella would want to know why she was asking and would surely insist that Eve take the letter to the police.

If the authorities were alerted and they decided to, say, stake out the P.O. box Warren had provided, what would happen? Warren probably didn't check his own P.O. box, even all these years later. But still, if the authorities knew that Warren was alive and somewhere in the vicinity of Oakland and they managed to capture and arrest him, twelve years after he had supposedly died, would that be considered national news? Would it warrant coverage not just in California but all over? Of course it would. Just look at what happened when Cathy Wilkerson turned herself in a few years ago. Her face was everywhere, and she hadn't even murdered anyone.

And if Warren were caught, what would keep him from talking? She knew from her own experience that Warren would be encouraged to reveal all pertinent information he possessed. Hadn't she shared everything she knew about Smash when she turned herself in? At the time, all past charges against her had been dropped, and no new charges were filed. But could that change? Cathy Wilkerson served time for unlicensed possession of explosives. Could she retroactively be charged with that, having known that Warren was in possession of stolen dynamite? But she had told the police about the dynamite. They couldn't press charges all of these years later, after she fully cooperated back in the day. Even if they wanted to, wasn't there some sort of statute of limitations that would protect her?

If somehow she were charged, would a judge or a jury understand that the Eve who joined the Smash Collective was not the same person she was today? That she had been seduced and brainwashed? Half of the time, she had just been trying to survive; she had just been trying to avoid being the point of focus during a Smash session.

She could not think about that time. She could not allow her memories to take her there, not for one more minute. It was unbearable to think of being that girl. *That* Eve was as dead to her as Warren St. Clair was supposed to be.

If Warren were to talk or, worse, pen some sort of prison memoir outlining all of the deranged things they used to do, she could lose everything, including the carefully constructed life she and Bob had built together, with Anna at its center. If Bob knew of the grittier details of her time in Smash, would he still love her? She remembered how outraged he had been when he had learned that Abby was a law professor. At the time, Eve had been surprised that Bob didn't seem to remember her connection to Abby. Surely she had spoken of Abby back when he and Daniella were her lawyers, back when she first surfaced. But Bob had no memory of that. He only knew about Abby because one of the talk radio shows he listened to featured her on a segment called "Dangerous Radicals in Academia." Except the talking heads got it wrong; they said Abby had been a member of the Weather Underground. Eve had kept her mouth shut. There was no need to correct their mistake.

Couldn't she simply pretend that Warren's letter had never arrived? Couldn't she toss the cheap piece of notebook paper it was written on into the fire, assume it was only a mean prank, written by some peripheral Smash member who was trying to mess with her in the wake of the *New York Times* piece? (She *knew* she should have said no to being in the article. But Bob was so excited! So thrilled by who they both had become!)

If the letter was from Warren, if he was actually still alive, it seemed he had a lot more at stake than she did. He had murdered J. T. Higgins, after all, and he had probably murdered a second person to stand in his stead and wear his dog tags. Were he to show up at her house, God forbid, he would be immediately arrested and he would be sent to jail for the rest of his life. He might even receive the death penalty. He wouldn't risk it. Eve was almost certain he wouldn't risk it.

Chapter 18

COVENTRY

Atlanta, 1987–1990

During the fall of my freshman year of high school, I finally convinced Mom to let me apply to Coventry by sitting her down after dinner one night and arguing my case as if I were a lawyer before a judge. I had all sorts of exhibits to present, including my grades and academic awards, as well as promotional materials from Coventry highlighting their 12:1 student-teacher ratio, their zillions of AP classes, their state-of-the-art facilities, and their generous financial aid program aimed at helping "bright students in need." After showing Mom what Coventry could offer, I reminded her that they had changed their hiring policy the year before and now hired teachers from all religious backgrounds, and not just Christians. (Their hiring policy had always been a sticking point for Mom.) I also reminded her that the previous year two members of their debate team had won the national tournament, meaning the school was clearly molding great future lawyers, which I might want to become. But my final argument was one of free will and choice.

"You always said that you wanted to help me grow into the person I was supposed to become, not a fantasy of the person you wanted me to be. Well, I want to do this, Mom. I want to try it. And if you don't let me, it will be what you want, not me."

Tears sprang into her eyes. Still, she made a lame joke, saying, "Don't be surprised if they offer courses in golf and wine tasting."

But then she held up her hands in surrender. "Okay, okay, you win. You presented your case brilliantly, sweetheart, tying facts with heart. I'm proud of you."

Later that spring, I was offered admission with generous financial aid, surely funded in part by years of donations made by Aunt Eve.

In terms of academics, I loved Coventry from day one. Most of my humanities classes were taught seminar-style, meaning we sat around a big, round table discussing whatever text we were reading as if our opinions really mattered. The setup for Algebra II and physics was more traditional, but the classes were so small that whenever I got confused the teacher was right there, ready to explain the equation again. And teachers had to stay in their classrooms for an hour after school was over in case anyone wanted to come by for extra help. Apparently I had actually learned a lot during my years in the Gifted and Talented program in the Atlanta public school system, because by the time midsemester reports came out I had some version of an A in every subject but PE, in which I had a B+.

Things were trickier socially. Though Anna took me under her wing the moment I arrived as a new sophomore on campus and even outfitted me in the right clothes (she was as generous with her wardrobe as she had once been with her Barbies), I felt like an oddball at Coventry from the very beginning. For one thing, I didn't have a mom and a dad, as everyone else seemed to, and worse, my mother worked—and not at some cushy job like interior design. And I was attending Coventry on a need-based scholarship (a fact I mentioned to no one) and we lived not in Buckhead or Ansley Park, but in a small house in Morningside with a basement apartment we rented out because we needed the extra income. And I was not given a car for my sixteenth birthday, as Anna and her friends were. My mom could barely afford the upkeep on her own ten-year-old Toyota. Nor did we have a second home at Lake Rabun or Highlands or Sea Island. Mom reassured me that we did have a nest egg, thanks to the prudence of my father, but that it was reserved for my college education and Mom's retirement and was not to be touched.

Anna welcomed me into her circle of friends, many of whom I'd already met at Anna's birthday parties over the years. Some were cheerleaders, like Anna. All were pretty girls who wore real jewelry from Maier & Berkele, made good grades, and always seemed to be on diets. I didn't click with any of them, not on any real level, but they were popular, and I recognized that there was a certain cachet to being seen with them. Still, after those first few months I found myself gritting my teeth every time I had to endure another lunchtime discussion concerning how many calories were in plain versus chocolate frozen yogurt. I would distract myself by watching Lizzie and Sake, who always sat at a table by themselves, best friends who didn't seem to give a damn about what anyone else thought of them, a fact made especially obvious when their band, Ümlaut, played.

Ümlaut was the only girl band on campus. They were inspired by the DIY ethic of the punk scene—just grab a guitar and do it. Neither Lizzie nor Sake was particularly musically talented, but they made up for it with sheer nerve. Somehow they managed to perform at nearly every on-campus concert Coventry hosted. Actually, the reason was fairly obvious: Lizzie's full name was Elizabeth Lee Calhoun, as in the Coca-Cola Calhouns, as in the Calhoun Auditorium, where all of Coventry's plays and concerts were staged.

Lizzie's family connections aside, Ümlaut rarely managed to stay onstage for long. Their acts were nearly always cut short due to "vulgar language." At the Planned Famine Concert, during which bands played all day to distract students from the fact that they had skipped lunch in order to Think About Hunger, their mic was cut as soon as Lizzie started screaming the lyrics to "Fuck You, Peggy Sue!" And at Coventry's Battle of the Bands, they earned a month of detention for their performance of "If I Had a Scrotum," a song that began with an audience call-and-response: "You say 'my' / I say 'scrotum!' / My! / Scrotum! / My! / Scrotum!"

They were glorious.

One day in December when Anna was out sick, I bypassed my usual seat with Anna's calorie-conscious friends, thrust back my shoulders, and headed toward Lizzie and Sake, plopping down at their table rather than asking permission to join. Their heads were bent over a black-and-white-speckled notebook, and they were laughing. I spent a long time putting ketchup on my chicken sandwich, scrolling a loopy design on its breaded crust.

Lizzie looked up at me and smiled. "No, no, not another doughnut for me," she said graciously.

I blinked. There were no doughnuts at the table.

"I can't wait to run six miles after lunch!" said Sake.

"Wow," I said. "Who do you have for PE?"

"Gosh, I found this morning's devotional very inspiring."

"The guy who talked about how our virginity was like an apple, and if you take a premarital bite out of it, the flesh turns brown and rots?"

"Oh, yes! So uplifting!" said Lizzie. And then she and Sake cracked up.

"We're playing 'Things We Never Say,'" Lizzie finally explained.

"Ha," I said. "As in, 'Gee, Miss Ellis's hair looks different today'?"

Miss Ellis, the dean of girls, was known for her perennial hairstyle, with feathered bangs in front and a flip in the back that looked like a ducktail.

"Exactly," said Lizzie, and just like that I was in.

By junior year, Sake, Lizzie, and I were a known trio. Anna and I still considered each other good friends—sisters, really—but we didn't have any classes together, and we rarely spent time with each other outside of school, except for occasional get-togethers with our moms. We would smile and say "hi" when we passed in the hall, and we would sometimes sit together in the cafeteria, but our paths had clearly split. Anna had become really involved with Young Life, which was the mainstream, upbeat Christian group on campus, the other being the Agape Fellowship, which tended to fixate more on sin and the evils of abortion.

I did go to one Young Life meeting with Anna, after she told me how fun it was. The meeting was held at night, in the basement rec room of some cheerleader friend of Anna's. All around me preppy kids scratched each other's backs while listening to the devotional, which was given by the cute young history teacher, Mr. Woods, who told a story about being saved by Jesus during a fraternity prank gone wrong, when he and some other Phi Delts tried to steal the lion from in front of the SAE house. I couldn't wait to get home so I could call Lizzie and tell her all about it. She immediately went to work on a new Ümlaut song: "Christ rescued me / from a pissed-off SAE!"

During the spring of my junior year, I began to worry that no one was going to ask me to prom. Prom was a Really Big Deal at Coventry that pretty much everyone went to, even the Doc Marten–wearing stoners who typically avoided doing *anything* that gave off the slightest whiff of school spirit. I wanted Dean to ask me, a track star who also happened to be crazy smart, but he was in a serious relationship with an artsy senior named *Zoe* (ugh).

"Boys are a snore," Lizzie proclaimed whenever I moaned about how much happier Dean would be with me. Of course, her dismissal of boys didn't stop half of the guys in our class from being in love with her. In fact, Lizzie was one of the first girls asked to the prom, by the captain of the soccer team, McKitrick Davis. Soon after, Robert Cho asked Sake, because at Coventry white kids and nonwhite kids didn't really date. It wasn't until a few weeks later that George Simmons, who was headed to UVA in the fall, approached me in the stairwell after fourth period and asked if I would go with him.

"Anna's already going with Chip," he said. "The four of us could go together."

"So you already asked Anna and I'm Plan B?" I joked.

George looked so uncomfortable that I dropped it. The fact was that Anna already had a boyfriend, Stuart, who went to Episcopal, a boarding school in Virginia.

But surely George knew that. He and Anna had known each other their whole lives. Their moms played on a tennis team together, and he also lived in Ansley Park. I remembered playing Marco Polo with George and his brother the summer my dad died, when Aunt Eve took us to the Driving Club to swim nearly every afternoon, thinking that the sun and the exercise would be therapeutic for me.

The weekend after George issued his invitation, Aunt Eve took Anna and me to Neiman's to look for dresses. Anna immediately grabbed a scoop-neck dress embellished with thousands of tiny pink sequins. It was the perfect bubblegum-pink prom dress, short and fun, the sort of sparkly thing I would have dreamed of wearing when I was eight and loved nothing more than to braid my Barbie's hair. While pink sequins were perfect for Anna, my style had grown more understated, and I filled my dressing room with black sheaths. None was cheaper than two hundred dollars, and the one I loved—a simple black dress, sleeveless with a high neck and low back, cost over three hundred. It was impossible. My mom had given me a hundred-dollar bill for the shopping trip and told me I could spend all of it. The corners of her mouth had turned up when she said that, and I knew that in her mind she was giving me a tremendous gift.

"Come out and let us see how pretty you look!" Aunt Eve called from the other side of the dressing room door. Anna's pink dress was already sheathed in plastic and waiting for her, hanging on the rack by the cash register.

I walked out, shrugging.

"It's perfect!" cried Anna.

"Oh, sweetheart!" Aunt Eve exclaimed. "That dress is gorgeous on you! And it shows off your lovely figure!"

"It's okay," I said, looking at myself in the three-way mirror, turning so that I could see the effect of the low-cut back. The dress skimmed my body, and the high neck was fluted so that my clavicle bones were visible on each side. I looked different in this dress, elegant, as if I should be wearing a tumble of pearls and clutching a cigarette in a long holder, like Audrey Hepburn in *Breakfast at Tiffany's*, a movie Aunt Eve had introduced to Anna and me, saying it had always been one of her favorites, even though she thought Mickey Rooney as Mr. Yunioshi was "a cringe."

Aunt Eve stared at me for a moment. "Sarah, honey," she said, her voice soft. "May I buy it for you?"

Of course I said yes. Of course I was thrilled. And of course I didn't tell my mom that Aunt Eve paid for the dress. I thought of offering Aunt Eve the money that Mom had given me, but I knew she would refuse it. What was a hundred dollars to Aunt Eve? Instead, I cut off the price tag and told Mom I got the dress on sale. I was positive Aunt Eve wouldn't mention anything about it, and I was right. She never did. I hid the hundred-dollar bill deep in my sock drawer. I felt guilty and I had no idea what to do with it.

On the day of the prom, Anna picked me up early and drove me back to her house, where we would get dressed. Anna had spent the afternoon at Van Michael Salon, having her hair shaped into curls so fat and springy I could not help but pull one. "Quit it," said Anna, playfully slapping my hand away. "You'll mess them up."

Mom walked out to the car with us, holding my makeup bag in her hand. "You two have fun," she said. "And make sure you don't do anything that could result in pregnancy."

"Jesus, Mom!" I said. I rolled my eyes but did not state the obvious, that Anna was planning to save herself for marriage and I certainly was not going to have prom sex with George Simmons.

"Sorry, Sarah, but it had to be said."

"Bye, Mom."

"Bye, sweetheart," she said, giving me a quick hug. "Be good."

Mom would not be at Aunt Eve's to see us off, though Chip's and George's parents would, drinking wine and taking photos. One of Mom's clients had just had his execution date scheduled, and she was swamped with work on his appeal, was planning, in fact, to pull an all-nighter. But it wasn't just work that kept her from the send-off party at Aunt Eve's. Most Coventry parents made her uncomfortable. They didn't share her politics, her frugality, or her sense of humor. Also, she would be the only one there without a husband.

After what seemed like hours of standing around and taking pictures—of each couple, of just Anna and me, of just Chip and George, and of the entire group—we finally piled into the limo the boys had sprung for and made a slow progression down Anna's steep driveway. As soon as we turned off Anna's street, George and Chip pulled out a plastic bottle of vodka, an engraved silver flask filled with bourbon, and a six-pack of strawberry wine coolers. Anna and I each took a wine cooler. George handed the limo driver a mixtape he had made for the occasion. As soon as the driver pushed it into the cassette player, the opening scream of Guns N' Roses' "Welcome to the Jungle" blasted out and Chip and George gave each other a high five. Anna and I laughed at what dorks they were.

All I remember about the dance itself was trying to avoid talking to any of the teachers, who were mandated to turn you in if it was obvious you had been drinking. Eventually, we headed to the official after party, a casino-themed extravaganza held at some rec center, with blackjack, poker, and craps tables. You played for lottery tickets, which you then entered into drawings for various prizes. Lizzie, who looked awesome in a floor-length yellow vintage dress, begged for my winning tickets. I gave them to her and she stuffed them, along with every other begged and borrowed ticket she could manage to get her hands on, into the drawing for a private flying lesson.

There was a DJ at the casino party, and when Tone-Loc's "Wild Thing" came on, George pulled me onto the dance floor, his groin pressing into mine. He had taken off his bow tie and his eyes were red. He tried to kiss me, but I turned my head away and he did not try again. I scanned the crowd for Dean, my crush. The other day at school he had told me that I was the smartest girl he knew.

"Girl?" I had joked. "You have to qualify your compliment by gender?"

"You don't understand," he said. "I live with my mom and my aunt Linda. It's a total matriarchy at my house. A smart woman is like the highest form of intelligence."

I was flattered. Especially because his girlfriend, Zoe, was brilliant—brilliant and beautiful, with her black hair cut in a severe bob, her heart-shaped lips always painted bright red. Zoe starred in all of the school plays and was headed to Yale in the fall. I was looking forward to the following year, when she would be more than a thousand miles away. But that was months from now, and that night whenever I saw the two of them together they were touching, his hand on the small of her back, her arm wrapped around his waist. It occurred to me that not only had they surely had sex, but they were *lovers*.

At some point Lizzie won the flying lesson. At some point I went outside with George and Chip and drank bourbon from George's flask. At some point we left the casino party and headed to someone's house whose parents were out of town, the same place Lizzie and Sake were also headed. Maybe it was one of their dates' houses; I don't recall. All I remember is sitting on a well-worn couch with Anna in a basement with wall-to-wall carpeting. And then I looked up and saw Dean, sans Zoe, getting a glass of water from the little basement kitchenette and then walking down the hall toward the sliding glass door that led outside.

I nudged Anna and pointed to Dean. She looked at me with wide eyes. "Go get 'em, tiger," she said.

"Grrr," I answered.

"Dork!"

I stood and followed Dean down the hall and out into the fenced backyard. A security light spotlighted my crush. His tux fit him well. He looked comfortable in it, like a grown man at a wedding, not like a kid playing dress-up.

"Hey!" I said.

"Hey," he said, smiling at me. "Nice dress. Understated."

"Thanks. Where's Zoe?" I was drunk enough to be bold.

"Home. She'd had enough forced revelry for one evening."

"She's not going to the breakfast?"

There was a breakfast at six that morning, still a few hours away, an annual thing that the Coventry moms hosted. Aunt Eve would be there with her famous French toast casserole.

"Zoe doesn't eat breakfast."

I wasn't sure, but it almost sounded as if he was mocking her.

"How sophisticated. Does she survive solely on coffee and cigarettes?"

He smiled. "Something like that."

"I guess it's going to be hard on y'all next year."

"Well, she's already told me that she doesn't want to be attached to anyone when she heads to New Haven, so I wouldn't worry too much about Zoetrope. She'll find someone to keep her warm."

"Oh," I said, and I moved a little closer to him. "That sucks. I'm sorry."

"Don't be," he said, and he smiled, squeezing my arm for just a minute before he glanced at his watch and said he had to go.

"Wait, why? Aren't you going to the breakfast?"

"Nope. I'm tired of being around drunk people. I'm going to stop at Waffle House on my way home, get an egg sandwich. Wanna come?"

I did. I really, really did. "Let me just tell my friends, okay?"

"Sure. I'll meet you by my car. It's the extremely sexy powder-blue mini-van parked in front of the house, Gwinnett County license tags and all."

"Gwinnett is definitely sexy," I said, acknowledging Dean's dig on the unfashionable suburb where he lived. But in my head I was thinking, *Oh my God, oh my God, oh my God.* I was going to go to breakfast with Dean. I was going to eat an egg and cheese sandwich with him! I couldn't wait to tell Anna, though I had a feeling she would disapprove of me leaving prom with someone other than my date. But it wasn't as if George and I were a couple.

I returned to the basement where she and I had been sitting, but she was no longer there. Chip was slumped on the couch with his eyes closed, bow tie in hand.

"Hey, Chip," I said, but he didn't respond. I put my hand on his forearm and shook it. He opened his eyes, blinked.

"Huh?" he mumbled.

"Do you know where Anna is?"

He yawned, shook his head. "I think she went to lie down? Or maybe she went outside. Some guys are smoking a joint out there."

Anna might have an occasional wine cooler, but there was no way she would smoke a joint. I left Chip and went to the bathroom to see if Anna was in there. The door was locked, and no one answered when I knocked. I knocked again, and I heard Sake call, "Just a minute!" And then she and Lizzie stumbled out, the straps of Lizzie's yellow dress haphazardly placed. "Are you okay?" I asked, thinking that maybe Lizzie had gotten sick.

"I'm fine. Just too much tequila," said Lizzie.

"Have you seen Anna?" I asked.

"I think she went to lay down," said Sake.

"Lie," corrected Lizzie. "Lie down."

"Oh my God, you're so annoying!" said Sake, but she said it in a gushing, flirty way. "Let's go see if Robert has another joint."

I had a strange sense as I watched them walk off, something about the way they were interacting with each other. It reminded me of Dean and Zoe, how he casually placed his hand on her waist, his knowledge of her body a foregone conclusion. And then it dawned on me, quickly and without warning: They had been making out in the bathroom. *Oh God.* Were they *lovers?* Did that mean they were gay? Did people think *I* was gay for hanging out with them? Or was I their camouflage, let into their friendship for the sake of optics, so people wouldn't suspect them of being a couple? But no. Sake and Lizzie loved me. I was sure of that. But they probably loved each other more.

I stood alone for a moment, feeling an odd sense of abandonment, but then I remembered that I was supposed to be going to breakfast with Dean—Dean!—that is, unless he had already left. I contemplated leaving right then, maybe scribbling a note and leaving it on Chip's chest for Anna to find whenever she returned from wherever she was. There was a short hallway off the bathroom that led to several doors, which I presumed were bedrooms. I would check in each of them to see if Anna had fallen asleep on one of the beds, and if I still didn't find her I would go. I opened the first door. No Anna, just a neatly made bed. I pushed open the second door. There was George, bent over the foot of the bed. He turned to look at me, the whites of his eyes visible in the dark. He looked panicked. It took me a moment to realize why. It took me a moment to realize anything, to make sense of the scene I had stumbled upon.

Anna was on the bed, on her back, her legs hanging off the end. Her eyes were closed and her cheek was turned to the side, as if she were sleeping. Her pink sequined dress was hiked around her waist and she didn't have on any underwear, a fact I could deduce even in the unlit room.

"What are you doing?" I asked dumbly.

"I was just looking," George said.

"She's passed out," I said slowly, still uncertain of what I was witnessing.

"It just happened. We were kissing and then she passed out—like, just now."

"Oh my God," I said.

"I swear to God, Sarah, I wasn't doing anything. I didn't even realize she'd passed out, I swear."

He was standing upright now, in his tuxedo pants, cummerbund, and white shirt. Did he pull up his pants in between my opening the door and this moment? I did not know. I could not make sense of anything. He was so tall. He was so much taller than either Anna or me. He was looking at me plaintively, his eyes huge and scared. "Don't say anything, okay? You can't say anything. We'd all get in trouble for drinking. We'd all get kicked out."

I couldn't think. I couldn't think with Anna half-dressed and passed out and George towering above me in his tuxedo, begging me not to say anything. What was it, exactly, that I wasn't supposed to say? I didn't know. I didn't know what I had walked in on. I didn't know what had happened before I walked in. All I knew was that I needed a minute. I needed to catch my breath.

"Just leave me alone with Anna for a minute, okay? It's going to be all right. I just need to be alone with Anna."

"You're the best, Sarah," he said before slipping out of the room, leaving me with Anna, who had not yet stirred.

I sat on the bed beside her. My eyes had adjusted to the dimness of the room, lit only by the glow of a streetlight coming in through the window. I stared at the window. The blinds were open. This seemed important. If George had intended to rape her, wouldn't he have closed the blinds?

I put my hand on Anna's shoulder, bare except for the thin pink strap of her dress. How was she this drunk? I had never seen Anna this drunk. She rarely drank, and when she did she would have one or two wine coolers and then dance wildly to Madonna.

I turned on the overhead light, hoping it would rouse her. It did not. I found Anna's panties crumpled on the floor. They were bright pink, to match her outfit. Her bra was bright pink, too. On the same day that Aunt Eve had bought both of our prom dresses, we had gone to Victoria's Secret to look for coordinating underwear, not to be sexy, but because southern girls match at every level. I hadn't purchased anything, saying that I already had black underwear at home.

When Aunt Eve was handing her credit card to the cashier at Victoria's Secret, did she have any notion that a boy might see the bra and panties she was purchasing for her daughter? My own mother's advice had certainly acknowledged the possibility of sex on prom night, and I had laughed away the suggestion, knowing that I was not going to have prom night sex with George Simmons. But George might have had sex with Anna, while she was passed out. Did I walk in on a rape? I had the sudden thought to bend down and sniff her vagina, to see if it smelled of semen, which I had heard smelled of bleach. But what if someone were to walk in? What if someone were to think I was doing the same things with Anna that Lizzie and Sake were probably doing with each other in the bathroom? I mean, I knew it was okay to be a lesbian—Mom had certainly schooled me on "the beautiful diversity of sexual desire" during our sex talks—but it wouldn't fly at Coventry, at least not with Anna's more mainstream crowd. I pushed the button on the door handle to lock it and then shook Anna's shoulders again, less gently this time, determined to wake her. It took a fair amount of jostling, but finally her eyes flickered and she looked at me, only half there.

"Where are we?" she finally asked.

"I'm not sure," I said. "Someone's house. Will's, maybe? Listen, Anna, do you remember anything that happened with George tonight?"

"I'm so thirsty," she said. "Can you get me a glass of water?"

"I will. In a minute. I promise. But first we have to figure something out. Look, I don't know how to tell you this, but I came in here a few minutes ago and George, well, George was in here and your underwear was on the floor and your dress was pulled up around your waist."

"What?"

"Your underwear was off. He said he was just 'looking.' He said he was just curious."

"I don't understand."

"He had your underwear off, Anna. He said he was just looking down there, but I don't actually know what he did."

"Looking at what?"

"Down there. Your . . . you know." Mom had used the word "vagina" with me ever since I was little, but I was having a hard time saying it to Anna, as if she would think I was being crude. Or maybe it was just that to say it would make the situation real.

"Wait, my rhymes with Carolina?"

"Yeah."

I was trying not to cry, but it was all so awful. We were all so drunk. And Lizzie and Sake might be some sort of a couple—a couple without me. And something horrible had happened to Anna with my prom date, in the home of someone I didn't even know, in some crappy basement. And Anna had no memory of what happened. George could have done anything.

I thought again of how semen was supposed to smell of bleach.

"Do you think you could put your finger in your—in your vagina and let me smell it?"

"*What?*"

"Just do it, Anna. Trust me."

"You're weird," she murmured, but then she sighed and did as I asked, and I remember thinking, *Compliant.* Anna was always compliant. When I smelled her finger, I did not pick up on any bleachy smell, thank God, but I did see a small spot of blood. *Oh God.* What did it mean that I saw blood?

Did it mean he jammed a finger inside her with enough force to make her bleed? Did it mean he jammed his penis inside her but didn't ejaculate?

"Are you sore?" I asked. "Do you hurt?"

Wasn't it supposed to hurt the first time you had sex?

"I'm just really thirsty."

There was a bathroom connected to the room. I found some paper cups in the medicine cabinet, filled one, and ran warm water on a washcloth. I brought both to Anna, who was sitting up on the edge of the bed, her dress now properly on. She took a sip from the cup, then put the cloth against her head. I had been thinking she would use it to clean herself.

"I can't believe I passed out."

"How much did you drink?" I asked.

She shrugged. "Um, the wine coolers in the limo, then something at the casino party, and then whatever was in George's flask."

"Bourbon," I said. Unless he had given her something else.

"Oh my God," Anna said, looking stricken. "I must have cheated on Stuart."

"Jesus, Anna, you did not cheat on Stuart. You were passed-out drunk. George took advantage of you. God, he *assaulted* you."

"I've known George Simmons forever. He didn't assault me."

"Anna, listen to me. George hiked up your dress and took off your underwear. And we don't actually know what he did then."

"That doesn't make any sense," she mumbled.

And then she leaned over and threw up on the floor.

Later, after I got Anna and the carpet relatively cleaned up and after we both sobered up a little, we attended the breakfast. I did not know what else to do. George had left whoever's house we were at, and so had Dean, Sake, and Lizzie, but someone had a car that Chip, Anna, and I piled into. I stayed by Anna's side the whole time. Pale and shaky, she drank Sprite after Sprite but only nibbled on a little fruit, whereas I gorged on Aunt Eve's French toast casserole, brioche soaked in custard, then baked with blueberries and served with maple syrup. Aunt Eve, who was there helping to serve, smiled at us from across the room and gave a little wave but kept her distance, not wanting to catch us with alcohol on our breath, I imagine. Eventually, a girl Anna knew from Young Life offered to give us a ride home. Before Anna got out of the car, I hugged her.

"Call me tonight," I whispered. "We'll figure it out."

Chapter 19

WILDERNESS ADVENTURE

Atlanta, 1990

Anna did not call that weekend, and I didn't call her, either, thinking that she needed a little time to process what had happened. But the Monday after prom, after Mom and I ate Stouffer's French bread pizzas in front of the *PBS NewsHour*, I borrowed Mom's car and drove to Anna's house. Not that she was expecting me. Uncle Bob answered the door with a surprised grin, proclaimed that I looked just as pretty as I had on prom night, and said that Anna was upstairs studying. Once upstairs I turned right at the hall, which took me to Anna's room. Her door was closed, and on the handle hung a small sign that read: *"Un peu d'intimité, s'il vous plaît,"* which had surely been picked up in Paris, where Anna and her parents had gone for spring break.

I knocked just to let her know I was coming in, and then pushed open the door. Anna was sitting on her bed, leaning against an oversized pillow covered in a floral sham. The duvet on her bed was in the same floral pattern. On the wall across from her bed was a corkboard pinned with hundreds of photos of Anna laughing with friends. I was only in a few of the pictures, which stung, even though I had been the one to drift away from her group and attach myself to Lizzie and Sake.

"Move over, bacon," I said.

Anna did not acknowledge my reference to the old Sizzlean commercial, only wordlessly moved over a few inches as I kicked off my shoes and climbed up onto her antique wrought-iron bed, a family heirloom given to her on her sixteenth birthday, along with an opal and diamond ring that had once been her mother's, and a new Honda Civic. It had been a while since I had last spent the night at Anna's, but I imagined the sheets were still soft and clean and smelled subtly of lavender. And her pillows—at least the non-decorative ones—were packed tight with goose down.

I sat so close to Anna that our arms touched. Her skin was tanner than mine.

"How are you?" I asked, trying to sound concerned but not pitying.

"Busy. Trying to figure out something to say about Elizabeth Bennet." She held a clicker pen in one hand and a notebook in the other. *Pride and Prejudice* lay facedown on the comforter. Like me, Anna was a top student, but she was in a different section of honors English than I was and my class had already completed its unit on Jane Austen. I had received an A on my paper, in which I argued that in Austen's world a woman's single moment of power was when she chose a husband. Get tripped up by lust or impulse and your life was, if not ruined, limited.

"Can we talk about what happened on Friday?"

She turned and looked at me with a blank face. "I don't know what happened on Friday. I don't remember anything. I'm just glad it's no longer Friday and we can put it behind us."

"Look, I think we should turn George in. I don't think they'll kick us out for drinking in light of the circumstances, and even if they did . . . well, it would suck, but we would deal with it. We could write our college application essays on choosing justice over our own self-interest, you know?"

Anna clicked the top of her pen over and over, making the tip pop out, then recede.

"I can't believe you would even consider using this experience for your college essay. Wow. That's just . . . that's just *rotten*."

She was crying, tears spilling down her cheeks.

"Oh my God, that's not what I meant! I just meant if we got kicked out, we'd figure out a way to make things okay. That's all."

She turned to face me straight on and I turned to face her, too, so that now my knees grazed against hers. She had a bright red pimple on her cheek, rare for Anna, or at least rare for Anna to show herself without any makeup on to cover it. "Listen," she said. "You have got to promise me, swear to me, that you won't tell anyone about this. Not anyone at school, not Lizzie, not your mom. You have to promise."

"And just let George get away with it?"

"Don't you understand that he's going to get away with it no matter what? Think about it: If we turned him in, at most he would get kicked out of Coventry for drinking. He's not going to face any other punishment. It's not like we have a criminal case against him. He was in the room with me with my underwear off. That's all you saw, and anyway, he could just deny it, say that it wasn't true."

"You were passed out on the bed and he was bent over you."

She didn't respond. I tried again. "UVA might rescind their offer of admission."

"Yeah, and all of his friends would hate me if that happened, and so would his mom, who I've known my whole life. The truth is, we were all drunk, and I don't even remember any of it. The only thing I know for sure is that if we turned him in, I would be the one who got punished. I would be humiliated—again—and we would probably get kicked out. And Sarah, I know you've only been at Coventry since sophomore year, but I've been going there since I was five years old, and damn it, I am not going to get kicked out because of something George Simmons may or may not have done! You have to promise me you won't tell anyone. You have to promise."

She was gripping my forearms tightly, her face a mess of tears and snot. There was a box of tissues on her bedside table. I wanted to get one for her, but I didn't want to pull away while she was holding on to me.

"Can I get you a Kleenex?" I finally asked.

"Yeah," she said, between choking little sobs.

I reached toward the box and handed one to her. She blew her nose, folded up the tissue, and then blew into it again. "Can I have another?" she asked.

I handed her another one. She wrapped it around her index finger and used the dressed finger to dig out a huge booger. She held it up for me to see. "I picked something special just for you," she said, alluding to a birthday card I gave her when she turned thirteen, which showed a little boy with a booger on his finger.

"Gross," I said.

"Yeah," she said, sniffing.

"Anna," I said. "I promise I won't tell anyone if you don't want me to. But I really want you to think about this some more."

"Do you think I've thought about anything else? Sarah, I *hate* that this happened. But I'm not going to let George ruin the rest of my time at Coventry. We're seniors next year and there's so much to look forward to and I just refuse to be dragged down by all of this during my final year of school. Can't you understand that?"

I could. And I admit there was a part of me that was relieved that Anna didn't want me to tell anyone at Coventry about what I had witnessed on prom night. Anna's determination to keep everything under wraps kept me safe, too.

I did not see Anna at all that summer. She had enrolled, last minute, in an outdoor leadership course trekking through the Rockies, leaving for Colorado two days after school let out. She *had* been looking forward to summer in Atlanta because Stuart would be home from Episcopal and they could spend their days making eyes at each other while swimming laps at the Driving Club, or batting a tennis ball back and forth across the net, or playing squash, or doing whatever else they did to help them avoid the temptation of going off somewhere alone and having sex. But instead she broke up with Stuart over the phone that spring, saying that she just couldn't handle the long distance anymore.

Anna returned from Colorado ten pounds thinner and with her blond hair cut to her chin. Dean and I had started dating over the summer, news I was nervous about sharing with Anna considering that our relationship had really gotten its start on prom night. But Anna was her usual exuberant self when I told her that we were a couple. "I'm so happy for you!" she enthused. Lizzie and Sake also liked Dean. They thought he was wry, and occasionally the four of us would all hang out together. But the truth was that more and more I found myself wanting to spend time alone with him, which was surely all right with Lizzie and Sake because it meant they could go off on their own, too.

That fall, Anna dropped the cheerleading squad and she kept dropping weight, even though she was no longer burning a million calories a day practicing cheer routines. She took to wearing dark clothes: black jeans, black T-shirts, gray sweaters, despite Aunt Eve's urging that she liven things up a little with a colorful purse or scarf. She drifted from her popular, earnest friends and started hanging out with Redburn Connor, who was known to light up a cigarette the instant his car turned off campus. I liked Redburn; we were in AP history together and I thought he was funny, especially when he asked if the London cabbies who drove soldiers to the front lines during World War II were paid a fare. But he was Anna's polar opposite: an avowed atheist, an LSD enthusiast, and one of two members of Coventry's Young Socialists Club.

That Anna was hanging out with an atheist druggie was not as unusual as it might seem but, rather, matched the pattern of blurred lines that defined the social dynamics of our class in its senior year. The captain of the football team auditioned for, and was cast in, the school play. The home-coming queen—Anna was on the court but was not crowned queen—broke up with him not because of his thespian impulses, but rather so that she could date a wiry junior who was on the fencing team. The closer we got to graduation, the more the hierarchy seemed to be breaking down, and nowhere was that more apparent than at Chastain Memorial Park on a Saturday night, where the bulk of our class often wound up, parking our cars in the lot by the stone pavilion, where there was a fire pit and, beyond that, acres of woods.

I don't know how it was that a sizable group of minors could gather in the wooded area of a large suburban park, build a bonfire, play loud music, and drink for hours without drawing the attention of the authorities, but most likely it had something to do with the sea of "Coventry" bumper stickers on the backs of our cars—protecting us even from the Atlanta police, who surely did not want to deal with entitled prep school kids any more than they wanted to deal with their powerful, entitled parents. In any event, we gathered at the park nearly every weekend of our senior year, playing the B-52s and R.E.M. from our car stereos, warming ourselves by the fire, venturing into the woods, either to kiss or to pee.

There was an older man who would sometimes show up, a rugged, athletic-looking guy with bushy silver hair and a thick beard. Dean and I called him Mountain Man because the first time we saw him he looked as if he had just come from hiking the Appalachian Trail, what with his oversized backpack, dusty boots, and flannel shirt. Initially, Mountain Man lingered on the periphery of our gatherings, but eventually he drew closer. One night Dean and I talked to him at length. He implored us to read some book called *The Sociological Imagination*, explaining that it had helped him jettison the corporate life in order to live in the woods with no possessions other than what he carried on his back. He claimed to have once been an executive at Coca-Cola but to have burnt out on corporate America, on its "shortsightedness, greed, and bullshit macho culture." And then he made direct eye contact with me and said, "Speaking of bullshit macho culture, don't let this guy pressure you into doing anything you don't want to do."

"Excuse me?" I asked, indignant. If anything, *I* was the one pressuring Dean.

"I'm just saying there's this insidious thing that gets passed from one generation to the next—believe me, I know—where boys are taught that in order to be a real man they have to dominate a woman, whether by force or by putting her onto such a high pedestal that she can't move. But that's bullshit. A real man respects a woman's choices. A real man isn't afraid of a strong woman."

"Um, okay," I said. "Thanks for the tutorial on Feminism 101."

"Do you consider yourself a feminist?" he asked, his eyes lighting up.

"Well, yeah," I said, though I'd never claimed the title before. "Weaned on *Our Bodies, Ourselves.*"

This was not exactly true. Yes, Mom had a copy of *Our Bodies, Ourselves* that she kept on the bookshelf by her bed, but she never showed it to me or encouraged me to look at it. In fact, the few times I'd flipped through it—usually to gawk at the up-close photos of women giving birth—were times she wasn't at home. But I wanted to show up Mountain Man, to prove I wasn't some clueless prep.

"Right on!" he cheered. "I didn't know kids still read that!"

A few Saturdays later, we spotted Mountain Man at Chastain again, this time talking to Redburn Connor and Anna near the bonfire. I thought about going over and joining them, if for no other reason than to see if Redburn and Mountain Man were duking it out to see who hated corporate America more. But I was waiting for Dean, who'd gone in search of more beer. From where I stood, it looked like Mountain Man was doing all of the talking, which seemed par for the course. But then Anna said something, animatedly. Maybe she was responding to Mountain Man having asked her if she was a feminist. I remembered once hearing Anna say that feminists were "just bitter women with hairy armpits who couldn't get dates," which was probably a line she picked up from one of the talk radio shows her dad listened to. But that was a while ago. Maybe her feelings had changed because of George, her summer spent hiking in Colorado, her friendship with Redburn. It occurred to me that I didn't really know Anna anymore.

Dean walked up holding a Busch tall boy and offered me a sip.

"I have to pee first. Will you come and keep an eye out?"

I didn't like to venture into the woods alone. I knew too many details of grisly murders, thanks to Mom's work with men on death row, all of whom, obviously, were not innocent.

We walked into the woods and away from the bonfire and the various clusters of people from Coventry.

"Is he for real?" I asked.

"Who?"

"Mountain Man."

"Yes. He definitely exists."

"I *mean*, do you think he was really a Coca-Cola exec who dropped out of the 'rat race'?"

"It's possible. Your mom quit her job at a corporate law firm."

"Yeah, but she didn't just quit working; she immediately took another job."

"Maybe he made enough money not to have to work anymore."

"But if Mountain Man really had enough money just to quit and not find other work, what's he doing here? Why spend his time hiking around Chastain Park? Why not go to a private island somewhere, or at least go hiking in the actual mountains?"

I almost tripped over a tree root, but Dean caught me and then kept his hand on my arm. I liked the way Dean smelled, both earthy and sweet, like the smell of freshly baked sourdough bread, which the woman who was currently renting our basement apartment made each week.

"Maybe he has someone in Atlanta who keeps him here," Dean said. "A sick mother or a kid."

"You're like a dog with a bone. Tenacious."

"Nice SAT word," said Dean.

"My mom is going out of town in two weeks," I said, blurting out what I had been both nervous and excited to tell him all night.

"Oh, really?"

Dean held back a branch with thorns on it so I wouldn't get stung as I walked past it.

"There's some ACLU conference in D.C. She's on a panel or something. Do you want to spend the night?"

He glanced at me, smiled. "Yes. I want."

We had not yet had sex, but the night before he had come over to my house to watch a movie and afterward, once we were sure Mom had gone to bed, he had pulled down the straps of my tank top, which I wore without a bra. He put my right breast into his mouth, kissing and sucking the nipple, before moving on to the left one. It felt so good, so startling. I kept think-ing, *How does he know to do this?*

"I think this is far enough," I said. "Turn around."

I pulled down my shorts and underwear and squatted. It took a minute for my pee to start because I was self-conscious about Dean being so near, but eventually it did. A little splashed on my Birkenstocks, which I chose to ignore.

I stood and pulled my underwear and shorts back on. "Okay."

Dean turned back toward me. He smiled and I smiled back, holding his gaze. In two weeks he would sleep over at my house and we could do whatever we wanted in my mother's queen-size bed. Mine was just a twin and not really big enough for the two of us.

I stepped up close to him, took in his familiar smell, ran my hand along his cheek, which was rough with stubble. "Hi," I said.

And then we heard the crunching of dead leaves and turned to see Anna walking in our direction, a burly figure heading the opposite way. In the moonlight I could make out his plaid flannel shirt.

"Hey! Anna! Over here."

Anna walked toward us, her short hair clipped back on each side with a little barrette, making her look like a young girl.

"Were you out here with Mountain Man?" I asked, not meaning to sound as judgmental as I did.

"I was with Miles, if that's what you mean."

"Oh, he's Miles now?" I asked.

"That's his name," she said. Mountain Man had actually told me that, but I hadn't bothered to remember. He was a caricature, someone interesting to talk to in a group, to muse about with Dean, certainly not someone to go alone with into the woods.

"Jesus, Anna, you have to be more careful. He's super creepy."

"Oh gee, thanks, Sarah," she said. "It's *awesome* how good you are at keeping me safe and sound."

She stormed off, back in the direction of the bonfire.

I turned toward Dean. "Oh my God."

"What was that about?"

"She's losing it. I have to tell her mom."

And then I told Dean about what George had done to her or, at least, the part of it I saw.

The next afternoon, after what seemed like hours, I finally heard the sound of the key in the lock. I ran to the front door to greet Mom, who looked sad and weary.

"Well?" I said.

"It didn't go quite as I expected," she said.

"Was she mad at me for not having said something sooner?"

"No, she wasn't. Come with me to the kitchen. I'd like a glass of wine. Would you like to have a small one with me?"

Mom had never offered me wine before. I had so much homework left to do, but how could I refuse this moment? "Um, sure."

We went to the kitchen, where Mom pulled an open bottle of white Zinfandel from the refrigerator. "Eve already knew about what happened with George," she said, reaching for two glasses from the cabinet above the dishwasher.

"What? Then why hasn't anything happened?"

Mom poured us each half a glass, then hesitated and filled them all the way. "Let's not make this a habit," she said, handing my glass to me.

"Did Anna tell her? When? After she got back from her wilderness thing?"

"Anna told her last spring, the morning after prom. Eve said that Anna was terrified of getting kicked out of Coventry over what happened, and Eve agreed that Anna shouldn't subject herself to possible expulsion over 'one bad night,' that Anna would be punished more than George, and that the best thing Anna could do was to move on, to not let George's actions ruin her senior year, especially since George would have already graduated, meaning she wouldn't have to worry about running into him at school."

I could hear the distaste in Mom's voice. I took a sip of my pale pink wine and then took another.

"It was Eve who suggested Anna go to Colorado. She thought a summer spent hiking would help Anna recover, would sort of wash the slate clean."

"Did she at least tell George's mom about what happened? I mean, they're friends. And neighbors! She sees her all the time."

"I doubt it, sweetie."

"But that's just awful. Why would Aunt Eve let George get away with doing that to her daughter?"

"I think she felt that she was protecting Anna by letting it go, protecting her from scandal, I guess, and from whatever backlash there might be were George to face expulsion or lose his college admission. A part of me thinks that she didn't really want to deal with the scandal, either, but I'm hoping that wasn't the case. She said she thought the mountains would clear Anna's head, but she realizes now that Anna needs therapy."

"Well, that's good at least. God, I don't think I like Aunt Eve very much right now."

Mom sighed. "Eve is the most fragmented person I know. She has all of these parts of herself locked away that she can't bear to look at."

"Like what?"

Mom was quiet for so long that I began to wonder if she had heard my question. Just as I was about to ask again, she spoke. "That's probably not mine to share, sweetie. But I suppose what I'm trying to say about Eve is that it's easy to fall short of your ideals."

"Do I?"

"Of course not," said Mom. "You're nerfect."

It was a joke between the two of us, a reference to the little figurine I had given her for Mother's Day years ago, before my father died. It was shaped sort of like a peanut with legs, arms, and googly eyes. A plaque on its base read: "Pobody's Nerfect."

Mom hugged me and kissed the top of my head, told me I was her brave girl and that she was so sorry Anna had experienced what she did. I leaned into her, breathing in the familiar scent of her perfume, a mix of essential oils that smelled of orange blossom and clove.

Chapter 20

OUR BODIES, OURSELVES

Atlanta, 1990

"Remember, Eve said you are welcome to come over to their house if you get lonely," Mom said, zipping up her carry-on suitcase.

"I'll be fine, I promise. I have to finish my personal statement, and if I stay with Anna I won't get any work done. Aunt Eve would keep barging into our room with a soufflé or something."

Mom smiled distractedly before checking her purse one more time to make sure it contained her airline ticket. "Well, call Eve if you need anything. And Pat said she'd keep an eye out for you while I'm gone."

Pat, our next-door neighbor, was a single woman in her fifties who taught art at the White Oak school and was fond of whimsical scarves and goddess statues. I doubted Pat would care about Dean coming over, but I made a mental note to tell Dean to park his car down the street so Pat wouldn't notice it in the driveway.

I watched Mom wrap her own scarf around her neck. She looked pretty. Her skin glowed and her cheekbones seemed more prominent. She had started taking classes at Pierce Yoga, and I supposed the effects of her practice were beginning to show.

"You look nice," I said.

She grinned. "Thank you, sweetheart! Now remember, I'm staying at the Days Inn Connecticut Ave. The number is written on the notepad in the kitchen."

"Got it. I'm really going to be fine. And we should go."

After I returned home from dropping Mom off at the airport, I sat at the kitchen table working on my personal statement for college applications, just as I said I would—at least until 8:00 p.m., when Dean was coming over. I was trying to figure out how to write about the death of my father in a meaningful way, to show how his death had shaped me. But how to write about it and not seem opportunistic, as if I were playing the "Dead Dad Card"?

I had spoken with my therapist, Ruth, about this during our last session. Ruth suggested I focus on a specific memory of my dad, like how the two of us would go for walks on Sunday mornings at Johnson Estates, the woods near our house. (It was usually just the two of us, as Mom would either sleep in or go to services at the UUCA.) Ruth said the memory could be a totally ordinary one, but that if I allowed my mind to concentrate on the specifics I would surely unearth some detail that encapsulated something true about our relationship, something true about his love for me, even if he was often distracted by his own work.

It was a good idea, but I was having trouble focusing on any one memory of my father. Instead, I kept thinking about something else Ruth had said during that session. We had moved on to the subject of anxiety and how I might not ever get rid of mine, but how I could learn to live with it. I mentioned that Mom believed my anxiety was rooted in Dad's sudden death and how that was true, of course, but that some of my anxiety was connected to the life the two of us shared: how I worried there would never be enough money, how I was haunted by some of Mom's cases, how excruciating it was to witness Mom get wrapped up in the fates of men who were most likely going to die in the electric chair.

"Yet would you want a different mother?" Ruth had prodded, gently.

I had thought of Aunt Eve and how I used to wish Mom were more like her, with her bubbly personality and her open wallet, always ready to buy Anna and me little gifts. And then I thought of that day last July, when Mom had invited me to accompany a group from the Southern Center for Human Rights to Jackson State Prison to greet Leroy Evans upon his release.

Leroy Evans was a client of hers who had been sentenced to die fifteen years earlier for a murder he could not possibly have committed, for a number of reasons. For one, he was the pit master at a church BBQ during the time of the murder. Literally dozens of people could vouch for him, and several did just that, under oath. But the white prosecuting attorney, by God, needed a conviction. And the sworn testimony of black witnesses clearly held no sway with the all-white jury who declared Leroy Evans guilty. After years dedicated to his case, Mom and her team had gotten his conviction overturned. And so we showed up to greet Mr. Evans as he took his first steps as a freed man. We cheered and wept as he walked out from behind the metal fence, wearing the navy suit my mother had brought for him, a shy smile on his face, tears rolling down his cheeks. And there was my mother beside him, my mother who had driven down to Jackson State hours earlier, in order to accompany him through his release, to stay by his side and assure him that yes, it was really happening.

It occurred to me that maybe I should write my essay about my mom, about how I used to resent her for taking on such hard things, especially after such a hard thing had happened to us with the death of my dad. But I was beginning to realize that Mom had taught me something essential: That sometimes it *is* possible to right a wrong, but you have to work for it. Justice does not simply show up on its own, gliding in on the wings of platitudes. Had Mom not *worked* as tirelessly as she did, Leroy Evans might well have been put to death by the state. But he wasn't. He was not.

And then my mind shifted to thoughts of Dean and what would happen once he arrived. I was planning on losing my virginity, on that very night! Would I seem different afterward? Would something about me exude "woman" instead of "girl"? Would I have an extra stride in my step, a deep knowing in my eyes? Would Mom be able to tell when she came home from her trip to D.C.?

And would it feel good? Would I have an orgasm? *Our Bodies, Ourselves*, which I had revisited after my last conversation with Mountain Man, said that women often don't climax the first time. And a few weeks earlier, Mom—after remarking that I certainly was "spending a lot of time with Dean"—had launched into a mortifying discussion about sex, during which she told me that it took her a little while to learn how to "be fully satisfied," but that finally she and my father tried it with her on top and something clicked. At that point I had covered my ears and yelled, "Stop talking! Stop talking!"

I closed my notebook, as I had stopped jotting down ideas for my essay and instead had started doodling Dean's name all over the page. I wished, suddenly, for a sibling to confide in. A sister. Anna and I used to think of ourselves as sisters, but even if she and I had been on good terms, I would never talk to her about this. Sex was too fraught a subject. Not just because of George, but also because she would probably say I should wait until marriage. I thought briefly of calling Lizzie—but I didn't really want to talk about sex with her, because that would open the door to talking about her and Sake, and for some reason I just felt really uncomfortable doing that. I *knew* it was okay for them to be together, but I just didn't really want to think about it.

I glanced at my watch. It was 6:45. Dean would arrive in an hour and fifteen minutes. I had a sundress I wanted to change into that I had bought from a shop in Little Five Points. It was made of soft white cotton and printed with little pink strawberries. Really, it was too summery for an October night, but I didn't care. I stood from my seat at the kitchen table and went to my room, standing in front of the full-length mirror mounted on the back of the closet door. Here I was. Seventeen. I allowed myself the acknowledgment that I was pretty. And then the doorbell rang. God, was he here already? It wasn't even seven. *Shit.* I ran my hands through my hair and walked to the back door, but when I opened it, there stood Anna, Anna who had not talked to me since I scolded her for embracing Mountain Man in the woods nearly two weeks ago. Did she know that afterward I had sent Mom over to tell Aunt Eve about what had happened with George? Surely she did.

"Hey!" I said. "Come in! I'm glad to see you."

"Hey," she said, flashing me a bright, toothy Anna smile.

We walked into the kitchen together. "I *still* haven't finished my personal statement," I said, motioning to the notebook and pens on the table. "It's so hard to figure out what to write!"

"I haven't finished mine, either."

"Are you still thinking UVA or Chapel Hill?" I asked.

"I've actually been thinking about applying to schools out west. In California, maybe."

"Wow," I said as I rummaged through the pantry, pulling out a bag of Chessmen cookies. I broke the seal, pulled one out for myself, and offered the bag to Anna, who shook her head.

"Do you have any wine?" she asked.

"Uh, sure, I guess." I pulled Mom's open bottle of Chardonnay out of the fridge and poured us each a small serving into the jelly glasses Mom and I used for orange juice. I was kind of bummed to be giving it to Anna— I had been thinking Dean and I could share the rest of the bottle—but I didn't want to say no to her request, not when she was actually sitting down and talking to me.

"So where in California? Pepperdine?"

She took a sip of her wine. "They don't allow dancing."

"Seriously?"

"Yeah, it's like, super Christian."

"Um, aren't you super Christian?"

"I'm not 'no dancing' Christian! I was thinking more like UC Santa Cruz or Berkeley."

"Really?"

Neither was a place I pictured Anna. I pictured her tucked inside a columned sorority house on some beautiful southern campus, giggling as she tried on outfits with her roommate before a mixer.

Of course, that was what I had imagined before last year's prom. Before George.

"I've just been thinking about how there's this big world out there and I ought to see more of it."

"Wow. Would your parents let you go? California is so far away, and both places are really lefty, aren't they?" Anna's dad was a bigwig in the Republican Party of Georgia.

"They're giving me some pushback, but I think I can talk them into it. If I get into Berkeley, that will help with Dad. He's big into rankings. And I'll tell Mom that going out west will help me get over everything that happened last year."

It occurred to me that Anna had just acknowledged that I knew that Aunt Eve knew about George.

"Anna, I'm so sorry about what happened that night—"

She cut me off. "It's okay. Seriously. Mom's making me go see a counselor, and it's been good."

"Who are you seeing?"

"Her name's Ruth. Ruth Stein."

"Oh my God, she's mine, too! Mom must have given her number to your mom. What do you think about all of her Hershey's Kisses wrappers?"

"Huh. I guess I noticed, but I never really thought about them. I like her, though. She's easy to talk to."

"Yeah, she's great."

"Listen," Anna asked. "Do you have any money?"

"Wait, what? Why?"

"It's for Miss Ada."

"Aw! I miss her."

Miss Ada had retired from working for Aunt Eve earlier that year. Her back had started giving her real trouble.

"Mom and I went and visited her last month. Some of the apartments around hers have boarded-up windows, and she told Mom to always telephone when she sends money so she can watch out for it. She says there are boys in her project who steal letters straight out of her mailbox."

"That's awful!"

"The whole time we were visiting, Ada kept grimacing and making these awful faces. Mom finally asked if her back was acting up, and Ada told us she was in terrible pain. Like, shooting pain that went from the middle of her back all the way down her leg."

"God, poor Ada."

"I think acupuncture might help. Of course, when I mentioned this to Dad he was totally against it—he acted as if I had suggested witchcraft—and Mom is siding with him, per usual. So they won't help pay for it. But I was thinking that if we pooled our money . . ."

"For Miss Ada to get acupuncture? That doesn't sound very 'Ada.' Unless the practitioner is also, I don't know, a Baptist deacon."

"I think when you're in a lot of pain you're willing to try anything. And everything I've read about acupuncture says it can be really helpful. Doctors don't want to admit it works because they don't want people to stop believing in Western medicine. But look, if she doesn't want to try it, she can always just keep the money."

"Why are you reading up on acupuncture?"

"Oh, one of the guys I met on my NOLS trip was really into it. It helped him get over a ski injury."

I thought of the hundred-dollar bill hidden in the back of my drawer, tucked inside an old pair of wool socks. Actually, it was perfect. I couldn't spend it on myself without feeling guilty, and I couldn't give it back to Mom without confessing that Aunt Eve had bought me a three-hundred-dollar prom dress, something that would offend Mom on multiple levels. So why not give the money to Ada, who certainly deserved more than a bad back and a boarded-up housing project for her retirement?

"I'd love to contribute," I said. Anna grinned.

Just as I was returning from my bedroom, cash in hand, the doorbell rang. Anna had walked to the living room, where she was looking at the framed photos on the mantel, one of which was of us as little girls, wearing matching rainbow-striped T-shirts.

"Here you go," I said, handing her the hundred-dollar bill.

"Oh my gosh, Sarah! This is incredibly generous! Thank you!"

"When are you going to give it to Ada? Maybe I could come with you."

"I thought I'd go by there tonight."

"God, are you sure that's safe?" I asked. "I mean, it's getting dark, and didn't Ada say there's a lot of crime at her apartment building?"

"I'll be fine," she said. "Sometimes the places that seem the safest are the least safe of all."

Like a party in someone's basement after prom.

The doorbell rang again. "That's probably Dean," I said. "We're going to watch a movie."

I opened the door. There was Dean with a pizza box in one hand and a Ball jar filled with pink tulips in the other.

"Pretty!" exclaimed Anna.

"They're from Aunt Linda," said Dean. "She bought a dozen, kept six, and sent the other half to you."

"How romantic of your aunt to send me flowers," I joked.

"Smartass," Dean said. He looked cute, freshly showered. He was wearing my favorite T-shirt, the dark blue one that matched his eyes.

"I'm going to go!" called Anna.

"Bye," I said. "Love you. Please be careful."

Dean set the pizza box on the counter while I cleared my work stuff off the kitchen table. And then he walked to me, draped his arms over my shoulders, and kissed me lightly on the lips.

"You look really pretty."

"I was going to put on a dress, but then Anna showed up totally out of the blue."

"I like you in jeans," he said. "They look good on your butt."

"So what kind of pizza did you get?" I asked, ignoring his comment, which didn't sound like Dean, but rather like some guy in a John Hughes movie.

"Meat Lover's Delight!" he exclaimed. "Ground beef, pepperoni, sausage."

I must have made a face.

"Wait, what?"

"That's just, that's a *lot* of meat."

"I can go get us a different pizza," he offered.

"Don't worry about it. I'll just pick some of it off. Do you want a Coke, or a glass of wine? There's some left in the fridge."

"I'll have a Coke," he said. "Although mostly I just want you." I tried not to wince. He sounded so corny.

"There's Cokes in the fridge. Grab one for me, too."

I walked to the cabinet to pull down plates. "Let's watch while we eat."

We were going to watch *Harold and Maude*, a movie Mom and I owned and had viewed no fewer than one thousand times but Dean had never seen.

"Sure."

I put two big slices of pizza on each of our plates, then started picking off most of the toppings from mine.

"I feel like a jerk about the Meat Lover's," he said. "It's just they were having a special and I thought it sounded really good."

"It's fine," I said, but in my mind I was thinking, *You're looking for discounts on this particular night?*

"Listen, don't eat too much, okay?"

"What, are you afraid I'm going to get fat?"

"Jesus. No. It's just that if you're overly full when you're, you know . . . it can make for an extremely awkward digestive situation."

Still holding the piece of pepperoni I had just plucked off, I looked at him. "Did Zoe fart while y'all were having sex?"

We had never actually discussed whether or not he and Zoe had had sex, but I assumed they had since they had dated for two years and neither of them was evangelical.

"Let's just say, digestive issues can be tricky."

"Great," I said, taking our plates and walking to the living room where the movie was already loaded into the VCR. "Now I'm terrified I'm going to fart."

Dean laughed, following me with the Cokes in hand. "This is *probably* the world's most sexy conversation."

"I know. Let's continue! Let's allude to more awkward sex with your ex! You guys did have sex, right?"

It was a question I had both wanted to ask and wanted to avoid. I knew from *Our Bodies, Ourselves* that it was really important to talk with your "lover" (ugh) about any fears or anxieties you might have. But I also really didn't want to think about Dean having sex with Zoe. I put Dean's plate on the coffee table and sat down with my plate of pizza on my lap. Dean put down our sodas and then sat beside me, our legs touching.

"So you really want to talk about who we've had sex with?"

"I do," I said. "I mean, it seems like the right thing to do."

But did it? Zoe was so striking, so dynamic, so *fucking* talented, and now I was going to hear about all of the awesome, wild sex they used to have.

"All right. You first," said Dean.

"Okay," I said. "So, I wouldn't sleep with anyone unless I was serious about him, and you're the first guy I've ever seriously dated. You do the math."

"Cool. Mine's pretty easy, too. I've just got Zoe."

"And y'all did have sex, right?"

"Once. The condom broke, and she got really freaked out that she might get pregnant. She's Catholic, and she knew that she wouldn't be able to have an abortion. So, after that we stopped having sex in the, um, conventional manner."

I chewed my pizza while he talked, feeling relieved that Zoe and Dean didn't have some epic sexual history that I could never live up to. "So y'all didn't have sex except for that one time? Wow. Cool! Is it weird to say that that makes me really happy? I mean, she's kind of intimidating."

"Please. She's got nothing on you."

I kissed him on the cheek.

"We did have other kinds of sex. . . ."

"Oh. Of course. You had oral. That makes sense."

"And anal."

"What?"

"Sarah, it's just another erogenous zone."

"Ew, ew, ew! Oh my God!" I actually felt myself scooting away from him, as if he were contaminated. "You don't think I want to have anal sex, do you?"

"Well, from your reaction I guess not."

"Ew. Seriously, *nothing* appeals to me about anal sex. Nothing. And honestly, it kind of freaks me out that you did that. Like, more than once?"

Dean's jaw tightened. "You know that most gay men have anal sex, right?"

"What does that have to do with anything? Are you telling me you're gay?"

"Jesus, Sarah, no. I'm just saying that you're kind of coming across as homophobic."

"That's so mean! I'm not saying I'm against *other* people having anal sex. We're talking about *us* and what *I'm* comfortable with, and how I'm clearly different from *Zoe*, who's just *so* experimental and open and artsy."

"Sweetie." He put a hand on my forearm.

"Yes, *sweetie*?" I answered as sarcastically as I could.

"You know what, Sarah?" he said, placing his plate on the coffee table and standing so that he loomed above me. "You don't want to have sex? Fine. You don't want to have anal sex? No problem. But don't get all biting and sarcastic just because you've got issues with gay people."

I glared at the remaining pizza on my plate, that ridiculous pizza with all of its stupid meat that I had to pick off. I was no longer hungry. I stood and walked to the kitchen. As I put the plate in the sink I called out over my shoulder, "My objection to you having had anal sex with your ex has nothing to do with how I feel about gay people. You're the one making this about gay people!"

He followed me into the kitchen. "When was the last time you hung out with Lizzie?"

I turned to face him. "What?"

"You guys used to hang out all of the time, and now you never do, and she thinks it's because she and Sake are together."

"Wait, what? When did she say that?"

"Last week. I was talking to her about my moms. . . ."

"Your mom's what?"

"My moms. Look, my mom is gay. Aunt Linda is not my aunt. She's my mom's partner. They've been together since I was two. I don't tell most people at Coventry. I mean, it's not like I'm from the Buckhead world. It would just be one more thing about me that was off."

Oh my God. Aunt Linda was Dean's mom's *lover?* I could not imagine. It wasn't that I couldn't imagine two women having sex—Sake and Lizzie practically glowed from all of the sex they were presumably having—but I couldn't imagine those two no-nonsense women with their sensible haircuts and their sensible shoes and their sensible diets doing anything together in bed but sleeping.

"Wait, do they share a room?"

"Of course they do. They've been together for fifteen years."

"You don't have to get all pissy. I'm just thinking about the fact that you lied to me about them."

"I never once lied to you about them. I never said *anything* to you about them."

"You called her 'Aunt' Linda. How is that not a lie? You showed me *Aunt* Linda's room, down the hall from your mom's. You pointed it out the first time I went to your house. And if they sleep in the same bed, then obviously that's *not* her room, so that's a lie. And then you went and told Lizzie about them before you told me. And *I'm* your girlfriend!"

"I only told her last week at Chastain. You were at that thing with your mom, and Sake had cousins in town or something, so it was just the two of us. We started talking, and I knew from what you had told me that she and Sake were a couple, plus I could kind of sense it on my own, so I just went ahead and told her about my moms. It actually felt really good to tell someone. And then she said that, yeah, she and Sake were in love and she was pretty sure that you knew and she was pretty sure you were freaked out by it. She said she figured that was why the three of you weren't hanging out together as much this year."

"She told you that?"

"She said she misses you."

Suddenly I felt so sad. Was I losing all of my friends, first Anna and now Lizzie and Sake, and maybe even Dean? I could feel tears welling in my eyes. How had we gotten here? How was it that Dean and I were yelling at each other on the night we were supposed to have sex for the first time?

"I'm happy for Sake and Lizzie. I really am. It's just, it's an adjustment, you know? But I'll call Lizzie tomorrow. I will. Honestly, though, I think I'm more of a bad friend than homophobic. I mean, I think the real reason I haven't been hanging out with them as much is because I want to spend all of my time with you."

I watched as his jaw unclenched and his face softened into a half smile. "You're sweet," he said.

We finished the pizza—now cold—and watched *Harold and Maude*. Dean almost fell off the couch during the bubble-blowing scene, when it's made obvious that twenty-year-old Harold and seventy-nine-year-old Maude just consummated their relationship. Dean and I did not end up consummating our relationship that night. I told him that I wasn't actually sure if I was ready, and he acted like the opposite of a guy from a John Hughes movie, assuring me that he was fine doing whatever. And then we started kissing, ending up on the living room rug. Dean touched my breasts, just stroked them lightly, and told me I was beautiful. I pressed my hand against the hollow of his chest. For some reason I loved that part of his body in particular.

We fell asleep on the floor and probably would have slept there all night if Argus 2 hadn't woken me, butting his head against mine. It was after midnight and the house had that odd, haunted feeling it gets when the rest of the neighborhood is asleep.

"You awake?" I asked Dean.

Silence.

I poked him until he opened his eyes. "Where did you tell your mom you were sleeping?"

"Here," he said.

"God, it really is different for boys. Even *my* mom would not be cool with you staying overnight."

"My moms are just happy I'm straight," said Dean sleepily.

"Wait, what? Wouldn't they be super supportive if you were gay?"

"They would, of course. But they know how hard it is, so they don't want that for their kid. You realize I'm telling you a dirty secret about gay parents, don't you?"

"All the secrets are coming out, huh?"

Argus 2 settled against my chest and Dean flopped an arm over my shoulder. Even in the dark I could make out the shape of the furniture in the room, including my dad's old leather recliner, which carried his essence, still.

"I was surprised to see Anna here," Dean said.

"Me, too. I think she was offering an olive branch. It was so funny, though, she came to me to tell me about how she wants to give money to our old nanny so she can get acupuncture. Which is just so not Anna. Nor is it Ada. But I contributed. It was my own peace offering."

"Huh," said Dean.

"What?"

"Did you know there was someone waiting for her in her car while she was in here with you?"

I sat up, Argus 2 darting out of the room as soon as I moved. "What are you talking about?"

Dean sat up, too. "I parked down the street like you asked me to. Anna's Volvo was parked down there, too. It didn't really register with me at the time, not consciously. But shit. That was her car. And there was someone in the front seat. Just sitting there. Wearing a ball cap. Fuck, Sarah. Do you know who's really into acupuncture?"

I could feel my heart tighten inside my chest even though my brain hadn't quite caught up. "Who?"

"Mountain Man. He gave me a whole lecture about it one night, about how doctors try to suppress the evidence of its efficacy because they're scared Western medicine will die out."

"Anna said something just like that to me. Oh my God, Dean. Do you think she's still hanging out with him?"

"Do you really think she's collecting money to give to your nanny for *acupuncture?*"

"I don't understand. What else would she do with it?"

"Give it to Mountain Man?"

Had Anna come by my house earlier that night because she was collecting money for Mountain Man? God, if that was the case, then he was definitely lying when he said he was once some higher-up at Coke. Shit. Was Anna *dating* him? Was she planning to spend the night with him, maybe use the money I gave her for a hotel room, telling her mom she was sleeping at my house, an easy cover since my own mom was away?

I stood and raced to the phone, dialing Anna's house, praying she was at home to answer.

Chapter 21

SURFACE

Atlanta, 1990

Anna's family had two phone lines, one for Anna and one for her parents. I dialed hers first and let it ring a bunch of times before hanging up. I dialed again. No answer. I took a deep breath and dialed the main number, the one that would sound in her parents' bedroom, the number I had committed to memory by the time I was five.

Uncle Bob answered on the second ring. "Yes? Who's calling?"

"I'm sorry to be calling so late. It's Sarah. Sarah Strum."

"Sarah!" he said, his voice suddenly full of warmth and concern. "What's going on? Are you girls all right?"

"I need to get ahold of Anna and she didn't pick up when I called her line."

I heard Aunt Eve's voice in the background. "Is everything okay?"

"Isn't Anna with you?" asked Uncle Bob, and it felt as if all the air was squeezed out of my lungs.

"No, she's not. She came by earlier tonight, a little before seven. She was looking for money to help Ada."

I heard Aunt Eve again, her voice panicked: "Anna's not with Sarah?"

And then I heard Uncle Bob say, "Go check her room," before he resumed talking to me.

"Anna said that she was spending the night at your house and the two of you were meeting Ada for lunch tomorrow at Deacon Burton's. She said y'all were collecting money for Ada. We gave her two hundred and fifty dollars."

"You gave money for Ada's acupuncture?"

"Acupuncture? No. Nursing care. Anna said she was having back surgery and needed a home nurse to assist her afterward."

I could feel the tightening in my throat that often signaled the onset of a panic attack. I was thinking of Mountain Man—Miles—and how idiotic it was that we all just sort of accepted him as a fixture of Chastain Park, how we let him hang around, how we engaged him in conversation, and no one ever told a parent or anyone with any authority about the fact that there was a grown man lurking in the woods. I was thinking of how I dutifully sent my mom to tell Aunt Eve about what had happened with George, but I had kept secret Anna's interactions with Mountain Man, so as not to get our whole class in trouble, so as not to shut down the whole Chastain Park Senior Experience.

What if Miles did something terrible to Anna? Men did terrible things to women all the time. I knew this from some of the cases Mom took on, details of which she had started sharing with me over the last year, because I had started asking. These particular clients were insane, Mom claimed, and should spend their lives in prison, but still she did not believe they should die at the hands of the state. I thought of her client who pushed his way into a strange woman's house when she answered his knock, bound her feet and hands, raped her repeatedly, cut off her nipples, and then stabbed her to death, puncturing her body again and again.

I heard a muffled noise and then Aunt Eve's voice was on the phone. "Sarah, are you certain that Anna is not at your house right now?"

"No. She's not."

"And y'all never had plans for her to spend the night with you tonight, to keep you company while your mom is out of town?"

"No. I mean, she came by earlier, but I didn't know she was coming. She was never supposed to spend the night."

"Do you have any idea where Anna might be or who she might be with?" asked Aunt Eve.

"She said she was going to visit Ada, bring her money, but I don't think she really was. And then later my friend Dean, who came over just as she was leaving, told me he saw someone in her car."

And then I told her about Mountain Man, as I should have done weeks ago.

"Stay right where you are, sweetie, and don't answer the door to anyone but Anna or me. I'm coming over."

Twenty minutes later there was a knock on the front door, and when I peered through the peephole Aunt Eve was on the other side.

I unlocked the bolt and she stormed in, and if she noticed Dean standing beside me she made no mention of it.

"No word?"

I shook my head.

"Bob stayed home in case Anna shows up. I need you to take a look at something, something that might help us find her."

"Okay, sure."

She strode into the kitchen and sat down at the table. "Could you get me a glass of water?" she asked Dean.

Dean wordlessly filled a glass with water and placed it on the table in front of her.

Aunt Eve took an envelope out of her purse and from the envelope an old photograph of her as a young woman, rail thin, with short-cropped hair and granny glasses. She was looking straight at the camera, her expression fierce, unsmiling. Next to her was a man, maybe twenty-five years old, with long curly hair and a smirk. It took me a minute to make the connection because in the photograph the man was much younger and thinner, but then it hit me: It was Mountain Man.

"How do you know Mountain Man? I mean, Miles?"

"His name isn't Miles," said Aunt Eve. "It's Warren. Warren St. Clair. I knew him a lifetime ago. For a long time I thought he was dead. Oh, sweetie, there's more to tell you, but for now we have *got* to find Anna. Think, Sarah. Think of anywhere they might be."

"Chastain Park," I said, feeling like an idiot for not having suggested it the first moment we realized Anna may have been with Mountain Man— Warren. "Look in the woods around Chastain Park, near the stone pavilion."

Aunt Eve called Uncle Bob, who contacted someone high up in the Atlanta Police Department, and soon an APB was sent out that Warren St. Clair, a man who was supposed to have died eighteen years ago, had been seen earlier that evening in seventeen-year-old Anna Powers's 1987 Volvo station wagon. Warren St. Clair had a laundry list of charges against him, including murder and assault, and now he was wanted for the possible abduction of Anna Powers.

Eve returned home on the slim chance that Anna might miraculously show up there, while instructing Dean and me to stay at my house just in case she returned. Meanwhile, the police sent a swarm of officers to Chastain Park. They did not find Anna or Warren but instead encountered a couple of kids from our class, stragglers who still hadn't called it a night, though it was after 2:00 a.m. They were brought to the police station, where they were questioned about their knowledge of the whereabouts of Anna Powers before their parents were called to come pick them up. Everyone was talking about it at school on Monday.

When they finally did find Anna, she was within two miles of both of our homes, at the Majestic Diner, where two cops had happened to stop for a cup of coffee. The cops had both read the APB and were pretty sure the burly man in a City Lights T-shirt sitting at a table with a pretty teen fit the description. The officer asked the waitress, who was pouring drinks behind the counter, how long the two of them had been there, and she rolled her eyes, saying they had been there all night, first ordering eggs, then pancakes, then endless refills of coffee.

Warren surely noticed the officers as soon as they walked in. Later Anna told me that throughout the night his eyes kept glancing at the door, as if he was expecting someone. It was probably when the cops started conferring with the waitress that he had placed a twenty-dollar bill on the table and stood to leave, perhaps believing that he and Anna could just hustle out. His decision to make a sudden departure confused Anna, especially because he offered no explanation, but she stood and followed him to the door. One of the officers stepped in front of it, blocking Warren's exit, and when Warren turned to see if there was another way out, the other officer, gun pulled, told him to freeze. Warren did not try to run for it or reach for a weapon or pull Anna in front of him as a shield. Instead, he complied, almost as if he had been anticipating this moment. They made him get down on the ground, face-first, before cuffing him. All the while Anna was crying for them to stop, insisting that he had done nothing wrong, that they were just talking, just talking about books. She held up Noam Chomsky's *Manufacturing Consent*, along with a collection of feminist essays titled *This Bridge Called My Back*, both of which Warren had recommended to Anna, and which she had purchased a few days earlier from A Cappella Books in Little Five Points. They planned to talk all night before he headed back to California, taking with him the six hundred dollars she had managed to gather from her savings, her parents, and me. Warren had told her he was going to use the money to continue with his antiracism work, which Anna said helped her justify lying about collecting it for Ada. "I figured it would go to someone *like* Ada in California," Anna later told me.

The officers insisted Anna come in for questioning. She asked if she could ride in the back of the patrol car with Warren, but of course they said no. At the station they were gentle with her, one officer getting her a blanket and another bringing her a cup of water. It was very late and she was scared and exhausted. She told me that they kept asking if Warren had tried anything sexually improper with her and that she kept explaining that they just liked to get together and talk.

It turned out that their meeting at the Majestic was the third time they had met one-on-one, ever since he had choked up while talking about his daughter with her and Redburn at Chastain. She had vanished from his life when she was eleven, taken by her mother to her home country of Guatemala, where they had disappeared into a culture he had no access to. What could he do, Warren had said, his eyes wet with tears, besides hope that Julianna—his daughter—chose to contact him once she was eighteen? (His half-Guatemalan daughter was, of course, a fiction. He was readying Anna to tell her, one day, that she was the daughter he was searching for.)

He told Anna that she reminded him of his lost daughter, and she shyly told him that they shared similar names—hers was short for "Joannah." He told her that he hoped she was being careful at Chastain with so many careless, drunken boys around. "All women should take self-defense classes," he said. "Learn judo."

Sometime during that conversation about his fictitious daughter, after Redburn had wandered away, Anna told him about what had happened with George, or at least as much as she knew, and how she had kept quiet about it, hoping the shame would pass. "Maybe if I had known judo . . . ," she said.

He looked at her sternly and said very clearly, "You did nothing wrong.

Nothing. Your body is yours, period. You have nothing to be ashamed of. That little shit is who should feel shame."

She told me that, at that moment, she had felt a great surge of love for this strange man whom she knew she was not even supposed to be talking to, but who made her feel better than anyone had in a long time.

After being questioned, Anna was released into the custody of her parents, and sometime over the next day Aunt Eve told Anna that Warren St. Clair was her biological father, come to find her.

But I didn't know that when I called Mom's hotel room early the next morning, after Eve had called to say that Anna had been found. All I knew was that Anna had been in danger and now Anna was safe. A man answered, and then Mom, clearly flustered, grabbed the line. "I'm sorry, sweetie. We thought you were the wake-up call. Meet Bruce, my friend."

"Oh, Mama," I said, and I started weeping.

"Sweetie, I had no idea you would be so upset. Look, Bruce is wonderful, but no one is ever going to try to replace your father."

I actually laughed. "God, no. That's not what I'm upset about." And then I told her about what happened with Anna and Mountain Man, who turned out to be Warren St. Clair.

"Do not let that man get near you," said my mom.

"He can't. He's in jail. They arrested him last night."

"How much of the story did Eve tell you?"

"She said she once knew him, a long time ago."

"Oh, baby. I can't believe that bastard is still alive."

Chapter 22

BELMONT GIRLS

Roanoke, Virginia, 1993

I begin the drive feeling melancholy about Dean. Though we broke up after our first year of college, made miserable because we tried to maintain a long-distance relationship, whenever we're back in Atlanta we hang out, ostensibly as friends. Last night we had "good-bye sex." I regretted it the moment we finished, regretted that I still can't quite let go of him, even though our lives—at least right now—no longer intersect.

But the farther Mom's Toyota carries us from Atlanta, the less I think about Dean and the more excited I become about returning to Brown. I love who I'm going to be living with, three fun friends, all of whom were in my freshman dorm. We lucked out with the housing lottery and got a suite in Young Orchard, where we will each have our own bedroom, with a kitchen and a living room to share. Best of all, Lizzie, after two years kicking ass academically at the University of Colorado, is transferring to Brown. Lizzie joined a sorority her freshman year at Boulder in order to please her mom but got kicked out or, rather, "encouraged to deactivate" after another member walked in on Lizzie and her "Big Sis" Natalie naked in Natalie's bed.

Lizzie's rendition of the story is funny—after they got busted, there was a formal meeting held by the officers of the house, during which everyone but Lizzie and Natalie painstakingly avoided any actual discussion of lesbian sex—still, the censure from her sorority stung. But now she will be at a place where the LGBT Alliance annually hosts the hugely popular "Prom You Never Had." I'm happy for her; also, I'm just really happy that she will be in my daily life again.

Mom recently installed a CD player in the Camry. After listening to my selection of R.E.M.'s *Out of Time*, followed by the Indigo Girls' *Rites of Passage*, Mom insists on choosing the next CD. I groan when she slides *Jesus Christ Superstar* into the player, but I secretly love the music, and even start singing along to "What's the Buzz" / "Strange Thing Mystifying."

Our plan is to stop in Roanoke, where we will visit Anna at Belmont College, then spend the night at a historic hotel downtown, which is a splurge, but one that Mom says she can handle, adding, "I get a Triple A discount." Anna is only in her second year at Belmont, having taken a year off after graduating from Coventry. During that time she embarked on a ten-month NOLS course in Patagonia, where she hiked all over Argentina and Chile, putting as much distance as possible between herself, her parents (well, her mother and her nonbiological father), and the media buzz around Warren's trial.

Aunt Eve and Bob dutifully paid for her exile, hoping, I imagine, that she might be ready to forgive them when she returned. She wasn't. Two years later, Anna still rarely visits Atlanta, and when she does she stays with Mom, having moved in with us during our final semester at Coventry, unable, she said, to bear being in the same space as her mother. Anna will meet Bob for dinner when she is in town (she no longer calls him Dad), but she won't see Aunt Eve. Mom says that Eve gets teary speaking of Anna but reacts to her daughter's rejection with resignation, as if it is something she must simply endure, a painful but necessary punishment, which will one day, she hopes, end.

Warren St. Clair truly *is* serving his punishment, twenty to life at a state penitentiary in eastern Kentucky, a bleak fortress that Anna visits every few months, making the five-hour drive. Belmont's relative proximity to the prison was one of the reasons she decided to go to college there, that and she got a newly established merit scholarship intended to lure girls who otherwise might go to UVA or Washington and Lee now that those universities admit women, causing Belmont's enrollment to decline each year. The scholarship helped free her, at least temporarily, from her parents' purse strings, and for Anna, the fact that Belmont only admitted women was a plus: there were no men around to molest you, for instance, if you happened to pass out after drinking too much. Still, her decision to attend the same college as did her mother, grandmother, and even great-grandmother surprised Mom and me. We thought she wanted as much distance as possible from her family, after all that had happened. "If he hadn't shown up, I never would have known," she would say, of Warren. "I would have lived my whole life as a lie."

I suppose she's at Belmont to try and piece together her story. She lives in Hanker House, informally called "Write House" because it's filled with creative-writing majors, which Anna plans to be. The women in her dorm tend to be more fringy than other Belmont students. They are not the ones who go through sorority rush, as our mothers did so many years ago. When I asked Anna if she was planning to join a sorority, she barked an emphatic, "Fuck no!"

Anna has changed.

During the drive Mom and I talk mostly of her upcoming wedding to Bruce, which will be held at North Oak Presbyterian, the church Bruce joined shortly after accepting the position of in-house counsel at the ACLU of Georgia so that he could move to Atlanta to be near Mom. Before Bruce relocated from D.C., he told Mom that he really needed to be part of a faith community in Atlanta and he needed it to be a bit more Jesus-y than

Unitarian. North Oak was one of the few churches he visited where the congregation is pretty much an equal mix of black and white. Mom goes with him most Sundays but can't go so far as to join. She doesn't want to abandon her Jewish half. The one time I went with them, the sermon was all about liberation theology—essentially that Jesus aligns with the oppressed and that any ideology that asserts the supremacy of one group over another stands in direct conflict with the will of God.

Bruce is black, a fact that seems to matter to Mom both a great deal and not much at all. Born to a poor family in Jackson, Mississippi, and educated at Jackson State on an ROTC scholarship (followed by a tour in Vietnam), Bruce shares none of my dad's patrician background but is very similar to him in terms of kindness and steadiness. The word "solid" popped into my brain the first time we met. He and Mom are planning on selling our house in Morningside and moving to College Park, a majority-black city just south of Atlanta that includes a designated historic district, where old bungalows, some in better shape than others, dot the leafy streets. The one Mom has her eye on has a huge front porch and a gorgeous stained-glass window that is original to the house. College Park is right by the airport, which is good considering how much they both travel for their jobs. But more important, Bruce will no longer stand out as one of the few black men in a mostly white neighborhood. "I don't want a neighbor calling the police every time I come home late," he said. At first I thought he was making a joke, but then Mom explained that, no, someone really had called the police once when Bruce had arrived home from work after dark and sat in the car listening to the end of an interview on *Fresh Air*.

Aunt Eve and Bob separated after Warren's trial and recently finalized their divorce. Eve moved out of the Ansley Park house and into what she refers to as a "cottage" in Buckhead near the Duck Pond, which she and Mom walk around once a month or so, catching up while getting a little exercise. I imagine they won't get together as often once Mom and Bruce move. College Park is really far from Buckhead.

I was surprised when I learned of the divorce, having always thought of Aunt Eve and Bob as a paragon of blue-blood stability. But Mom says that the national media attention surrounding Warren's trial, and all it dredged up about Eve's past, was just too much for Bob to handle. "He could no longer cast her as his helpless little debutante, led astray," said Mom. Plus, Eve had lied to Bob for years, keeping secret the fact that Warren had written her when Anna was eleven, saying he wanted to get to know Anna, asking for her photo. Eve ignored his letter, hoping he would simply disappear, the way he had disappeared all those years ago after he blew up the house at Linwood Avenue, killing J. T. Higgins and an unidentified man around whose neck Warren surely placed the dog tags that read: *Minh, Ho Chi.*

Mom says that if Warren had been charged with those two murders, she is certain he would have been found guilty. But it turned out the state of Georgia didn't have to build a case against him, for he was already wanted in the state of Kentucky for the murder of Leroy Butts McGee. Mr. McGee, whose head Warren had smashed with a pistol during an armed robbery in 1972, was the owner of a restaurant/filling station just south of Lexington. He did not die instantly but later, at the hospital. His only son, who had walked in on the robbery, testified for the prosecution. Warren did not deny the charges but pled insanity, claiming the depravity of the Vietnam War had driven him literally crazy, that he never would have committed such a heinous act if our country hadn't been concurrently scorching the bodies of Vietnamese villagers with napalm.

"Your moral relativism disgusts me," the judge decreed before handing down the sentence.

As we approach Roanoke, Mom launches into her latest tirade against Eve, that she has become an absolute zealot, having switched her membership from St. Luke's to a newly established evangelical church near Coventry, led by a celebrity preacher who published a book about himself called *The*

Prophet Among Us. In the book, he claims that he is indeed a modern-day prophet and that God routinely speaks to him, with great urgency, about the heresy of the modern Episcopal Church, particularly its decision to ordain first women, then homosexuals as priests. Mom says that though Eve was granted membership at her new church, there are certain things she can't do there as a divorced woman, such as teach Sunday school. But regardless of her second-class status, she remains committed to her newfound orthodoxy and is forever talking of her "innate depravity" and the fact that she had to hit "rock bottom" in order to have a chance at salvation.

"Have you ever considered the possibility that she might be right?" I ask. I am goading, but it seems wrong of Mom to dismiss Aunt Eve's beliefs so out of hand when they are clearly coming from a place of need.

"If she's right, then you and I and everyone else we know are going to hell," Mom says.

"I know, and that's really disturbing, but isn't that kind of the heart of the Christian faith? I mean, at its core, doesn't Bruce's church teach the same thing, that you have to accept Jesus in order to be saved?"

"It depends on what your definition of salvation is. Bruce would argue that a Christianity focused exclusively on individual salvation and the after-life, available only to those who claim a certain creed, is missing the point entirely."

"So what's the point?"

"Ugh. You know Unitarians don't like to talk about this stuff!"

"You *love* to talk about this stuff," I say. "Besides, aren't you, like, half-Presbyterian now?"

"Okay, fine. Anything for my darling child." She glances at me, smiles. "Bruce takes Jesus at face value when he says to welcome the stranger, feed the hungry, visit the prisoner, et cetera. He sees that as the point. He sees building a beloved community as the point. He thinks that if the concerns of this world didn't matter, the Bible never would have said anything about

God loving it. He thinks the end game will be the reconciliation of all people, rather than the divvying up of the saved and the damned."

"Does he believe in heaven?"

"I think so. He has his moments of doubt like most of us, but ultimately he believes in an immortal soul and an eternal love. And because of that he trusts that this life is not the full story."

"What about hell?"

"Nope. He finds it anathema to the spirit of a loving creator that anyone would be condemned to an eternity of suffering."

"Even Hitler?" I ask. "Even child pornographers? Even corrupt prosecutors?"

"You just pinpointed *exactly* where it gets tricky for me."

"Huh," I say.

We ride in silence for a minute. I'm thinking about Aunt Eve, and how she once assured me that heaven was real and that my father was in it, and how much I needed her certainty at that particular time in my life.

"You know," I finally say. "St. Luke's was all about Aunt Eve's family, where Anna was baptized and confirmed, where the three of them sat in the same pew every single Sunday. But now she doesn't really have her family anymore. So it makes sense that she would need a new church where she could start over. She's probably just looking to replace what she lost, to find some stability."

"Yes, but why *that* particular church, led by such an arrogant, self-satisfied man? It drives me crazy how easily Eve is taken in!"

"You could invite her to services with you and Bruce. Give her another option."

"I did, actually. A few months ago. And she came. Afterward, she mailed me a copy of *The Prophet Among Us*."

We exit the freeway at the signs for Belmont College. We have a Triple A book of maps outlining our entire trip, but Mom says she doesn't need me to navigate, she remembers the way. Ten minutes later, we arrive, Mom turning the car into the long driveway that winds through green hills dotted with trees and eventually leads to a quadrangle of pretty old redbrick buildings. Gentle mountains surround the campus, and I remember, as I do every time I visit Anna, why she loves this place and why Mom loved it, too, during her one year here. We park in the visitors' lot and walk along a path to University Hall, where the Blue Room is located, the formal parlor where the creative writing department is hosting a reading as part of a convocation for new students to give them a glimpse into what the writing program is all about. Anna is one of the presenting poets.

It's dusk. The sky is beginning to turn pink against the mountains and the air takes on just the slightest chill. I feel hope rise in my chest like helium. It is uplifting to be somewhere so beautiful.

"God, does this place bring back memories," says Mom as we walk up the short flight of stairs that lead to University Hall.

I think of the story she often told about how her dorm mother and Rush Counselor arrived at her room early one morning to inform her that she had been cut from Fleur and Pansy. Eve defended her and fought hard for her to be included in her sorority, and then dropped out when she realized Mom wasn't offered a bid because she was half-Jewish. I think of all of the meals Aunt Eve brought to Mom and me during the year after Dad died, how she nourished us during that dry, desert time, how she took me to the pool nearly every day that summer, knowing that the more exhausted my body was by nightfall, the more likely I might actually sleep. I think of her buying me a three-hundred-dollar prom dress when I was sixteen; I think of the delight she always took in making Anna and me happy. And now she is alone—divorced by her husband of twenty years, her only child no longer speaking to her.

"I feel so sorry for Aunt Eve," I say as we make our way through the stately old building.

"I'd take Eve's fate any day over Warren's," Mom snaps.

"They're not equivalent cases. Warren killed people. Aunt Eve didn't."

"God only knows what all Eve did."

"Jesus, Mom. Do you realize that you're harder on her than you are on anyone else? You spend your whole life trying to find mitigating factors for why convicts did what they did. But you won't do that for your oldest friend."

"It's just that she frustrates me endlessly. Her life has offered her so many opportunities, so many second chances—second chances no person of color would *ever* get, by the way. Yet she continues to bury herself again and again in the dogma of whoever has captured her attention at the moment."

"That doesn't mean I can't feel sorry for her."

There is a large crowd gathered in the Blue Room, and the prep factor is high—lots of headbands and pink-and-green plaid. A few minutes after we arrive, Anna enters with a posse from Hanker House, diluting the clean-cut vibe. With her is a black woman with short hair and dark liner inked around her eyes wearing Doc Marten boots and a flannel shirt over baggy shorts, a wispy white girl so pale and thin she looks to me as if she spent her youth trapped inside a dark, damp basement, and a freckled redhead who looks more or less like a standard-issue prep, save for the oversized pin she wears on her button-up shirt proclaiming, "Well-Behaved Women Seldom Make History."

And then there is Anna, in sweats, flip-flops, and a T-shirt that reads: "This Is Your Brain on Drugs with a Side Order of Bacon" over a fried egg with a strip of bacon beside it. Anna is a good twenty pounds heavier than the last time I saw her. She became skeletal during her year in Patagonia, but she has been making up for it ever since. It occurs to me that George might not have assaulted her had she been overweight. Or maybe he would have.

Maybe he would have felt even more entitled to violate her, figuring she was less valuable than a pretty, popular girl.

"You're here!" Anna says to Mom and me, walking over to give us a hug. She smells a little sweaty, earthy.

"Is Belmont the same as you remember it?" she asks Mom.

"Better," says Mom. "They don't have maids living in the basement anymore, do they?"

"No, but all of the cafeteria ladies are black and they get paid crap."

"Oh," says Mom. "Different station, same song."

There are rows of fold-up chairs facing the podium. We grab three seats up front, Anna sitting with us. At the beginning of the reading the head of the creative writing department, a no-nonsense woman with short dark hair, gives a brief overview of the program and then introduces Anna to kick things off, calling her "a bold Belmont woman finding her voice." Anna walks solemnly to the podium, looks straight at Mom and me, and smiles briefly in acknowledgment.

"This one is called 'Raised Right,'" she says, her voice loud and clear and steady.

> *"No white shoes after Labor Day!*
> *Say, 'Yes, ma'am,' and 'No, sir'!*
> *I was raised right in the shadow of lies*
> *I believed I was saved; I thought I was*
> *blessed; I cleaned up the mess you made*
> *My life an illusion—proof you were okay*
>
> *"In lieu of knowledge you gave me a downy bed*
> *to sleep on, to weep on, to keep on*
> *telling myself that it didn't matter*

when hands—not my own—plowed me
the seed had long been sown
I was to swallow the burden as my own
You wonder now why I can't go home?
Atone. Atone."

Chapter 23

MISS EUGENIA'S ROOM

Roanoke, Virginia, 1993

Anna reads four poems in total, though none that move Daniella so much as the first one. Applause sounding around them, Anna makes her way back to Daniella and Sarah. Daniella hugs her goddaughter, exclaiming, "You were fabulous!" And then, as Anna takes the seat beside her and the next student-poet makes her way to the podium, Daniella whispers, "I'm going to slip out and find a restroom."

She doesn't actually need a bathroom, just air. She can't breathe in the tightly packed Blue Room, hemmed in by both students and ghosts. She walks to the main door of University Hall and lets herself out into the night, a little chilly, though it's only September. She gazes at the mountains that surround the campus. She always thought of the mountains as nurturing, enfolding the students in a gentle embrace. She remembers Eve declaring, after they had both decided to transfer to Barnard, that Belmont was nothing more than a fancy prison for girls, the mountains standing guard. She thinks of Warren St. Clair, locked inside a metal cage within an honest-to-God prison, just one state away.

Over the course of the past decade, she has spent a lot of time visiting men who live in metal cages. Most of their hopes are humble. They want to remain living inside of their cells rather than be escorted in chains to their death. She met Bruce while working on the case of Malcolm Jones, a man sentenced to die whose IQ was 67. The ACLU had partnered with the SCHR in the lawsuit against the state of Georgia, and they sent Bruce down from D.C. She was drawn to Bruce immediately: his runner's build, his precision of manner and dress—cultivated by his time in the armed forces—his deadpan sense of humor. On their first date he solemnly stated that he only dated women who also worked for organizations with letters for names.

On impulse, she walks toward Monty House, the brick Colonial where she and Eve first met, thirty-one years ago almost to the day. It looks more like the home of some wealthy southern landowner than it does a dormitory. But that was the point, wasn't it? Monty House reflected the sort of home Belmont girls grew up in and the sort of home they would one day be in charge of managing, financed by their husbands, all doctors and lawyers and captains of industry. At least that was the expectation back when she was a student. Pushing on the front door, she realizes that it's locked. There is a punch pad where the doorbell should be, but she doesn't know the code. She smiles inwardly, thinking that she never really knew the code at Belmont. As she contemplates whether or not to push the "Help" button, the door swings open and two pretty girls tumble out, laughing, one wearing a sweatshirt with "Fleur" embroidered across its front. She has blond hair pulled into a long, straight ponytail and the clearest skin Daniella has ever seen on a teenager. The other is dark haired and petite, wearing a T-shirt from the Salty Dog Cafe in Hilton Head. Daniella thanks the Fleur for holding open the door. "Yes, ma'am," she replies.

Surely Anna would have become like this pretty girl, had life not taken a different turn.

And now Daniella is back inside. There is the portrait of Georgina

March, and there is the grandfather clock, ticking away. The Oriental rug looks to be the same one that graced the foyer when she was a student, though she now knows to refer to it as "Persian" and not "Oriental." And surely the rug has been rewoven, mended, because she remembers it being thinner and more tattered, a sign of old money. Or at least, that's what her mother used to say, her mother who was always a little breathless over such things.

The air is still redolent of orange oil.

Her first thought is to head up the front staircase, to try to take a peek in her old room. Instead, she pivots, walks to the door leading to the base-ment stairs. There are no longer maids living in the basements, thank God, so who or what now occupies the space?

It's dark, but she finds the light switch by feeling along the wall, and after a moment long fluorescent bulbs flicker on from the ceiling. She hears the tumbling of laundry, and sure enough, there are several coin-operated machines in the room adjacent to what had once been Miss Eugenia's. Breath held, she looks in Miss Eugenia's old room. There are several wooden desks stacked inside, along with a twin mattress propped against the wall and countless cardboard boxes sealed up with packing tape. She turns on the bare bulb in the center of what is now, clearly, a storage space. There is no window. How could she forget that Miss Eugenia's room had no window? Had she simply overlooked that detail when, at age eighteen, her own life was flooded with so much light?

Daniella walks back out into the open basement, sliding her back down the rough wall until she is sitting on the floor. Her bad hip protests only a little from the sudden movement. Has it really been thirty-one years since she and Eve sat together with their backs against this same basement wall, aghast at what had happened to Miss Eugenia, and yet still able to wipe away their tears and rejoin the world above?

Daniella pictures Eve back in the day. She can't help but smile. How bold she was standing up for Miss Eugenia. How bold she was standing up for Daniella when she was cut from Fleur! How glorious she once had been, a bright, golden sunflower, stretching toward the sky, determined to grow beyond what her roots would allow.

Now Eve, at nearly fifty, reminds Daniella of a woman made of wax, still beautiful if observed from enough distance, but frozen, locked, her ash-blond hair touched up every three weeks, her body forced daily through grueling workouts, under the direction of her personal trainer, Caesar, a gay black man Eve declares "so darling!" seemingly with no self-consciousness about the fact that the conservative church to which she now belongs was created in outraged reaction to the Episcopal Church's decision to ordain an openly gay priest.

Oh, Eve. Is this really where you've landed?

Sarah says she is too hard on her old friend, and perhaps she's right. But doesn't the fact that she's hard on Eve prove that she still loves her? Or is her love for Eve an artifact from the past, a habit she can't quite seem to break?

Once, they lived together in this very building. During the waking hours they shared their every thought. At night they lay across from each other in their respective twin beds, inhaling and exhaling the same air. And when that air became too stifling, they linked arms and jumped from the insulated world of Belmont to Barnard and all it exposed them to. And then they lost each other. Again and again they lost each other. There were moments when it seemed they might find their way back to what they once had—when Eve came to her, pregnant, her old life literally burned to the ground. When Pete died and the grief was unbearable and Eve showed up day after day with food, tucking Sarah under her maternal wing, keeping her busy and loved. But their connection never lasted. The rope that held them together grew increasingly frayed. And now the only thread that seems to remain is their shared love for Sarah and Anna.

But that's a tenacious thread.

Daniella pictures the now-fierce Anna reading her aching, sophomoric poems, poems that were surely intended for the one person she no longer speaks to. Daniella wonders what trajectory Anna will follow. She hopes her goddaughter will continue to dig for the truth of her life, to integrate her past into her present. The cynic in her imagines she'll try for a few years and then grow weary of the effort and instead find a stable boy from a good family from Hampden-Sydney or Washington and Lee to rescue her from her fractured past. What a seductive belief—that one can start fresh simply by jettisoning one's history, that one can leave all that is painful or unsavory behind.

And what of Daniella's own part in an unsavory past? What of her own role in what happened to Miss Eugenia, how she despaired over the fired maid's fate but did nothing else to help her? When she told the story to Bruce, his eyes had pooled with tears.

"She could have been Mama," he said. He was not being hyperbolic. His mother had worked as a maid, not at a white college but at a white woman's house. Like Ada.

Ada. Ten years ago, Daniella had failed to step up and help Ada purchase a modest house, after Bob and Eve refused to co-sign her loan. At the time, Daniella was about to leave her well-paying job to work for the Southern Center for Human Rights. Money *had* been tight. But she had always had the comfort of knowing that Pete had left her enough to pay for Sarah's college and some of her retirement. And she always knew, too, in the back of her head, that one day—far in the future, she hoped—her parents would die and she and her brother would split their assets. And one day Stockton Strum would die (Pete's father had died years ago) and she would leave money for Sarah, only daughter of her beloved son.

But in those years immediately following Pete's death, Daniella had not been able to trust that she and her daughter were going to be okay. To trust that things would be okay would be to relinquish some of her grief over losing Pete, and that would mean relinquishing Pete himself, something it had taken her a long time to do.

But she did, finally. And then came Bruce. Bruce, with whom she will start a new chapter in College Park, in a bungalow purchased with cash, thanks to the profit she will earn selling the Morningside house. And Ada—whose life was, of course, so much bigger than the work she did to support herself—Ada raised not only Eve but also Sarah and Anna, the two girls Daniella loves most. And what does her final chapter hold? An apartment in a run-down housing project where half of the windows are boarded up.

It isn't right.

She should have co-signed the loan. It wasn't too great a risk. And now it's too late. The house is long gone, and Ada is in her seventies, with a bad back. But Ada *could* move into a nicer apartment, one with an elevator so she wouldn't have to manage stairs, maybe even a high-quality assisted-living unit, so there would be someone to care for her if her body keeps giving out. Daniella's mind flashes to the Sunday before, at Bruce's church, when a woman spoke to the congregation about donating funds to help build an after-school center in a high-crime neighborhood. "Give as much as you can," she urged. "Then give more."

Daniella would give Ada as much as she could. And the world would remain unjust. But she would do it anyway—acknowledge Ada's humanity while claiming her own.

Was it Eve's humanity that drove her to write a letter in support of Miss Eugenia, to drop out of Fleur, to (temporarily) relinquish all comfort to protest imperialism both here and abroad? How much easier to think of Eve as egotistical, naïve—to think of her as nothing more than a silly child. How much easier to pin her to a board, dissect her under a harsh light, declare her deficient, and throw away the remains. But instead she pictured her friend as she found her thirty-one years ago, slumped against this same basement wall, having just watched the banishment of Miss Eugenia, overcome with pure grief.

Daniella's eyes pool with tears. Eve's instincts *were* once pure. It was just that so much got in the way. Daniella allows herself the hope that the girl Eve once was still lives inside the woman, buried but breathing.

ACKNOWLEDGMENTS

It is with humility that I lift up the names of some of the very real people mentioned in this book who dedicated their lives to the ongoing struggle to end systematic racism and racial oppression, including: Medgar Evers, James Chaney, Michael Schwerner, Andrew Goodman, and Fannie Lou Hamer. Gratitude goes to the (then) youth, led by Bob Moses and others, who journeyed to Mississippi during the summer of 1964 to work in tandem with the black citizens of that state to attempt to bring their voting rights to fruition. I would not have been able to write about that summer with any clarity had I not viewed director Stanley Nelson's excellent documentary, *Freedom Summer*, or read Elizabeth Sutherland Martínez's *Letters from Mississippi: Reports from Civil Rights Volunteers & Poetry of the 1964 Freedom Summer*. Also helpful was the "Timeline for the 1964 Freedom Summer Project" published by the Wisconsin Historical Society.

The Smash Collective was loosely inspired by the radical leftist group Weatherman. Instrumental in my understanding of both the genesis and the ideology of this group was Sam Green and Bill Siegel's gripping 2003 documentary, *The Weather Underground*. I also read several memoirs written by former members, including: Cathy Wilkerson's *Flying Close to the Sun: My Life and Times as a Weatherman*; Bill Ayers's *Fugitive Days: Memoirs of an Antiwar*

Activist and *Public Enemy: Confessions of an American Dissident*; and Mark Rudd's *Underground: My Life with SDS and the Weathermen*. Indeed, in the chapter "Called Home," Eve references a story in which the real-life David Gilbert links the oppression of blacks in America to the bombing of villagers in Vietnam. The story of Mr. Gilbert's revelation came from the chapter titled "A Good German" in Mr. Rudd's excellent autobiography. Additionally, I gleaned much from Lucinda Franks and Thomas Powers's five-part series about Diana Oughton, "Diana: The Making of a Terrorist," first published in *The Boston Globe* in 1971. It was through their account of Oughton's life that I first read of members of Weatherman killing, skinning, and eating a tomcat in order to show how ruthless they had become. The cat story might be apocryphal—Bill Ayers adamantly denies that it happened—but in any event, reading about it both troubled me *and* sparked my imagination.

Other books that helped me get a handle on that era include Todd Gitlin's *The Sixties: Years of Hope, Days of Rage*; Abe Peck's *Uncovering the Sixties: The Life and Times of the Underground Press*; Bryan Burrough's *Days of Rage: America's Radical Underground, the FBI, and the Forgotten Age of Revolutionary Violence*; Dan Berger's *Outlaws of America: The Weather Underground and the Politics of Solidarity*; Joan Didion's *Slouching Towards Bethlehem* and *The White Album*; Minrose Gwin's *Remembering Medgar Evers: Writing the Long Civil Rights Movement*; Jamal Joseph's *Panther Baby: A Life of Rebellion and Reinvention*; and Betty Medsger's *The Burglary: The Discovery of J. Edgar Hoover's Secret FBI*. Pete Strum's dissertation on Reconstruction is directly inspired by Eric Foner's 1989 masterpiece, *Reconstruction: America's Unfinished Revolution, 1863–1877*. Much of Daniella Strum's work defending indigent prisoners on death row was inspired by Bryan Stevenson's transformative memoir, *Just Mercy: A Story of Justice and Redemption*. On a lighter note, like Anna and Sarah, I, too, read all of Lois Duncan's thrillers when I was growing up, and enjoyed rereading *Stranger with My Face* for the purpose of writing this book. Similarly, it was fun to revisit the seminal *Our Bodies, Ourselves* by the Boston Women's Health Book Collective.

My son was born in the middle of my writing this book, and it took me a few years to acclimate to being both a mother and a writer. Thank you to my stalwart editor, Trish Todd, who told me that she cared more about me getting the book "right" than turning it in on time. Thanks also to my fierce advocates at William Morris Endeavor, and especially to my lovely agent, Claudia Ballard.

Thank you to Katharine Roman who shared the experience her mother, Sharon Powell, went through as a Jewish woman going through sorority rush at a southern university in the 1960s. Sharon, your harrowing story inspired Daniella's experience with Fleur. Thanks also to my loyal writing group—Beth Gylys, Peter McDade, Jessica Handler, and Sheri Joseph—who read and critiqued much of this book in progress. Special thanks to Sheri, who read the whole novel once I completed a draft, and offered me exhaustive notes for revision. Sheri, the book is *so* much better because of your diligence and care! Joshilyn Jackson also read the book in early form, and her brilliant sense of story significantly improved the final version. Not only that, but Joshilyn suggested the title. My eagle-eyed husband, Sam Reid, swept in at the end of this project and read the manuscript line by line with pencil in hand, making it approximately a thousand times more graceful and cohesive than it was originally.

Thanks always to my loving parents, Ruth and Tim White, who offered their enthusiastic support for this book early on. And thank you, Mom and Dad, for being such loving grandparents. Thanks also to my wonderful in-laws, Barbara and Ron Reid, who have made me feel such a part of their family and who regularly care for my son. Your steadfast commitment to him helps me continue to be a writer. Thanks for making our little boy feel so special and loved. (Truly, Ronnie, it takes a village!)

On that note, I can think of no better "village" in which Sam and I can raise our little boy than the one offered by my loving and inclusive church. Church family: Y'all humble me and help me believe in an eternal love that is ultimately more powerful than the forces of hate and division.

ABOUT THE AUTHOR

An Atlanta native and current Atlanta resident, Susan Rebecca White is the author of three critically acclaimed novels, *Bound South*, *A Soft Place to Land*, and *A Place at the Table*. A graduate of Brown University and the MFA program at Hollins University, Susan has taught creative writing at Hollins, Emory, SCAD, and Mercer University, where she was the Ferrol A. Sams, Jr., Distinguished Chair of English. Susan is married to Sam Reid. They have one son.